The
Secret
Message

BOOKS BY ANNA STUART

Women of War
The Midwife of Auschwitz
The Midwife of Berlin
The War Orphan

The Bletchley Park Girls
The Bletchley Girls
Code Name Elodie

The Berlin Zookeeper
The Secret Diary
A Letter from Pearl Harbor

The
Secret
Message

ANNA STUART

Bookouture

Published by Bookouture in 2024

An imprint of Storyfire Ltd.
Carmelite House
50 Victoria Embankment
London EC4Y 0DZ

www.bookouture.com

Storyfire Ltd's authorised representative in the EEA is Hachette Ireland
8 Castlecourt Centre
Castleknock Road
Castleknock
Dublin 15 D15 YF6A
Ireland

Copyright © Anna Stuart, 2024

Anna Stuart has asserted her right to be identified
as the author of this work.

All rights reserved. No part of this publication may be reproduced, stored in
any retrieval system, or transmitted, in any form or by any means, electronic,
mechanical, photocopying, recording or otherwise, without the prior written
permission of the publishers.

ISBN: 978-1-83618-673-1
eBook ISBN: 978-1-83525-656-5

Previously published as *The Resistance Sisters*
(978-1-83525-657-2)

This book is a work of fiction. Whilst some characters and circumstances
portrayed by the author are based on real people and historical fact, references
to real people, events, establishments, organizations or locales are intended
only to provide a sense of authenticity and are used fictitiously. All other
characters and all incidents and dialogue are drawn from the author's
imagination and are not to be construed as real.

For my sisters in words – Julie, Tracy, Debbie, Helen and Sharon. Always there for advice, comfort, wisdom and, of course, karaoke...

PROLOGUE

WARSAW | 5 NOVEMBER 1939

Hana Dąbrowska staggers into the family bakery and the sweetly familiar scents of home embrace her. She inhales wafts of butter, sugar and cinnamon, willing their sweetness to take away the pain in her heart, but nothing can do that today. As her younger sisters, Zuzi and Orla, follow her inside she pulls them close – the family must stay together now, more than ever.

'We're safe here,' Magda, their mother, says, though her voice trembles.

She leads them to the kitchen where the family has for so long eaten, worked, and played together. Her mother-in-law, Babcia Kamilla follows, her eyes fiercely dry and her back ramrod straight as she guides young Jacob before her. The family take their seats around the table and look to the empty chair at its head. Their Papa, Kaczper, has been in prison for two months, so they've become accustomed to seeing his place empty, but the knowledge that he's now gone and will never fill it again sharpens the pain of his loss.

Orla, the youngest sister at just thirteen, puts her blonde head in her hands and weeps. Her tears fall into the ever-present dusting of sugar on the worn oak table, making dark splatters, and Jacob slides up against her, tracing shapes between them. She puts her arm around him and he strokes her blonde hair. He is only eight and confused by all that has happened on this dark morning.

It started at dawn, when they were awakened by vicious knocks on the cheery red door of their bakery.

'Get up,' the Nazi soldier snarled at them. 'You're going to see your father.'

Oh, they were excited then. They scrambled to dress and follow him to the prison where Kaczper Dąbrowski had been kept out of sight ever since the Nazis occupied Warsaw at the start of September. They all gabbled about how much they had to say to him, how they'd hug him and promise him they were doing all they could to secure his return to the family bakery, the family home. But it was a cruel trick. Kaczper was not waiting in a room to see them, but shoved onto a noose-lined balcony while they were herded, at gunpoint, into the yard below.

'Why did they have to kill him?' Jacob sobs now, his grief released in the comfort of home.

'Because he's a good man,' Hana, the eldest at eighteen, replies. 'And the Nazis hate good men.'

'Not as much as we hate the Nazis,' Zuzi, a fiery seventeen-year-old, spits, making them all hiss at her to keep quiet. You never know who might be listening.

Magda makes tea in a big pot, lays out cups as she does every morning, and finds a loaf of fruit bread, Kaczper's speciality. She's been running the bakery for the last two months, lovingly following her husband's recipes until he could resume his work. Now he never will. Her hands shake and Hana rushes to help her. This has been the worst morning of any of their lives and they are all quivering. She focuses hard on cutting the bread, but all she can see is that dark prison yard.

'Kaczper!' Magda called out the moment she saw him and he looked down in surprise, his eyes filled with infinite sorrow.

'Sweetheart,' he said softly, as if they were meeting in a park on a rose-tinged summer evening and not on the brink of his brutal death at the hands of Warsaw's occupiers. 'It's so very good to see you. And you, son. Look after your mother.'

Little Jacob, crushed against Magda nodded, his lip caught in his teeth to stop it wobbling.

'Good lad. And my girls.' Kaczper turned his smile on Hana, Zuzi and Orla, then corrected himself, 'Young women now and beautiful, every one of you.'

They shifted, not willing to see any beauty in that hateful morning but loving him for doing so. Kaczper Dąbrowski, master baker and dedicated town councillor, had always seen the best in any situation. His light doughs and pastries had only ever been bettered by his optimistic plans for the city he loved – plans which were about to cost him his life.

'Mother.' Kaczper's final smile was for Babcia Kamilla, standing stiffly at Magda's side. 'Carry on the fight.'

'Always, son.'

'I know it. They cannot cuff us for long.'

Kamilla nodded determinedly, the lump of her tears almost visible in her long throat as she fought to keep them inside. She lost her husband, Aleksander, in the initial fight against the invaders and must now be robbed of her son too.

'Stay strong,' Kaczper instructed his family, as gloating soldiers thrust the nearest noose around his neck. 'Do not weep for me. I do not want you to weep, but to live and to love – and to fight. Will you do that for me?' They nodded obediently, but then his voice cracked and tears filled his brown eyes. 'I'm sorry,' he said. 'I'm sorry to leave you. I'm so, so sorry to leave you.'

Orla sobbed, tears streamed silently down Zuzi's cheeks, and Hana held them both protectively close.

'I love you, Kaczper,' Magda cried defiantly.

'I love you,' Hana echoed her mother, then they'd all been saying it. They said it as the guards took the once big man and shoved him over the edge. They said it louder and louder to fill his last breaths with as much care as they could until, blessedly quickly, it was done. He was gone.

Now, in the cosy kitchen of the home and business he and Magda created when they were first married, they look again to his chair. The cushion still bears the imprint of his big body and the arms are worn smooth with the touch of his skilful baker's hands.

'He's not gone,' Hana says defiantly, reaching out to stroke the wood. 'He's not gone because he's here, in our hearts.'

She beats her hand against her chest and her sisters follow, Zuzi with an audible slap, Orla a soft press, as if seeking to keep her own aching heart within her breast. Jacob copies them, standing up as straight as a little soldier and, unexpectedly, they laugh. The sound fills the bakery, just as it did for so many years, and they look at each other, then instinctively reach out to clasp hands around the table. Kamilla hesitates but today even their guarded grandmother needs the comfort of a human touch, and she joins the circle.

'You heard him,' she tells them. 'We fight and we live and we love.'

'He said,' Orla dares to correct her, 'we should live and love and fight.'

Kamilla tosses her head. 'Fighting first. Tomorrow, we join the underground resistance. Agreed?'

Orla still looks uncertain and Magda grips her fingers tight.

'Not all resistance is with guns, sweet one. We can fight in our own ways.'

The three sisters look at each other, then at their mother and their wide-eyed little brother. Zuzi's eyes blaze with rage, Orla's swim with tears, and Hana's darken with worry. Grief for their lost father quivers between them, a twine around their bruised hearts, holding them even tighter than before.

'We fight in our own ways,' they agree. 'And together. That way, when the time is finally right, we will rise up. And we will win.'

PART ONE

Before God the Almighty, before the Holy Virgin Mary, Queen of the Crown of Poland, I put my hand on this Holy Cross, the symbol of martyrdom and salvation, and I swear that I will defend the honour of Poland with all my might, that I will fight with arms in hand to liberate her from slavery, notwithstanding the sacrifice of my own life, that I will be absolutely obedient to my superiors, and that I will keep the secret whatever the cost may be.

THE OATH OF ALLEGIANCE OF THE ARMIA KRAJOWA (THE POLISH UNDERGROUND ARMY)

ONE

30 JULY 1944

HANA

Hana pressed her face against the tram window, unable to believe what she was seeing outside. She and her sisters were striving to look calm as they made their way to their AK stations for training, but it was hard for there was a curious panic in Warsaw's air. German soldiers were marching up Jerusalem Avenue, but they were like no Germans she'd ever seen before. They were shuffling their muddy jackboots and keeping their eyes trained on the pavement of the city they'd arrogantly marched into five years ago. Their uniforms were torn and skewed and permeated with an air of defeat. She grabbed Zuzi and Orla and nodded at the astonishing sight beyond the window.

Zuzi beamed. 'Look at them, crawling in the dirt where they belong!'

'Zuzi, hush!'

Hana looked nervously around, aware, as always, of her duty as the eldest sister to keep the other two safe. They were in the Polish carriage, the only one of the three that made up the tram, with the front two reserved as Nur für Deutsche – only for Germans – but you never knew who might be listening. No Pole would snitch on their own but there were soldiers everywhere.

'Don't worry about the Deutsche,' Zuzi shot back. 'They're far too busy fleeing to listen to us. Look.'

Sure enough, the tram was pulling up at Warsaw's main station in the heart of Śródmieście, the modern city centre, and out of the front two carriages spilled a great mass of well-dressed Volksdeutsche, lugging suitcases, bags and packing crates, and hurrying at speed into the station.

'They're leaving?'

Hana pressed her face even tighter against the glass. It was hot from the midsummer sun but she had to see this. The German families departing from their tram were joining many more arriving at the station in fancy motor cars, on foot or even by horse and cart. It was an exodus surely only matched by the poor Jews forced from the ghetto last year.

'Shame there's no gas chamber for these gits,' Zuzi muttered.

'Zuzi! Hush.'

Hana tugged desperately at her sister's sleeve, willing her to be less reckless. She understood her sentiments, of course she did, but they were better expressed in the safety of their mother's bakery.

'They look so sad,' Orla said, putting her hands up to the glass, as if she might reach out and help.

Following the direction of her younger sister's blue eyes, Hana saw a mother juggling a baby and a toddler as she tried to drag a giant case towards the station. The baby was wailing, the toddler dragging her feet and the mother looked terrified. Even as they watched, however, a burly soldier bent down to offer the toddler chocolate and took the case, instantly easing the blonde woman's load.

'My heart bleeds,' Zuzi said sarcastically, and Orla shifted.

'I know. Sorry. It's just so horrible. They're people too.'

Orla was right about that, Hana thought, and she squirmed for the space to give her a hug as the tram finally got going again. Orla looked up at her. Her youngest sister had recently turned eighteen and was a lovely woman with the softest colouring of the three of them. Zuzi's hair was as near-black as their father's had been, Hana's own was a sort of dirty straw colour – hazel, if you asked her fond mother – but Orla's, like Magda's, was the bright blonde of an angel and her blue eyes were always ready with a smile – or a tear, especially when it came to children.

'It looks like it might soon be over, my little Lania,' Hana told her.

Orla smiled at the family nickname: Lania – doe – after the deer she'd loved to spot on childhood walks in the woods north of Warsaw. These days, those woods were filled with men and women of the AK – short for Armia Krajowa, or Home Army – and 'Lania' was Orla's AK pseudonym. Not that she would fight, thank heavens – or, at least, only in her own way, as their mother had taught them, for the youngest, gentlest Dąbrowska sister was training as a nurse. Perhaps her skills would be needed soon.

'Look at them,' Zuzi hissed, pointing to another set of soldiers on the street, as bedraggled as the last ones. 'They're fleeing the Russians. The Red Army must be close. We have to rise up and take the city while this lot are in tatters.'

'When the time is right, we will,' Hana said, trying to keep her hot-headed middle sister calm.

'How could it be more right than this?' Zuzi demanded, dark eyes flashing.

She had a point. Hana worked as a liaison girl, delivering underground messages between the many AK units in Warsaw's forty-thousand-strong underground army, and she knew that the appetite to attack was growing in intensity. Yesterday, Gouverneur Fischer, the Nazi ruling Warsaw, had put out an order for all Polish males to report for 'defensive duties' and she'd been busy all day passing along the AK's command to ignore the summons. It had been a risk, as the Germans were often swift to execute brutal reprisals, but not as much of a risk as letting all their fighting men head into possible custody. In the event, no action had been taken; the Germans truly seemed to be on the ropes.

Hana fidgeted with the loaf of bread under her arm, wondering what today's instructions would be. Carrying secret messages was work that suited her well, allowing her to use her near-perfect mind-map of the city to get around, but it was risky as anyone caught carrying AK instructions was executed as a traitor. So far, her policy of carrying official orders buried deep in one of her mother's freshly baked loaves had kept her safe but as the Germans got more edgy, and the AK more volatile, the risk worsened. Something had to break.

Everyone in the tram was watching the mass of departing Volksdeutsche and Hana could feel the mood lifting, as if the electric tramlines were running not just above the Warsawians' heads, but through their bodies too. For so long they had been oppressed by the Germans, for so long they had been made to feel like second-class citizens in their own city, refused entry to the best restaurants, theatres and cinemas, banned from government, banned even from having an education.

The Volksdeutsche were the German-born civilians who'd been shipped into occupied Warsaw in their thousands and swanned around the city as if they owned it. The Nazis had taken many businesses off Poles, handing centuries-old family concerns to these upstarts with no consideration or compensation. Even worse, they'd taken houses and apartments from the Jews, crushing them into a ghetto and ushering German cuckoos into their precious homes. It was barbaric and the

Warsawians hated the Volksdeutsche almost as much as the Nazi soldiers.

Polish schools and universities had all been shut down. Between her liaison work, Hana was doing a degree in architecture, but doing it in underground lessons, taught at great risk by brave men and women who could be arrested at any moment. She'd seen three of her teachers go the way of her dear father in the last year and was desperate to defeat the hated occupiers so she could study in the open again and rescue the city she loved from the ravages of war. Her father would have been proud to see her do that, she was sure, just as he would have been proud to see her marry her darling Emil…

Hana gave herself a small hug, as she always did when she thought of her fiancé, a Polish pilot who'd had to flee occupied Warsaw back in 1939. That had been five long years ago. She knew he'd found safety in Great Britain and was flying bravely with their RAF but she hadn't seen him since. Back then, he'd had broad shoulders, a strong frame and a crooked smile that had filled her heart with joy every time it came her way, but she had no idea what he looked like now. Had war made her dear Emil as thin as it had herself? Had so long in a foreign land bowed his shoulders? Had the dangerous work of a pilot robbed him of that wonderful smile? Was he even still alive? His last letter had arrived weeks ago but the post was impossible and she refused to give up hope. She was desperate for liberation to find him once more. And yet…

'We have to be careful,' she whispered to her sisters. 'The Russians are slippery.'

'The Russians are our friends,' Orla said stoutly. 'Our allies.'

Hana smiled fondly at her.

'The Russians are not *our* allies but our allies' allies,' she corrected. 'Stalin has no diplomatic relations with Poland and he wants to take Her into his empire, just as Russians always have.'

'Which is why we have to rise up and take Warsaw ourselves,' Zuzi insisted, pushing her dark hair impatiently off her face. 'Come on, you two, don't you want to smash them out of here?'

'I don't know about "smash",' Orla hedged.

Zuzi tossed her head. 'Well, you should.'

'Yes, Żelazo.'

Hana smiled at the retort. Żelazo – iron – was Zuzi's AK pseudonym, chosen when they'd all joined the resistance a few days after their father's execution back in 1939. The middle Dąbrowska sister was fighting in the most traditional way as part of the Minerki, an all-female sapper unit, trained in explosives. She and her fellows had sent many German trains off the rails, or factories sky-high in the last two years, and the work suited her fiery personality. She'd chosen the code name Żelazo because, so she'd said, her heart was iron and would stay so until the Nazis were defeated. It made Hana sad that Zuzi was still resolutely single at twenty-two but perhaps, in wartime, her sister was right to prefer mines to men.

'Come on,' Zuzi said, 'this is our stop.'

Hana tumbled out of the tram with her sisters and instinctively looked to the blue skies above. Maybe if the Allies had heard that the Germans were on the ropes, they would send planes. Maybe the Polish pilots would return to help liberate Warsaw as they had vowed.

'I wish I didn't have to leave you,' Emil had told her on the day they'd been torn apart, holding her so close that she'd felt him against almost every point of her body – and wanted more.

'If you stay, they'll kill you.'

They'd both known that; their planned wedding would have swiftly become a funeral. The impressive reputation of the Polish pilots was too great for them to be allowed to live and, indeed, once they'd escaped, they'd gone on to prove themselves in the Battle of Britain. News in Warsaw had been provided through the Nazis' street-speakers, trumpeting tinny narratives of Luftwaffe daring and brilliance, but the underground radios had picked up a different story – of Spitfires and Hurricanes defying the Messerschmitts and keeping the treasured sliver of sea between Great Britain and the rest of Europe free of Nazi invasion.

For months, Hana had been on tenterhooks, dreading news of Emil's death, but what had finally come had been a precious letter from him, modestly reporting 'some success' and telling her of the violet he had painted on the underside of his plane in tribute to her. Fiolet was the pet name he'd given her in the heady summer of '39 because, he'd said, the little flower's petals were shaped like hearts and she had his. But then the Germans had invaded, the Russians hot on their tails, and everything had changed.

Hana had taken Fiolet as her code name, for Emil's sake, and his letters had kept arriving, scrawled with the censor's dark pen but rich with love all the same. Then last year had come the news that, with the Allies invading Italy, Emil was being posted to Brindisi. *We are coming, my love*, he'd written. *Keep your eyes on the skies and when you see my violet you will know I am close.* Might that be soon? It was almost too wonderful to hope for.

Hana shook herself and turned to hug her sisters goodbye before they went, separately, to their secret AK training, Zuzi to the Kampinos woods north of the city, Orla to her hospital on the edge of Stare Miasto, the medieval old town, and Hana to her liaison hub here in Śródmieście.

'The Russians are coming,' Zuzi hissed into their communal embrace. 'They've covered seven hundred kilometres in the last six weeks – why would they stop at Warsaw? We're going to be free, girls, we're really going to be free!'

'You think?'

'I *know*. Tata must be looking down on the city with elation.'

The mention of their beloved father thudded through Hana's heart and she instinctively glanced towards the Pawiak prison, standing dark and menacing just down the road. If she looked closely, she would see the corpses that forever hung there, as Kaczper's had once hung, but she kept her eyes resolutely off the dangling shapes casting their tragic shadows over Warsaw, and kissed Zuzi.

'Stay safe.'

'Stay *alert*,' Zuzi corrected. 'See you at sunfall.'

'See you at sunfall,' Orla agreed, and skipped off for her onwards tram to the John of God Hospital.

Hana stood, watching her sisters go, their words echoing in her ears. 'See you at sunfall,' was a phrase the family always used – a reminder that whatever challenges the day held for them as individuals, they would be together again before it ended. They'd said it in increasingly determined hope since the occupation had made the simple joy of sitting safely around the table at the end of the day less secure than it should be, and Hana couldn't help worrying. But what could she do?

'See you at sunfall,' she called after them.

Tucking her hollowed-out loaf under her arm, she traced the back alleyways through to her liaison hub, hidden above a small beauty salon, deliberately too scruffy to attract the Volksdeutsche. Upstairs she found her fellow liaison girls in a state of high excitement.

'What's going on?' she asked, looking around them all.

'Everything!' one of them told her, handing her a slip of paper. 'Read today's message.'

Hana looked down. There, in bold black letters, stamped by Commander Bór himself, were the words that all of Warsaw had, surely, been awaiting:

From Commander Bór to all AK operatives in the Warsaw area – I announce a State of Alert. All troops and ancillaries stand by for action. W-hour is near.

W-hour: W for Wystąpienie – outbreak. At last! Hana thought of Zuzi and how she would welcome this; of Orla, who would fret about what it might mean; of Babcia Kamilla, who would cry revolution; her teenage brother Jacob, who would be reckless in his desire to be involved; and their mother, Magda, waiting in the bakery for them to come home every sunfall. Suddenly the chances of them all doing so felt dangerously diminished, but what could they do? If the Nazis were weakening, the AK had to act.

Tata had told them to keep up the fight and Hana was determined to do her duty by him and by everyone trapped in this viciously occupied city. If the Russians were coming, they must rise up, claim Warsaw, and welcome them in as allies. It shouldn't be more than a few days of fighting and it would be worth it to be free again at last.

Free to be with Emil.

Hana reached eagerly for ten of the officially stamped orders to get to her assigned AK platoon commanders, hidden around the city, and slid them into her loaf. Her hands were shaking, but she thought of her father and the vow her family had made to avenge his death, and they steadied. It was time to take the news to all Warsaw; time to strike at last.

TWO

ZUZI

Zuzi leaped off the tram and strode up the road towards the Kampinos Forest as fast as her athletic legs would take her. She felt wired up, alive, bursting with energy. The once-cocksure German soldiers were dribbling back through Warsaw, broken and bent by the advancing Red Army, and she couldn't wait to help crush them completely.

'We'll avenge you, Tata,' she swore under her breath.

She pictured her father, standing proudly on that bitter prison balcony, his bare shoulders squared despite the lurid lash-marks across them, and his eyes bright as he'd looked down on his family.

'They cannot cuff us for long,' he'd told them and he'd been right, though, God help them all, it had felt long enough. Zuzi had been seventeen when the Nazis had stormed into Warsaw; now she was twenty-two and a trained saboteur. At school she'd been desperate to study the 'not for girls' subjects of science and maths and, thanks to the AK, she'd learned more about chemistry than she'd ever have been allowed at school. She was ready to strike.

Zuzi pictured the shackles on her grandmother's wall. Babcia Kamilla often told them the story of her own father's imprisonment in Siberia, of how he'd been made to lay rail tracks through snowy plains in temperatures many degrees below zero, his thinly clad legs bound to the supply trucks with the cruel cuffs and chains now on the wall in her grand house in Stare Miasto. She told of how he'd worked, day by day, to chip a link of the great chain away and how, finally, when his Russian guards had been warming themselves in a shepherd's hut, he'd broken it with one swipe of his hammer and run. For months he'd trodden the Siberian wastelands, living on animal scraps and the kindness of peasant families before, somehow, he'd reached the Polish border and found his way back to Warsaw.

It was a tale of great courage, always recounted by Babcia Kamilla with envy, as if she wished she'd had the chance to prove herself in the same way. Zuzi had little doubt that Kamilla would have been just as successful as her legendary father and would probably have killed the guards with her bare hands besides.

Kamilla had been very encouraging of Zuzi's activities with the Minerki and was always keen to hear of their acts of sabotage. She'd wanted to join herself, citing her expertise in making filipinkas – home-made grenades fashioned out of explosive stuffed into household cans – in the First War. But the AK had strict age limits and at sixty-eight, albeit a wonderfully fit and ferocious sixty-eight, she fell well outside them. Zuzi was always happy to relate Minerki stories for her grandmother to live vicariously and maybe now it would be the biggest story of them all – the story of freedom.

Reaching the edge of the forest, she stepped in at her designated entry point and counted off the oaks to find the path down to the current training point. It was a relief to be under the trees, away from the roasting heat of the city, and she slowed her steps, listening to the rustle of the leaves, not to mention of the many AK groups training, and often actually living, out here in the welcome shade of the vast Kampinos.

'Password.'

The girl standing in the path knew Zuzi perfectly well but was a stickler for procedure. With a roll of her eyes, Zuzi gave today's word, żonkile – daffodils – and was allowed to proceed. In the clearing beyond, well-shaded by incongruously colourful rhododendrons, were the Minerki – a circle of twenty explosives experts, their skills honed over the last two years by the painstaking teaching of their brilliant leader, Tosia.

Tosia beckoned Zuzi into the circle as another girl arrived behind her. They had to come separately to avoid detection, and the thought that they might soon be able to fight in the open thrilled Zuzi. She wasn't the only one.

'I am authorised to tell you that we are now in a state of alert,' Tosia said, to muted cheers. 'HQ have eyes on the advancing Russians and will call W-hour when they believe an uprising to have the greatest chance of success. Warsaw is on the brink of liberation.'

Around the circle everyone's eyes shone. They'd been robbed of the freedom of their youth by the occupiers, subjected to brutal rationing, and deprived of their education. The one thing they'd managed to hold onto was the Scouting movement. Deemed wholesome by the regimented Nazis, the Scouts had allowed the AK to train up thousands of young people in the key elements of warfare under the guise of campfires and odd jobs. Zuzi and her sisters had come through the 'grey ranks' – so called because of the colour of their uniform – and moved into the full adult AK in their own chosen areas. Explosives suited Zuzi perfectly and she was honoured to be part of the Minerki.

'Rome has been free for weeks,' she said. 'And I hear the

Allies are close to Paris. Imagine if we can kick the Nazis out of our capital before the French clear theirs!'

'It would be wonderful,' Tosia agreed solemnly, 'and only fitting. Our government *never* went grovelling to the Nazis like that bastard collaborator Pétain, but fought on from exile. And Warsaw *never* capitulated, not even when they murdered us in cold blood. This city had 1.3 million souls in it before the Nazis marched in and I'm told we're down to 900,000. That's too many lives lost – but still plenty left to take it back!'

The girls gave another whispered cheer.

'War!' Nina, the youngest of them all, hissed, her eyes gleaming.

But at that Tosia put up a warning hand. 'War, yes, but not as the world knows it. This will be guerrilla fighting, up narrow streets and through tricky buildings.' She looked around them and smiled. 'And what do we need to manage tricky buildings?'

'Sappers!' the girls chorused happily.

'Sappers,' Tosia agreed. 'Expert sappers. The Minerki will prove our worth to the AK in the days ahead, ladies!'

They looked proudly at each other. They were an all-female group and, in Zuzi's opinion, better for it. Much of their daring work wouldn't have been allowed if there had been so-called 'superior' men to do it and she considered the loss of cocky male company a small price. Plus, it saved her from any nonsense about romance. Orla was always reading silly novels with dark-eyed heroes sweeping girls off their feet, but that did not appeal to Zuzi at all. Her legs worked fine, thank you very much, and she certainly did not need some man deciding what direction she travelled in.

'We will have to be brave,' Tosia warned. 'I have been given our initial target.' The girls drew in a collective breath and leaned forward. 'We are to be part of the unit attacking the Prudential tower.'

Zuzi couldn't believe her ears. The Prudential tower in Śródmieście – the modern, downtown area of the city – was the highest building in all Europe. Hana was always mumbling about its innovative design but, more importantly, it was a key Nazi stronghold in the heart of Warsaw. And *they* were being entrusted with helping to take it!

'It's an honour,' Tosia acknowledged, 'but a deserved one. Time and again we have proven ourselves the best sapper unit in the AK.' She allowed another muted cheer then put up her hand for silence. The girls obeyed instantly. 'But this will be our biggest test. The Prudential has thick walls so we will need all our most devious tricks to breach it. And all our supplies.'

She paused and the girls looked at each other awkwardly. For the last few months, the AK commanders had instructed that the uprising would take place on the open roads, sabotaging the Wehrmacht as they retreated from the Soviets. The AK had therefore smuggled weapons and explosives out of the city, where they were made in daring underground factories, and into stashes buried in the countryside. The Red Army had moved so fast, however, that such assistance had not been needed and the strategy had switched back to a city-based uprising. If that was to be soon, they needed to get those weapons back.

'Today's mission,' Tosia confirmed, 'is to locate a cache of high-grade mines and grenades and smuggle it into our designated position in an AK apartment opposite the Prudential. It is risky, ladies, and will need all your ingenuity and courage. It's not traditional sapper work and if anyone doesn't wish to take part, please leave now, with no aspersions on your value as part of this unit.' No one moved an inch. Tosia smiled. 'Thank you.'

'So,' Zuzi asked eagerly, 'where are the goods?'

Tosia looked unusually discomfited. 'We don't know.'

'We don't *know*?' Nina cried.

'We don't know *yet*,' Tosia corrected herself. 'As you're aware, the location of any cache is, according to strict AK protocol, only known by two people in a platoon. This particular one was located by Sofia and Roza.' A sigh rippled through the group and Tosia acknowledged it. 'Sadly, Sofia was lost to us last week—'

'Not lost,' Zuzi said. 'Murdered.'

The girl had not even been on Minerki duties, but had seen a lame hare in the forest and dared to catch it and take it home for her hungry family's pot. An SS officer, fancying her prize for himself, had shot the animal dead in her arms, not caring that the bullet had gone through the beast and straight into Sofia's heart.

'Murdered,' Tosia agreed, nodding to Zuzi. 'And Roza is on a mission to Lublin so has been unable to pass on the knowledge to a second member.'

Zuzi groaned. She understood the need for secrecy. The Gestapo tortured anyone suspected of being part of the AK and it was best if you had as little information as possible to release under their cruel ministrations, but it created a practical problem.

'What do we do?' she demanded.

'We wait. Roza is due back any moment and, in the meantime, it won't hurt us to do some wall-breaking drills. On your feet, ladies.'

The girls pushed themselves up reluctantly.

'Who needs more drills?' one girl grumbled.

'Especially without actual explosives,' another agreed as they rolled out the fake wooden mines and pretend string fuses.

'We have too few to waste,' Tosia said sharply. 'And, besides, you don't want the Nazis in on us, do you?'

Still the grumbles went on and it made Zuzi cross. She put her hands on her hips. 'Drills today, ladies, Nazis tomorrow!'

The other girls moved faster and Tosia threw her a grateful look but Zuzi wasn't just saying it to calm things down. She meant every word. Those beasts had thrown her tata to his death and she was coming for them as soon as she possibly could.

THREE

ORLA

Orla stood in the linen cupboard, taking as long as possible to select the right sheets for the twenty new beds they'd set up in the cellar below the John of God Hospital. She'd go out there again very soon, really she would, she just needed a minute to herself. There was something about that row of innocent beds waiting greedily for patients to fill them that made her feel dizzy and she didn't want to have to admit that to anyone. If fresh linen made her faint, how would she cope once it was covered in blood and pus? Sister Maria kept describing it to them all in lurid detail to 'prepare you,' but Orla didn't want preparing. She didn't want any of it.

Her father would be disappointed in her, she was sure, but she couldn't help being keener on the living and loving of Kaczper's final exhortation to his family than the fighting. She hated having the Nazis ruling Warsaw as much as anyone, but surely meeting their hate-filled guns with more, equally hate-filled ones wouldn't do anyone any good? Who was she to know, though? She'd turned eighteen a few weeks ago so was supposedly an adult, but she still felt more like the thirteen-year-old who'd clung to her big sisters as the shadow of their dying father had been thrown across them.

Orla was in awe of Hana running around the city with secret messages, forever in danger of being found out and arrested, or Zuzi, blowing up enemy trains and headquarters with home-made explosives. They'd both been very certain about what roles they wanted to take in the AK when they'd graduated from the Scouts, but Orla had had no idea, save that it should be as far from the fighting as possible, and nursing had seemed the most caring of the other options.

She was lacking the courage and conviction of her big sisters, that was the problem. She admired them for wanting to pursue 'proper professions' and for fighting their way into predominantly male fields but all Orla really wanted was a kind husband, a nice house and some babies to love. Right now, with the young men either off fighting in other countries or running around their secret AK bases with guns and grenades, that was a foolish dream.

'Lania? Where are you, girl?'

Orla jumped at the sound of Sister Maria's voice and, hastily grabbing at the nearest pile of sheets, stumbled out.

'Right here, Sister. Just making sure I had the correct size.'

The head nurse looked her up and down.

'They're all the same size, girl. Now, get them on the beds and let me see nice, sharp corners. We don't want anyone bleeding onto creases, do we?'

'No, Sister. Of course not, Sister.'

Orla ducked past her and set to making up the beds, wondering which wounded man would care about creases, but not wanting to test her boss's minimal patience. The order of the task was, at least, soothing but she was distracted on the final bed by a very unpleasant smell drifting out of the makeshift hospital kitchen on a disturbing waft of dark smoke.

Abandoning her sheet, she ran across and flung open the door to find Alicja, a young orderly, flapping ineffectually at a burning pan. Alicja's nine-month-old daughter, Daniella, was sitting in a high chair, wide-eyed at the pretty patterns of light, and Orla leaped forward.

'What's in it?' she demanded.

'Oil.'

'Then you're only going to make it worse. Stand back.'

Snatching the tea towel from Alicja, Orla drenched it in water from the bucket in the corner and threw it over the smoking pan. The oil gave an angry hiss of protest and the flames licked at the underside of the tea towel. Alicja snatched up her baby and Orla bundled them both out of the door in case it went up but, deprived of fuel, the flames sank sulkily into nothing.

'Why did you let the oil get so hot?' Orla asked her.

'I wanted to make kopytka with this left-over potato, didn't I?'

'You were doing kopytka in oil?'

Orla stared at the rough potato dumplings in Alicja's bowl in astonishment.

'Of course,' Alicja said, though she sounded less sure now. 'I wanted them crispy on the outside.'

Orla rolled her eyes. 'On the outside, yes, but you do that on a griddle.'

'You do?'

'Yes! After you've boiled them. Do you not know how to cook?'

Alicja looked close to tears. 'I've not had time to learn. Daniel and I were living with Mama and Tata after we wed and I was learning to keep house, really I was, but then he... he...'

Orla put a hand on the girl's shoulder. 'He was killed?'

Alicja gave a sob. 'They all were. A bomb. I was eight months pregnant and for months I couldn't do anything but birth Daniella and care for her. I've lived on bread and cheese mainly, so I'm useless with actual cooking. But then, with all the talk of an uprising, I thought I should volunteer. That was yesterday. They put me on catering, cos of having a baby and looking like I ought to know how to feed a family – which I did ought to – but I... I don't, and I didn't dare say.'

Orla felt mean for giving Alicja a hard time. The girl looked younger than she was. She'd been through so much and she was still here, baby in tow, doing her best.

'You will,' she assured her. 'All you need is a bit of training. Come on, I'll show you how to make them the easy way.'

A few minutes later, Daniella happily absorbed with a pot of raisins, they were rolling out her father's best kopytka – what the master baker had called 'busy dumplings' because they were made in a long sausage and cut up swiftly into bite-sized lumps that boiled in seconds. They weren't as smart as stuffed pierogi, but Kaczper had taught his children to make them because they were far quicker and that was surely going to count for something in the days ahead. Alicja, at least, looked happier and she carried her first batch out to the workers, beaming with pride.

'It was all Lania,' she said as everyone gathered to enjoy the little treats.

'Nonsense,' Orla said briskly. 'I'm just a nurse.'

'No one is *just* a nurse,' a young doctor said, chewing earnestly on a kopytka.

'I didn't mean—'

'Healing people is a very noble profession.'

'Of course it is. Absolutely. That is...' She tailed off, suspecting she was about to say something foolish, but the earnest-faced young doctor looked at her so intently that it felt even more foolish to stop. 'I simply wonder if it would be more noble to work in a profession that prevented people from hurting each other, rather than mopping up the mess afterwards.'

The doctor gave a bark of a laugh.

'A very good point. You wish to be a politician?'

'Goodness no!' Was this young man wilfully misunderstanding her? 'I don't wish to be anything very much, but that's not really an option right now, is it?'

'It's not,' he agreed grimly. 'We have to liberate our country, liberate all Europe.'

'Yes, yes, I suppose we do. That is, do we? I mean, we in Warsaw specifically?'

'Oh yes. Everyone must, if, and when, they can. Normandy is free now, southern Italy is free. We're closing in on the Nazis but not fast enough, not for me.'

His earnest face was flushed, his hands shaking, and she put out her own to still them.

'For a special reason?'

He nodded. 'Very special. My mother is in a concentration camp.'

Orla gasped. 'I'm so sorry. How come? I mean...' She looked at him, seeing a solidly Polish young man. 'Your family aren't Jewish, are they?'

'No,' he agreed fiercely, 'but we are human.'

Orla flinched at the ferocity of his voice. 'What do you mean?'

He shook himself. 'Sorry. I get a bit passionate about this. The Jews in my hometown, Łódź, were put into a ghetto, just like they were here. They were treated terribly and so we – my mother, father, brothers and I – tried to help. We smuggled in supplies and, and advice.'

'Advice?'

'My mother was – *is* – a midwife. She was trying to help a young nurse called Ester – a little like you, actually – to assist the birthing mothers in the ghetto. She was caught, my younger brothers with her, and they were all sent off to camps. Mama is in one called Auschwitz. I've no idea what sort it is, but its name comes up more and more often in underground reports, so I fear the worst. The last thing I heard, she was still alive, but they say conditions in those hellholes are abysmal. They say...' he swallowed hard, 'that they are burning people in there, like we think they burned the Jews of Warsaw at Treblinka.'

Orla sucked in her breath. The walling off of part of Warsaw to create a Jewish ghetto in 1939 had seemed horrific enough, but then the Nazis had started shipping the poor people to Treblinka, supposedly for healthier outdoor work and more spacious living conditions. Several of the AK had tracked the Nazi trains at the start of 1943 and reported back that thousands of Jews were sent up the branch line to the camp, but none ever came out. No food ever went in either and those stark facts, along with the sickening smells of meat and ash reported from the area, had pointed to only one conclusion – the Nazis were exterminating the Jews.

It would have been impossible to believe, but after four years living with the barbarically callous way their occupiers treated anyone but their own kind, few Poles had doubted the truth of it. The AK had been in touch with ZOB, a brave resistance movement within the ghetto walls, and when it had become apparent the Nazis were about to empty the last of the inhabitants into Treblinka last April, ZOB had risen up. Their rebellion against the German tanks and guns had been tragically futile and Orla had hated hearing the endless shots and cries of pain from behind the walls in the long month of their struggle.

'At least they died on their own terms instead of clawing the cages of a gas chamber,' Babcia Kamilla had said stoutly, but it had not seemed much of an improvement to Orla. And this poor man's mother was now in one of those same, hateful camps.

'So, you see,' he concluded, 'we have to get rid of the Nazis so that I can get Mama out.'

'I do see,' Orla agreed, horrified. 'Your poor mother. She was only trying to help.'

'To mop up the mess?' he suggested.

'I didn't mean to offend,' she said hastily. 'I'm sure your mother is a wonderful nurse – far better than I am.'

'You'll be fine.' He stuck out a hand. 'Bronislaw Kaminski at your service. They call me Dr Bronislaw around here, though, in truth, I'd only done three years of my medical degree when Tata and I had to flee from the Gestapo, so I'm improvising as much as you.'

He winked, suddenly looking far more human, and Orla laughed.

'Orla Dąbrowska,' she offered, then clapped her hand over her mouth. 'That is, Lania, I'm Lania. That's my code name, I keep forgetting to use it.'

'Me too,' Bronislaw said. 'I'm Łukasz – patron saint of doctors. Arrogant?'

'Confident,' Orla corrected.

He smiled and held out a hand.

'Well then, Lania, how about us trainee medics help each other out?'

'Perfect.'

Orla took Bronislaw's hand and shook it firmly, thinking that the stark, secret hospital suddenly felt far more manageable. The Poles would do this uprising as they did everything – together. The Nazis might parade in perfectly matching goose-steps, but their hearts did not beat as one in the way the Warsawians' did and that, Orla prayed, would count for much in the days ahead.

FOUR

HANA

Hana paused at the innocuous-looking apartment door to catch her breath. On the wall, the AK symbol had been proudly scrawled and she touched her fingers briefly to it. It was an anchor made out of an entwined P and W, originally for Polska Walcząca – Fighting Poland – but increasingly read as Powstanie Warszawskie – Warsaw Uprising. She'd seen so many of them as she'd been carrying the official 'state of alert' message around the city today. Warsaw, it was clear, was ready to rise.

Hana wasn't sure *she* was ready and she certainly wasn't ready for her younger sisters to get involved. Mama was wonderful but had been so busy with the bakery since Tata's death that Hana had always felt responsible for Zuzi and Orla. It had been fine when they were still children running around with the Scouts, but every day now she worried that one of them wouldn't make it back for sunfall. The uprising would only make that fear more acute and she was grateful to have other things to think about this evening.

Surreptitiously checking for any watching patrols, she

pushed open the door and ran up the steps to the third floor where, under the guise of a drafting class (considered suitably manual to be permitted for Poles), she would continue her architectural studies. There were four people there already, all boys, plus their tutor – the man they were only permitted to call Agaton, his AK pseudonym, though they knew him to be Stanisław Jankowski, an up-and-coming architect. He had inspiring ideas about modern design that had seen him win several of the underground competitions run beneath the Nazis' noses in the last few years and Hana was honoured to learn from him.

'The time is close,' he was saying as she slid into her seat. 'We are in a state of alert and will reclaim Warsaw very soon. When we do, we must be positioned to make her great again. Every Warsawian will do this in their own way. Our politicians will return to fill the parliament, our lawyers will come out of the underground courts and run a fair, transparent justice system, and our architects – *us* – will take back the streets and continue our work of making Warsaw into a vibrant, modern, forward-looking urban space.'

The class cheered in a practised whisper and Agaton beamed round at them. He was always animated but today he was visibly buzzing.

'We have plans,' he said, his voice low and his eyes darting to the door, ever alert for SS intrusion. 'Great plans for a new, latitudinal expressway, linking the bridges in the east to the roads to the west, with buildings along it.'

'New designs?' Hana asked eagerly.

'Of course,' Agaton agreed. 'We must look forward, not back. And you, my dear students, will be the people to create them. Here.'

He drew out a small sheaf of papers from a secret pocket in his briefcase and, after checking the windows and doors, spread the top one on the desk between them. It clearly showed

Warsaw, blooming westwards from the north–south line of the Vistula, with the suburbs of Żoliborz in the north, Wola in the west, and Czerniaków in the south, like petals around the central hub of Stare Miasto, the medieval old town, and, directly below it, Śródmieście, the modern city centre where they were now.

'These are maps of the city as it stands now and this' – Agaton tapped one sheet proudly, running his pen along a bright east–west line through the centre – 'is the blueprint for the new expressway we will build once She is ours again. Your homework for our next class is to come up with a design for one section. Think big. I want housing projects, office buildings, playgrounds, parks, communal spaces and civic buildings. I want—'

The loud rap of heavy boots on the staircase cut his words dead. They all froze, then Agaton leapt into life.

'Drafting books!'

They whipped them out as Agaton stuffed the secret maps into a folder and fumbled to fit it back into his briefcase.

'Let me.' Marek, the oldest of their group, took the folder and made for the fire escape. It was risky heading for the street that way, but what choice did they have?

Hana leapt up to close it behind him but as he scrambled out, one of the sheets fell from the folder and fluttered lazily back into the classroom. She snatched it up, the rap of the boots getting louder as the dreaded SS reached their floor. Marek was gone and Hana was holding a map that might incriminate them all – what could she do?

Heart pounding, she slid onto the fire escape and heard the door shut behind her. She felt horribly exposed on the slim metal staircase. Looking down, she could see Marek almost at the pavement, and chased after him as the sounds of shouting above told her the SS were in the classroom. She prayed they'd removed everything incriminating, prayed Agaton and her fellow students would convince them they were mere donkey drafters, and prayed that she escaped attention. She'd urged her sisters to stay safe then plunged herself straight into danger! But she had to catch Marek and restore the last of the sheaf of maps to him.

He was off down Królewska Street, his long legs covering the ground far more easily than hers, and she hastened after, hoping to keep him in sight and catch him at a road crossing. Sure enough, as he turned onto Zielna Street, heading bravely in front of the Telephone Exchange – the forbidding concrete tower in which the Nazis housed vast comms links to their rapidly collapsing eastern front – he was stopped by traffic lights. At the same time, the doors of the Exchange opened and a troop of Gestapo came out. They eyed the Poles calmly waiting to cross the road and exchanged ominous glances.

Her blood chilling, Hana slid into a shop doorway and watched as they sauntered forward, demanding papers. Marek looked terrified and she knew that feeling all too well. Often, she'd been stopped for a check with an incriminating message tucked into the loaf under her arm, feeling as if it were pulsing out its presence to the dark-browed guards. She'd always got away with it with a sweet smile, a blush, or the offer of a pastry, but the Wehrmacht soldiers were well-known for going easier on girls. It was one of the reasons the AK used so many of them to carry their messages. It did not stop them from their merciless attacks if they found something, however – and these were the men the whole city was about to rise up against. Hana felt nausea rise in her throat and pressed herself against the wall as she watched Marek.

The lights changed but no one dared step away from the dark-coated men. They began shuffling their ID cards and work permits out of their pockets and Marek did the same. Hana willed him to stay calm but even from fifty metres away, she could see his hands shaking around the incriminating folder.

He kept cleverly to the back, hoping the Gestapo would tire of harassing Poles before they reached him, but this lot kept doggedly on, staving off boredom with a few kicks and punches along the way. Marek looked surreptitiously around but it was a wide, open street and there was nowhere to stash the folder, even had he dared attempt it.

'You! Papers.'

Marek handed them over and Hana dug her nails into the very mortar of the shop, willing the Gestapo to move on. They shut his ID card with a snap and handed it back, the same with the work permit. Hana allowed herself to breathe but, just as they were about to turn on their shiny heels and leave, one of them, perhaps sensing Marek's fear with his vicious Nazi nose, pointed to the folder.

'What's that?'

Marek tried to say something but what was there to say? The lead Gestapo had it off him in a moment and flipped it open. He sneered.

'Maps of the city? And future plans besides! What are you doing with these, Pole?' He stepped up to Marek, pressing his face close into that of the trembling student. 'How dare you, you arrogant bastard? This is not your city to map out. It's ours. You shouldn't even be here, any of you. Hitler wants you gone. He wants Warsaw turned into a transit post for our empire in the east.'

'What empire?' Even from her hiding place down the road, Hana heard Marek's voice, loud and clear and defiant. He had clearly decided that if he was to be arrested, he would say his piece first and she strained to listen; to bear witness. 'Your precious Third Reich is crumbling. Your soldiers are being whipped down the road by the Red Army and they'll be here to whip the rest of you any day now.'

She couldn't help admiring his bravery but cringed back from the likely consequences. The rest of the Poles were shuffling away, keen to distance themselves from this brave rebellion, and Marek was left alone before the furious Gestapo.

'You think the Russians will help you?' their leader sneered. 'You think they'll hand Warsaw over and let you make it pretty with your pathetic, futuristic maps? Fool! They're treacherous, back-stabbing Slavs and they'll enslave you.'

'As you have tried to enslave us,' Marek shot back. 'But you won't succeed. No one will succeed. Poland will be free-eee.'

The last word gurgled out on a wave of blood as the Nazi shot him, point-blank, in his stomach, ramming the gun against his flesh in a dark thrust. Marek crumpled to the ground, screaming in frothing agony as his lungs clogged and his body jerked on the pavement between the impassive Nazis.

'Serves you right, ignorant Pole, with your ridiculous, egotistical little maps.' The Gestapo tapped the folder. 'The boss will have a good laugh at these.'

He turned and rapped back into the Telephone Exchange, leaving Marek on the pavement, thankfully still as God scooped his soul out of his crumpled body. People hurried nervously around him and Hana looked down at the single map in her hand. Terrified, she shoved it into her knickers, her head spinning with grief and fury. She longed to carry Marek to the hero's burial he deserved, but did not dare. All she could do was report his loss to Agaton and hope the AK would be able to retrieve his broken body for his family under shadow of darkness.

Turning sadly away, she swore that this hateful reign of terror would be stopped. The Russians were close and, if they advanced further, Warsaw *must* rise. It was all down to Moscow now, Moscow and the AK. Picturing Marek spewing up blood for the simple crime of daring to dream of a better city, she hardened her quaking heart.

Whatever it meant for her family, she was ready now; it was time.

FIVE

ZUZI

Zuzi crouched in the forest, staring at the radio sitting on a tree stump like a primitive god, awaiting the promised broadcast from Moscow. The Minerki had grown bored of waiting for Roza to return with the location of the weapons, and been delighted when a nearby AK platoon had called them into their leafy den, saying Stalin was about to send a message to Warsaw.

This was vital. If Stalin backed the Poles, they could rise. If Stalin approved the use of force, it meant the Red Army were on their way and the insurgents would only need to hold out for a few days. They could do that, Zuzi was sure. The AK could take their city and they could keep Her safe until the Soviet troops brought their vast numbers in to shore them up. If Stalin did not offer his support, however...

'I can't bear it much longer,' one of the AK moaned. 'Every day under the jackboot feels like a year. We *have* to strike.'

'We have to have Stalin's backing,' his leader told him repressively. 'A fight cannot be won on will alone.'

The man sighed rough assent. They knew that too well

from the terrible events of September 1939 when they'd resisted the invaders with three weeks of passionate fighting that had served only to see far too many of them dead. For months, Poland had been clothed in a cloud of shame until, the following spring, they'd seen Blitzkrieg – the unstoppable German tank-led assault – rage through Denmark, Norway, Belgium and finally France even quicker than it had flattened Poland. No one had stood a chance. Fierce love for your country was a strong force, but not as strong as a machine gun or a tank. Cold steel beat warm hearts every time and they must remember that now. But, oh, Zuzi knew how the young man felt and she gripped at a gnarled tree root as she willed the radio to produce the support they longed for.

'Ssh,' Nina said, 'that's the Moscow march. Stalin will be on in a minute.'

They all shut up as the Russian music crackled out of the set and then, at last, came the voice of Marshal Stalin, overlaid by a translator turning his words into Polish for them all to understand. Zuzi dug her fingers into the root and prayed for this to be the message they sought.

'Warsaw is shaking to the foundations from the roar of guns,' the speech started. 'Soviet forces are coming to bring you freedom. People of the Capital – to arms!'

Zuzi looked to her fellows, and saw the same spark in their eyes that she felt in her own. Stalin was backing them!

'May the whole population rise like a stone wall around the capital's underground army,' the voice went on. 'Strike at the Nazis! Obstruct their plans to blow up public buildings. Assist the Red Army in the crossing of the Vistula. Send them information. Show them the way!'

'Yes!' the people around Zuzi were calling, fists pumping the air and cheers growing in volume as Stalin's voice rose. The Vistula River was the final barrier keeping the Russians out of Warsaw, but not, it seemed for long.

'May your million-strong population become a million soldiers who will drive out the Nazi invaders and win freedom!'

'Freedom!' they all echoed, leaping to their feet and hugging each other.

Zuzi flung herself into the communal embrace, feeling excitement fizz inside her like home-made wine.

'What is it?' someone demanded, running into the clearing. 'What's happened?'

'Roza!'

They ran to greet her, babbling about Soviet backing, and she laughed out loud.

'Well then, Minerki,' she said, 'we'd better go and get ourselves some weapons!'

Saying goodbye to the men with cries of, 'see you on the frontline', they split into two groups – ten to find transport for the weapons and ten to follow Roza to the cache. Zuzi was glad to make it into the second group, although less impressed when the weapons turned out to be buried beneath someone's courgettes in a vast allotment. She found herself in a crusty pair of overalls, spade in hand, but nothing could dampen her excitement and she dug into the soil with enthusiasm.

'Steady, Żelazo,' Tosia warned. 'You don't want to strike a mine.'

Zuzi forced herself to probe more carefully, gently digging up the ripe courgettes and lifting them high as if they were the treasure she was seeking, before prising out the mines and grenades stashed beneath. The allotments were busy with the Volksdeutsche still left in Warsaw and the Minerki had to slide the weaponry into a handy shed in secret. Luckily, the German civilians seemed to be digging up their own boxes in even more of a frenzy than the Minerki and paid them little attention.

'Look at them, grabbing their family jewels to flee the city,'

Roza whispered, pointing to a mother and two daughters scrabbling in the dark soil nearby.

'We should go over and shove their fine diamonds up their tight arses,' Zuzi growled.

Tosia put a warning hand on her shoulder. 'And have every guard in Warsaw onto our treasures before we have a chance to attack? You must be calm.'

Zuzi knew her leader spoke the truth but, God help her, it was hard. She wanted to attack now, as Stalin had exhorted, and every second of waiting was torture.

'Dig,' Tosia urged and, with a groan, Zuzi did so.

Evening was falling by the time they had all the boxes into the shed. Zuzi was dizzy from the heat and had had to eat several raw courgettes to overcome both her thirst and hunger. Holding the weapons with which they would destroy the Nazis, however, kept her going and she was swift to volunteer to smuggle them across the city.

Curfew was only an hour away so it was vital to do a first run to the apartment opposite the Prudential before it struck. W-hour could come at any time and they had to be ready. The others of their troop had gathered several means of transportation and they hastily stashed the weapons in the seemingly innocuous containers – in a basket beneath fruit, inside a bundle of soft toys destined for an orphanage, and even in a box of sanitary towels.

'Careful with those,' Nina laughed, indicating the towels. 'They're precious.'

'Not for Poles,' Zuzi joked in a mock-German accent. 'Poles aren't worth enough to menstruate!'

The others laughed bitterly.

'I tell you,' Zuzi went on, 'the Germans will need these soon enough to use as white flags for surrender!'

The others cheered and, encouraged, she bent to grab one, but as her fingers closed around the nearest pad and she lifted it in a pretend wave of capitulation, the girls gasped. In her hand was the pin of a hidden grenade, wrenched free with her 'joke' of a sanitary towel. Zuzi moved fast, spotting the relevant grenade and hurling it from the shed into the mound of dug-up courgettes. The vegetables exploded in a gruesome green mash, splattering them all with juice but, praise God, no blood. Zuzi peered out, horrified at herself. The Volksdeutsche had thankfully all gone and only an elderly couple were still working their patch. They looked over, shook their heads, and went back to their weeding. Zuzi sank to the floor, shocked and ashamed.

'I'm sorry,' she said, the adrenaline of the hyped-up day draining rapidly out of her. 'I'm so, so sorry.' She'd been foolish and reckless and she'd nearly killed their entire troop. What was wrong with her? 'I'm sorry,' she said again, burying her head in her knees.

'This is a valuable lesson for us all in treating these weapons with respect,' Tosia said sternly.

'Yes, Tosia,' the group agreed, also muted. 'Sorry, Tosia.'

'Be very sensible transporting these and very careful. Anyone gets caught, you know what it means?'

'Death?'

'Precisely. Death and, worse than that, less weapons for W-hour. So, off you go – last one back makes the tea, right?'

It was what she always said at the start of a mission and they all smiled and headed out. Zuzi made to go with them but Tosia stepped in front of her. 'I think you'd better sit this one out.'

'No!' Zuzi cried. 'No, please. I've learned, Tosia, I promise.'

Their leader, however, folded her arms. 'Not today. You can play the fool when we've won.'

Zuzi felt rare tears prick her eyes and looked hurriedly down. She deserved this but it still hurt.

'Yes, Tosia.'

Tosia lifted up her chin. 'But you can carry the medical

supplies we found beneath the mines. The John of God Hospital are setting up a hidden ward.'

She held out a box of dressings. Zuzi took them, humiliation complete, but then something jogged in her mind. Orla was working in the John of God and suddenly the thought of seeing her kindly little sister felt like the best thing she'd heard all day.

'Yes, Tosia,' she said again, more firmly.

She could still feel Stalin's urge to rise up rushing around her blood and she still wanted to do it right here, right now, but she was a part of a far larger, more coordinated attack, a cog in a vast and carefully constructed wheel, and she must learn to play her part calmly. Bending to very carefully arrange a few of the sanitary towels on top of the bandages as camouflage, she headed, alone, over the splatter of courgette.

The mess was a garish reminder of the dangers of the explosives in which she would soon be dealing. Entering the war, she saw now, might be more blood than glory, but, even so, it had to be better than this endless, grinding captivity and she was determined, come what may, to do her bit to escape it.

SIX

ORLA

'Oh honestly, this is ridiculous!' The voice came from outside the hospital, high-pitched with indignation and very, very familiar to Orla. 'I know "żonkil" is the password,' it went on, with an accompanying foot stamp, 'because I've used it once already today. If it's good enough for the Minerki, it's good enough for a few medics.'

Orla, doing an inventory of their supplies, bit her lip to stop herself laughing.

'That sounds like my sister,' she said to Bronislaw.

'Poor you!'

They both paused to listen.

'What's that? Plural? Oh fine – "żonkile". Will that do you? Good. Now, let me deliver my supplies, you idiot.'

Orla laughed again and raced to greet Zuzi as she came down the stairs into their secret ward.

'Why are the people on the door always so pedantic?' her dark-haired sister demanded indignantly as soon as she saw Orla.

'Because that's their job. Security is paramount, as you know.'

'I suppose, but who cares if there's one daffodil or many?'

'An undercover Nazi with a grenade?' Bronislaw suggested, joining them.

Zuzi turned her black eyes furiously on him and Orla braced herself.

'Because the Nazis always operate undercover around here, don't they?' her dark-eyed sister fired out. 'It's not like they own the city, is it? It's not like they can rap on any old door and shoot whoever answers without so much as a by-your-leave, is it?'

Orla cringed but Bronislaw did not seem at all fazed.

'Good point. There's always the communists though.'

Zuzi sniffed. 'Hmm. That's a good point too.' She looked up at him. 'Who are you anyway?'

'Dr Br—'

'Łukasz,' Orla supplied swiftly.

Zuzi looked at her in confusion, almost as if she'd forgotten she was there. Was that the dazzling effect of the Łódź doctor? He was handsome, Orla supposed, if you liked the brooding type, which she definitely didn't. Zuzi, however, might well do, if she'd only let herself. Orla felt a smile tug at her lips but fought it, knowing her spiky sister would hate being the cause of any amusement.

'Well, Dr Łukasz, I've brought you some supplies.' Zuzi was holding a large box which she held out towards him and then blushed – actually blushed. Orla didn't think she'd ever seen her sister do that before. 'Sorry, they're, er, hidden beneath, er...'

Orla lifted the lid to see a neat row of sanitary towels and understood her sister's embarrassment but Bronislaw, again, was not fazed.

'Perfect, thank you. I'm sure it will all come in very handy. This is most resourceful of you.'

'Oh, we dug them up from under some courgettes. That is...'

Zuzi was stumbling over her words again and Orla was definitely going to smile if she didn't get away.

'Just getting some fresh air,' she excused herself and made a dash for the door into the hospital proper. Her uniform was the same as those working in this official area, so she was able to blend in before any prying eyes. Thankfully there were no Nazis patrolling today, so she headed outside for some fresh air.

She looked up and down the road. Hundreds of Volksdeutsche were still fleeing west, back into the heart of the Third Reich, but there were no more bedraggled Wehrmacht soldiers. Indeed, up ahead she caught the distinctive sound of jackboots rapping confidently along and, peering into the evening sun, saw lines of them marching smartly past the end of Bonifraterska Street, presumably heading to shore up their defences against the approaching Red Army. Orla put up a hand to see more clearly, mesmerised by the rapped-out rhythm, and was nearly sent flying by a young boy moving at high speed and giggling fit to burst.

'Jacob?!'

'Orla! Oh, Orla, we've done the funniest thing.'

Her younger brother leaned over, gasping breath into his lungs as two of his friends came panting up to join him, also giggling.

'Why were you running?' Orla demanded.

'So we don't get caught, of course.'

'Doing what?'

They started giggling again as they tried to explain.

'Fleas,' was all Orla caught at first, and then, 'itching', and it slowly came out that the three of them had spent days collecting dog fleas into two big jars. These they had smuggled into the German-only cinema down the road, releasing them mid-film and sitting quietly at the back to watch the resultant chaos.

'It was so funny, Orla,' Jacob laughed. 'First one started scratching, then his neighbour and then the row in front, until they were all at it like dogs. We had to leave before we burst out laughing and gave ourselves away.'

'And you don't think running from the cinema did that?'

'Nah. They were too busy...' Jacob paled. 'Is that that fat officer from the end of the row?'

His friends stared at the man lumbering up the road towards them. He was in a uniform decorated with scary amounts of braiding and was scratching at his fat neck as he scoured every face on the street. Two dark-coated Gestapo stood at his shoulders, guns held menacingly before them.

'Oh God,' Jacob gasped, 'we have to run.'

'No.' Orla put a hand on his shoulder. 'They've not seen you yet. This way.'

Heart racing, she steered them into the hospital, making for the secret entrance to the cellar at the back. If the itching officer caught them, the punishment for humiliating him would be unimaginable and she couldn't bear the thought of her little brother suffering – or worse.

'Down here.'

All three boys went meekly where she led, their appearance so ghastly that even the password girl didn't stop them. Zuzi was still talking to Bronislaw but came over immediately.

'Jacob? What are you doing here?'

'He's volunteering for bandage practice,' Orla said, spotting her boss. 'Sister Maria, these three young men are here for the nurses to practise on.'

'Excellent.'

The stern-faced head nurse swept in and the boys turned even paler, but let themselves be led to the newly made-up beds to have slings and tourniquets applied to their thankfully still intact bodies.

'What have they been up to?' Zuzi whispered to Orla.

'Setting fleas on Germans.'

'Neat.'

'Not when they nearly got caught it's not.'

Zuzi shivered and slid an arm through Orla's.

'I blew up some courgettes today,' she confided.

'Courgettes?'

'Long story. Let's just say it made me realise the dangers of fighting.'

'Good,' Orla said stoutly. 'Hana wouldn't like you being reckless.'

'She worries too much,' Zuzi said lightly, but Orla knew that if her bold sister was afraid, it must be bad.

'Must we rise up, Zuzi?' she whispered.

Zuzi squeezed her arm.

'We must, Orla. We cannot live in a world in which young lads could be executed for a mere prank, can we?'

She indicated their little brother. Jacob was relaxing now, even enjoying the attentions of the young nurse wrapping a bandage around his scalp, but his could have been a very different fate. Orla thought of the Wehrmacht reinforcements marching past the end of the road, of the fury of the officer, and the dark truncheons and pistols of his Gestapo guards. Suddenly, all she could see was Jacob's precious young blood leaking out of that pristine white bandage and onto those pristine white sheets – a hideous parody of the bold Polish flag.

'You're right,' she agreed. 'I just pray it doesn't last too long.'

'Oh, it won't,' Zuzi told her confidently. 'Stalin has sent out a broadcast urging us on. He'll be here within days, Orls, and the main thing we can do is make sure we rise up first. Come on, let's get ourselves home, hey?'

'Just in time to see the others before sunfall?'

'Exactly that.'

Orla smiled. Calling Jacob to them, she waved goodbye to Bronislaw – amusedly noting Zuzi having to stop herself doing the same – and headed home to Piekarnia Dąbrowska and the safety of her family.

SEVEN

31 JULY

HANA

Hana picked at a slice of her mother's beautiful fruit bread as her family chattered excitedly over breakfast. Raisins were rare now and she was trying to summon up an appetite for this precious treat, but it was hard. All night long the image of Marek spewing the last of his blood onto the pavement in front of the Telephone Exchange had haunted her and she wasn't sure whether it made her more sad or angry. The anger, at least, was easier and she was trying to focus on that. The radio, under the cover of the morning news, was broadcasting today's AK password: wojownik – warrior. It was hard not to read things into that choice; were they all truly to become warriors today?

Hana edged towards the door, getting up the energy to pull on her boots and head to work, but at that moment her grandmother burst in.

'I come bearing gifts!'

Babcia Kamilla stepped over the threshold and paused, awaiting the attention of the family. Hana sighed. Usually, she found her grandmother's self-important ways amusing but she wasn't in the mood today. The others, however, were all ears.

'Are you eating?' Kamilla trilled, looking round the table. 'So sorry to interrupt. Fruit bread? Goodness no, Magda, I don't do breakfast, you know that.' She frowned at Magda who, even with the ravages of grief and rationing, was still softer and more buxom than determinedly skinny Kamilla had ever been. But then she gave a condescending nod of her head. 'Well, maybe a small coffee if there is one? And, I suppose it would be a shame to let that last slice go to waste. There's precious little food with the bastard Nazis controlling us.'

Again, Hana suppressed a sigh. It was always the same. Babcia had never truly got over her precious son choosing to become a baker and, even worse, a baker in the working-class suburb of Wola instead of her own elegant Stare Miasto. Her father had always said it was more down to earth in the west of the city which was, of course, precisely what Kamilla preferred to avoid but, whatever she claimed, she had a weak spot for Magda's baking and almost always condescended to visit at mealtimes.

'What's this gift?' Hana demanded.

Everyone looked at her, surprised. Hana was usually the calm one, but she hadn't the energy for it today. Kamilla bristled but, perhaps sensing her mood, put her coffee down. Slowly and deliberately, she clutched the hem of her calf-length skirt and lifted it up.

'Babcia!' Magda protested, but Kamilla waved her off.

'It was the only way to get it here,' she said, and they saw, wrapped around her slim hips, a large Polish flag. Zuzi leapt up to grab the end of it, and Kamilla spun gracefully, as if carrying out a trick on a sophisticated dance floor, not unravelling an illegal flag in the back of a bakery.

'Why?' Hana stuttered.

'I asked her for it,' Zuzi said excitedly. 'My unit have been assigned to attack the Prudential tower at W-hour and we wanted a really big flag to fly from the top when we take it.'

'*If* you take it,' Hana corrected.

Zuzi huffed. 'Thanks for the vote of confidence, sis.'

Hana rubbed a weary hand across her eyes. 'Sorry. I didn't sleep well.' She slid her feet into her boots. 'I'd better get to my post.'

'You better had,' Babcia Kamilla agreed. 'Communication will be key in this uprising. Armies are like orchestras, your grandfather always said – they work best in concert. You, my dear Hana, are one of the conductors.'

Hana gave her grandmother a reluctant smile. 'Thank you, Babcia, but I'm nothing so grand. I merely carry messages from the conductors.'

Kamilla was not to be put off. 'You are, my dear, the very baton.'

She gave a flourish of her slim wrist and Zuzi laughed.

'We're all batons, these days,' she said, indicating their frames, far too skinny from the rationing and only kept whole with their mother's clever use of her baking allowances.

Anger ground in Hana's stomach again. The rations allowed to a Pole were half that allowed to a Volksdeutsch, as if they were half the people which, indeed, is how the arrogant Nazis saw them.

She stamped her foot. 'How have we allowed this to go on for so long?'

The rest of her family jumped.

'Are you all right, Hana?' her mother asked, coming over and putting an arm around her shoulders.

She forced herself to smile. 'I'm fine, Mama. Just... frustrated.'

'It's a good question,' Zuzi said.

'To which the answer is...?'

'Guns,' Jacob said promptly. 'Their guns are bigger and better than ours. Well, the ones that we have and that I'm not allowed to use.'

'Quite right,' Orla admonished him. 'You're reckless enough with fleas, so you don't deserve bullets.'

Jacob pouted.

'If I had something important to do, I wouldn't need to mess around with insects.' He leaped over to Zuzi. 'I helped Orla's lot in the hospital yesterday, so can I come with you today, Zuzi? Please.'

'Sorry, Jacob,' Zuzi said, chucking him under the chin. 'The AK doesn't have enough weapons for the trained soldiers, let alone upstart Scouts.'

'Filipinkas then. I could carry filipinkas, right?'

'That still takes training.'

'So train me! We fight in our own ways, right, Mama? And I want to fight with you. Please, Zuzi.'

He dropped comically to his knees before her and she groaned.

'If we need you when the uprising actually breaks out, Jacob, I'll train you.'

'Really?'

'Course. But hopefully we won't. Hopefully, our brave Polish pilots will come to our aid.'

She threw a wink Hana's way and Hana's heart ached.

'Do you think they'll come?' she couldn't resist asking.

'Of course they will. They've worked hard for the Allies throughout the war so must, surely, be allowed to come to the assistance of their own country?'

Hana's heart lifted.

'You're right,' she agreed, lacing her boots up with new determination. 'The Russians will march over the Vistula and the RAF will fill the skies and they'll help us chase the Wehrmacht and the Luftwaffe out of Warsaw, right?'

'Right,' the others chorused.

'And in the meantime,' Zuzi said, 'your job, Jacob, is to keep spirits up.'

'Fine,' Jacob grunted. 'I'll stick to paint – for now.'

He lifted an olive oil tin he'd filled with black paint and tucked a paintbrush into the waistband of his shorts, ready to head out scrawling PWs onto Warsaw's walls.

'Take care,' Magda urged, kissing him.

He squirmed away. 'I will, Mama. I always do.'

She hugged him again. 'Just remember you're precious to me.' She looked around the breakfast table and blinked her big eyes, as blue as Orla's. 'You are all precious to me.'

Jacob ducked hastily out the door, though not before he'd given his mother a quick peck on the cheek. Hana hugged all her family, bar Babcia, who did not like vulgar displays of emotion.

'Your bread,' Magda said.

'Perfect.' She wrapped the loaf in a linen cloth and tucked it into her bag. 'See you all at sunfall.'

'See you at sunfall,' came back the determined chorus. She prayed it was true.

The sun was beating down on Warsaw and Hana pulled her hat low, not wanting to burn. She hopped onto a tram heading west into Śródmieście and her liaison hub behind the beauty salon. There were many such hubs all over the city and today liaison girls and boys like her would be hurrying to build an undercover network of communication ready to carry word of W-hour to the forty thousand AK troops currently polishing their guns across the Polish capital.

The tram reached her stop and Hana jumped off, looking around for guards and finding far more than she'd like. There were markedly fewer Volksdeutsche making for the station today too. Perhaps they'd all gone already, or perhaps they were bolstered by the fresh troops marching down Jerusalem Avenue, shiny boots on their feet and shiny guns across their shoulders. Hana felt a coil of unease in her stomach. The Nazis no longer looked to be leaving Warsaw and she prayed the AK command knew what they were doing. Everyone would be at risk if this didn't work, including her own family. Dear Tata had urged them to fight, yes, but he had urged them to live too and, as the eldest child, Hana knew she owed it to him to prevent harm coming to the others.

Forcing herself on, she chose the quieter side alleys to wind her way towards her post but as she walked, she heard footsteps close behind and, when she stopped to look back, thought she saw someone duck into a doorway. Was she being followed?

She tutted at herself. She was hardly important enough for a tail and yet, when she set off again, the footsteps also renewed.

'It's a city,' she told herself, 'There are people everywhere.'

But again, she looked back and again she caught the shadow of a figure ducking out of sight. Her heart snagged. Had someone seen her watching Marek's death yesterday? Did someone know she had a map for a new expressway tucked deep into her knicker-drawer in their home above the bakery? And yet, if so, why were they not arresting her? Remembering her training, she stepped into a shop doorway, forcing herself to casually peruse the goods in the window, while keeping an eye on the street for any suspicious figures coming past. And then, suddenly there was one – and Hana nearly laughed out loud.

'Got you!'

She jumped out, grabbing her hunter by the collar.

He squirmed. 'Get off me, Hana.'

'No. Why are you following me, Jacob?'

Her little brother squirmed harder.

'I just wanted to know where you were going. It's boring painting anchors. I want a more important job.'

'What could be more important than lifting the fighting spirit of the city?'

He pouted. 'Shooting Nazis?'

Hana shushed him, looking anxiously around, but they were alone for now.

'It's not about simply shooting individuals, Jacob,' she hissed, 'it's about defeating the regime.'

He kicked at the ground.

'That too, I guess, though I'd still like to shoot some Nazis. They killed Tata, Hana.'

'I know that, but—'

'I barely remember him.' He looked up at her, his mischievous eyes for once deeply serious. 'I lie in bed at night trying to picture him. Not the... the last time. Just him, when he was here with us, baking bread and playing football in the street and carrying me on his back. I know he did those things and if I work really hard, I can sort of see it in my mind, but I can't feel it, Hana. I can't feel *him*.'

Hana squeezed his shoulder.

'I'm sorry, Jacob. He was so proud of you, I know that. He was so pleased he'd got a son after three girls.'

Jacob stood up straighter, his eyes taking on their familiar cheeky sparkle. 'Boys *are* better than girls.'

'That's why they pull silly stunts with fleas?'

He shrugged. 'It was very funny, Han. You should have seen them all itching away, the officers and the soldiers and their big fat girlfriends.'

Despite herself, Hana smiled.

'I'm sure it was. Just don't take too many risks, Jacob.'

'Don't we all have to take risks now, though? Isn't that what an uprising's all about?' Hana shushed him hastily, but he had a point. 'Can I come with you?' he pressed. 'Please. I'd be really good with messages. I know the city well and I'm fast. I bet I could get a message all the way from Żoliborz to Czerniaków in half an hour.'

'I bet you could, Jacob,' she agreed, 'but it's not possible. There are systems to get through.'

'For now,' Jacob said.

'What do you mean?'

'Once we're at war it'll be different. They'll need people like me if...' He tailed awkwardly off.

'If people like me get killed?' Hana supplied, the possibility chilling her blood.

Jacob flung his arms around her waist. 'Not that. Definitely not that. Sorry, Hana. I didn't mean it. I don't want you to get killed, not today, not in the uprising, not ever.'

Hana hugged him close, feeling the new strength in his wiry young body, and knew that they had to free Warsaw for Jacob and all the other youngsters growing up to believe guns, killing and rebellion were a normal part of life.

'I won't,' she promised, then felt compelled to amend it to, 'I'll try really hard not to.'

Jacob nodded his head fiercely against her shoulder then pulled back and lifted his tin.

'Best deliver this oil, hey?'

She smiled at him.

'I'm sure it will be much appreciated.'

He groaned but smiled again and then he was off, haring down the street to find his chums and paint their rebellion loud and proud in strong PWs onto Warsaw's walls. Hana watched until he turned the corner, out of sight, and then made her way cautiously to her post.

'Fiolet, at last! You're wanted in there.'

One of the girls in the apartment room above the beauty salon nodded to the bedroom that stood as their leader's office.

'Me?'

'Yep. Must be something serious cos Czajnik has asked for you twice.'

Hana cursed herself for lingering with Jacob, but what could she have done? Hurrying to the door, she knocked.

'Ah, Fiolet, come in, close the door.'

Her boss, code name Czajnik – Kettle – was a stern-faced lady of around forty who must surely have been a headteacher before the occupation put a stop to such innocent professions.

'Sorry I'm late. I had to shake off a tail.'

She regretted the over-dramatic pronouncement immediately but luckily Czajnik paid it zero attention.

'You are one of our top girls, Fiolet.'

'Thank you, ma'am.'

'Fleet of foot, I'm told, with an excellent sense of direction and a clever way of keeping messages secret.'

Hana glanced down at her mother's loaf and smiled.

'I do my best.'

'And do it so well that I have a new assignment for you. An important one. First, however, I must be sure of your commitment to your role.'

Hana shifted.

'I'm totally committed, Czajnik ma'am. I'm ready to rise and prepared to do everything it takes to keep the AK units in communication with each other.' She remembered Babcia's pronouncement at breakfast and drew herself up to channel her dignified grandmother. 'Armies, like orchestras, work best in concert.'

Czajnik looked taken aback.

'Quite. Well put, my dear. And you have no, erm, romantic entanglements that might impair your ability to give fully to your job?'

Hana blinked; this was an unusually probing set of questions.

'I'm engaged, ma'am, but my fiancé is a pilot stationed in Italy so unlikely to be demanding my attention.'

Czajnik nodded.

'Good. Excellent.' Hana was not sure she could agree but said nothing. Czajnik steepled her fingers self-importantly and leaned forward. 'I would, therefore, like you, Fiolet, to report to Commander Bór's HQ.'

'Commander...?'

Commander Bór was the head of the whole AK, not just in Warsaw but right across Poland. What could he want with her?

'Your role will be to carry his top-level messages to core hubs for distribution. It will be demanding and it will be dangerous, but you will be involved at the highest possible level. Will you do it?'

She fixed Hana with a gimlet-stare that left her little choice, not that she wanted it. This was an honour indeed and she saluted smartly.

'Yes, ma'am.'

'Excellent. Here's the HQ address.' She handed over a slip of paper. 'Memorise it.' Hana scanned the address three times, nodded and handed it back. Czajnik tore it into pieces and set fire to them in a copper tray on her desk, clearly not averse to a little drama herself. 'Good. Report in at 1700 hours.'

'This evening?'

'Of course. W-hour could be upon us at any time, girl, and it will be your job to tell all Warsaw. Off you go!'

Hana scrambled from the room and out to her rapt fellows. The day passed in a blur as she trawled around Warsaw, delivering messages hidden in Magda's loaf. She noted many more PWs on walls and smiled to see them, but the hours seemed to drag until, finally, she could make her way to AK HQ, her head spinning with the fact that she, Hana Dąbrowska, was to be

Commander Bór's very own liaison officer. Wait until she told her sisters. Wait until she told Babcia Kamilla! Maybe she really was a conductor now.

She went up to the address she'd memorised – a hardware shop, full of the sort of tools that labouring Poles were still permitted to buy – and cautiously gave the password to the brown-coated man behind the counter. With a small smile, he ushered her to a side door and she found herself in a store cupboard with, as he hastily showed her, another secret door at the back. Feeling ridiculously excited, she slid through it and headed up dusty stairs. She gave the password again at the top, this time to a young man with dark eyes and a pistol at his belt, and then she was in a large room furnished with several smart desks. They were all empty.

'Sit there,' the guard said, pointing to a chair. Hana did as she was told and realised she could hear voices from an adjoining room. Commander Bór was evidently in a meeting with the Homeland Council – the high-level generals and government delegates running the AK – and she sat very still and did her best not to eavesdrop.

She did not succeed, though, to be fair to her, their voices were all raised, their debate clearly heated.

'We must not rise up until the Russians cross the bridges,' one man said. 'That is the point of no-return for the Red Army.'

'And quite possibly the point at which they take Warsaw,' someone else argued. 'If we wait until then it will be too late. They will claim the victory and we will be vassals once more, just to a different master.'

'We have to seize the city first,' a third man agreed. 'We have to welcome the Russians as holders of our own capital, not let them roll in and take it as conquerors.'

'You assume,' another voice said, run through with urgency, 'that we *can* seize the city.'

'Of course we can. Have you not seen the Wehrmacht fleeing east? They're on their knees.'

'Those ones might be, but not the fresh platoons they're shipping from the Reich. My sources tell me Hitler has put Himmler in charge of defending Warsaw. That means he'll be sending in the SS with all their brutal, dirty tactics.'

'Which is why,' the first man said, 'we have to take Warsaw *now*, before they get a hold on it.'

The arguments went round and round and Hana sat listening, her heart sinking into the chair. Everything they said, on all sides, made sense. Poland was caught between two enemies, as She had been for centuries, and they had to tread a fine line to escape them both.

There was a bang as someone struck a desk next door. It made her jump, it made the dark-eyed guard jump, and it silenced the voices.

'Gentlemen.' This voice was calm and refined, if run through with tiredness. 'We are faced with an impossible choice. The government in London are supporting an uprising, our generals are supporting an uprising—'

'Not all of them, Bór,' someone objected.

'*Some* of our generals are supporting an uprising,' the first man – Commander Bór himself – corrected, unbending, 'but most importantly of all, our people are supporting an uprising. Not just supporting it, but begging for it. They are sick of the occupation. They are sick of oppression and cruelty. They are sick of having their favourite bits of their city barred to them, sick of being deprived of education for their youth, and sick, above all, of seeing their loved ones hung for no fair reason. They are champing at the bit to rise up and kick out their oppressors and I do not think, gentlemen, that we will stop them. If we order the rising, we can, at least, do it in an orderly, military fashion. I believe we owe it to our people, who have been patient in their suffering for far too long, to step up and lead them out of it.'

Hana felt a lump in her throat and looked over to the guard to see him wiping a surreptitious tear. She thought of Zuzi raring to fight, of Jacob, begging to be allowed a gun, of even gracious Babcia Kamilla asking to be allowed to make grenades. The commander was absolutely right and next door, to her relief, she heard a rumble of male voices agreeing.

The door flung open and she leaped to her feet to see a tall, wiry man, around the age her father would have been were he still with them. He wore a handyman's overalls, but had an unmistakable air of authority as he stepped up to shake her hand.

'Good evening,' he said politely. 'You must be my new liaison officer?'

'Yes, sir. I'm Fiolet, sir.'

'Fiolet. What a lovely choice. Welcome to the job, Fiolet. You join us on a propitious day.'

He sat at his desk and wrote with a firm, loping script as Warsaw's other top commanders and politicians emerged, also in the workmen's gear that would allow them to filter onto the street unnoticed by the Nazi patrols. Bór completed his message and handed it to Hana with a tight smile.

'Take care of this with your life.'

She nodded firmly and looked down to read the few simple but weighty words:

Order from Commander Bór and the Homeland Council:

W-hour is set for 17:00 hours tomorrow, 1 August 1944.

Prepare yourselves well and may God go with us.

Here, in her hands, was the order that would, tomorrow,

take her city, her people, and her family to war. Already Bór's aides were copying it out and stamping the slips to make them official. Her job now was to carry them to the core hubs from whence they would be distributed to all the others and from them to every underground soldier in Warsaw.

Five years ago, sorrowing for their lost father, the Dąbrowskas had joined the AK, swearing revenge. 'When it is time,' Babcia Kamilla had told them, 'we will strike.'

Now, it seemed, it was time. May God help them all.

EIGHT

1 AUGUST 1944

ZUZI

Zuzi sat, eyes fixed on the Prudential building as if she might bore into it with them though, of course, it would be the mines stacked neatly at her side that would do that. They were checked and ready and could be easily primed come W-hour in – she glanced at her watch – an hour's time. The message the Minerki had been waiting for had come to their unit via, of all people, her sister, Hana, apparently now something fancy in the liaison-girl world. Zuzi was pleased of course, but all the more determined to excel at her own role and make her father proud.

Her fingers went to her sleeve, feeling the red-and-white armband that marked her out as part of the AK. Units of less explosively minded girls had been diligently sewing these for weeks and Tosia had handed the Minerki theirs on arrival at their strike point. Zuzi stroked it proudly. This was all the AK had in the way of uniform. They had no fancy tunics, no standard-issue boots, no smart gun holders or regulation caps, just this simple red-and-white band.

The girls had put theirs on proudly, admiring themselves

and even posing for a photo with a camera Tosia had borrowed from one of the many reporters roving Warsaw. If W-hour went well, they would be able to wear them out in the open – miniature mirrors of the giant flag Zuzi intended to fly from the top of that building right across the street. She couldn't wait to replace the hated swastika. All they had to do first was chuck the Nazis out of the tallest building in Europe...

Zuzi's heart clenched and she gave it a stern talking-to. She was Żelazo; she was iron. She'd been waiting for a chance to strike at the Nazi monsters ever since they'd thrown her beloved father off the prison balcony and, at last, that chance was here. All around the city other units would be poised, just like theirs, and come 1700 hours they would rise up. There were forty thousand of them to only ten thousand Wehrmacht and they had surprise on their side. It would work; it had to.

Beside her, Roza's fingers ran over her rosary beads, her lips moving in silent prayer. Zuzi wasn't the only nervous one, then! Looking around the room in the heart of Śródmieście, she could see that their entire band was caught in private contemplation – or, at least, those of them that were here. They were several women down and Zuzi had no idea if they'd chickened out, been caught trying to get here, or not yet even got the message. There had been little time, last night, to distribute the order before curfew had fallen on the city. Hana had come home frustrated and been up and out as soon as it was lifted this morning, but Warsaw was a huge city and the AK were, of necessity, hard to find.

'Where are they?' she heard Tosia murmur to the leader of the AK sharing the attack with them.

This was the Kilinski platoon, one of the crack units that had made a name for themselves in various acts of sabotage over the last two years. The Minerki had worked with them on several occasions before so had been glad to welcome them into their apartment base. Their leader, an older man called Bartek, had proved himself both brave and resourceful and would be a good man to work with. This afternoon, as they'd been trying to divert themselves from the mammoth task ahead, he'd mentioned a son who was a doctor in the John of God Hospital and Zuzi had instantly seen the likeness. This Bartek, then, was the father of the intriguing Dr Łukasz, Orla's friend. Not that he was that intriguing, of course, not to her at least. She was iron.

Zuzi focused again on the Prudential tower. Two Nazi guards were goose-stepping across the grand entrance and she salivated at the thought of blowing them up. That wasn't nice, was it? But the time for being nice was long gone and, in an hour, they would be able to prove that to the occupying Germans, to the arriving Russians and to the whole world. Poland might be the first country to have been invaded by Hitler but they wouldn't be the last to be liberated – and they certainly wouldn't sit and wait for other people to do it for them.

'We need the whole platoon with us to do a professional job,' she heard Tosia complaining to Bartek, and leaned back to listen in to their conversation.

'It's a nonsense,' he agreed. 'We've been planning this uprising for five years so why are we rushing into it at the last minute? We needed at least forty-eight hours' notice to properly prepare. Half of our division are still out in the forests. Two of my men are printers and have been shut in their cellar for the last week because the Nazis have got wind of their press and set a guard on the entrance. I guess at least they'll stop worrying about that once we strike and we can get the poor buggers out.'

Across the city, the cathedral clock struck – just the soft, short chime of 1630 hours but Zuzi felt the city snap to attention. She could hear stray shots in various places as men got overexcited at having real weapons in their hands. Honestly! They had no control. The AK would be far better with more women in its ranks – as the Minerki would prove in half an hour.

Down below, a door banged and they all looked round, nerves jangling. Zuzi heard someone mumble today's password and then, to her joy, the last two of their tight-knit band tumbled into the room and Tosia hugged them in a most un-Tosia-like way, saying something about her 'little family' being complete. Zuzi joined in the welcome, but the word 'family' caught at her.

Her sisters would be at their posts now. Orla would be in the John of God Hospital on the edge of Stare Miasto, and Hana in the new AK HQ, at the famous Kammler furniture factory in their own suburb of Wola. Magda would be in the bakery, frantically kneading dough to feed the resistants – and to ease her fears for her children. Jacob would, hopefully, be with her, finding some outlet for his restless energy that did not involve aggravating the Gestapo. And Babcia Kamilla – she would be in her home in Stare Miasto, sipping a sherry, with her father's handcuffs on the wall above her head and her eyes fixed on the clock, waiting, as she had done several times in her life before, for the Poles to regain their independence.

Zuzi reached for the flag, wrapped up into a tight cylinder, and pushed it into the waistband of her trousers, buckling her belt tightly around it so it would not shift when they attacked.

'Gather in,' Tosia told her girls and they immediately formed a tight circle as they always did before a strike, though there had never been one as big, or as unpredictable as this. 'You know the drill,' she told them. 'You've done it a thousand times before. In fifteen minutes we will creep downstairs and, when the clock strikes five, we'll go. Bartek's men will take out the guards to cover us as we cross the street, place our explosives around the door, and set them off. You must move fast but with care. No heroics. Job done, we flatten ourselves to the walls to let the Kilinski inside and follow when ordered. From there, no drills can help us. You carry your weapons and you do as asked – blast staircases, walls, doors, whatever the Kilinski require. Our job is to open up their way and, ladies, we are damned good at it.'

She held up a hand and the Minerki clasped theirs around it until they formed one giant fist. Zuzi felt the power of her comrades quivering through their joined fingers and drew in a long, slow breath. They could do this. They had blown up train tracks, cars and supply trucks; they could manage a building, even one as big as the Prudential tower, especially when every other AK member in Warsaw would be striking at the same time.

Outside, the cathedral clock struck the merry note of quarter to the hour – quarter to *W-hour*.

'Mines at the ready, ladies,' Tosia said. 'This is it – this is the big one.' She smiled at them. 'Last one to the top makes the tea, right?'

'Last one to the top makes the tea,' Zuzi echoed, unpeeling her hand and going to fetch her mines and grenades. She was ready, she was definitely ready, but her not-so-iron heart was beating harder than ever before as she made for the stairs. She thought of her real family, sitting around the breakfast table yesterday morning while Babcia flamboyantly unrolled the flag that was now clasped sweatily in her waistband and wished she could be back there. But then she reminded herself of her father, flung to an ignominious death over a prison balcony by the evil Nazis, and her heart stilled.

'We will not be cuffed for long,' she muttered into the endless silence before the strike of five.

NINE

HANA

'You're taking that?!'

The words burst from Hana in a most unseemly way, especially given that she was addressing Bór's aide-de-camp, an imposingly military man with three medals pinned to the inside of his overcoat. But, really, they were moving the Homeland Council to a battle HQ, so why on earth was he packing a gramophone case? There would hardly be time to dance.

'Of course,' he replied lightly. 'An innocent man going to visit his friend on a normal summer afternoon, with little time for thoughts of anything as foolish as insurrection, would naturally want a few merry tunes, yes?'

She stared at him and, with a broad wink, he lifted up the edge of the gramophone to reveal, nestled into a secret compartment, two shiny pistols.

'Ah. Of course. Sorry, sir. Shouldn't have questioned you. I'm a little flustered.'

He patted her on the shoulder.

'Aren't we all, dear girl. It's not every day a whole city rises up – and under *our* direction.'

He winked again and went back to packing up the gramophone, inserting several ostentatiously German records into the lid. Hana thought he seemed quite the reverse of flustered, radiating an excitement that those used to army life must experience as battle drew close. Many of the men in HQ were the same, moving with purpose and charge, and she supposed that sitting around for five years running an underground militia must have been extremely frustrating for those used to leading the way. The only Poles fighting in this massive war were those who'd escaped the Motherland in 1939 and joined either the Russians or the British – like Emil.

Hana stepped to the window to look to the sky as she always did when she thought of her fiancé. It was foolish as he was hardly likely to be there, but it made her feel closer to him all the same. God, he loved flying. She could still remember him taking her out to dinner when he'd got back from his first training with the Polish air force in the summer of 1939. She'd been eighteen and still in her last year at school and had thought Emil Andrysiak, at twenty, so glamorous in his delicious uniform. She'd felt like the luckiest girl alive that he'd chosen to court her.

'It's magical, Hana,' he'd said. 'The planes are so light and responsive, it's almost as if they aren't there at all and you're flying freely. You must let me take you up when I'm fully qualified – if your father will trust me with you.'

She'd laughed. Emil had met Kaczper and they'd got on famously so she'd been sure he would trust Emil with her, both in a plane and in life. Emil hadn't declared himself at that stage, but he'd been dropping hints, asking her about her visions for the future which by then, frankly, had been mainly filled with thoughts of him.

'Do you want to make a career in the air force?' she'd asked him that night.

'Oh no,' he'd said. 'It's wonderful but I'd hate to be in the military when I had a family. That is...' he'd flushed gorgeously, '*if* I'm lucky enough to have a family.'

'What would you like to do then?' she'd asked.

'I want to teach history. Ideally at university level but maybe in schools, if I'm not good enough.' He'd flushed again. 'Sorry. Do you think that's terribly dull?'

Oh, she'd loved him then.

'I don't think it's dull at all. Why would I?'

'Because you're always talking about contemporary design and modern technology and looking to the future, so you probably think studying the past is silly.'

'Of course not,' she'd told him. 'Studying the past is the best way to look to the future.'

'Oh. Oh yes, I love that. I... I love you, Hana Dąbrowska.'

'I love you too, Emil.'

It had been the first time either of them had said it out loud and thank heavens their main courses had arrived because they'd had no idea what to do with themselves and been grateful to divert into discussion of pork belly and dumplings.

Hana smiled at the memory. It felt so very long ago. It *was* so very long ago. Emil had paid a formal visit to her father a month later and then come to find her with the beautiful amethyst ring she was twisting around on her finger now.

'You're all the future I want,' he'd said, down on one knee before her, and she'd scooped him up and kissed her seal of approval onto his lips.

A month later, Hitler had invaded and he'd had to flee for his life as the Nazis ran roughshod over Warsaw, trampling their wedding plans with everything else in their path. How Hana hated them but, at last, the chance had come to throw them out and she was foolish to hesitate.

She pulled herself away from the window and went to Bór. 'What can I carry, sir?'

They went into the street at carefully spaced intervals so as not to draw the attention of the Nazi patrols all over the city. Hana watched the cream of Poland's military and political leaders slink their way out of the apartment in a motley collection of overalls, smocks and catering uniforms, and admired their dedication. Most of these men were well into their fifties and could have been sitting out the occupation with their feet up but no, they were determined to liberate Poland and Hana was proud to be amongst them.

She left with Bór's ADC just after 1500 hours, her arm linked into his as he cradled the gramophone on the other side, looking for all the world like a couple out for a happy summer excursion. Bór came behind in paint-splattered overalls with an array of radio equipment squirrelled into the pots he carried in both hands. The ADC was whistling and she admired his aplomb but could offer little accompaniment bar the frantic beating of her heart.

The city felt electric. She'd seen it all day as she'd gone from hub to hub, speaking today's loaded password, przeznaczenie – destiny – at every secret apartment, house and shed to get in and pass on the momentous order: *W-hour at 1700 hours today.* It had not been easy. The Germans, although boorish, were not stupid and they, too, had picked up the excitement in the air and were checking papers everywhere.

She'd had to change her route many times to avoid them and had not got to her last delivery point until 1300 hours, giving the men and women on duty only four hours to find and muster their troops. People were scurrying everywhere and Hana's knowledgeable eye could see baskets of apparently very heavy fruit being lugged around, and the bulge in many an overcoat – far too warm for this hot August day – as guns were hastily taken into position in whatever way could be improvised.

She tried not to look at anyone bar her supposed beau but was still hugely relieved when they reached their destination – the Kammler furniture factory. Before the war, this renowned manufacturer had provided high-quality furniture for the finest homes all over Europe (Babcia Kamilla had a Kammler dresser of which she was especially proud), and during the occupation, for the Reich alone. Mr Kammler, however, had joined the AK right at the start and been quietly recruiting and training a staff that doubled as a fighting unit. Now, he welcomed the Homeland Council in, enthusing about the honour, and showed them up to a suitably grand office above the main workshop.

Hana looked around at the smart desks, laid out for the various commanders and government delegates, at the wardrobes doubling as document cupboards, and the dressers being set up as vital radio stations for comms with the AK control centres and the outside world, and felt a thrill at being a part of this. Who'd have thought little Hana Dąbrowska would find herself at the very heart of the uprising, positioned to carry Bór's orders to the whole of the AK? She went to the corner desk assigned specifically to her and looked around proudly.

And that's when the shots rang out.

Hana looked frantically at the grandfather clock in the corner. It wasn't even four yet – far too soon for W-hour to be erupting. Even worse, the shots seemed to be coming from the doors through which they had entered the factory not ten minutes ago.

'Get down,' someone shouted and Hana found herself flung to the floor.

'Where are the Radosław lot?' the ADC hissed at Bór. The 'Radosław' elite platoon was assigned as the Homeland Council's personal guard but there was no sign of them in the factory.

'Perhaps that's them now?' Bór suggested.

'If so, there's nothing elite about them. Only a fool would shoot early; it could break the entire plan.'

Two more shots sounded and then silence.

'The plan seems intact,' Bór said drily, picking himself up. 'Shall we go and investigate?'

Hana crept down at the back of their group to find Kammler and his men standing over a heap of dead Wehrmacht soldiers.

'Sentry lost his nerve when this lot patrolled too close for comfort,' Kammler said, rushing over to Bór. 'But don't worry, sir, we took out the rest and we've commandeered the jeep for good measure.'

He pointed to the German vehicle parked in the corner and Bór nodded.

'Good work.'

He went over to the dead men and Hana crept after him, morbidly fascinated. She'd never seen a dead body so close before. She'd got sickeningly used to corpses dangling from Nazi nooses and the other day she'd watched Marek die in a crumpled heap on the pavement, but there was something about these men, limp and pale at her feet, that felt so horribly real. She stared down at them – empty husks of people who had, until fifteen minutes ago, been breathing, dreaming humans – and felt the true power of a gun. One tiny bullet fired from afar, and a person could be gone forever.

'Good riddance.'

One of Mr Kammler's men kicked at the nearest body and it flopped helplessly, an arm falling limply to the warehouse floor. Hana shivered. Yes, the man had been a Nazi, and yes, if he wasn't lying dead on the floor, then they might be doing so instead, but it still seemed such a waste. Bór stepped forward.

'Treat the dead with respect, please,' he said sharply. 'He may be a Nazi but he's still someone's son.'

'Pity they didn't bring him up better then,' the man muttered, but he stepped back all the same.

Bór looked at his watch.

'Right, 1630 hours. We have to get back upstairs. We'll bury them tomorrow.'

'Bury them?' another man protested. 'I don't see why we should give them the respect they've not accorded us for the last five years.'

'You don't?' Bór looked at him in concern. 'I'm sorry for that, but the way I see it, we are trying to win Warsaw back to justice and fairness and we should start here.'

The man shuffled his feet. Bór simply looked at his watch again, then around the warehouse, but there was still no sign of their elite defenders. He shrugged.

'Come, let us get ready for W-hour. It seems we must face it on our own.'

He strode from the ground-floor warehouse and back up the stairs, Hana scurrying in his wake.

'I'm sorry, sir,' she panted, struggling to keep up.

He looked back at her. 'For what?'

'For not getting the command out in time.'

He shook his head.

'Oh no, Fiolet, *I* am sorry for not giving it sooner, but if there is one thing I have learned from my many years in the military, it is that regret, at least during battle, is a waste of time. The current situation is all that matters and we must deal with it as best we can to ensure a favourable future one. I am in no doubt that our platoon will be doing their best to reach us and, until then, we have Kammler and his men who know this factory inside out and, as they have already proved, are trained to kill. Besides, it's not just up to us now, but to every single brave member of the AK. Come here, to the window, and let us see the uprising begin.'

Hana did as she was bid, marvelling that she was standing with the top people at this pivotal point in history. The commander was a fascinating man, inscrutably calm but radiating energy. She'd heard tell that he had a wife in Warsaw but that they lived separately to avoid detection, only seeing each other once a week. Even so, the poor woman had given birth once during the occupation and was pregnant again. She had, it was whispered, refused to leave Warsaw and the knowledge that she was in the city with his children must give the uprising a personal edge for the commander. If so, he showed little sign.

Standing there at his side, Hana thought of Orla in her hospital and Zuzi poised to attack the Prudential tower, Babcia's flag optimistically ready to fly from the top. Her heart shuddered with its usual protective fear for her little sisters and she wished she was fretting about nothing more than unsuitable boyfriends, but that was not the hand God had dealt them. She prayed her mother and brother were safe in Wola and her grandmother was at her window in Stare Miasto to see the sparks fly when, at any moment now, the cathedral clock struck five. She looked up into the skies, serenely blue, with a few streaks of cloud hanging over the Vistula, and prayed to God and, as always, to Emil, for their blessing. It was probably blasphemous to petition her fiancé alongside the Almighty, but it brought her comfort and, in these hard times, that did not seem such a sin.

Hana closed her eyes, twisting her ring on her finger as she imagined Emil tomorrow, when news of the capital's rising reached his base in the toe of Italy. Would he and his fellow pilots be sent north immediately? The Red Army must be taking air bases from the Nazis as they advanced, so there had to be one they could use. The thought of her fiancé of five unseen years being within reach felt thrilling, and she gripped at the windowsill as, below her, the city waited.

And then the first chime of five from the cathedral clock dropped into the summer evening. There must have been four more, but they were drowned out as Warsaw erupted in one giant explosion – five chimes lost in five years of pent-up fury and pride, pointed down barrels and fired with calculated expertise. All around them, the sun flashed in a thousand windows as they were flung open to let the snipers begin their deadly work, and the city shook to the crash of grenades flung into the heart of the enemy.

Hana thought, briefly, of the corpses down below and knew that every cry going up from the sudden war-spots all over the city could mean another person, German or Polish, to put into the soil. She wondered how much blood it could absorb, but this was not the time to think negatively. This was not the time to think at all. This was W-hour and it was time, after five oppressive years, to act.

TEN

ZUZI

Zuzi felt the chimes of five ring through every part of her. It was the music of insurrection and it was glorious. Barely had the first one sounded before it was backed up by an orchestra of shots and blasts as Warsaw exploded in long-suppressed fury.

'Let's go, ladies!' Tosia cried and flung open the apartment door as shots from Bartek's men above them took out the two guards at the Prudential's grand doors.

Zuzi paid them no regard, save to be sure they were dead as she stuck her mine to the door frame and unrolled the fuse at speed. She could feel her heart pounding and her legs shaking and was grateful for those endless drills as her fingers did their tasks almost without her knowing. The windows above them had opened and Nazis were shooting at the AK on the opposite side but they had not looked down at the Minerki directly below.

She flattened herself against the wall and put a match to the fuse as, next to her, Roza did the same and across the way, two others lit their side. Zuzi watched, mesmerised, as the tiny flames flicked merrily up the wires and then braced herself as the Minerki entered the orchestra of the uprising. The doors blasted open, their glass shattering so that Zuzi had to turn herself into the bricks to avoid shards of it hitting her face. She felt pinpricks across her back as they bit but she was wearing Tata's old uniform jacket, tailored to fit by Orla, and they made little true impression through the thick fabric.

'Good work,' Bartek called as he led his men inside.

There were some sixty of them and they fanned out in small groups, leading the way into the building to hunt down Nazis. As they passed through, Tosia signalled the Minerki to follow Bartek's main platoon of twenty men and Zuzi felt the first shudder of fear. They had done no drills for the next part of the action because they had no idea what it might involve. Intel suggested there was a small but well-trained group holding the building but if so, they must be holding it from the upper floors because the big entrance hall was deserted.

'This way.'

Bartek motioned them up the sweeping staircase. The men pressed to the wall, pointing their guns around the turns ahead of them, and Zuzi followed with the other girls. Battle continued to ring out around Warsaw but within this, the central building, there was an eerie silence.

'Door,' Bartek hissed, looking round his men to Tosia.

She nodded and nudged Zuzi and Roza forward. They trod past the men to stick plastic explosive to the hinges and insert a detonator, rolling the wire back to a safe distance for lighting.

'Get down,' Zuzi hissed to the nearest men and had the satisfaction of watching them rush to obey as she lit the fuse.

This door, too, blew open at a first attempt and the AK rushed in but there was nothing in the big room bar a slumped body at the window. Someone darted across, gleefully grabbing a big Sten gun, but they could not pause to glory in small finds. They were here for the building.

Slowly, meticulously, they swept through the rooms on this floor. The building was vast and the German defenders seemed to be strung out in pairs.

'Trapped like flies in a web,' one of the AK growled as he passed Zuzi to shoot two of them down with the guns taken from their own guards.

First floor cleared, they swept upwards. It was a hot day and someone had opened the windows on the landings to let in some air. Through them, Zuzi could hear shouts of triumph and pain in both Polish and German and longed to know how the AK were faring elsewhere across the city. But there would be time enough for that at the end of this first outbreak; for now, she must concentrate on her objective.

She felt for Babcia Kamilla's flag, tucked into her waistband, and looked upwards. The stairs spiralled towards a huge roof-light at the top. Briefly Zuzi found herself thinking that Hana would be interested in that – she was always going on about something she called 'skylights' – but this was not the time for interior design.

'Let's go,' she urged and they pushed on.

Another turn in the stairs, another landing, another door. Zuzi and Roza ran up to stick plastic explosive along the hinges again. But as they were pressing their detonators into the mould, there was a furious rattle of a machine gun from beyond. Holes sprayed across the door and Zuzi shrank away as Roza, moving too late, was flung backwards, blood spraying from matching holes across her stomach.

'Roza!' Zuzi cried, diving for her friend, but Tosia held her back as more bullets came through the door, battering the girl's prostrate form.

'Roza!' Zuzi said again, but this time it came out on a sob.

Her friend lay there, eyes staring blankly up the endless stairs as her blood drained from her like a sieve. Zuzi felt herself start to shake all over.

'That could have been me,' she whimpered.

'But it wasn't,' Tosia said crisply. 'Sorry to be harsh, but you have to stay strong. There will be time to grieve later – and let's do it for as few of us as possible.'

Her words made sense but, trapped in the staircase, with the enemy all around them, fear felt like a far more logical response. Zuzi glanced downwards but some Nazis had emerged from hiding and were engaging their men in the room directly below. There was no escape; they had to go on.

'Can you light that?' Bartek asked, indicating the fuse dangling limply from the riddled door.

Zuzi fumbled for her matches but the first one caught against the box and it broke in two.

'Slowly does it,' Bartek said, though he looked nervously to his men, strung out along the staircase like ducks in a fairground. They were depending on Zuzi to do this and fast.

She struck a second match and it caught easily. Steadying her breathing, she put the match to the fuse, then pulled Bartek down several steps as it crackled merrily towards the explosive. It blew with a loud blast and men rushed past her, firing into the room. One of them fell, dead, as if giving himself to Roza as a partner in the grim dance of eternity, but they took the floor with ease and breathed again. Two bright-eyed young men went up the stairs to scout ahead and returned a minute later.

'Main garrison on the fifth floor, sir. Sounds like they're preparing to make a stand.'

'Good work.' Bartek clapped him on the back. 'Let's make sure none of them ever stand again, yes, lads?'

The forced bravado should have sounded ridiculous, but here, with shots echoing around the vast building as the enemy hid who knows where, Zuzi felt it rush through her.

'You're not having Warsaw any longer,' she whispered in the Nazis' general direction. 'It's ours. It's all—'

A shot rang down the stairs, pinging off the iron balustrade right next to Zuzi and she flattened herself against the wall, all bravado instantly gone. At her side, Tosia flung a grenade, along with a ripe line of expletives, in the direction of the shot and a cry of agony told them she'd hit her mark.

'Good,' Bartek said. 'Let's go!'

They stormed up the stairs, shooting as they went and seizing guns from any Nazi they felled. On the third floor, Zuzi had a machine gun thrust into her hands and she had to admit that, although it terrified her with its merciless power, holding it gave her courage.

'Watch out!'

Three enemy soldiers came from a side room and Zuzi dropped to her knees and squeezed the trigger. A blast of fire knocked her backwards but their attackers fell, whether by her hand or one of the others she had no way of knowing – and was glad of it. They'd been shown the workings of all sorts of guns in training but studying their mechanics and firing them into someone's heart were very different matters. More than ever, Zuzi wanted to flee this hideous building and run home to the comforting yeasty warmth of their beloved bakery, Piekarnia Dąbrowska, and the safety of her family.

'This is the big one, folks,' Bartek said. 'We can do this. Stick together and listen for orders.'

They were going on up and there was no means of escape, bar via the pearly gates. The image of Roza riddled with bullets lurked around the edges of her vision but she could not let it in. Everything was moving at pace now. Automatically, she set explosives to the doors of Floor Five, inserted detonators, ran out fuse wire, lit the end. Automatically, she followed close behind Tosia as they brought up the rear of the AK charge on the garrison that had held the Prudential tower for five long years. Automatically, she flung grenades into their position behind a rough table barricade and threw herself to the ground to avoid the blast.

Her mouth was full of dust and smoke, her ears ringing with explosions, her eyes stinging in the acrid air, but she was still alive. When, finally, the shots stopped and the smoke cleared, she found herself standing with Bartek's small group, all looking dazedly around the empty building. Victory, it seemed, came not with trumpets or even cheers but with silence. Beautiful silence.

'Did we do it?' she gasped out. 'Is it ours?'

'We need to sweep the building,' Bartek said cautiously. 'But, yes, it seems that it is. You did well. You all did very well.'

He sounded stunned and Zuzi knew exactly how he felt. She had no idea how much time had passed but it looked as if the light was fading from the sky over Warsaw.

'The roof!' she cried. 'We have to get to the roof!'

Bartek went first, forcing a cautious speed on them as he checked every entrance for lurking enemies. One man leapt out at them, making Zuzi scream embarrassingly, but his hands were up and he babbled for mercy in frightened German. Bartek took him prisoner, securing his wrists with rope and leading him, like a dog, up the final staircase.

The door was unlocked and Zuzi stepped through to find herself in a flat, open space with a three-hundred-and-sixty-degree view of Warsaw. The sun was dropping below the horizon, painting the city an aptly blood red. Fighting was still going on in many streets, marked out with tracer fire, but it was impossible to tell who was commanding the different areas. The Germans could have beaten back the AK and might, even now, be coming for them here in the Prudential. If that was the case, they would be the ones trapped like flies in a web and their hours of fighting would be for nothing.

'The flag, Żelazo?'

Tosia's crisp voice snapped her out of her panic and she turned and saluted smartly, pushing her foolish fears aside.

'Right here, ma'am.'

'Excellent. Let's get it up this flagpole and show Warsaw that she's Polish once more!'

Zuzi smiled and ran to help her fellow Minerki pull down the hated Nazi swastika. Only eighteen of their original twenty had made it, Roza shot down on the stairs and young Nina in the fight for the fifth floor. But now they were at the top, and, in honour of their lost comrades, they must shout out their victory to the city.

'I can see them building barricades,' one of the AK called, scanning the city with binoculars. 'That must mean we've taken some of Warsaw.'

'Over here too,' another called from the far side, and Zuzi felt her heart lift.

With the other girls, she tore the Nazi flag from the ropes, tying their simple red-and-white one in its place. Zuzi remembered Babcia Kamilla unrolling it from beneath her skirts yesterday morning, when Warsaw had still been an occupied city, and felt a rush of something she thought might be freedom. Heaving on the ropes, she helped send it up the pole where it caught the evening breeze and flapped proudly above their city, a sign to all. From below she thought she heard cheers and, putting a hand on the flagpole to steady herself, she let out a shout of her own.

'We did it! We're free!'

'We've taken the *first steps* to freedom,' Bartek corrected her cautiously, but he was smiling too and grabbed her hands to jig her madly around the top of the Prudential tower. Their feet caught in the Nazi flag, flapping around the flagstones. Zuzi drew her knife and began slashing it to pieces.

'Get out of our city!' she cried, throwing a fragment to the winds. 'Get out, get out, get out!'

To the west, the sun was setting, pulling the curtain over the first day of the uprising and to the east, fires lit up the Russian camp. The Red Army leaders would see the flag and they would know that, as Moscow had asked, the Poles had risen up to pave the way for Russian firepower to drive the Germans out fully. The uprising was far from over but today they had fought and today they had won. Warsaw was theirs once more and, whatever the battles ahead, Zuzi would revel in it.

ELEVEN

ORLA

'The flag!' The door of the underground hospital burst open and there stood Alicja, Daniella strapped to her chest with a large scarf, and her eyes shining. 'I can see the flag.'

Leaving the door to the underground hospital defiantly open, she grabbed Orla's hand and pulled her upstairs. It felt strange to do something so impulsive, but when they tumbled outside, there were no Germans to be seen. AK soldiers were firing from windows at the far end of the street but behind them, the sun was sinking over a Warsaw that was cautiously filling with curious civilians.

'Look – up there!'

Alicja pointed south and Orla's eyes roved across the roofs to the tip of the giant Prudential tower. Sure enough, atop it, flapping in the rosy light of dusk, was an equally giant Polish flag.

'Zuzi!' Orla gasped.

Someone passed her a pair of binoculars and she trained them eagerly on the glorious sight. Below the flagpole a group of slim figures was silhouetted against the sky, proclaiming Polish independence at last, and Orla squinted at them, praying one was her sister. She could have watched forever, but others were impatient to see and she handed the binoculars back with a thank you and hugged Alicja.

'They did it!' she said.

'It worked,' Alicja agreed, stroking her baby's head.

Listening to the incredulity in her new friend's voice, Orla realised how much they'd all feared it might not. She could still hear explosions across the city but she was standing in the open with her neighbours, free to say and do whatever she wished for the first time since she'd turned thirteen. It was like having a glorious bucket of cool water thrown over you on a sweaty summer's day and she put back her head and laughed.

'They did it!'

From the top of the tower, scraps of something began to fall.

'What's that?' Alicja asked the man with the binoculars.

He peered into them and gave a broad smile. 'It's the Nazi flag. They're tearing up the Nazi flag.'

Orla's smile was even broader. That would be Zuzi, no doubt about it. She looked at the tiny figures casting torn-up swastika to the rising wind and smiled. She couldn't wait to get back to the bakery and hear her sisters' experiences of W-hour. They were bound to be more exciting than her own, sitting by empty beds waiting for news. They would both have the sort of tales you could regale an eager father with and Orla felt a tremor of familiar inadequacy, but then reminded herself that in a hospital, empty beds were far better than full ones. Besides, this feeling of freedom was excitement enough.

Opposite the hospital, someone flung open a window and set a gramophone on the sill, sending glorious, trilling loops of Chopin out to the people below. For years the city's greatest composer had been banned and the beautiful notes seemed to dance on the air. Orla took Alicja's hands and danced her round and round, little Nella laughing between them, but their merriment was interrupted by the jangle of a bell as an ambulance came round the corner at top speed.

'Nurse! Over here at once.'

Sister Maria's voice brooked no opposition and Orla dropped Alicja's hands and ran back to the hospital as two girls leaped out of the van and opened the back doors. Inside, lying on stretchers slotted like bunks into the high sides, were four young men, all moaning hideously and clutching at wounds that were dripping blood onto the metal floor.

'There's more where they came from,' one of the girls said. 'Loads more.'

Nausea rose in Orla's stomach but the men were suffering and she had to move fast. Stepping into the van, she held her breath to try and block the tinny smell of blood, and leaned over the first patient.

'We're going to get you help,' she told him. 'We'll have to lift you and it's probably going to hurt, but there are excellent doctors inside to treat you.'

The young man looked trustingly up at her and she prayed she was telling him the truth. Taking one end of the stretcher as a driver took the other, she eased him out into the fading light and saw that his left leg was crushed badly below the knee. Nausea rose again and, as she rushed him inside, she glanced back to the flag flying proudly over Warsaw, and wondered what this giddy freedom was going to cost them all.

'We'll have to operate.' Bronislaw looked at the leg and across to Orla. 'Will you assist?'

Orla hesitated. They'd got the first men inside but more were coming, in ambulances, on stretchers, and leaning on the shoulders of frightened friends. Many of them were young –

boys Orla should have been finishing school with if it hadn't been for the occupation. Now they were bleeding their lives away.

'Lania? Orla?!'

The sound of her real name snapped her out of her reverie and she tutted at herself. There was no need for code names now they were out of hiding, but there was every need for action.

'Of course, Doctor,' she said, and was grateful when he smiled at her.

'We can do this. We *have* to do this.'

She nodded and set her jaw, willing herself not to cry as Bronislaw tied a tourniquet above the poor lad's knee.

'What do you need me to do?'

He grimaced.

'I need you to hold him down here, on his thigh, and lift his foot up so that I can get decent purchase.'

Orla looked at the disfigured foot and cursed herself for choosing nursing. She'd known she was too soft to be able to blow people up but hadn't thought she might, instead, find herself dealing with the results of those explosions. She remembered Sister Maria describing the injuries they would deal with. She'd thought the head nurse had been embellishing to shock them, trying, perhaps, to exaggerate her own experiences in the First War, but she hadn't told them the half of it. She longed to run out of the hospital and all the way home, but this boy was in pain and she could not turn her back on him.

Bronislaw lifted a syringe and injected their patient with a carefully measured amount of their small supplies of morphine. The boy was half unconscious already and the drug made him smile woozily.

'This is going to hurt,' Bronislaw warned.

'Hurt,' he agreed, but as the young doctor lifted the jagged-edged saw, his eyes filled with tears.

'I don't think—'

'Nurse!'

Bronislaw shoved a wooden stick into his mouth and waved Orla urgently forward. Trying not to think about anything other than her direct instructions, she laid one hand on the boy's thigh and, with a shudder, gripped at the exposed bone of his foot. He let out an instant yell, spitting the stick aside, but it was nothing to the moment Bronislaw's saw bit his flesh and he roared in pain.

'Hold him steady,' Bronislaw gasped. 'The quicker we do this, the better.'

Orla gripped tight but closed her eyes and tried to imagine herself away from here. She fought to picture her usual happy places – the back of the bakery, a wood full of deer, the faces of her family – but none of it would penetrate through the distress of the man she was helping to mutilate.

'Helping to *live*,' she reminded herself, but then Bronislaw made his last cut and the lower leg came off in Orla's hand.

Her eyes flew open and, dropping it to the floor, she staggered back against the operating table, sucking in frantic breaths as the rapidly filling hospital ward seemed to fracture into a hundred hazy squares before her. The man had passed out so was spared the horror of having the gaping wound cauterised with a hot iron but Orla smelled the sizzle of his flesh and barely had time to whip away from the table before she threw up.

'Sorry,' she gasped as Sister Maria hurried across. 'I'm so sorry. I'll learn. I'll get better. I'll—'

She felt a warm, steady hand on her back.

'You did very well, Orla. Very well indeed. You're a brave girl and you'll make an excellent nurse.' Orla was not sure either of those things were true, but was thankful the man's screams had stopped. There were others though and she slowly raised her head and looked around the packed ward. This, then, was the reality of the uprising – the red and white of the proud Polish flag high up on the tower, sickeningly mirrored in the blood and bandages down here in the city's hospitals. It would be a long night.

'I'll clean this up,' she said, 'and get back to work.'

She ran for a mop and bucket, nausea swirling in her stomach and dread swirling even faster in her mind – what had they started here? And how on earth were they going to get out of it alive?

TWELVE

HANA

'It's working!'

It was the quiet awe in Bór's voice that made Hana realise quite how tense the AK commander had been.

'Of course it's working, sir,' she said. 'The AK have been brilliantly trained.'

'And are passionate in the love of their country. That, Fiolet, has been our advantage tonight.'

On their smart dressers, the radio sets were alive with messages coming in from all over the city reporting victories – areas taken, streets secured, buildings seized. It wasn't universal good news. The two key bridges over the Vistula had been too heavily defended to take but the AK had occupied most of the city, including the main routes through to those bridges, so German links with their eastern front were all but severed. The Russians would thank them for easing their way into Warsaw.

'Have you told the Allies, sir?' Hana asked.

'Tried to. The long-range transmitter is playing up so I'm

not sure the messages have got through yet but we'll keep working at it.'

Hana felt a shiver of unease pass over her skin. Warsaw had risen up and nobody beyond her borders knew? That felt precarious, but, glancing over to the technicians, working frantically on the big set in the corner, she was sure it was one they would conquer as effectively as they had conquered so much of their city tonight.

'In the morning,' Bór said confidently, 'I will be able to send London a true appraisal of the situation on the ground and ask the Allied Forces for assistance. It's not as if we will be asking for anything more than our own men. We have many good Poles marching with the Red Army and our pilots, of course, have long been doing brave deeds with the RAF. Now, with Warsaw free, we can call them home to us.'

Hana closed her eyes, savouring the words: Call them home to us! How many times in the last five years had she longed to call Emil home to her side and been stopped only by the thought of the risk to him if she did so. He had offered, early on, suggesting he came back to Warsaw under a false name and worked as a labourer.

I would not care what work I did if I could come home to you each night, he'd written and her heart had sung at the words, but she'd seen what he had not – how brutal the occupying Nazis were to anyone with any spark. And Emil had more sparks than a New Year's Eve firework display. She'd written, with a heavy heart, to warn him to stay away and assure him that one day he *would* come home to her. Was that day finally close? By next week, might Hana be dancing in a no longer German-only dance hall wrapped in Emil's arms and—

'Enemy above! Enemy above!' One of Kammler's men came running into the room. 'Take cover.'

Hana dived beneath a desk, all thoughts of dancing gone in an instant.

Bór strode forward. 'What do you mean, "above"?'

'In the attic, Commander, sir. They got in over the roof!'

The man was clearly panicking and, with a sharp curse, Bór drew his gun and pushed past him. Hana had seen the attics when they'd toured the building on arrival – long, low storerooms beneath the eaves, lit up by dormer windows along both sides. She pressed herself against the side of the desk, imagining crack SS troops pouring through them, and grabbed for the rosary at her belt, rubbing the familiar beads and trying to breathe as the sound of shooting came down the stairs.

'Mama,' she whimpered.

The shooting was increasing. How many of them were there? And was this happening all over Warsaw? Were her sisters already limp, empty corpses, devoid of...

'Stop it!' she told herself again.

Hysteria would help no one. She had to fight, had to protect herself. What would Babcia Kamilla do? she asked herself and, edging to the front of the desk, looked around the room. Behind the door, Kammler had placed a smart oak stand, equipped with several ornately handled umbrellas and walking sticks so, darting out, Hana grabbed one then pressed herself into the gap between two wardrobes.

The men around her were positioned with their guns trained on the door, but still the fighting continued in the rooms above their heads, the raps of gunfire and booms of grenades echoing out around a city filled with the same sounds of death. Hana tried to breathe but her head filled with a picture of Marek, bleeding out of a bullet-hole in his stomach; she did not want to die that way.

But then, through the chaos, came a beautiful sound – a low, gloriously confident voice, saying in bright, clear Polish: 'Radosław division reporting for duty, Commander Bór, sir. Apologies for the late arrival.'

All around Hana, the men of the Homeland Council put

down their pistols and went forward, shaking the hands of the troop of young men striding into the room. Hana stared as they brushed dust from their red-and-white armbands and talked of crawling through attics and over rooftops to reach their post just in time to stop the Germans attempting to do the same.

'Sentries at all posts, sir,' their leader announced. 'The building is secure.'

'Good work,' Bór told them. 'Now, let's see how the rest of the city is getting on.'

He went back to the window as if, Hana thought weakly, he was on a night out at the theatre. For herself, her legs felt too weak to support her without the solid oak of the wardrobes to lean on and she stayed in her hidey-hole, drawing as much air as possible into her constricted lungs until, at Bór's side, the AK leader pointed.

'Look, sir – the flag! We're flying the Polish flag!'

On a rush of joy, Hana darted forward, joining the men at the window, and sure enough there, right in the very centre of Warsaw, flapping proudly in the rising breeze, was the big red and white flag she'd last seen beneath her grandmother's skirts.

'God be praised,' she gasped, 'you did it, Zuzi – you really did it.'

'Fiolet,' Bór called, and she snapped to attention. He smiled. 'What's your real name?'

'My real one?'

'Of course – the time for subterfuge is over, is it not? We are free – or, at least, we are fighting freely.'

She nodded, unable to take it all in.

'It's Hana, sir.'

'Excellent. Well, Hana, it's time to send out a message.'

Bór strode to his desk and grabbed a pen. In bold strokes he wrote:

People of Warsaw, you were called to rise and you have risen with all the strength of your bodies and all the bravery of your souls. The Homeland Council salutes you. Much of the city is ours and we must hold it with resilience and courage for the few days it will take the Allied Forces to come to our side. They will bring the might of their firepower but know, tonight, that Warsaw has been won with the might of your great hearts. God bless and keep you all.

Commander Bór

Hana read it over and over as copies were made and stamped, then an AK sentry held the door open for her and she stepped, awed, into a street no longer patrolled by Germans. There was no need for subterfuge now, no need for ducking around checkpoints and concealing messages in stale bread. She would have to find her way along a safe route but already she could see AK men stationed at every street corner to mark out their territory so, holding the message up high before her, she set out.

It was a strange night, tracing her way around Warsaw in the darkness, but a heartening one. It soon became clear that the AK had secured a vast area, many kilometres square, encompassing Żoliborz in the north, Czerniaków in the south, Stare Miasto and Śródmieście in the middle, and her own dear Wola in the west. Rough barricades were being thrown up by whistling soldiers everywhere and people were venturing onto the streets to test their new freedom and to help secure it for the days ahead.

There was still danger from Nazi snipers hiding in apartment buildings and a few strongholds they'd managed to hold onto, but Hana had a clear map of her birth city held in her head and was swiftly able to mark out the best routes between the AK hubs. By dawn, she had delivered Bór's message of thanks and hope to all her appointed areas and was able to turn for home. She'd have to be back on duty later but for now, she desperately needed rest.

Gratefully, she headed west. The sun was rising behind her and it looked set to be a glorious summer day but all she wanted was bed. She pictured the big, soft double up in the eaves of the bakery that she shared with her sisters and felt a rush of fear. What if one of them hadn't made it? The Prudential had been a notorious Nazi stronghold and although Zuzi's flag was flying from the roof, there was no way of knowing if she'd placed it there or if someone had taken it from her corpse. Even Orla might not have been safe. She'd heard shocked whispers of retreating enemy soldiers targeting hospitals with grenades – what if one of those had exploded in the John of God?

The hospital was barely two streets' diversion from Hana's route home and she turned towards it, homing in on the low, white-painted building with her heart hammering. She'd seen too many dead bodies this long night to know that many would never wake to the freedom of 2 August 1944, but the thought that one of her own family might not do so was like a bullet in her heart.

She hastened up the steps, fear battering her weary body, but at that moment the door swung open and out came her little sister, looking as tired as she felt but gloriously, wonderfully whole.

'Orla!'

'Hana!'

They fell into each other's arms, gasping out snippets of their respective nights. Hana told Orla of the brave young soldiers manning flimsy barricades and Orla spoke of unspeakable injuries. One young man had had to have his leg amputated and Hana shivered at what it must feel like to have a part of yourself literally cut away.

'Don't think of it,' Orla urged, tucking a hand through her

arm. 'It's more sunrise than sunfall, but it's time to be together all the same. Warsaw is taken and, now, let's go home.'

Hana nodded. Home: the word had never sounded so sweet and she just prayed the whole family would be there waiting for them.

THIRTEEN

ORLA

Orla clutched tight at Hana's arm as they rounded the corner and caught their first glimpse of Piekarnia Dąbrowska.

'It's open!' she cried delightedly.

Both girls picked up their pace, ducking through the happy crowds filling the streets, drawn towards the glorious smells of fresh bread that meant they were home. The sun was climbing over the houses, casting bright light into the street, and Orla blinked, drinking in the merriment all around and feeling it help cast off some of the horror of last night.

The darkness had, at least, brought a halt to most of the fighting, giving the nurses time to stabilise those of their patients who had not succumbed to their injuries. Sister Maria had made a makeshift morgue but the young man without a leg had not, thankfully, been moved there. The last thing Orla had done before she'd left the hospital had been to check up on him and to her delight his eyes had fluttered open and he'd grabbed at her hand.

'Thank you,' he'd whispered through parched lips.

Orla had hastily held a glass of water to them.

'Just get better. That's all the thanks I need.'

He'd looked down at his lost leg and his eyes had filled with tears.

'I won't be fighting again, will I?'

Orla had smiled.

'Hopefully within a few days, none of us will. You've done your bit.'

'I've done my bit,' he'd agreed and drifted back to sleep with a half-smile on his face.

It had been enough to release Orla from the endless pressure of care and, ripping off her apron, she'd run to stash it in the staffroom. Alicja had been in there, sleeping curled up around her baby in a nest of sheets, and she'd blown them a kiss, then headed thankfully out of the hospital to the wonderful sight of her big sister. And now, at last, they were home.

'Mama!' she cried, flinging herself inside.

'Orla! Oh, my beautiful Orla, you're safe.'

'I'm safe,' she agreed, 'and so's Hana.' She pulled her sister after her, pushing aside the thought of all those who, sadly, would not be going back to their mothers today. 'Zuzi?' she asked nervously, and was answered by someone slamming into her back.

'You're here, little doe. You made it!'

'Zuzi!' Orla hugged her so tight that she felt her weary limbs begin to shake but it didn't seem to matter because Zuzi was holding her up. 'You got your flag to the top.'

'We did!'

'Was it hard?' Hana asked, hugging her too.

Zuzi stepped back with a grimace.

'It was brutal. Two of our girls were killed, one of them right in front of me. She went up the stairs first. If it had been me, I'd—'

'But it wasn't you,' Orla told her fiercely. 'You're here and you're safe.'

'I am!' Zuzi visibly drew herself up. 'How was the hospital?'

'Brutal too.' Orla swallowed. 'I had to hold a man's leg while Bronislaw cut it off.'

'Bronislaw?'

'Dr Łukasz to you, though I don't suppose we need code names any more, do we?'

'Maybe not. His name's Bronislaw then?'

'It is, and he's an excellent doctor. I only had to hold the leg, he had to actually saw through it while the man was writhing and screaming. God save us, Zuzi, it was terrible. We're so lucky to be here.'

'I had to step over several bodies to get to the top of the Prudential,' she said. 'And you know what the worst thing is – I got used to it really quickly. On the way back down, I barely even noticed.'

Hana shivered.

'I thought I was a goner at one point. All these Nazis penetrated the attic and I had to...' She looked shamefaced but pushed on, 'I had to hide between two wardrobes.'

'Good,' Magda said, throwing her broad baker's arms around them all. 'Courage is one thing, but recklessness is another.'

'Quite right,' an imperious voice agreed. 'If you've got to die, at least die well, that's what your grandfather always used to say.'

'Babcia!'

Their grandmother stepped inside and smiled at them as they ran to her, but put up her hands to ward off any foolish attempts at hugging.

'No need to get over-emotional. Everything went to plan. The AK have the city and I saw the flag, Zuzi – it looks very fine up there.'

'It does, Babcia.'

'You've all done marvellously well. We must celebrate. Where's young Jacob – what's he doing lying in bed when there's a free city to enjoy?'

'I'll go and get him,' Magda said. 'You girls sit down, eat!'

They sank gladly around the kitchen table. All over Wola people were waking up and they could hear voices rising in joyous celebration in every street but for this moment they were content to be here together, their own little unit.

'Your father would be so proud,' Kamilla said and if Orla hadn't known her better, she could have sworn she wiped a tear from one of her perfectly made-up eyes. She put out a hand and, to her surprise, her grandmother took it.

'We've done the fighting,' Orla said. 'Let's pray to God that we can now do the living and the loving.' Her sisters put their hands out too and, clasping onto each other, bowed their heads.

'Dear Lord...' Kamilla started but she got no further before Magda burst back down the stairs.

'He's gone! Jacob's gone!'

They were up in an instant.

'Gone where?' Orla demanded.

'I don't know,' Magda wailed. 'I thought he was in his room.'

The sisters looked at each other.

'He followed me the other day,' Hana admitted. 'Said he wanted to be more involved. I sent him off to paint PWs.'

'Remember him begging to go with me too?' Zuzi said. 'He was desperate to fight.'

Orla groaned.

'He was so full of himself when he set the fleas into the cinema, bless him. He wanted to do something active. He's thirteen after all.' She looked around. 'Where the hell has he gone?'

'To anyone who would have him,' Zuzi said grimly, then her face clouded. 'Wait a minute.' She raced up to the bedroom the three of them shared and then came clattering back. 'My mines are gone.'

'Your...?' Magda put a hand to her forehead. 'You've been keeping mines in our home?'

'Not primed ones.'

'Does Jacob know how to prime them?'

'No idea.'

Zuzi ran to the door. So many people were out, filling the streets. Someone was playing the national anthem, and many were gathering to sing it loud and proud. It would have been a glorious sound save for their fear for their little brother. They moved between their neighbours, asking everyone, 'Have you seen Jacob?' But no one had.

Orla sank onto the steps around the fountain in the middle of their housing block. It had been built by the innovative architects regenerating Warsaw after the First War – Hana was always going on about it – and was set around a lovely open space of lawns and pathways with the fountain at the centre. For the last five years it had been shut off by the Nazis, the Poles not deemed worthy of something as indulgently pretty as a water feature, but someone had found the tap and it was joyously spurting water once more. Children were dancing in it, flinging merry droplets around, and Orla saw the two lads who'd been flea-releasing with Jacob and felt tears sting her eyes.

'No point in panicking,' Babcia Kamilla told her, but even she looked agitated, her be-ringed fingers plucking at her lacy sleeves as she scrutinised the happy children for any sign of their lad.

A strange noise sounded further up the street and the children jumped from the fountain and ran out to see what was making it. The Dąbrowskas went with them, Orla clinging to her mother's arm and praying desperately that it was not some dark form of funeral procession. But there was, surely, too much cheering for that?

Sure enough, rolling down the road from Śródmieście was a German tank, a troop of giddy AK soldiers on its roof and a Polish flag flapping from the gun turret. Someone had thrown roses onto it so that it looked as gaudy as a carnival float and there, astride the gun, a steel hat at a jaunty angle on his young head and his arms raised in giddy triumph, was Jacob.

Orla fell to her knees.

'Thank God,' she breathed. 'Thank God, thank God, thank God.'

Hana and Magda dropped down beside her, Babcia placing her hands on their shoulders, but Zuzi ran at their little brother, dragging him from the turret and shaking him.

'Don't you dare ever make me think I've lost you again,' she shouted over the cries of celebration. 'Don't you dare!'

Then she was tugging him over to them and they were fussing around him and he was shaking them off, embarrassed in front of his adopted platoon, but touched all the same by their care.

'Come and see my tank,' he said proudly. 'I blew it up all myself with one of your mines, Zuzi.'

'Which you should not have taken.'

'I blew it up,' he repeated stubbornly. 'Papa would be proud.'

'He would,' Zuzi conceded, letting herself be pulled over to their brother's prize, the rest of the family following. Orla brought up the rear, glancing to the skies.

'If you're watching, Tata, this is for you. This is all for you.'

She'd done nothing more heroic herself than hold some poor man's mangled limb, but it didn't matter. You fought in your own way. It wasn't about personal glory, but about freedom. And today, praise God and the AK, Warsaw felt free indeed. She just hoped it stayed that way…

FOURTEEN

2 AUGUST

ZUZI

Zuzi stood astride the barricade and screamed her joy to the world. On top of the Prudential building yesterday she'd felt like a conquering warrior but here, in Wola, with the ordinary people of her neighbourhood dancing in sheer relief, she felt totally and utterly happy. It made her realise how rare that had been in the last five years. Oh, she'd had good times of course, with her family, with her friends, but there had always been the creeping fear that some Nazi was looking in on your happiness, ready to snatch it away with the flick of a Luger.

Finally, those Nazis had been pushed to the very edges of Warsaw and it was surely only a day or two before the Russians picked them off and the liberation of Warsaw was complete. Zuzi could hear the rumble of Red Army guns over the Vistula as they rode roughshod over whatever paltry German reinforcements had been sent to try and stop them, and was pleased they would be able to invite them in as conquerors, not grovel as grateful subjects. She pictured the handcuffs on Babcia Kamilla's wall and smiled.

'Carry on the fight,' their father had said before his brutal death and that was precisely what they were doing. Every minute more news was trickling in about AK successes. The *Information Bulletin*, the underground paper that had been produced and distributed at huge risk for the last five years, was being openly sold in the street and hundreds of people were buying it to devour the list of targets taken.

Most of Stare Miasto was secure, the Nazis easily driven out of its narrow streets, and flags were flying from every window of the beautiful medieval market square. It was a similar story in Zoliborz in the north, Czerniakow in the south, and their own dear Wola in the west. In all three suburbs, Nazi battalions had been caught by surprise and forced out of large residential areas which could now be secured with barricades.

Fighting had been hardest in the key modern centre of Śródmieście but the AK had secured most major buildings. The Prudential was at the top of the list of successes, Zuzi's unit credited alongside Bartek's Kilinski platoon, but there were many more. The central post office had also fallen to the Kilinski, and other units had taken City Hall, the Court of Appeal, the Królikarnia Palace, and a huge SS supply warehouse at Stawki. It seemed the AK had secured most major buildings, setting up a grand frontline on Plac Teatralny overlooking the Brühl Palace. This was the headquarters for Generalleutnant Stahel, the Nazi Commander of Warsaw, and had been too fiercely protected to capture, but the AK were holding Stahel and his staff under siege, which amounted to much the same thing.

Perhaps the biggest success of all (bar the Prudential, of course) had been the taking of the electric power station out on the banks of the Vistula. That had been an operation long in the planning, the Krybar battalion infiltrating the plant as workers over the last year and smuggling in weapons so that, come W-hour, they'd been able to rise up from inside and overcome the surprised German guards. Several of the enemy had, apparently, been blasted away with steam from the cooling stacks and, after hours of hard fighting – half the troop manning the guns and the other half keeping the station running to fill fighting Warsaw with light – they had secured it. It was a huge victory for the insurgents, who were now guaranteed power.

There had, sadly, been less success at the waterworks and the Nazis had turned off the mains supply, but there were wells aplenty for a few days and most people had been sensible enough to fill their bathtubs and buckets when the fighting broke out. The Telephone Exchange, a near-impregnable concrete tower, was still in Nazi hands, neither of the main railway stations had been secured, and attacks on both airports had been repulsed with German heavy arms. The casualties, people whispered, had been enormous, and the Warsawians had established little means of contact with the outer world. But they did hold the city and that, for now, was enough.

Certainly, the civilians were delighted and had showed up in their hundreds to help build barricades to keep their newly Nazi-free streets secure. Zuzi's Minerki were in Wola to help shore up their enthusiastic but amateurish efforts at the western edges of the AK-held city and Zuzi was loving it. All around people were throwing things from their windows – tables, chairs, wardrobes, even old-fashioned chamber pots and iron fireplace surrounds they must have ripped from their walls. Now, Zuzi was commanding them in an operation to shore up the motley collection with something big and solid.

'Push!' Zuzi urged from her vantage point.

A huge gang of people were lined up along the side of a tramcar and, at her urging, gave it such a great heave that, with a creak of metal, it slid off the rails and fell almost gracefully onto the side of the barricade. It looked sad there, deprived of its tracks, but it would be more use against a tank than a Louis XVI dining table, and could, surely, be restored once this was all over. A Scout ran up and painted a PW onto it, bold and proud, and Zuzi clapped.

'Great work everyone. Now – sandbags.'

Several of her Minerki wheeled over barrowloads of sand and the householders began shovelling it into every bag and sack they could find to stack around – and inside – the tramcar. Slowly, the barricade went up. Some wag wheeled a piano onto the far side and Orla clambered up to play Chopin on it as the barricade-builders stacked sandbags around her. It was hot work in the August sunshine but people brought jugs of lemonade and Magda handed around jewelled kolacky, as if Christmas had come half a year early to Wola. And, indeed, it felt as if it had.

Jacob proudly regaled them with the tale of his tank capture. He had, it had emerged, snuck from his room at the first threads of dawn, taking a detour via the girls' room to help himself to Zuzi's mines. Then, entirely on his own initiative and apparently based on a story he'd read in the *Information Bulletin*, he'd waited in one of the myriad coal cellars with hatches straight onto the street. When a German tank had rumbled into view, he'd waited until it was right overhead, darted from the hatch and wedged the mine into the track before darting below once more, leaving himself a sliver of a view from which to watch the track explode twenty metres down the road, sending the tank skewing sideways. A troop of AK in an apartment nearby had seized on the opportunity to shoot down the Nazi operatives fleeing from the gun turret and the tank had been theirs.

Jacob had made it sound so simple but Magda, not usually ruffled by much, had been taken over all faint and had to sit down, and he'd laughed, delighted at this appreciation of his manly talents. It hadn't helped that the AK platoon had adopted him instantly, finding him a hat and an armband and dubbing him 'mały orzeł' – little eagle – so Zuzi had turned her fury on their leader.

'You think it's clever, do you, to encourage a child to sneak out of home and throw themselves into the path of danger?'

The man had shrunk back. 'How old is he?'

'Thirteen.'

'Thirteen? That's barely the age of my own Amelia.'

'And is she off planting mines under tanks?'

'Of course not. At least – I hope not. They're all so keen to get involved, aren't they?' He'd stuck out his hand. 'Kapitan Szymon Ancel, pleased to meet you. And I apologise. I'm not sure I'm going to be able to keep your brother from the platoon now, but I will do my very best to give him the least dangerous tasks.'

Now, Zuzi looked along to where he was mustering his men to drag two smart motor cars – left behind by Volksdeutsche – into the barricade, and saw Jacob working as hard as the rest, his young muscles straining to keep up with his new gang, but a huge beam on his young face. That, at least, was good to see.

Szymon Ancel, it had emerged, was Jewish, a rare survivor of the ghetto. He and his family had escaped in the early days of the Ghetto Uprising and, with the aid of fake papers provided by the AK, had lived undercover ever since. Szymon was, if possible, buzzing more than the rest of them with being part of an uprising that actually looked set to succeed. His family had come out to join him: a beautiful woman called Lydia with a glorious shock of red hair; a matching red-headed teenage daughter called Tasha; and a sweet-faced younger girl, Amelia, wide-eyed at being allowed out in the open. They were all getting stuck in with everyone else, the barricades going higher and higher, locking the Poles into their reclaimed city with ready exuberance.

A shout of laughter went up and Zuzi turned to see Babcia Kamilla standing on the barricade, the Dąbrowska portrait of Hitler in her hands. All Poles had had to keep one on their walls (you could be shot for failing to display the expected adoration for the 'Führer' who'd stolen your country) and they all hated them. In Zuzi's house, Magda had hung a shawl over the man (easily whipped away if the Gestapo came calling), but you'd still been able to sense him peering out at you through its pretty weave. Until now.

'You sit there, you bastard!' Kamilla cried, loud and clear, and Zuzi flinched at the unusual obscenity from her dignified grandmother. 'Your precious soldiers can shoot you right between your weaselly eyes if they ever try and get back into Warsaw again.'

The crowd cheered and darted off to rip their portraits down and line them up along the top, like ducks at a fair, waiting to be shot down – except that Zuzi prayed no Germans got close enough to even try.

'Zuzi!' Hana called, and she looked down to see both her sisters standing below her. 'I'm afraid Orla and I have to go.'

Her heart wrenched. Here behind their community barricades, it was possible to believe that the uprising was over, the victory won, but those barricades were there for a reason. The Nazis were not defeated yet and on the edges of the AK's hard-won space, men and women were fighting to keep them intact. There might only be a day or two more to hold on, but duty called her precious sisters into the fray again.

Hana was going out to thread her way between AK posts, forever at risk from an enemy sniper, and Orla was heading into the heart of the city, a ready target for any attack. Elsewhere in the war, hospitals, marked with red crosses, were protected under the Geneva Convention but this was a city battle, every target too close to the next one to be definable, and she would be horribly at risk. Zuzi slid down the barricade and grabbed them both.

'Stay safe,' she begged them.

'Don't you mean stay alert?' Hana corrected her with a half-smile.

'Both,' she said stoutly. 'I want to see you back here tomorrow, yes?'

'Yes, Captain!'

Hana saluted and Zuzi forced herself to laugh but, as she watched the pair of them head out of the safety of their merry streets and back into the heart of the battle, she felt only fear.

'Minerki!'

Tosia was calling them to her and it seemed it was time for her to depart too. She thought of the Prudential yesterday – of the satisfaction of fixing the plastic explosive to the door and watching it blow apart. That had been the highlight. The rest had been smoke and darkness and fumbling with fuses in the perpetual fear of not being the first to your weapon. Afterwards, standing on top with the flag, Zuzi had kidded herself that she'd enjoyed it, but she had to admit that the thought of going into battle again did not fill her with the angry energy she'd had in the build-up to W-hour.

'Yes, Tosia?'

She reported in dutifully with the others. There were two gaping spaces where Roza and Nina should have been and the Minerki shuffled closer, trying to cover their loss.

'We're on duty, ladies. Attack on Gęsiówka with our friends with the tank here.'

She waved to Szymon, who saluted back. Zuzi could imagine why he would want to take Gęsiówka. It was the last remaining Jewish labour camp, holding out on the wasteland of the one-time ghetto to process what bricks and stones the Nazis needed to build their hateful pillboxes. Not that many of those were left now. The younger AK had apparently perfected the art of jumping onto them from above and throwing grenades into the slits while the Germans inside were preoccupied with shooting at their comrades. It was effective but they had to be very quick to get away before the bunkers blew and Zuzi supposed she should be glad Jacob had chosen taking out tanks instead.

'Our job will be to blast the walls while the tank takes the watchtowers, then it will be able to roll on inside and free the prisoners. Who's in, ladies?'

The cheer was, Zuzi noted, more muted than before. Then she heard a new voice and turned in horror to see Babcia Kamilla stepping determinedly into the circle.

'I would like to volunteer for service,' she said to Tosia.

'I see.' Tosia looked Zuzi's aristocratic grandmother up and down, taking in her designer trousers, silk blouse and pearl brooch. 'And you are?'

'Kamilla Dąbrowska, reporting for service, ma'am. I may look old and weak to you but, trust me, I'm a whizz with a filipinka – am I not, Zuzi?'

And there it was – their connection confirmed. Zuzi considered refusing to answer but Babcia was staring straight at her and there was no avoiding it.

'She is,' she confirmed, though she had only Babcia's word for it. 'She made them in the First War. Killed over fifty Germans,' she improvised.

Babcia did not even flinch.

'And a good few Russians besides. I can throw with the accuracy of an Olympic athlete.'

There was no faulting her confidence and Zuzi saw Tosia wavering but the Minerki had been in training for years and it wouldn't look good to bring a novice in at this critical point.

'I thank you for your brave offer, but—'

'Tell you what, give me that grenade.' Kamilla nudged imperiously at Zuzi who, stomach curling with embarrassment, handed it over. 'See that pigeon up there.' Kamilla pointed into a tree this side of the barricade where a fat pigeon, attracted by the crumbs from Magda's kolatzy, was looking curiously down at them. 'Prepare to eat it in a pie.'

Before any of them could object, she pulled the pin, lined herself up and, with perfect precision, sent the grenade in a sweet arc, tip over tail, towards the very branch on which the creature was perched. It went up in a cloud of leaves and feathers and the Minerki burst out in spontaneous applause.

'Some pie,' Zuzi muttered, looking at the splattered remains on the ground, but the local dogs were rushing delightedly to the feast, while, with a clap on the back, Tosia welcomed Kamilla into the Minerki. Zuzi groaned and looked across to her mother, who mouthed, 'Sorry'. It made her smile. She'd always loved and admired Babcia Kamilla and, if she had to take anyone into an attack on an impregnable Nazi labour camp, someone who could throw a bomb like that was probably a good choice.

'Working together, hey, Zuzi,' Babcia said, linking arms with her. 'Sorry to push in, but I was going mad sitting around. I have to *do* something and, besides, this way I can watch over your brother.'

'My brother?'

Zuzi groaned again as she saw Szymon's tank lead them out, Jacob still sitting at his side.

'I thought you said you'd keep him safe,' she called up.

Szymon shrugged apologetically. 'What can I say? Attack is the best form of defence.'

Glancing back at Magda, standing alone on the doorstep of Piekarnia Dąbrowska as her entire family went once more into battle, Zuzi wasn't so sure, but they were in this now and they had to see it through. She waved to her mother.

'See you at sunfall, Mama.'

'See you at sunfall,' Magda cried back, the words choked

with the tears she would be praying all day she did not have to spill, and Zuzi had to turn her head forward to keep her own inside. Cocking an ear for the continued rumblings of the Russians across the Vistula, she sent up a fervent prayer for their swift aid. The Poles had risen up as Moscow had demanded, so now Moscow must send the Red Army in to save Warsaw – and soon, or there wouldn't be much left to save.

FIFTEEN

5 AUGUST

HANA

'And then Babcia threw this grenade right into the watchtower and it exploded – boom – sending bits of guard everywhere. It was even better than the pigeon!'

Jacob laughed in lurid delight and Hana looked at him in concern. She was cuddled up in bed with Zuzi and Orla, their younger brother sitting at their feet, and had been loving this family togetherness after four hard days of insurgence, but listening to her brother's glee as he retold the taking of Gęsiówka for the fiftieth time, she felt uneasy.

'You know it's not good to blow people up, Jacob?'

'Of course,' he agreed quickly. 'Not *people*. Not nice, normal people. Nazis, though – they're different.'

Hana sighed. He had a point, she supposed, but his delight in the killing was still disturbing. The sooner the Russians arrived and they could take the city and get lads like Jacob out of the underground and back into school, the better, she thought. But then he crawled up the bed to cuddle in against her and said, 'I only want to protect us, Han-Han, as Tata would have done if he were here,' and her heart melted.

'I know, Jacob, and that's lovely, but it's not down to you. We all have to look after each other.'

'We do,' Zuzi and Orla agreed either side.

Jacob looked from one to the other with a frown. 'But I'm the man now, right?'

Hana tutted. 'And we're the women – women can protect each other too.'

'True,' he agreed. 'I'd take Babcia over half the lads around here – and Zuzi. You should have seen her blowing that wall apart. The look on the Germans' faces when we drove in through the gap!'

He was off again but Zuzi was looking proud so Hana didn't want to stop him. The Gęsiówka raid seemed to have been a resounding success, the walls blown apart, the German guards taken prisoner and the Jewish prisoners dancing with joy when they'd realised this raid was not death, but liberation.

'You should have seen them,' Zuzi was saying. 'They wept, every one of them, and hugged us and thanked us over and over. I've never seen Babcia look more uncomfortable, but even she had enough compassion to smile and pat their backs.'

'She liked it better when a group of them lined up, saluted Szymon and told them they were "ZOB Battalion reporting for duty, sir!"' Jacob put in.

'She did,' Zuzi agreed. 'Saluted right back as if she'd been doing it all her life.' They smiled at each other. 'Mind you, she admitted she could "do with a little sit-down" afterwards. I bet she's been asleep ever since.'

'I hope she wakes up in time for the liberation party,' Orla said, and they all raised their mugs of tea in a silent toast to the longed-for moment.

Surely the Russians would be here very soon? There had been talk of some German resistance on the other side of the

Vistula but that was over now and the Allied force had to cross the river, and fast. Warsawians had all watched, horrified, at the barbaric way the Nazis had exterminated the brave Jews when they'd tried to stand up against the clearing of the ghetto last year, so they knew where their own rebellion would end up without external aid.

Hana had spent the last four days carrying messages from AK central to all the liaison hubs and commanders they could reach. The men in the northern suburb of Żoliborz had their area secured, but the Germans had held onto the Gdansk railway station and the vast stone citadel that separated it from Stare Miasto so they were cut off from everyone else. Other units were trapped in pockets of German attack, or struggling to hold isolated buildings, and keeping everyone connected was hard work. A number of units had radios but bombs were taking out more and more sets every day and, besides, they weren't sure how secure the airwaves were, so important operational plans were safer carried by hand. Alongside the liaison workers, the Scouts were running an amazing postal service, carrying hundreds of letters between families, friends and sweethearts every day, but that, too, was dangerous work.

Hana's one-time lecturer, Agaton, had been in HQ yesterday with an old map of Warsaw's sewer system and was talking about trying to trace a route beneath the ground. It looked an exciting option to Hana but a sanitation engineer had explained that the sewers, although solid and extensive, were dangerously full. The level would, apparently, be dropping now that the Nazis had cut off the water supply to the city, but the risk was still very high for anyone attempting to navigate them and they were all hoping it would not be needed.

In the meantime, Hana and her fellow liaison girls had to make their way, heads low and rosary beads clutched firmly in their sweaty fingers, along the backs of barricades, or across the enjoyably clear areas held behind them. Yesterday, she'd crossed the beautiful market square right out in the open, her messages held in her satchel for all to see, and had felt liberated.

She'd paused in the middle, spinning slowly and taking in the eighteenth-century townhouses on all sides. They were pretty, she supposed, but very fiddly and impractical. It was time to build Agaton's new expressway and carve out a modern style of living for the Polish people. She'd felt the sting of Marek's pointless death and wondered what the Gestapo had done with the paltry set of maps they'd taken his life for, but then she'd heard a burst of fire down somewhere nearby, and run for cover. You never knew where a Nazi sniper might turn up; both sides, now, were fighting undercover.

The Saxon Gardens, between Śródmieście and Stare Miasto, was the trickiest area to negotiate. The parkland was largely held by the AK, but at the centre stood the Brühl Palace where Generalleutnant Stahel was holed up with a small guard, and the Wehrmacht were attacking hard to try and break him out of the siege. They had many snipers and several rocket launchers trained on the area from the impregnable citadel, and it was precarious getting past them. Yesterday, Hana had had to dive into a bush to escape a run of bullets and crawl on her belly along the back of a fountain before she felt brave enough to dash for the next barricade. Already, her days of cowering between wardrobes felt long ago but it was tiring and she was treasuring this rest back at home.

She looked around the bedroom she'd shared with Zuzi and Orla throughout their childhood. It was tucked under the eaves on the top floor of their apartment above the bakery. Mama (and Tata in the happy days when he'd still been with them) slept below with Jacob on a truckle bed at her feet, and there was a cosy sitting room alongside. The kitchen was on the ground floor, behind the bakery, and was always so warm and delicious-smelling that the family spent much of their time in there, but Hana loved it up in the girls' cosy nest.

It had two dormer windows that let in the sun when it rose on one side and as it set on the other. Given the money, Hana would love to install some of the fancy new 'skylights' that Agaton had showed the class the other day. Until recently, roof windows had only been installed in churches or palaces – such as the celebrated run in the Versailles palace – but several architects were looking to bring them to normal homes. Agaton had told them about a man in Denmark, a Mr Rasmussen, who was trying to perfect an affordable design he was calling VELUX, to capture the perfect combination of ventilation and light he claimed would transform dull attics into modern living spaces. Hana thought he was absolutely right and longed to try it for herself, but first there was a war to win.

'Are the planes going to come, Hana?' Jacob asked, bringing her back to the present with a sickening thud.

'How's she meant to know?' Zuzi snapped at him, as Orla slid a warm arm around her shoulders.

Hana leaned into it. She was usually the protective one in the family, but when it came to Emil, her younger sisters shielded her, understanding the pain of his absence. For once, however, she did have some information – albeit not the sort she'd hoped for.

'I asked the commander yesterday,' she admitted, twisting her ring round and round on her wedding finger.

'He lets you do that?' Orla asked.

Hana nodded. Bór was a very open man, especially considering his background. Noble by birth, he'd lived before the war on his wife's fine family estate, and had made his name as a cavalryman in the First War and an Olympic equestrian after it. He was educated and cultured but he listened to people, even lowly liaison girls like her, and all yesterday she'd been plucking up the courage to ask him about the planes. In the end, the agony of not knowing about Emil and his squadron had outweighed her fear of sounding disrespectful and she'd dared to step forward.

'What did he say?' Zuzi demanded.

Hana knew this word for word, for it had stuck in her mind ever since.

'He said that he sends a plea to the government in London every morning and every evening. He said that he's sent personal transmissions to the head of the RAF, the War Council and Mr Churchill himself.'

'And...?'

Hana swallowed hard. 'And they say no.'

'No? Just that – no?'

'They say that the Polish squadron is already assigned to some mission in France.'

'In France?' Zuzi exploded angrily. 'France already has a million Allied troops swarming over it since their precious D-Day. What about us? What about Poland? They're *Polish* pilots, *our* pilots.'

'I know,' Hana said miserably and Orla's arm tightened around her shoulders.

'I suppose they didn't realise we had the uprising planned, with it having to be done in secret?' she said.

'Oh, they did,' Hana told her. She loved her little sister's generous nature but this was just naive. 'Bór says our government gave us the go-ahead to rise on July twenty-fifth – our government *in London*. They briefed the bloody war council about it themselves.'

'Hana!' Orla objected, and Hana bit on her lip. She tried not to curse but, really, this was enough to push anyone to the limit.

Bór had been furious about it. He'd raged, entirely fairly in Hana's very personal opinion, about the glorious service the Polish pilots had given the British in defending their precious little island and how the British surely owed them the courtesy of returning them for this, Poland's most vital battle. Hana had stood in his office, picturing Emil getting into his plane, lovingly painted with a vivid violet on the underside, launching into the skies and then turning, not north to help his fiancée, but west to aid the French. She'd almost cried right where she stood. Especially once she'd heard why.

'The government have told Bór there's nowhere nearer than Brindisi to base them,' she said to her sisters.

'Surely the Russians must have captured a few airbases?' Zuzi protested.

'Oh, they have, but they don't want us using them.'

'Us? The Poles?'

'Us – anyone. Not the British or the Americans either. The Americans flew their great big Liberator planes out of several of them earlier in the war and are willing to help but permission has been retracted. Stalin won't let them land on his territory.'

They went quiet, taking this in. Jacob looked around at them all.

'You mean,' he said slowly, 'that Stalin doesn't want to help us?'

Said that way, in her brother's high-pitched young voice, it sounded very stark.

'It's probably more that he wants the Red Army to do it themselves,' Orla said hastily.

'You think?' Zuzi held up a hand towards the window, open to let in the fresh morning air before the day heated up once more. 'Listen.'

They all cocked their heads.

'What?' Orla asked. 'I can't hear anything.'

Zuzi nodded grimly.

'Exactly. What's missing?'

Hana strained her weary brain to work it out. The air was filled with the twitter of birdsong and the chatter of the people of Wola waking eagerly up to another day as masters of their own lives. Across the city there were a few gunshots as the AK and the Wehrmacht started fighting around the barricades but out here all was quiet. Too quiet.

'The Russian guns!' she cried. 'I can't hear the Russian guns!'

For weeks, the life of the city had been punctuated by the rumble of the Russian advance creeping inexorably closer but this morning, five days into the uprising that was intended to ease the Soviet entry into Poland's capital, they had stopped.

'But he said we were to rise,' Orla gasped. 'Stalin said we were to rise to, to...'

'To show the Red Army the way,' Zuzi finished. 'He did. I heard it myself, out in the Kampinos Forest, the day before the Homeland Council called W-hour.'

'So, what, he didn't mean it?' Hana stuttered.

Zuzi shook her head grimly.

'I'm afraid it looks horribly as if he didn't mean a single word. Stalin is going to leave us here to fight the Germans so that we're both destroyed and he can take Warsaw for himself.'

Hana reached her hands out to her younger sisters and they grasped at them and huddled in close, tugging Jacob with them as they all tried to process what this meant. Warsaw, it seemed, was on her own and the Dąbrowskas were stuck right in the middle of it. How would they ever make it out alive now?

SIXTEEN

ORLA

Orla cuddled against Hana, listening hard to the sounds from outside their window. Zuzi was right; there were no Russian guns rumbling over the Vistula, although there was something else, an almost eerie sound totally at odds with the sunny morning.

'What's that?' she asked.

Jacob leaped over the window.

'It sounds like... screaming?' he suggested.

Orla swallowed. It sounded exactly like that and not so very far away either. Then suddenly the air was filled with a roar of an engine and a gut-wrenching whine before somewhere, barely three or four streets away, there came a ground-shaking explosion. The dark shadow of a thin-bodied plane fell across Jacob and he ducked back, but it pulled up and away over the rooftops with another smug roar.

'The Luftwaffe!' Jacob cried. 'That was a Stuka dive-bomber, I swear it was!' He sounded almost thrilled, until another one flew in and an explosion shook the ground even closer to their bakery. 'They're going to kill us,' he whispered as the reality of the sleek bomber's lethal firepower hit home.

Hana and Zuzi were out of bed too and pulling skirts and blouses on over their slips at speed.

'We should go down to the cellar,' Hana said. 'Get dressed, Orla.'

Orla grabbed the nearest dress from the wardrobe. It was a pretty thing with a pattern of sprigged blossoms, far too nice for the gore of hospital work, though perhaps it would cheer up some poor patient. She grabbed her shoes as Hana hustled them to the stairs but halfway down they met Magda flying towards them, her eyes wide with fear.

'We have to go, girls.'

'Go?' Zuzi asked. 'Go where?'

'Away. Anywhere. Just away. The Germans are attacking.'

'We saw a plane,' Jacob told her. 'It was so close I thought it was going to smash right into—'

'Not the planes.'

Their mother, usually so smiley, was rigid with fear and Orla grabbed her shoulders.

'Then what, Mama? What is it?'

'In the streets,' she gasped out. 'They're in the streets of Wola, attacking from the west. Mrs Gorska just came running to tell me. Some sort of wild gang, she says, with great big guns. They're pulling people out of their houses and shooting them.'

Orla stared at her. 'They're murdering the AK?'

Magda shook her head furiously.

'Not only the AK, Orla – everyone. Women, children, old folk. Everyone. Listen!'

She ran into her bedroom and threw open the window. Orla could hear the screaming more loudly and it chilled her blood. It wasn't in their street yet but it sounded closer than before. The Germans must have broken through the barricades at the edge of their suburb and the menacing planes were clearly supporting a huge ground offensive heading right for their home.

'We have to go!' she gasped.

Up until now, despite the unspeakable injuries she'd seen in the hospital, the uprising had felt like something happening around the edges of the city, but suddenly it was thundering in on their own family and it was truly terrifying. She led the way down to the bakery where, out of the big shop window, they could clearly see people fleeing east towards Stare Miasto, horror writ across their faces. One woman glanced in and saw Orla.

'Run!' she shouted. 'You have to run. They're monsters.'

Orla needed no second urging.

'Come on,' she said, grabbing Jacob by the hand. 'We can go to Babcia's. It'll be safer there.'

Babcia Kamilla's house was on one of the pretty cobbled streets off the market square at the heart of Stare Miasto, so narrow and high-walled that it would surely be far harder for the German troops to storm. They all ran to the door, but then Magda paused.

'Kaczper's baking equipment,' she moaned, looking back into the cosy shop with its lovingly carved wooden counter and bright shelves full of breads and cakes.

'We'll come back for it,' Zuzi assured her. 'But right now – we have to run.'

The streets were filling, hundreds of people pouring away from who knows what horrors. Orla saw one of their regular customers, a kindly older man, hobbling along on his walking stick, and went to help him but he pushed her away.

'Don't worry about me, just go, girl. They're doing terrible things to women back there. Terrible.'

Orla glanced to her sisters and saw her own fear reflected in their eyes. What was this? Surely soldiers took people prisoner, not... Louder screams sounded out and, looking back through the fleeing crowds, she saw several manic, ragged soldiers turn into their street. They fired and she heard screams of pain and, more chilling even than that, manic laughter in response.

'Come on.'

She was still holding Jacob's hand and was glad when he reached his other one back for Magda, Magda for Zuzi and Zuzi for Hana. It made them an unwieldy caterpillar but kept them tight together and she focused ahead, picking a path through the crazed people. More and more were spilling out of their houses at the cacophony of terror, and the way was becoming dangerously blocked. Orla glanced down several side streets but they led to who knows what and they were surely safer on the main route. If nothing else, she thought darkly, there was a mass of people to kill before the attackers got to them.

She picked up snippets of information as they fought their way east.

'They're making for the river, cutting the AK areas in two.'

'They're trying to get to Stahel in the Brühl Palace.'

'They're SS bandits. Hitler's put Himmler in charge and he's sending all his most vicious troops.'

Orla had no idea if any of this was true but it made horrible sense. The Russians had stopped attacking and the Nazis had started and her family were right in the firing line.

They hit a junction with Zelazna Street coming across. Hundreds of people were converging and the crowd built. Orla felt the press threatening to pull Jacob's hand from her increasingly sweaty grasp and looked frantically back for him.

'I'm here, Orla,' he panted, eyes screwed up in an attempt at bravery. 'Keep going.'

She nodded and turned but then a surge of people from their right shoved her sideways and her brother's hand was forced from hers. She thought she heard her name shouted but it was all she could do to stay on her feet and by the time she'd righted herself, she could see none of her family. At her side, a little girl had fallen, weeping for her mama, and Orla bent to scoop her up before she was crushed.

'Don't worry, sweetheart,' she told her. 'We'll find, Mama. We'll—'

'Thank you,' someone said and the girl was whisked out of her arms by, she could only assume, one of her parents. The press of people was worse than a tram at rush hour and, with the sun beating down, Orla felt dizzy. She forced herself to keep going, making for the walls along the shaded side of Chłodna Street. At last, she made it and paused, pressing herself against the cool bricks to draw breath. She scanned the crowds but could see none of her family. No matter. She knew where they were going, all she had to do was stay calm and make for Babcia's house as fast as possible.

She began to slowly edge her way along the houses but had not gone far when, just up ahead, five men in a semblance of uniform burst from a side street and started spraying bullets into the helpless mass. Orla pressed herself into an archway, tears filling her eyes. A large, black PW was painted onto the bricks and the paint rubbed onto her dress. She tried to brush it off but only succeeded in coating her hands in a black mockery of the brief joy of the initial uprising. The Nazis were ploughing into the crowd, firing at point-blank range and people were falling to the street, some instantly dead, others writhing in an agony that seemed to amuse their tormentors.

'Please God,' Orla begged, 'let it be a clean bullet.'

But the five attackers mercifully passed her, heading back the way she'd come, perhaps seeking to pincer the inhabitants of Wola against their fellows coming the other way – or perhaps simply rampaging, for there looked to be no order to their merciless killing. Her breaths came in short, sharp gasps as she prayed the rest of her family had been past the junction before the killers had emerged.

She forced herself to look at the bodies littering the area but could see none she recognised. It did not lessen the tragedy but made it slightly easier to bear, and she forced herself to plough on. She had to get to Stare Miasto. Wola was breached by wild SS and the only safety was beyond the next barricades. She could see one up ahead, manned by young AK who were peering over the top with terrified eyes but were, at least, working to get the fleeing people through, covering their escape with long guns.

'A few more steps,' Orla urged herself but there was only room for single-file through the gap in the barricade and the crowd was clogging behind it.

She prayed for patience but more shots fired out, from above this time, and she realised the enemy had penetrated the houses left by those fleeing for their life and were using them as vantage points. Up ahead she thought she saw a flash of dark hair as a young woman leaped over the barricade and prayed it was Zuzi, the others with her, but she was too far back and everyone was pushing and shoving. Gritting her teeth and sticking out her elbows, she fought forward but then, just as the barricade was within her reach, more men burst from another side street. Orla felt an arm go tight around her waist and breath hot on her neck as she was lifted bodily and dragged sideways.

'Get off me!' she shrieked, kicking her feet in a desperate attempt to hit her captor's shins, but he laughed.

'No chance, darling. You're mine now.'

Orla's heart pounded with fear and she remembered their customer's stark words back at the house: *They're doing terrible things to women back there. Terrible.*

She kicked harder as the man dragged her down the side street and into a small square. She tried to look around but he covered her eyes as he pressed himself, hard, into her back. Her tears leached through his fingers as his other hand scrabbled at the hem of her pretty dress, ripping it in his haste. Orla tried to pray but she was too frightened to breathe let alone talk to God. And then, somewhere nearby, a voice rapped something in sharp German and her captor let her go with a curse.

She scrubbed at her eyes, trying to focus, but now another man had hold of her arms and was marching her forward. Parked at the side of the square was a tank – a big, burly German panzer, soldiers astride it with machine guns. In front of it, to her confusion, was a ladder, turned horizontally and propped up on several chairs. People, almost all young women like herself, were being pushed against it and she feared she'd been released from one horror to be exposed to a far worse one. What were these Nazis doing?

There was little time to wonder as she was rammed against the far end of the ladder and a German command was rapped out. Orla felt her wrists taken from behind, with far less force than before but still too tightly to escape, and then some sort of tie being wrapped around the left one.

'What are you doing?' she demanded furiously. If she was going to die, she was going to do it fighting.

'Stay still,' came back the reply in, to her surprise, fluent Polish.

She twisted, trying to see the man securing her to the ladder, but he turned his head away.

'Why are you doing this?' she tried. 'What have I done to you?'

The man made a strangled noise. 'They're forcing me.'

'And you're forcing *me*.'

'Sorry.'

'Sorry?!'

She twisted further and this time he caught her eye and grimaced. 'Hold still, please.'

'Why should I?'

'Because,' he hissed, 'if you don't, they'll shoot you.'

'Right. And if I do, they'll just gang-rape me?'

He sucked in a breath and shook his head. 'Not that.'

'Then what?'

But now the chairs were being kicked away and the ladder was jerked backwards, taking all those tied on with it. Orla strained to see and realised, with fresh horror, that they were attaching the middle of it to the front of the tank. They were a human shield. She, Orla Dąbrowska, was part of a human shield.

'Who are you?' she demanded of her captor.

The men attaching the ladder were fumbling their job and it gave them a little time.

'Eduard,' came the reply. 'Eduard Mattner. I'm not part of this lot, honest I'm not.'

'Looks very like you are from where I'm standing.'

'It's true. I didn't ask to join. They pulled me in two weeks ago.'

'From where?'

'Prison.' Orla jerked away but his grip was tight on her bound wrists. 'Stay still,' he hissed. 'It's your best chance.'

'Lucky me! A prisoner as my saviour.'

'It's not like it sounds,' the soldier – Eduard – hissed back. 'I was imprisoned as a conscientious objector. I hate the Wehrmacht. I hate the war. I hate Hitler!'

His voice was low, frightened, and she felt him twisting around to look for his commanders and almost believed him. Not that it helped.

'Well, Eduard, your objecting doesn't look all that conscientious to me.'

'No.' He let go of her wrists. 'I'm sorry. I'll help, I promise. I'll get you out.'

He looked around again but he was as trapped within this little square as she was. Orla could still hear the screams of mass murder in the next streets and now the ladder was secured and the tank's engine started up, echoing like the roar of some medieval beast around the closed-in square.

'Walk!' a voice commanded in German and then again in Polish. 'Walk, bitches! Let's see how much your rebel boyfriends value their womenfolk, shall we?'

The tank began to move and Orla had little choice but to stumble forward. She heard Eduard call something but his voice was drowned in the shouted commands. She tugged frantically at the ties and found that Eduard had left them loose enough for her to free herself easily. She shrugged them off and looked for escape, but she could see clearly that if she threw herself aside, one of the men atop the tank would simply gun her down. She took the steps with her petrified neighbours, scanning the buildings for places to hide. There were none.

The tank turned onto the main street. The route was largely clear now, the snipers sending the crowds off to the sides, seeking safer ways to Stare Miasto, and the tank swung round to the right, forcing Orla, on the far side of the ladder, to run to stay on her feet. The woman next to her missed her footing and was dragged, legs scraping across the rough tarmac, until the tank paused to line up at the barricade, and she could stand again. The woman was weeping loudly and crying for mercy but Orla feared it would not be forthcoming. The AK on the barricade before them had a stark choice – save the fifteen women being driven towards them, or save the lives of themselves and all those cowering beyond their barricade. It was a grave choice but not, at the end of the day, a difficult one. Orla was going to die.

The tank began moving steadily towards the barricade and the AK lined up their guns. She looked frantically round again and spotted a doorway to her left. If she could dive into that then maybe she'd escape their firing. What happened after that she did not want to contemplate but one step at a time.

Up ahead, the AK were babbling a confusion of apologies

that might soothe their own souls but would do nothing for those they were about to release from their bodies. Orla held her hands against the ladder, gripping it for ironic support as she drew closer to the tiny gap in the wall. And then, over the ongoing screams from behind, she heard the click of guns being cocked, and let go. A single shot pinged off the metal of the tank and then many were ringing out and women were falling, their weight dragging at the ladder as the soldiers on its gun turret fired in return.

Orla flung herself sideways, scrabbling for the doorway as the tank rolled past. She thought she'd made it, but then all the air was knocked out of her as someone fell on top of her. She waited for the barrel in her neck but it didn't come.

'Stay down.'

She recognised the voice as his – Eduard's – and felt his arms wrap around her, not as captor but as protector. Her body started to shake and she pressed herself against the rough wood of the door, letting him shield her with his big, warm body as shots pinged relentlessly around them. The tank rolled past their hiding place but still the battle raged and Orla was sure the beast of a machine must, any moment, now, plough into the barricade and take it out. Were the others safely past it? she wondered desperately. Had they made it to Babcia's? They would be desperately looking for her, she was sure, and felt terrible for causing them such distress.

She was hot and sore but kept on sucking in breaths, certain each one would be her last, until suddenly, with a hideous bang, the oxygen was sucked right out of the street, replaced with the heat of fire. Eduard's body jerked against her own and she heard German curses on the frying air and the sound of jackboots hitting the pavement. Squirming out from under the limp German, she saw the tank blazing on one side, flames licking sickeningly along the ladder, lighting up the limp forms of the dead women still tied to it. She had almost been one of them.

'Eduard?' There was a nasty piece of shrapnel in his shoulder and she stared at it, knowing that, were it not for him, it would be embedded in herself. He had died to protect her. 'Thank you, Eduard,' she said, bending to pull it out, not wanting him to be laid to what little rest might be found in stricken Warsaw with tank stuck in his skin.

'Owww!' His howl of pain made her stagger backwards in surprise and he reached out and pulled her back in against him. 'Careful. This isn't over yet.'

'You're alive.'

'Just about. And you?'

He touched a hand to her cheek in what felt like a very intimate gesture but, when he pulled back, his finger was covered in blood. She put her own up to it and found a long cut down the side of her face. It hurt, now she'd noticed, but it didn't feel fatal.

'Come on,' Eduard said, 'we have to get you out of here.'

The Germans had abandoned the tank and the AK were swarming excitedly towards it but there were still snipers about and one young man was sent flying backwards, screaming in pain.

'Keep low,' Eduard urged, pulling her around the front of the tank and towards the barricade.

Shocked hands reached out to pull her through the slim gap at the side. She tried to scramble over but her legs had turned to jelly and it was only Eduard bodily lifting her into the AK's arms that saw her safe onto the other side.

'Thank you,' she said. He gave her a watery smile and turned away. 'Don't go!'

The AK looked at her like she was mad but, feeling stronger now, Orla reached out and pulled him after her, eyes scared, hands held high.

'What did you do that for?' one of the AK demanded, gun raised.

'He saved me,' she said. 'He promised he'd get me out and he did. He's not one of them. He's a conscientious objector.'

'Doesn't look like it to me.'

The AK leader pushed his gun into Eduard's chest.

'It's true,' Eduard pleaded in his perfect Polish. 'My mother is a Pole, my father German. I was forced into the Wehrmacht when the Nazis took our area, and then imprisoned for refusing to fight.'

'We don't need cowards,' the AK man sneered.

'Refusing to fight for *Hitler*,' Eduard said. 'I'll fight for you. I'll fight for Poland. I'll fight the animals doing this to our people.'

The AK men shifted. Orla looked around them, feeling faint. She could see the tank burning itself out beyond the barricade, the corpses of those women who had been less lucky than her burning with it, and she had to lean against the sandbags to stay upright.

'His story makes sense, sir,' one man said.

'Hmm.'

'Here.' Eduard reached for his gun and the AK all cocked their weapons. 'It's yours. For your fight.' He took it by the handle and flung it at their feet. The leader picked it up and looked to his platoon.

'I say he's genuine, sir.'

'Could be an act – they're devious bastards. Take him away for interrogation.'

He waved and two men stepped up and grabbed an unresisting Eduard, bundling him towards a nearby building. Orla watched him go, feeling a strange sense of loss. Why was that? Her cheek was stinging badly and her head was swimming, so most likely her judgement was impaired. This man had the hideous Nazi eagle on his chest. He was the enemy. And yet, he had saved her.

'Thank you,' she called, and Eduard looked back and gave her a shy smile.

'My pleasure,' he called back. 'God bless you.'

And then he was gone and the AK were returning to their barricade as the hideous fight continued beyond it. Orla's legs shook again and she was grateful when another liaison girl came running up and offered her an arm.

'Let's get you to hospital,' she heard her say.

'Hospital,' she agreed foggily. 'Yes. I'm a nurse. I have to nurse.'

The girl said something about being nursed for once and she wanted to object but felt too pathetically weak to do so. She thought of her family and fought to breathe, amazed she was still able to do so.

Then her legs gave way and she could think of nothing at all.

SEVENTEEN
6 AUGUST

ZUZI

Zuzi lifted the hammer and drove it, hard, into the wall. That was for the monsters running riot around Wola. And that – she brought down her hardest blow – was for whoever had got Orla. Her little sister had never done anything to hurt anyone. She was the kindest, gentlest person – the only one of their family, except perhaps their mother, who hadn't wanted the uprising – so why was she the one suffering?

Zuzi swung the hammer again and had the satisfaction of seeing it break into the next room. The Minerki were operating in Stare Miasto, breaking down walls between people's cellars to enable them to pass safely underground in the event of an air attack.

Zuzi had asked to be excused to look for Orla, but Tosia had taken her arm and said, 'Do you not think, if she's alive, she'll find you?'

'Yes,' Zuzi had agreed, 'but what if she's not?'

Tosia had spread her hands wide. 'Then I'm afraid it's too late to do anything.'

It had been a stark but honest truth.

'She might be injured,' Zuzi had objected. 'Maybe in a hospital somewhere.'

'In which case, the sooner we make Stare Miasto safer to travel around the better.'

There had been no denying the logic and, as the waiting had been all but breaking Zuzi, she'd agreed to put her nervous energy into breaking walls instead. So, here she was.

She adjusted the props keeping the cellar stable and took a hammer to the wall once more. The householders, a friendly couple with three young children, stood watching with their hands to their mouths and Zuzi offered them her best attempt at a reassuring smile. The cellars throughout Warsaw were solid and well-built, the interconnecting walls there for security not support. Already this family were connected on the far side with another, and another and another leading all the way along beneath the street so that liaison officers, AK soldiers and medical staff could pass easily through. Thanks to the brave Krybar battalion still holding the power plant, they could string lights along the passage, and underground Warsaw felt chaotic but safe. This final strike was into the John of God Hospital – the hospital in which Orla should be nursing the sick; the hospital in which Dr Bronislaw worked.

Zuzi felt a stupid judder inside herself and hid it with yet another smash of the wall. The hole was substantial now and she forced herself to prise away the loose bricks with her hands for a neater, more orderly job. One of the children, a girl of maybe ten, came shyly up at her side.

'Can I help you?'

'I'm not sure. I don't want you to get hurt.'

'I won't,' the girl insisted. 'I'm very careful. And besides' – she tugged on Zuzi's blouse – 'I really want to do something useful.'

Zuzi understood that and nodded.

'Prise the bricks out one at a time. If you feel anything sliding, drop it immediately and step back, yes?'

'Yes, ma'am.' The girl gave Zuzi a crooked salute and looked, for a second, so like Orla, that Zuzi had to grip at a brick to resist the urge to reach out and hug her.

'Thank you.'

Her father, an older man with a pronounced limp, also stepped up to offer help while his wife took the two younger children out of harm's way, promising to return with cups of tea. They would be very welcome, for it was a hot day and even beneath the ground, Zuzi was sweating at her task.

Now, however, the gap was big enough to step through and, leaving her helpers to keep widening it, she squeezed into the next cellar and looked around. She was in the once-secret part of the hospital where, unbelievably, just a week ago, she had brought medical supplies to her sister when she'd been in disgrace for pulling a pin out of a grenade. The loss of a few courgettes seemed laughable with all they'd been through since then, and the hospital was almost unrecognisable too.

Instead of neat rows of pristine beds, the place was crammed with people, the lucky few on mattresses, but the rest on an assortment of makeshift pallets in between. Most lay, aptly patient in their suffering, but a few moaned and cried out and the nurses scurried between them, doing their best to help. Zuzi couldn't stop herself scanning those that passed in the desperate hope one of them might be Orla but, of course, her sister was nowhere to be seen.

'Żelazo?'

She jumped at the soft touch on her arm and looked up into the warmest brown eyes she thought she'd ever seen.

'Dr, erm... Łukasz?'

He smiled gently.

'I think the time for code names is gone, don't you? Call me Bron.'

'Bron? Right. Yes. I will. And I'm Zuzi.'

'A lovely name.'

'Thank you.' She could think of little more to say, which was most unlike her and, frankly, most pathetic, but he made her insides burn as if someone had exploded a filipinka inside them and it made it very hard to concentrate. He was a man like any other, she told herself sternly, save that he did have those brown eyes and that lovely smile and he was a doctor, with the power to save lives and... She shook herself. 'How's it going? That is...' She looked around the packed ward and felt even more foolish. 'It's clear things are tough, but I meant with you. How are you doing?'

None of this was coming out right but then he smiled again and said, 'Better for seeing you,' and it didn't seem to matter.

'Just helping sort out your access,' she said, waving back to the hole. Her father and daughter helpers waved obligingly and she wondered what on earth this looked like. Not that Bron seemed to care.

'That will be a big help,' he said earnestly. 'Now the Nazis are bombing us, it's hard to get people into the hospital overground.'

'I don't think that's going to be a lot easier,' Zuzi said, grimacing at her rough hole.

He gave a wry laugh.

'Perhaps not, but it might reduce a soldier's chance of getting injured a second time before his wound can be treated, so that's a win, right?'

'I'm not sure about a win...'

'No.' He tipped his head on one side in a way that set the sparks going in Zuzi's stomach and, if she was honest, disturbingly lower. 'You're right, Zuzi. But maybe less of a loss.'

'Hmmm.' Zuzi thought perhaps she could stand here discussing linguistic pedantics for hours, but then he added,

'Where's Orla today?' and instantly she wanted to be anywhere else.

'She's missing,' she admitted, though it took about as much effort as three big hammer swings to get the words out.

'Missing? Oh no! Are you all right?'

His kindness was sweet, she supposed, but desperately misplaced. She'd lost her little sister and did not deserve any compassion.

'Course I'm not,' she snapped, 'but I'm probably more all right than she is.'

He didn't flinch in the way she'd expect, just nodded.

'What happened?' Zuzi felt herself choke up and had to lean on the nearest bedstead to support herself. 'Zuzi? Here, please, sit down.'

He'd pulled up a chair from who knows where and as she sank gratefully onto it, he crouched before her and unselfconsciously took her hands.

'You can talk to me,' he said, adding with half a smile, 'I'm a doctor.'

Zuzi tried to smile back, but she wanted to be able to talk to him because he thought she was worth his time, not just because everybody did. She tutted crossly at herself – what a time to be going soft.

'We had to flee our home,' she said tightly.

He squeezed her hands. 'You live in Wola?'

'Lived,' she said bitterly. 'We're with my babcia Kamilla now in Stare Miasto. At least, Mama, Hana, Jacob and I are. Orla...' She choked again but still his hands were holding hers and, although he didn't say any more, his warm presence was enough to calm her. 'We'd linked hands to stay together but there were so many people. It was panic. I mean, of course it was, there were Nazis running riot, shooting everyone and pulling girls aside to, to...'

'Rape them,' he said. He was a very straightforward man; she liked that.

'It was awful. We were trying to get out.'

'Of course you were.'

'But then there was a crush of people from another direction and Orla somehow got swept away. Jacob let her go. That's to say, he didn't let go. I don't mean it was his fault. He's only thirteen and his hands probably aren't all that big yet. I should have been holding her. She's my little sister, she's—'

'Eighteen, Zuzi. An adult. It's not your responsibility, not your fault.'

Zuzi looked into his eyes, wanting to believe him, but that was a nonsense.

'It's as much my fault as anyone's.'

'True, but it's *no one's* fault.'

There was nowhere to go with this man!

'It doesn't matter,' she said impatiently. 'The point is, Orla's gone. She was swept away. The rest of us got through the barrier and she didn't, which means she's still over there, in Wola, with those evil, evil men.' She clenched at his fingers. 'What if they're raping her? What if they're holding her down and, and...'

Now the tears came and there was no fighting them. Bron held her hands tight, his thumbs gently circling the tops of them as she wept. He didn't offer her false platitudes, didn't pretend it was all fine, and she appreciated that. Eventually she felt able to speak again.

'I wanted this, you know. I wanted the uprising. I was full of how I was going to smash in the Nazis, but now they've got my little sister and there's nothing I can do.'

'You can keep on smashing.'

'What?'

'So that she didn't die in vain – if she's dead, which she may well not be. It's chaos out there and I bet Orla won't have given in. From what I've seen of her, she's sweet, yes, and kind and caring and optimistic, but she's no pushover – is she?'

Zuzi looked into his eyes again. She thought of Orla and knew he was right.

'You're a wise man, Doctor.'

'Bron,' he said softly. 'I'd really like it if you called me Bron.'

'Bron,' she repeated.

'Where's your babcia's house?' She looked at him, confused. 'So that if Orla turns up here, I can come and let you know.'

'Oh. Right. Thank you. It's 113 Rybaki Street, off the market square towards the Vistula. She has a marvellous view of the Russian non-advance.'

She gave a bitter laugh and his fingers rubbed hers again.

'Got it.' A nurse was hovering and he looked awkwardly up. 'I'd better go now, I'm afraid. Will you be...?'

'Of course.' She felt ashamed. Here she was monopolising a doctor over her small concerns when there were people with horrific injuries all around who needed him far more. 'Of course you must. Sorry. I—'

She got to her feet but he was still holding her hands.

'Please don't apologise, Zuzi. Come and see me anytime, talk to me about anything.'

'Because you're a doctor, right?'

He shrugged.

'More because I like you.'

He was gone almost before the words were out, off with the nurse to bend over some patient across the crowded room. Zuzi stared after him, confused. He really was the most intriguing man and Orla was very lucky to work with him every day. Her heart squeezed.

'Orla,' she murmured under her breath and suddenly she had to get home.

The hole in the wall was plenty big enough. Her job was

done and she had to be with her family – what was left of it. Turning, she all but ran through the cellar wall, remembering to grab her hammer and thank her diligent helpers. She scrambled on through the next few houses to an easy staircase up and headed out to find that dusk was falling. A Stuka screamed overhead, flinging a bomb onto the roof of a church, and she flinched back as the spire cracked and, with a grating sound, collapsed in on itself, the golden cross tumbling from the top to cries of horror beneath. Zuzi crossed herself and, head low, made for Babcia's house at speed.

Magda was there, pacing up and down the elegant entrance hall, carving a maternal groove into the black and white tiles.

'She's not here?' Zuzi asked.

Magda shook her head. 'Sunfall came and went without her.'

'The sun's still there,' Zuzi said fiercely. 'We'll get her back before it goes down again.'

'How, Zuzi?'

To that, she had no answer. 'Is Hana here?' she asked instead.

'Out running messages.'

'Jacob?'

'Upstairs crying his eyes out, poor lad. He blames himself.'

'Don't we all?'

Magda nodded dumbly. She pulled on her blonde hair and Zuzi noticed streaks of grey running through it, as if her mother had aged years in this last day.

'Babcia Kamilla?' she asked.

'Harassing the "authorities" – whoever she thinks they are – into looking for Orla. We agreed someone should be here, in case she came back, but the waiting is killing me, Zuzi.'

Zuzi threw her arms around her mother.

'Someone very wise just told me that Orla is stronger than any of us give her credit for. He said—'

'No!'

'Honestly, he—'

But her mother was pushing her aside and stumbling to the door and there, looking dazed but definitely intact, was...

'Orla! Oh, Orla, you're here. You're alive. You made it. How did you make it?'

Zuzi couldn't stop the words tumbling out as she clutched at her little sister, patting her down to be sure she was whole. She had a nasty cut on one cheek but it had been washed and dressed and she looked otherwise well. Magda was kissing her too and then running inside to call Jacob, who came pounding down the gracious staircase two at a time and flung himself, bullet-like, into the hug.

'Orla. I let you go. I let you go and I thought they'd got you.'

'They nearly did,' she said. 'But it wasn't your fault, Jacob. *I* let go of *you*.' Her voice was so sweetly, perfectly her own that Zuzi felt tears scratching at her eyeballs and, after a brief battle, gave up and let them fall.

'They didn't, did they?' she asked, holding her sister at arm's length to look into her lovely blue eyes. 'They didn't get you?'

Orla shook her head.

'They tied me to a tank...'

'What?!'

'But I got away. That is, someone helped me get away. A German.'

'A German?' Zuzi spat.

'A nice German.'

'No such thing.'

'Oh, there is. He was... It doesn't matter.'

'Quite right,' Magda agreed. 'Nothing matters, save that

you are here and safe. Oh, my little girl.' She crushed her against her bosom. 'My little Orla.'

Orla smiled, then looked around. 'Where's Hana?'

'She'll be here. Babcia too. Come on through. I've made bread.'

Zuzi laughed at the glorious mundanity of it.

'Of course you have, Mama.'

Magda shrugged, wiping tears away.

'I had to have something to knead, or I'd have gone mad.'

Zuzi nodded.

'I smashed in a few walls,' she offered. 'One to your hospital actually, Orls. That doctor was there – what's his name?'

'Bronislaw,' Orla said, 'as well you know.'

Then she winked at her – actually winked – and Zuzi was so relieved that she was here and well and whole that she just smiled and guided her through to the kitchen as Hana and Babcia came running through the door, shouting in delight. They would have Orla's story around the table before sunfall, all of them together, as it should be.

She could only pray that it would stay that way.

PART TWO

I received your letter about Warsaw. I should inform you that a closer look at this case has convinced me that the Warsaw activity, which was undertaken unbeknownst to and without contacting the Soviet command, was a thoughtless adventure that caused pointless losses of population. On top of that, it resulted in a smear campaign by the Polish press that alluded to the Soviet command deceiving the citizens of Warsaw. In view of all this, the Soviet command has decided to publicly disassociate itself from the Warsaw adventure, as it should not and cannot bear any responsibility for Warsaw's affairs.

MARSHAL STALIN, TO STANISŁAW
MIKOŁAJCZYK, POLISH PRIME MINISTER,
MID-AUGUST 1944

EIGHTEEN

7 AUGUST

HANA

Hana stared into the night sky, looking for lights amongst the stars, but it was impossible. With no Allied air defence to stop them, the German Stukas had taken to attacking Warsaw every day, dropping incendiaries to set so much of Warsaw burning that the sky was a permanent dirty orange, like a nonstop sunset gone wrong. Hana was in the north-west area of the ruined ghetto, just inside the line of cemeteries that were proving a crucial line of defence around Stare Miasto.

She was waiting, with her comrades, for a miracle, but she was worried. These were far from ideal conditions for aeroplanes and for the first time since she'd heard the news that the RAF were to fly in supplies, she wished they wouldn't bother. The planes would be sitting ducks in the raging firelight – easy targets for the Germans' sophisticated anti-aircraft guns – and that was if they made it over the vast Nazi-held territories between here and Brindisi. It was, Agaton had told her earlier, a two thousand kilometre round trip, over hazardous terrain, but the Polish pilots were apparently determined to make the attempt and Mr Churchill was backing them to do so.

Hana's heart swelled with pride, then contracted once more with fear. If Emil was one of the pilots on tonight's mission, he would be so vulnerable up there above her. They needed the help, that much was true. The Russians had not retreated, but neither had they advanced, so the AK was having to hold the city and they were fast running out of the ammunition to do so. The vicious SS brigades had occupied Wola and carved a path across Warsaw, taking the Saxon Gardens and the Brühl Palace and pushing on to the Poniatowskiego Bridge, so they now had free access across the middle of the city.

It was, ironically, almost the route that had been proposed for the east–west expressway by the city planners before all this had started. Hana had lost her single sheet when they'd had to flee Wola and, as far as she knew, the rest of the maps, both of the existing city and the hoped-for future one, were still in the Telephone Exchange. That, sadly, was one of the strongholds the Wehrmacht still held. The AK had tried again and again to storm the concrete tower of a building but to no avail and it loomed over Śródmieście, bristling with snipers who would shoot at anyone trying to fetch water or bread to survive another day.

Hana shivered at the thought. They'd all got far too used to men – and women – sustaining horrible injuries. Orla was back at work after her narrow escape and came home every night whispering about the dire wounds she'd seen. It broke her beautiful heart every time, Hana could see, and she wished she could find a way to spare her little sister the pain, but for now they were all in this together.

She looked across to where her fellow liaison girls were crouched in hiding spots amongst the rubble of the ghetto, each clutching the lantern they would light when they heard the engines – *if* they heard the engines. The news had arrived three days ago that the RAF had been authorised to drop supplies. If the conditions were right, the BBC would play 'One More Mazurka' – a famous Polish folk song – at the end of its Polish broadcast at 8 p.m. Twice they'd eagerly listened for it and twice been disappointed, but tonight the strains of the city's special song had rung out and it had been all go. Hana, as Bór's liaison officer, should not really be part of the light troop but she'd begged Czajnik to let her join them and, with two girls in hospital, she'd been short-staffed enough to say yes.

Now, Hana had to admit, she was questioning her decision. On their first night in Stare Miasto when Orla had returned, they'd sat in Babcia's elegant living room, thanking God for keeping them all safe.

'We wept for your father,' Magda had said solemnly. 'Let us not weep again.'

Even Babcia Kamilla had been subdued and, although she'd said the usual things about doing their duty by Poland, she'd urged caution. The Warsaw Uprising was no longer a swift, heady victory, but a war of attrition and Hana had asked her precious family not to take unnecessary risks in the coming days. Babcia had a beautiful silver cross – a treasured family heirloom – and they'd all put their hands on it and made the oath to do their best to stay alive for each other. So why, then, had she volunteered to step into open land, a light clearly marking out her exact position for both friend and enemy?!

To her right, Czajnik, personally leading their little troop, looked at her watch in the eerie light of the fires.

'It's getting late,' she hissed. 'I'm not sure they're coming.'

Hana felt a stab of relief, swiftly followed by an even sharper pain. The music on the BBC told them the planes had taken off, so if they did not come, it was most likely because they'd been shot down.

'A little longer,' she urged. 'It's a long way.'

'Wouldn't be if they could use Russian bases,' came Czajnik's angry reply.

Hana nodded and clutched at the bricks of the small wall she was hiding behind. Why were Churchill and Roosevelt letting Stalin get away with such deceit? They were *allies*, surely, fighting on the same side – though not, perhaps, with the same aims for after the war.

'Pull yourself together,' Hana muttered under her breath. Yes, she was sitting amongst the remnants of a cruel ghetto, waiting for planes that might never come, bringing a few handguns to set against the myriad German tanks and dive bombers, but that didn't mean she had to give in to every dark fear. The Nazis might have carved a path through central Warsaw but the AK still held almost every other area and once these weapons arrived, they would attack again. There were plans to take the Telephone Exchange and that might mean they could rescue the city maps the Gestapo had snatched off Marek before the uprising. A new, regenerated Warsaw, that's what she had to focus on – that and staying alive long enough to be a part of creating it.

Somewhere from the German-held area beyond the cemeteries came the unmistakable rap of jackboots – a patrol. Hana threw herself on the ground, her head close to a rounded rock marked in chalk with a Star of David. Pulling back, she saw two names written beneath it with utmost care – Zachariah and Tobias and then dates next to their names, 1911–1943 for Zachariah, 1940–1943 for Tobias. Hana's heart clenched for what was surely a father and son somewhere beneath the rubble protecting her from Nazi fire.

The ghetto had been an affront to humanity and its liquidation the ultimate atrocity. Hana, along with the rest of the AK, had applauded the last of the Jews for their brave uprising but she couldn't help remembering how it had ended. Of the four hundred thousand people once crammed into this now-ruined area of Warsaw, the only ones who'd survived had been the fifty that Zuzi and her Minerki had freed from Gęsiówka last week. That and the brave people like Kapitan Szymon Ancel, who'd escaped and hidden elsewhere. What did he and his family make of this second, failing attempt at liberation?

'The British are coming,' Hana reminded herself sternly, but right now, with a torch beam shining across their exposed hiding places, the Germans felt far closer. Thankfully the beam couldn't quite reach their positions and it pulled away as the boots marched on.

'Right, ladies,' Czajnik hissed. 'I think we need to call it—'

She stopped as, quiet at first, but growing swiftly louder, they all heard the unmistakable sound of engines on the night air. Hana looked south and saw, silhouetted against the flames of Wola, the shape of an aircraft – a British aircraft. It was swiftly followed by two more, all three flying steadily towards them.

'Now!' Czajnik ordered. 'Lights, now!'

Hana fumbled with her matches, holding the flame to the gas, willing it to light. A gust took the first one and she struck a second. This time it caught and the flame flared in the glass box. Closing the door, she stepped from Zachariah and Tobias's final resting place to take up her position, forming a square with the others.

'Hold them up high, girls – we need these supplies!'

Hana lifted her arm, wishing she were taller. She could no longer hear the Nazi boots and had no idea if that meant they were gone, or had stopped to look into the ghetto area again. The anti-aircraft crews had located the planes and were sending powerful searchlights into the sky, picking them out like actors on a stage. The flak guns were firing, the black puffs of their shells blooming like doom-laden roses across the white beams, sharp against the orange glow of the city beneath. It was like a beautiful painting, save that it might bring death for any or all of them. Hana clutched at her lantern, holding it high above her head. Her arm ached but she refused to let it drop. If those men could fly two thousand kilometres over enemy territory to get to them, she could cope with a little muscle-pain to guide them safely in.

The flak shells were exploding overhead, raining pieces of shrapnel, and Hana was glad of the steel helmet one of the AK in their protective platoon had lent her as metal pinged against it, a parody of the sound of rain on canvas that she remembered from family camping trips as a child. Somewhere nearby there was a shout in German, and now the jackboots were coming. A shot was fired, and then more from the AK. Every bit of Hana shook but the planes were so close that she could almost see the pilots in their cockpits, leaning out to look for their lights.

'We're here!' she cried over the noise of the guns.

She saw the flaps in the underside of the first plane open and packages began to fall out. They were ominously bomb-shaped and for a dreadful heartbeat she thought this might be some lethal scam, but then strings strung out from them and miniature white parachutes opened, checking their fall so that they floated softly down like giant dandelion heads. It was a beautiful sight. In those cylinders were the guns and the ammo the AK would need to keep the Nazis out of Stare Miasto. It might be a risk for Hana right now, but in the long term it could save them all. A bullet pinged off a wall a metre to her left and she longed to dive for the ground but the AK on the far side took out her attacker and she held steady. The other two planes were closing in, their bays opening to release more magical packages.

'You see!' she flung in the general direction of the Nazis. 'We're not alone. We have friends. We have allies. And they're coming for you!'

Another bullet flew, so close it almost kissed her cheek, but the planes were closing up their bays again and swinging away, dodging the flak like pros, and their job was almost done. None of them had been Emil but perhaps she'd been foolish to hope for that anyway. There must be hundreds of pilots in Brindisi.

She sank back down behind her pile of rubble, wrapping her arms around herself as she tried to picture her fiancé. At first it felt impossible, but then an image came to her – Emil turning up at the bakery at the start of their courtship with a picnic basket and newly washed rug, asking if she would do him the honour of accompanying him out for lunch. 'It's hardly the Europejski Hotel is it?' she'd heard Zuzi giggling behind her but she hadn't cared. Sitting with Emil amongst the meadow-flowers on the bank of the Vistula had been the finest dining experience of her life. Especially when he'd leaned over and touched his lips to hers and… The glorious memory was pierced by an excited shout from one of the girls.

'There's another one!'

Sure enough, a fourth plane was coming in, travelling at speed to catch up with its fellows. The girls shot back into position and Hana screwed up her courage and joined them. She was desperate to get home to Babcia's pretty house with its soft carpets and elegant furnishings, to the comfy bed she shared with her sisters and the makeshift bakery her mother had set up out of the kitchen. A bullet pinged off her hat and she staggered sideways. Surely the plane knew where to drop now? Surely they could get back undercover before it was too late? She peered desperately upwards. It was very close and the bay doors flashed silver against the night sky as they opened.

And that's when she saw it – painted behind the doors in the most beautiful shade of purple, was a violet, its petals marked out with the utmost care and unmistakably heart-shaped.

'Emil!'

All thoughts of home vanished from Hana's head. All tiredness slipped from her arm. All fear was gone. She could think only of her fiancé, no more than fifty metres above her. He had come! He was alive and he had come to bring hope to Warsaw. Hope to Hana.

'Emil!' she cried again. He could not hear her but maybe, somehow, he would sense her, maybe he would feel her love beaming up to him brighter and stronger than any hateful searchlight.

'Fiolet! Get down!'

Czajnik tackled her to the ground just before bullets fired across the spot where she'd been standing. The lantern went crashing across Zachariah and Tobias' sweetly chalked stone, its light extinguished instantly, and she panted out her thanks to her boss as she sat cautiously up for a last look at her fiancé.

His bay was closing now, his packages floating down, and his plane tilting sideways, heading up and away across the Vistula. Hana felt the pain of his departure but willed him on – back to base, back to safety to live another day, as she would. The Russians must surely come now that they saw how serious their allies were about Warsaw. She touched her fingers to her ring, as prettily purple as the beautiful, hopeful flower on her fiancé's plane, and smiled as she watched him disappear into the safety of night. He would be back, she was sure, and she would do everything she could to be here for him.

NINETEEN

11 AUGUST

ORLA

'Down there?' Orla stared in horror at the dank, moss-strewn steps leading beneath the earth. It had been bad enough coming into the cemetery as night fell, but now she was expected to plunge into the tombs. She grimaced at Bronislaw. 'Seriously?'

He grimaced back.

'It's the best we're going to get out here.'

'Is it not some sort of bad omen to operate on people in a tomb?'

'Maybe it's a good omen. Maybe the dead are greedy of their space and will work to make sure no one else clogs it up.'

Orla peered at him to see if he was serious but, with the fading light and Bronislaw's deadpan delivery, it was impossible to tell.

'Let's hope so,' she said, looking around her again.

She and Bron had been tasked with setting up an operating theatre as part of the field hospital in the vast Protestant cemetery. This, along with the Catholic, Orthodox and Jewish cemeteries, formed a great band of open land curving around the western edge of Stare Miasto. They were all held by the AK but the Wehrmacht were attacking the edges, and intel suggested that tonight they were going to mount a big attack. The hospital was being set up in an area on the AK-secured east side which had once, a long time ago, been walled off by some wealthy family intent on privacy for their ancestors. It was as safe as possible but it still felt ominous to Orla.

'Shall we...?'

Bron waved to the steps and she moved cautiously onto the first one, peering into the inky depths in disbelief. A few weeks ago, she would have been petrified to even enter the cemetery at night. She and her friends used to tell each other horror stories about the ghosts roaming amongst the eerie tombs, clinging onto each other with girlie shrieks at the thought of long-dead Warsawians rising to torment the living, and now she was heading down into them. How things changed! Tonight, Orla would almost welcome the company of the ghosts of the past to defend their beloved city, and she'd certainly rather see a headless knight than a headless AK soldier.

Talking of which, they had a hospital to set up, and fast. The AK were taking up positions amongst the graves and there was an ominous rumble of tanks to the west. The battle was close so there was no time for being squeamish. Bronislaw shone a torch downwards and Orla had little choice but to follow its beam. She prayed that it would open out into some sort of pretty marble room, with elegant columns and maybe an altar, so that she could pretend she was in a chapel, but no such luck. The lower chamber was a thin, dark area with a packed earth floor and dripping ceiling. On either side were stone shelves and on them all rested iron coffins. The lid had fallen sideways off the nearest one, giving Orla a glimpse of an actual skeleton as Bronislaw's torch swept across it, and it was all she could do not to scream.

'They're a bit creepy,' Bron allowed, putting a steadying

arm around her and moving the beam hastily away, 'but try to think of them as our friends.'

'Our allies...?' Orla suggested darkly.

Hana had come home the other night raving about the RAF pilots who'd dropped supplies over the ghetto and it had, indeed, been a magnificent feat. From what Orla had picked up, mind you, most of the supplies had been blown over the German lines, their delicate parachutes wafting the AK's badly needed guns, bullets and bandages into the hands of their enemy. Plus, although those four planes – all flown by Poles – had made it, two others had not and there had been no more flights since. The net result had been less than half a day's worth of fighting equipment, now long gone.

Plus, Orla reminded herself, the beautiful glow in her sister's hazel eyes as she'd described seeing the violet on the bottom of the final plane. Orla could not begin to imagine how hard it must be for Hana. She'd been engaged for five years and was no closer to a wedding than she'd been before Emil had proposed. Seeing the evidence that he was still alive and missing his fiancée had invigorated the eldest Dąbrowska and that had been worth a lot to them all.

Four days later, however, and they were fighting for their lives amongst the dead. Zuzi and her Minerki were a key part of the team setting mines along the German side of the cemeteries to break up their advance. Babcia Kamilla was with her, in theory working from the back to provide equipment to the younger girls, but Orla worried what would happen once the action heated up. Jacob was firmly bedded into Szymon Ancel's platoon, who were deploying their stolen tank from the sidelines, and Hana was here too, poised to take messages back to other units as events unfolded. The Dąbrowskas were all, despite their vow to try and stay safe, tangled in the heart of the fighting and Magda had sent them out this afternoon with so many kisses that Orla swore her cheeks still stung. Not that she was complaining; there was, surely, no such thing as too much love?

Nor such a thing as too many cakes. Reaching into the pocket of her big, once-white apron, she drew out the slab of Magda's finest szarlotka she had sent with her 'for energy' and took a bite. Sugar was short so it was tarter than usual but the sweet cinnamon stickiness of the apple against the light, nut-topped dough was still almost enough to transport Orla to a nicer place. Mind you, there weren't many much worse places.

Bron had set a gas lamp on the top coffin-shelf and it cast a flickering light across their morbid hospital, lighting up her sneaky snack.

'What's that you've got there?' he demanded.

'Cake,' she admitted.

He pouted in the low light, exactly as Jacob might, and she laughed and tore off a hunk, handing it over. It was nice having this man as a sort of older brother, and would be even nicer to have him as an actual one if he and Zuzi ever… Not that this was the time to be thinking of romance.

'You're a wonder, Orla Dąbrowska,' Bron told her, scoffing the cake with moans of pleasure.

'My *mother* is a wonder,' she corrected, feeling better for the food. 'Now, Doctor, where in this chamber of the dead do you propose we set up our operating table?'

Bron looked around as he licked his fingers clean of the precious treat. 'Our options aren't vast.'

'No.'

'So…'

He indicated the lowest of the iron coffins, bending to take hold of a handle. Orla shuddered.

'We can't do that, Bron.'

'I don't think we have any choice. Come on.'

He tugged on the handle and Orla bent reluctantly to grab her end and help him pull it into the centre of the room.

'It's not high enough.'

'Not yet,' he agreed grimly and reached for the one on the next shelf up. Orla crossed herself at this desecration of the dead, but helped him position the second coffin on top of the first to make a perfect, waist-height table.

'I'm sorry for disturbing your rest,' she whispered to whoever was inside.

Bron gave her a wry smile. 'They've been stuck in here ages; they're probably bored sick.'

Orla groaned. 'I'd give anything to be bored.'

Bron gave her hand a quick squeeze.

'A few more days,' he said.

She didn't contradict him but they both knew that everyone had been saying that since the start of the uprising. Now they were a full two weeks in, with no sign of a conclusion, and the promise was wearing thin. But what could they do? No Pole would surrender, so they must fight on and pray the outside world came to their aid before... Orla pushed the thought away and went to help Bron arrange his instruments on the vacated shelf.

She thought again of her friends telling stupid ghost stories around campfires. If they could see her now, they'd never believe it. Then again, many of them were doing much the same. The Nazis had robbed them of the innocent joys of a normal childhood when they'd occupied their city, so here they were, fighting to get it back.

It would just be nice if they had a little help to do so.

Orla went to stand next to Bron, trying not to notice the way that the flickering gas light made the exposed skeleton seem to move. She was a nurse, here to do a very important job and not to...

Orla screamed as feet sounded out on the stone steps. Dear Mother of God she was trapped here, with the enemy sneaking in on them, coffins all but ready for her to tumble into. Her heart rattled against her ribs and she slid behind Bron – as if that would do her any good.

'Password,' Bron snapped, reaching for the only things he had with which to defend them – a scalpel and a two-inch needle.

'Rzepa,' came back the reply in a steady voice – turnip. Whoever had set today's password had a dark sense of humour. 'Stretcher-bearers reporting for duty, Dr Kaminski.'

Orla felt her heartbeat steady but then the second stretcher-bearer made it down into their tiny tomb and it shot right back up again.

'Eduard?'

'Angel!' His voice was warm and his eyes shone. 'I so hoped I'd see you again.'

She stared at him. 'Angel?'

He shifted. 'It's how I've thought about you in my head. I didn't know your name, you see – still don't, actually. May I ask...?'

'Orla,' she said, holding out her hand. 'Orla Dąbrowska.'

'Angel Orla!' He dropped a kiss onto the back of her hand and she felt the touch of his lips rush through her, as if it were packed with more sugar than fifty of her mother's szarlotka. 'Are you well?'

'Very well,' she agreed.

'Your cut is healing?'

He put up a finger to her cheek and she leaned into his touch. The cut was barely even there any more but it was as good an excuse as any to get close to this kindly man.

'It is. Your shoulder?' She almost reached for it but then realised that would put them in a full embrace which would be nice of course, but hardly appropriate in the circumstances.

'Healing well, thank you.'

'That's good. I hoped I'd see you again,' she admitted. It was probably far too forward, but when a man was pressed up close against you in the confines of an ancient tomb, the usual courting conventions didn't seem to matter as much. Besides, he *had* called her an angel...

'You wanted to see *me?*' he asked.

'To thank you.'

Even in the gaslight she could see him flush.

'For what? Tying you to a ladder and sending you to near-certain death?'

'No,' she said gently. 'For *barely* tying me to a ladder and then protecting me with your own body.'

'It was the least I could do, given, well...'

'The tying me to a ladder thing?'

He hit a hand to his forehead. 'You can joke about that? Already?'

She shrugged. 'If we don't laugh, we cry, right?'

Eduard nodded and stepped closer. The other stretcher-bearer had brought some bottles of antiseptic and thankfully he and Bron were in deep conversation, giving her a little longer with Eduard.

'The AK accepted you then?' she asked.

'Sort of. They didn't want me wielding a weapon, which is fair enough, but they offered me the role of stretcher-bearer and I agreed. It's hardly glamorous, but I wanted a chance to prove I was useful. I can tell you now though, Orla, if I'd known it would bring me to you, it would have been right at the top of my list – above bearing arms, above driving a tank, above even commanding all of Warsaw.'

Now it was Orla blushing; this was nonsensical.

'If you were commanding all Warsaw, Eduard, you would be able to see whomever you liked.'

'Only once I knew her name. I could hardly send the AK liaison officers out looking for an angel, could I?'

'You mean you don't think anyone else would see me that way?'

He shook his head. 'You're funny, Orla. Sharp.'

She laughed. 'My sisters are the sharp ones. Hana, the eldest, is so intelligent you can't get anything past her and Zuzi is as fierce as a mountain lion. It's all I can do to keep up.'

'Two sisters?'

'And a younger brother, yes. You should meet them.'

'I'd like that very much, if you'd let me, for tea maybe or, or...' He ground to a halt and looked around the tomb. Orla felt the urge to laugh again. What were they doing, talking about meeting her family for tea, when they were standing on the verge of a mighty battle that could, possibly, cost both of them their lives? And yet – what better time?

'We'll have tea,' she said, daring to reach out and take his hand. 'When this is over, Eduard, we'll all have tea.'

He smiled and kissed her hand once more but then, far above them, came a boom of a tank and the rattle of machine guns.

'I'd better go,' Eduard said. 'I'll see you soon, no doubt.'

Orla nodded, knowing that this would not be in his best suit, posy in one hand and cap in the other, but carrying bleeding, weeping young men to their coffin operating table. Tea suddenly felt a long, dark way away and Magda's szarlotka churned in her stomach as she moved round next to Bron and waited for whatever this dark night would bring.

TWENTY

ZUZI

'It's a what?'

Zuzi stared at Bartek, then back to the little square before them.

'A kill box,' the AK leader said again. It didn't sound any better the second time.

'How does it work?' Kamilla asked at Zuzi's side.

Bartek stepped into the middle of the area. It was flanked on two sides by tombs – fancy, ornate things full of nineteenth-century corpses. On the far edge, two big gravestones belonging to the slightly less fancy dead had been joined to the tombs with other gravestones, carried from their proper places and propped up against the standing ones to create a form of box.

'We will be fighting on this side.' Bartek pointed past the rearranged graves to a small group of AK crouched behind a barricade just visible through the slim gap between the standing stones. The Germans will approach from this side.' He indicated the far larger gap between the tombs. 'From there, especially in the dark, it will look like an easy passage through, but once they get into the kill box...'

'They'll be trapped,' Zuzi said.

'And that's when we fling in the grenades,' Kamilla supplied.

'Exactly, ' Bartek confirmed. Zuzi shuddered and he looked at her with an apologetic smile. 'It sounds rather grim, but this is the way we have to work, given the weaponry we have.'

Zuzi could see the truth of that. She thought back to the cache of weapons she and the other Minerki had found under the courgettes. That had only been two weeks ago but already it felt like forever. They'd been so pleased with themselves then, gloating over the clutch of guns and ammunition, but in truth that little lot, smuggled with such pride across occupied Warsaw, had barely been enough to keep a single platoon going for an hour.

The AK policy of only having any two people know about the location of a cache had backfired with the big losses of the renewed German attack. It seemed certain that there were weapons hidden, unknown and unfound, all around them while those they did have dwindled rapidly away. They desperately needed more supplies but until Emil and his mates were allowed to fly over the city again, they had little bar the homemade grenades at which Kamilla excelled. For the last two days Zuzi had worked alongside her in an underground workshop beneath the market square as the Minerki trained groups of civilian volunteers in the art of making the filipinkas.

They weren't hard. You simply mixed some explosive with improvised shrapnel and crammed it into the can, then passed it to an expert to insert the friction fuse – designed by two Polish engineers before the war – that would allow the mini-bomb to explode on impact. Some called them Sidolówka after the cans of Sidol metal polish that were the perfect size and shape for a grenade and came with a metal cap to prevent them going off by accident. These days, however, they had run out of polish cans and used anything they could get, improvising the lids with as much care as was possible. Even so, they were volatile things and the Minerki had carried their stash with the utmost care to the cemetery where they were lined up, ready for use in the AK's 'kill boxes'.

'So, we wait here,' Kamilla said, gesturing to the semi-protected area behind one of the tombs, 'and when they run in, we fling a grenade and, boom – dead Nazis!'

'Exactly.'

Kamilla nodded earnestly. Zuzi glanced at her in the growing gloom of the cemetery. Her grandmother was dressed in an improvised uniform fashioned from her dead husband's wardrobe, her AK armband worn proudly on top, and her eyes were shining. She'd been subdued after Orla's disappearance but seemed to be back on fine form now.

'Are you looking forward to this, Babcia?' Zuzi asked as Bartek went off to organise the other Minerki around their kill boxes.

'Of course. Those bastards shot my husband and executed my son – it's time they got a taste of their own medicine.'

Put like that, it was hard to deny, but Zuzi still found the idea of killing men hard. She'd signed up to build bombs, and to sabotage train lines, buildings and even cars, but actual hand-to-hand battle was something else altogether. She tutted at herself. They'd been busy all day laying mines along the western edges of the cemetery to take out the first wave of a German attack, which was exactly the same principle, just one step removed. And she'd known there were drivers in those trains and cars when she'd blasted them sky-high so it was surely disingenuous to pretend she'd not been killing. Even so, she took up her position between the graves in this dark battlefield of the dead with some trepidation.

'They're coming!'

It wasn't so much the rumble of the tanks or the rattle of guns that hit Zuzi as the enemy began their advance, but the blinding flash of the searchlights they trained onto the cemetery. Suddenly, their hiding places amongst the rickety graves and ghostly tombs felt dangerously exposed and she and Kamilla pressed themselves tight against the marble wall. As their eyes adjusted, they could see that, thankfully, the lights barely penetrated their position and were mainly illuminating the front line of German soldiers as they charged over the cemetery wall and towards the AK. Zuzi peeped out in time to see the first of the Minerki's mines throw one young man up in the air before Nazis were popping everywhere, bodies flying like swatted insects.

'Got them!' Kamilla breathed and Zuzi had to admit that, with the Nazis bearing down, there was a certain satisfaction to seeing them stopped.

Not that it would work for long. There were hundreds of troops pouring over the wall and she knew for a fact that they'd only had forty-eight mines to lay. The second wave had their way paved by their less fortunate comrades and they were charging in fast. The AK were firing where they could, but they were under severe instruction to only shoot if they had a clear sight of the enemy so as to save ammunition.

'This is hopeless,' she breathed.

'Nonsense,' Kamilla said crisply and she'd never been more grateful to have her grandmother at her side. 'The graves are holding them up nicely and look – our lure is working.'

Sure enough, a small troop were making their way, bent low, towards Bartek's AK platoon, clearly seen through the gap in the graves. Zuzi grabbed a grenade, pleased to see her hands were steady. For the first time, she could see how the men managed to fight, for here, with the stark choice between the enemies' lives or her own, her brain was clearing.

'Not yet,' Kamilla whispered as the soldiers got closer. 'Not yet, not yet... now!'

Three men had stepped into their kill zone and, confused by the gravestone blockade, were trying to turn back. As one, Zuzi and Kamilla uncapped their filipinkas, stood and threw them into the kill box with perfect accuracy. They'd only just crouched down again when the cans exploded, to cries of agony – and then silence. The other Germans backed hastily away, looking for another route, and Kamilla punched the air in silent glee.

'We did it, girl!' She peeped over the tomb. 'That's for Kaczper,' she hissed at their victims. 'And for Aleksander. When will you let us live in peace?!'

Zuzi had no idea if the men were alive to hear, but it stirred her soul and she was ready when the next group approached. Again, they struck, again, they killed, but the general German line was closing in on them, moving inexorably forward. With a loud crash, a tank smashed through the cemetery wall and began creaking across the graves, cracking them mercilessly beneath its grinding tracks. The searchlight truck came in its wake, sending a tank shadow, twice as large as the real monster, onto the trees and tombs like some ghastly cinema reel.

'Fall back,' she heard Bartek cry and grabbed at Kamilla's arm.

'Come on, Babcia.'

'In a minute. There are more coming – look.'

Sure enough, another group had been lured into the kill box. Their searchlight was shining straight through to the AK beyond and it was too clear a path to resist – or so they thought.

'Now!' Kamilla yelled and, for a third time, they flung their grenades between the tombs.

The men went up with a bang, but their comrades, close behind, did not move away. Instead, they shouted for back-up and curved sideways, heading straight for their hiding place.

'Come on, Babcia!!'

The Germans were so close now, Zuzi could smell their cologne over the reek of cordite and blood filling the cemetery. Bartek was frantically waving them towards the AK line. It was barely twenty metres away but, with all the graves and trees, it was impossible to run. Zuzi pulled Kamilla behind a large gravestone as bullets rang out. She heard them ping off the stone and blessed whoever's memorial this was for their care. It was down to the dead of Warsaw to offer protection to the living, but there was only so much they could do.

'We have to get back.'

Kamilla nodded at her. She had no smart words now. There was no fiery energy for killing in her dark eyes, just the same racing fear for her life that Zuzi was feeling.

'That grave next, yes?'

She pointed to another large one a few metres away. Kamilla nodded and glanced behind her. There were troops all over the cemetery, firing indiscriminately, and Zuzi's heart was racing furiously, desperate to keep beating.

'Go!'

They dived out, scrambling between the graves, the Nazi light exposing their positions but also guiding their feet. Zuzi dived behind the stone and heaved a sigh of relief when Kamilla slid in behind her. No bullets followed them and Zuzi listened to the heave of their breathing and sent up a prayer of thanks for it. But this was no time to sit around contemplating.

'That one.'

She picked out another of the larger gravestones. It was only a few metres from the AK barricades. If they could make it there, their next dash would be over the sandbags and into the relative protection of the Polish zone through which they could retreat to Stare Miasto.

'First one home gets their choice of Mama's cakes,' she gasped and felt Babcia grab for her hand and squeeze it hard.

'You're a good girl, Zuzi.'

'Not really, but I'm a fast girl and right now that's what counts. Ready?'

'Ready.'

'Go!'

She led the way. The light was lower here and the fighting seemed to be concentrated to her right. Her foot caught in a tree root and she stumbled but grabbed at a gravestone for support and pushed on. She heard a shout, 'Hier!' and bullets rained in on them but, bending low, she dived for the gravestone and made it. Heart pounding, she turned back to help Babcia Kamilla but her grandmother had paused, frozen at the bullets, and was huddled against a stone cross.

'Here, Babcia. I'm here. You can make it.'

Babcia was shaking but she looked to Zuzi, nodded, and visibly gathered herself.

'For Kaczper!' she shouted and then she was up and running. Zuzi reached out to grab her hand and Babcia held out her own but just as their fingers were about to touch, she gave a cry and, clutching at her stomach, fell to the ground.

'Babcia!'

Zuzi darted out and reached for her, dragging her forcibly behind the gravestone. She was alive but groaning agonisingly and Zuzi propped her up against the stone.

'Look at me, Babcia. Look into my eyes. You're here, you're alive.'

'It hurts.'

'Where? Here?' She reached down and gently pulled Babcia's hands away from her stomach. Blood spilled out and she had to fight not to scream. That would help no one right now.

'It's not too bad,' she lied. 'Here.'

She ripped off her jacket and tied it roughly around Babcia's middle. 'Now come on – we have to go again.'

She could see the AK waving her in and tried to get Babcia to her feet but her eyes were rolling back in her head and she could not lift her alone.

'Help,' she gasped. The Germans were closing and she could hear the screams of other Poles as they were hunted down and shot. 'Please, help.'

Kamilla's eyes half opened and she clawed at Zuzi. 'Leave me.'

'No.'

'You have to. I insist. I don't want to be responsible for your death. Leave me!'

'No!'

Zuzi tried to drag her but all the graves and roots made it impossible. Then suddenly someone was at her side.

'Let me.'

'Bartek! Oh, thank you, Bartek.'

'Quick.' He swept Babcia Kamilla up as if she weighed little more than a filipinka and glanced out. 'Now!'

He ran, Kamilla in his arms, and Zuzi ran after him, focusing on her grandmother's limbs dangling either side of his strong back and trying to ignore the bullets and bombs exploding around her. The AK opened up a gap in the barricade and Bartek dived through with Kamilla, then hands reached out and yanked Zuzi to safety. She fell to the ground, gasping, as they closed it behind her but there was no time to rest.

'We have to go,' Bartek said. 'We're falling back behind the second wall. Come on.'

She stumbled to her feet once more, following the others to a gate in a high wall, willing her legs to carry her that far. They were shaking like the leaves on the trees above but, somehow, she made it into the private cemetery and drew in breath after treasured breath. Then she remembered.

'Babcia?'

'She's still alive,' Bartek said. 'The stretcher crew are on their way.'

He had a torch which he waved in some coded pattern and Zuzi heard footsteps as two men ran up. One was older, his hair white in the half-light from the German searchlight, but the other was a young man who should, surely, have been fighting. Then again, thank God he wasn't.

'She's here,' she told him, grabbing his arm. 'Take care, she's old.'

'But tough, hey?' the man said. His Polish had a curious accent but he spoke kindly.

'How do you know that?'

'She must be, to be out in this. Don't worry – we have a field hospital over there and an excellent surgeon ready and waiting.'

'Bron?' Bartek asked.

The man gave a quick nod as Bartek laid Kamilla onto the stretcher. A part of Zuzi registered that the doctor was brown-eyed Bron, the son of the man who had carried Kamilla to safety.

'I owe your family a debt of gratitude,' she said to Bartek.

'Not yet,' he told her grimly. 'Now go!'

They were off again. Zuzi gave her legs a stern talking-to and they rose to the challenge and carried her after the stretcher-bearers, moving at pace towards the back of the cemetery. They paused by the biggest of the tombs, and the younger one pointed a torch into a hole in the earth.

'Down there?' Zuzi gasped.

'It's safe.'

It didn't look safe but they were carrying Kamilla down and there was little choice but to follow. The chamber was lit by a gas lamp which cast eerie flickers of light across a sombre scene. There were several coffins on shelves either side and, on the free shelves lay two AK men, both bandaged and, thankfully for them, out cold. The coffins that must have rested there before were stacked up to form an operating table onto which the stretcher-bearers were sliding Babcia.

'Oh God,' Zuzi moaned, but then someone threw warm arms around her and she looked up, confused, into wonderfully familiar blue eyes. 'Orla!'

'Zuzi. I'm so glad you're here.'

'But Babcia, she got shot. She's unconscious. She's—'

'In the best possible hands. Here, sit on the step and let us get on with our work.'

Zuzi's legs gave in to this welcome command. The stretcher-bearers slid past her to rescue other unfortunates and she was alone, with a ringside seat as Bronislaw untied her jacket from around Babcia and pulled back her blouse. Zuzi was too low to see the wound – and grateful for that – but she knew it was bad from Bron and Orla's faces.

Bron's settled into a look of intense concentration.

'Scalpel,' he said to Orla, who reached for it from the clutch of instruments at the feet of the coffin. 'Antiseptic.'

A bottle was produced and Zuzi watched Orla pour a careful amount onto a cloth and clean Babcia's wound with professional care. Zuzi thought of her sister as a child, always running around after her and Hana as the annoying 'little one', and realised she had well and truly grown up. She gripped her legs to her chest and willed her sister and the clever doctor on.

'Tweezers,' Bron said to Orla. 'We have to get the bullet out. Can you mop away the blood?'

Orla tried but it was clear to Zuzi that their handful of old towels were far from adequate. Kamilla was half awake and moaning piteously but Orla spoke to her soothingly, without once taking her eyes off her task, and suddenly Bron held up the tweezers. A bullet flashed, golden in the lamplight, and he gave a grim nod of satisfaction.

'Needle.'

Zuzi didn't want to look but his hands were mesmerising as he deftly sewed up her grandmother.

'More antiseptic,' he said to Orla and then, as she dabbed it on, he looked over to Zuzi. 'I think we've done it. The bullet is out and the bleeding stemmed. Now it's a matter of rest.' He looked around the tomb and gave her a wry smile. 'Probably not here.'

Zuzi pushed herself to standing.

'It's not the *most* restful place, I've ever been,' she agreed, daring to move closer to Babcia. Across her pale stomach was a line of stitches, very neat but in a coarse thread that spoke of the tricky conditions of the operation. Just then, though, her eyes flickered open.

'Good God,' she said, 'am I dead?'

'No, Babcia,' Zuzi assured her. 'You're very much alive.'

'Well, thank goodness. I'd hoped heaven was nicer than this.'

They all burst out laughing and Zuzi felt relief course through her. The first light of dawn was creeping down the steps and all sounded quiet outside. The Germans must have retreated – for tonight at least – and they would be able to get Babcia to a proper hospital to recover.

She turned shyly to Bron. 'You saved her life.'

He gave her a lopsided smile that did that funny exploding thing deep down inside her again.

'We don't know that yet, but the signs are promising.'

Babcia was trying to sit up and he put an authoritative hand to her shoulder and pushed her gently back down. 'Stay there please. You mustn't strain the stitches.'

Babcia subsided with a quiet 'Yes, Doctor', and Zuzi looked at him in awe.

'She never usually does what she's told.'

He smiled again.

'She's probably not usually in a tomb with a bullet in her stomach.'

'*Not* in her stomach,' Zuzi corrected. 'Thanks to you.'

'I was glad to help.'

He was close now, his brown eyes looking into hers, and she was painfully aware of Orla bustling around, deliberately not watching. There were more explosions inside her, lighting a fire in places where she was sure nice girls weren't mean to feel anything at all.

'Well, I owe you,' she managed stiffly. 'That is, *we* owe you. Our family. I'll bring you some cake from our bakery.'

'Or you could come for tea,' Orla suggested brightly and they both looked over at her. 'I've invited someone for tea so maybe Bron can come too.'

'Tea?' They both peered at her, then back at each other.

'She must be hallucinating,' Zuzi said to Bron.

'She must,' he agreed. 'Best play along. Shall I pour, my lady?'

He swept Orla a bow and Zuzi thought she'd never seen anything more handsome, but then one of the AK patients woke up with a groan of confusion and she reminded herself not to be ridiculous. They were as far away from afternoon tea as it was possible to be, and they had to stop playing around like children and get Babcia behind their lines before the Germans came at them again.

And yet, as more sunlight crept into this crazy hospital beneath the earth, casting rosy light across her grandmother, her sister and the clever, serious, surprisingly funny doctor who'd saved her life, Zuzi saw no reason to rush. The bullets would be back all too soon and for this strange, quiet moment it was enough to still be alive to see the new day.

TWENTY-ONE

15 AUGUST

HANA

> *God, the Father of Heaven,* have mercy on us.
> *On Poland, our fatherland,* have mercy, O Lord.
> *On the nation of Martyrs,*
> *On the people always faithful to You…*

As the priest intoned the litany for the Polish nation over the rumble of bombs nearby, Hana snuck a look between her clasped hands at his curious congregation. It was the Feast of the Assumption, a key festival in the Polish calendar, but this was not a normal high mass. The church was the cellar of the John of God Hospital, the pews were the lines of beds, and the altar was a rough table covered with a bedsheet, though at least topped with Kamilla's beautiful silver cross. Their grandmother had asked Jacob to fetch it to her bedside and was presiding proudly over the congregation from the front bed, the rest of the family perched around her for this most peculiar, but most welcome of services.

O Mary, Mother of God, Queen of Poland, pray
for us.
*St Stanislaus, Father of our land,
St Adalbert, Patron of Poland,
St...*

Hana gave the responses automatically, her thoughts elsewhere. The list of saints invested in Poland's safety was extremely long, although She might need the help of every one of them in the days ahead – and, perhaps more immediately, of the British and Americans. The RAF were apparently eager to fly from Brindisi again and they'd been told that the Americans had a host of supplies ready to drop on Warsaw in their fancy Liberator aircraft. Every night, Hana listened eagerly to the BBC Polish programme for the signal that more planes would be coming but so far 'One More Mazurka' had not sung out. The weather, someone had told her, had been very unsettled over Italy so that was hopefully the problem.

'Mary, Mother of God, Queen of Poland,' she whispered in her own prayer, 'please let them come tonight.' She crossed herself then added, 'As long as it's safe.'

The last thing she wanted was to pull Emil into danger but, oh, they needed the supplies he and his fellows could bring. The Germans had taken the cemeteries and, although they hadn't mounted a full assault on Stare Miasto yet, they were getting ready to do so. The Warsawians had all been feeling confident of the AK's ability to defend the narrow streets in which they were currently living a relatively normal life but lookouts had brought reports to HQ earlier today about a new Nazi weapon arriving by train.

It was something they called the Karl-Gerät and the reports had described it as a giant rocket launcher, so huge that its missiles each weighed two tonnes and were brought separately so as not to overbalance the train. They would be loaded into it via a crane and could, it was believed, fire up to a kilometre in distance. With Stare Miasto less than five hundred metres from this monster weapon's position in the Nazi citadel to the north, it did not bode well.

The priest had reached the end of his long list of saints and drew breath, looking solemnly around and, Hana suspected, checking all attention was on him – something that was hard with bombs above and several of his congregation needing ongoing nursing. He didn't let it faze him but pushed on with his litany.

> *From long and heavy penance of history,* deliver us, O Lord.
> *From the shackles of bondage,*
> *From the hour of doubt,*
> *From the instigation of betrayal...*

Hana glanced to Zuzi, intoning the responses with fierce pride, and knew they had reached the part of the Polish litany that most appealed to her sister. She, like Babcia, was determined in her opposition to oppression, although Hana knew that Babcia's dramatic injury and operation had shaken Zuzi's confidence and hoped this communal prayer would help her recover it.

Hovering at Zuzi's shoulder was the doctor, Bronislaw, and it was clear that his attention was more on Zuzi than the Almighty. Hana smiled to see it. Just past them, Orla stood with Eduard, the German-turned-insurgent who'd rescued her from the horrors of a human shield and become her stretcher-bearer and, if Hana's eyes did not deceive her, her very good friend. Maybe more. She smiled again. If love could still creep between the bombs and the bullets, there was hope for them all.

Hana bowed her head, trying not to let unchristian jealousy creep into her feelings about her sisters. Her pretty ring, symbol of her seemingly endless engagement, caught her eye and she had to admit that seeing Zuzi and Orla with young men made her yearn for Emil. This war had ripped away what should have been five years of married life for Hana and she longed to see an end to it.

She'd heard a few people muttering recently, saying that the Homeland Council had been wrong to call the uprising, but they were exactly the same people who'd been nagging to throw out the occupiers so she wasn't going to listen. The Allies would come. Churchill was sending planes, Roosevelt had his Liberators ready, and they would be working on Stalin to stop playing cat and mouse with Warsaw and bring the Red Army in to chase the Nazis out. The AK just had to stay strong.

> *Faith in you and trust in Mary,* grant us, O Lord.
> *Hope in the victory of the good cause...*

Hana looked up at the silver cross and prayed for the strength to do what she had to, and the wisdom to determine what that was. Her toes curled in her sturdy boots and she imagined she caught the smell of sewage on the hot August air. It was all in her imagination of course, as it so often had been in these last few days, but that didn't stop it worrying her.

Agaton had been down the sewers. He'd dropped into a manhole in Stare Miasto two days ago, making for Żoliborz in the north, and had not been seen for an agonisingly long time. Hana had imagined her one-time architecture teacher falling in the sewage, hitting his head on a sharp brick, or being sucked downstream with the city's waste. Perhaps, she'd tortured herself, the Nazis had booby-trapped the sewers, as they'd booby-trapped a tank the other day.

A platoon of triumphant AK had seized the tank when its driver had abandoned it in apparent panic, bringing it through the barrier and parading it up and down Kilińskiego Street, giving children rides on its sturdy sides. At least a hundred people had gathered to celebrate its capture and that's when, right outside the AK HQ, it had exploded. Hana had thankfully been out on her messages at the time, but she'd seen the aftermath and heard shaking witnesses talking about a nightmarish rain of blood and limbs.

The blast had not, thankfully, reached Bór and the rest of the Homeland Council on the third floor, but the backdraught had thrown them across the room, knocking several of them out. Bór had been forced to retire to bed with extreme headaches and deafness. He was battling valiantly on but it was hard to be a commander if you could not reach all areas under your command – which was why Agaton had gone into the sewers. And, to their great joy, he'd popped back up earlier today, having successfully completed the return trip underground. He'd been a sight to behold, mind you. Hana's once elegant teacher had become a veritable sewer rat, black with all manner of sludge, and stinking quite hideously. His white teeth had been the only clean part of him but had, at least, been well on show as he'd beamed around with pride.

'It's not easy down there,' he'd allowed, something of an understatement, given that it had taken him the best part of forty-eight hours to make the two-kilometre round trip. 'But we can make it safer with ropes and signs and maps.'

He'd looked at Hana then and she'd said she'd be delighted to help draw the maps.

'Excellent,' he'd replied, 'and, you know, it's really not as bad as it looks. I just slipped towards the end. With a decent pair of boots and a good torch you'll be absolutely fine.'

Hana had looked at him in horror. 'You want me to go down there?'

Agaton had shrugged.

'How else will you draw the maps, Fiolet?'

Agaton, like a number of the more cautious AK, was still using code names and it had caught at her heart, conjuring up the glorious image of the vibrant flower painted on the underside of Emil's plane. But it had also hardened her resolve.

'I'm happy to draw up the maps from others' sketches and descriptions, but I can't go down there. I just can't.'

She'd disappointed Agaton, she knew, and that had upset her but it hadn't changed her mind. She'd made her family swear an oath not to take unnecessary risks and she had to honour that – although what constituted a 'risk' was shifting all the time. The Stukas were roaring in on Stare Miasto every day now, dropping their bombs on the beautiful medieval streets with indiscriminate glee, and any one of the Dąbrowskas could fall victim. Nonetheless, they could limit the hazards they faced, and plunging into the dangers of the sewers was not doing that.

Hana looked up at the cross and then back to her beloved family, gathered around Kamilla's bed as the priest, finally, concluded his litany and moved to bless them all with the giving of the host. She would not enter the city's subterranean pipes, however much Agaton asked. She owed it to her family, to her hopes of regenerating Warsaw, and to Emil. If he could stay alive to fly aid to them, she could stay alive to – one day – become his wife.

TWENTY-TWO

ORLA

Orla crossed herself and slid quietly away from her family as the prayers concluded. There were patients needing tending although, God help them, a priest's blessing might bring them more aid than she could. She was getting more practised at nursing, but she hated seeing so much suffering, especially when it got personal. Mopping the blood out of Babcia Kamilla's stomach while Bron delved around inside her grandmother's innards to fish out the vicious Nazi bullet had done little to enhance her enjoyment of the caring profession, although she had to admit that the success of the operation had brought her some satisfaction. She'd noticed Zuzi watching her with something almost like admiration and that, after years in her big sisters' shadows, had been rather nice.

'Forgive me, Father, for the sin of pride,' she muttered under her breath. She wasn't going to waste the priest's time with her facile confession. The poor man had many services to get through, in various cellars, courtyards and improvised chapels around Stare Miasto, and the last thing he needed to worry about was her family insecurities.

'Let me change that dressing,' she said to a young man with blood oozing out of the bandage around his head.

She went to the dressing station, praying there would be fresh bandages but, as usual, there were only those they'd rescued off others who no longer needed them and washed in the dwindling supplies of water. With the mains cut off, they were relying on the wells a number of people had in their gardens, often ones dug in the three-week siege in 1939, but this summer had been so hot that many weren't reaching a decent supply and they were having to ration it.

The hospital had a good well in its rear courtyard but it was overlooked by German stations in the Saxon Gardens and all too often Nazi snipers took out innocent people as they queued for this most basic commodity of life. Orla hated them when they did that and then hated them even more for making her hate. All her life she'd tried to live by Christ's principal of 'love your neighbour as you love yourself', but when your neighbours were the sort of people who shot at children with water buckets and strapped women to the front of their tanks, it was hard. The Romans had been bad, but she was pretty sure Christ had never had to turn the other cheek to a Nazi.

With a sigh, she picked up the least dirty of the bandages and went back to her patient. Distracting him with chatter – the easiest part of the job – she unwound the linen and tried not to let her horror sound through her words as she clocked the gaping wound beneath. Bron's stitches were holding together but the flesh either side was swelling and straining between them, releasing a yellow pus that made Orla want to rush outside and be sick.

'That reeks,' the lad said. 'Is that me? Do I smell like that? Oh God, am I rotting?'

'No, no, no,' she said. 'It's just your body working to heal itself.'

'Nice try, Nurse,' he grunted. 'But better to accept it – I'm a goner, aren't I?'

'You are if you give up like that,' she told him crisply. 'Now, I'm going to clean it with some, erm, astringent.'

She opened the bottle behind his back so that he could see she wasn't using conventional antiseptic, but red wine – a rather fine red wine by the fruity smell of it. Zuzi's Minerki had blasted their way into the cellars of a grand wine merchant yesterday and found thousands of bottles. In the absence of water and other cleansers, they'd appropriated as much of it as possible for the various hospitals around the city and here at the John of God they'd been very grateful. If nothing else, it eased the patients' pain.

'This might sting a little,' she said, crossing her fingers at the gross misrepresentation as she poured the wine onto the pulsing wound.

'Aaaah!'

'Sorry,' she apologised but pushed on anyway. It washed the pus away, even if it did make him look even more like something out of a horror show.

'Please stop,' he begged, thrashing around, his arms flailing dangerously.

'Let me.' Eduard stepped up at her side and gently held him down. 'Let the nurse do her work, lad, and you can have a glug or two of this fine vintage after.'

Orla finished cleaning him up and Eduard held the bottle to his lips, letting him gulp enough down to hopefully sleep away his agony.

'Thank you,' Orla said, as they stepped away.

'My pleasure.'

'Hardly!'

'Anything is a pleasure if it's at your side. Why do you think I always bring my poor wounded to the John of God?'

Orla blushed. 'You charmer.' She glanced around the ward but the priest, bless him, was doing a round of all the beds and most of the patients were too busy waiting for their turn to need a nurse's attention right now. 'Cup of tea?'

'Please.'

They moved into the makeshift kitchen at the back to find Alicja jiggling Daniella on her hip while trying to stir a huge pan of eggs.

'Eggs?!' Eduard's eyes lit up and he rushed forward as if the pan held purest gold.

'One of the other stretcher-bearers found a pigeon loft full of them. Brought them to me as a treat for the patients on this feast day.'

'And the staff?' Eduard asked hopefully.

'If they help cook them, perhaps.'

'No problem at all.'

He reached for the spoon and Alicja handed it over with alacrity.

'Perfect. Perhaps I can calm Nella now. Can Mama calm you, poppet? Can she?'

She babbled kindly to the baby but Daniella was grizzling and who could blame her. The poor mite should have had her mother's undivided attention at this tender point in her life and instead she was forever being juggled with hospital work.

'Shall I take her for a bit?' Orla suggested.

Alicja's eyes lit up.

'Would you? Really?' She smiled gratefully as Orla took Nella into her own arms. 'I'd so love five minutes' fresh air. It's roasting in here.' She darted for the side door, then stopped and pointed at Eduard. 'Don't burn my eggs.'

'Wouldn't dream of it.'

He waved the wooden spoon merrily, then went back to stirring the precious food.

'Low and slow, that's the key with eggs,' he said to Orla.

'You cook eggs?'

'Oh yes. I grew up on a farm and my parents were always busy with the livestock. My job was to look after the chickens and that included making the breakfast eggs for all the family. I became quite the expert.'

She looked at him, trying to imagine him as a young boy, standing at a stove in a farmhouse kitchen.

'I'd like to have seen that. Do you have siblings?'

'I do. That is, I did.'

'What?'

His shoulders hunched and instinctively Orla took his hand, shifting Nella onto her hip. The baby seemed to have sensed the emotion in Eduard's voice too, as she had stopped grizzling and was gazing intently at him.

'Can you tell me?' Orla asked.

Eduard looked into her eyes. 'I haven't told anyone before. That is, there hasn't been anyone to tell. I...'

His eyes filled with tears and he dashed them crossly away.

'You can tell me,' Orla said firmly.

'Yes,' he said. 'I really think I can.' Even so he struggled to get the words out and his voice, when he did, was hoarse with years of unshed tears. 'The Wehrmacht attacked us at dawn, rampaged into our village, totally out of the blue. We were all up milking the cows or taking the sheep to pasture. It wasn't a big place, more a homestead than a village with not one person out to harm anyone or do anything more than raise a few of God's creatures for market. But in they came, firing at anyone in their sights as if we'd been put there for their amusement.

'We were German, Orla. We spoke German, our signs were in German, we had German houses, but they didn't see us that way. They were screaming at us – "ignorant Poles" or "ugly beasts". They went hunting around for schnapps and, once they had that down their neck, they were even worse. They gunned...' He swallowed but pushed on. 'They gunned my father down with his cows and my mother too when she went running out to him – though that might have been a blessing because I saw what they did to those women who survived their bullets and she was better in God's arms than having to go through that.'

He shuddered and Orla moved closer. Nella was still staring up at Eduard, as if taking in everything he said but the eggs were sticking. Orla quietly pulled them off the flames – some things, even in starving Warsaw, were more important than food.

'And your siblings?'

His hand gripped tightly at hers and she leaned against him to keep him steady.

'My little sister ran up a tree to hide. She loved trees, was always up and down them. We used to call her Eichhörnchen – squirrel. It was her natural safe place but those bastards they...' Now he was crying. 'They shot her out of the tree like a fairground game. I saw her fall, saw her thud to the ground. It was a clean shot at least, she didn't suffer, but she was gone so quickly. One minute there she was, scampering up a tree like she always did, and the next – limp and empty on the ground.'

'Her *body* was empty,' Orla said gently. 'Her soul had climbed the biggest tree to heaven.'

He smiled at her through his tears.

'That's beautiful, Orla. Thank you.' He put his arm around her in turn, pulling her in close against him and it felt so natural, so right, that Orla slotted into his embrace, Nella locked happily between them. 'They shot my brother as he ran for the hills,' he said, the words coming more easily now. 'So perhaps he climbed a hill to heaven too.'

'Of course he did. And you? Where were you, Eduard?'

'Oh, I was right there, in the middle of it all, but they didn't shoot me. They rounded me up with the other fit young men and they told us we had a choice – fight or die.' His arm tightened around her. 'I didn't want to die so, help me God, I agreed to fight. I took their uniform and swore allegiance to their evil Führer and I marched on with them. I left my parents and my little brother and sister dead in their own fields, and I marched away with their killers. What does that make me?'

'It makes you sensible,' she said. 'It makes you brave and strong.'

'To leave them?'

'They were dead, Eduard. There was nothing you could do for them, bar stay alive. That's what they'd want.'

'That's what I told myself.'

'And you were right. You were so, so right.'

'It didn't feel that way. I tried to desert at the first chance but they chased me down and threw me into prison. I broke rocks for two years and then they shoved me in with Dirlewanger's lot and, well – you know the rest.'

'I know that now you're here, with me... that is with, er, with us...'

'With *you*,' he said firmly. His face was bent to hers now, his lips centimetres from her own. 'Do you think, Orla, that one day, when this nightmare is over, we might, we might...'

'Take tea together?'

He laughed.

'Take tea, yes. Take tea every single day for the rest of our lives.'

She sucked in her breath.

'I'd like that,' she said. It wasn't ladylike, she knew, but time was far too short to mess around with formal manners.

'Oh Orla, my mother would love you.'

Then his lips were on hers and she let go of his hand to snake hers up around his neck and pull him even closer until Nella's squeaks of protest forced them apart with a laugh.

'Sorry, lass,' Eduard said, ruffling the baby's hair, 'but some things are too important to get in the way of.'

Nella squirmed and pointed determinedly to the eggs, making them laugh again.

'Fine,' Eduard said, 'food now, kisses later.'

He looked at Orla with such intensity that her entire self seemed to melt from the inside.

'Not too much later,' she said hopefully and Eduard leaned in and gave her another swift kiss before applying himself to the egg pan. Orla considered the pair of them, cooking eggs, a baby nestled between them. She wondered if this was how it might be, sometime in the future, and yearned to get there. She'd had enough of bombs and fires and bullet-torn flesh. She'd had enough...

'What on earth was that?'

She and Eduard looked at each other as a peculiar noise ripped through the air – a dark, pained sort of moo.

'Sounds like a cow giving birth,' Eduard said, confused, but then the sound stopped. A loaded silence filled the kitchen and, barely seconds later, six explosions in quick succession shook the walls.

'What are they firing at us now?' Eduard asked, rushing to the door.

Orla went with him, peering out. Down the road, two houses had cracked open and flames were spewing from the gaps. People were rushing from their Ascension Day prayers, crying out in horror, and Orla spotted Alicja between them. The young mother waved to baby Daniella and started to cross the road towards her daughter, but then came the dark sound from the sky once more.

'Take cover!' Eduard yelled.

He pulled Orla into the door frame of the hospital as the loaded silence fell and it was from there that she saw six small, sleek rockets arc over the building and head straight for them, flashing in the sunshine. Alicja pressed herself back against the opposite wall, her eyes fixed on Daniella.

'Mama's coming, Nella!' she called. 'Mama's just—'

Three of the rockets smashed straight into the wall, sucking the words out of the young woman and sending bricks flying until, with a creak of fury, the entire building collapsed, right on top of her.

'Alicja!'

Orla thrust Nella at Eduard and ran out, scrabbling at the bricks, but it was too late, she knew that even as she dug. No one could survive such an avalanche. Nella wailed piteously and Orla looked back at the baby in Eduard's arms and wanted to weep. Save that the strange, animalistic noise was filling the air once more, robbing them of even a chance to grieve.

'It sounds closer,' Eduard said. 'This way.'

He dragged her towards the hideous noise. It felt entirely the wrong thing to do but, sure enough, the rockets arced right over their heads.

And smashed straight into the John of God Hospital.

'No!' Orla screamed.

The ancient walls shook with seeming indignation as the shells pierced through the cream bricks right where they had been standing seconds before, then began collapsing in on themselves. Orla heard cries of terror from within and saw, as one wall dropped straight downwards, an entire ward exposed, the nearest beds teetering precariously on the open edge. Nurses ran to catch them but were too late for one and it fell, tipping its patient into the rubble before smashing down on top of him. The staff were pulling the other beds inwards but the building was old and, without its front wall, it was falling apart – with Orla's entire family in its basement.

She ran to the doorway that had sheltered her, Eduard and Daniella mere seconds before. It was now a teetering wooden frame, all the bricks fallen away, but the steps to the basement were intact. Patients were staggering out of it, clutching onto staff, and Orla gasped with relief as Magda emerged, propping up the young soldier with the bloodied head. Jacob was right behind her, carrying a young girl, and Orla ran to pull them away from the precarious remains of the hospital. Nella was wailing in Eduard's arms and now the eerie sound rent the skies again, louder than ever. These rockets passed over their heads to smash into the lives of some other pour souls in the next street but their damage had already been done in this one.

'Where's Hana?' Orla asked her mother.

'Trying to get Babcia out with Zuzi.'

Orla darted to the door but Magda clutched at her arm.

'Don't go in there, Orla. I can't lose all of you. I can't.'

But at that moment, Hana emerged, white with plaster. They rushed to her, to see tears streaking down her cheeks.

'I can't get to them,' she gasped. 'There's a beam down and I can't get to them.'

TWENTY-THREE

ZUZI

Zuzi's brain was buzzing with the sound of falling masonry, her mouth was clogged with dust and her eyes, however hard she strained them, could only make out vague shapes in the darkness. She couldn't feel her limbs, at least until a piece of plaster fell on her leg making her cry out in pain.

'You're alive then,' a crisp voice said through the darkness.

'Babcia? Is that you?'

'Of course it's me, Zuzi. Who else's bed were you sitting on?'

'Are you well?'

'I've been better.'

'Fine, yes. Me too. But are you whole? Has anything fallen on you?'

'Other than you?'

Zuzi felt a gentle push on her arm and realised that she was half-lying across her grandmother. The dust was clearing and slivers of light were creeping into whatever hole they'd got themselves into this time. She cautiously sat up and peered around. Two beams had come down, miraculously falling against each other above their heads and creating an alcove around the bed. On all sides, however, were piles of rubble with no obvious way out.

'Hello?' she called. 'Hello? Anyone there?' Silence. 'Hello!' she yelled as loud as she could with dust in her throat. And then, 'Help!'

The only response was one of the beams creaking above them and she looked up in concern.

'We're trapped, aren't we?' Babcia asked. Her voice was as robust as ever but Zuzi caught a shake around the edges and fumbled for her grandmother's hand.

'At the moment,' she said. 'But I'm sure the others will be trying to get us out.'

'If they're not under all that.' Kamilla waved both their hands towards the rubble and then squeezed Zuzi's fingers and said, 'Sorry. Not helpful. No point in being negative is there?'

'No,' Zuzi agreed cautiously, 'but practical might be a good idea. If we're going to clear a way out, we need to decide which way it should be.'

She got off the bed and peered at the rubble. It was a little like the dens she and Hana had made when they were younger – though with rather more bricks and beams than sheets and cushions. They'd never let Orla come in and play and it had made their little sister mad. One day, when Orla had been about five, she'd got so frustrated that she'd patiently and quietly laid stones all along the bottom of their sheet walls. Zuzi could still remember the panic she'd felt when she'd tried to lift the flap and been unable to do so. She and Hana had screamed until Magda had come running to set them free. But even if Magda was alive and out there trying to help them, this would be a far harder job than lifting a few stones off a bedsheet.

Zuzi forced herself to focus, applying all the principles she'd been taught with the Minerki. The engineering elements of their training had fascinated her and she had to remember them now.

'The light is coming from here,' she said, gesturing to the pinpricks between the bricks. 'So this must be our best chance.'

She prodded tentatively at the pile of bricks, trying to gauge how loose they were. The last thing they needed was for her to send them avalanching down. The larger of the two beams was providing some support and she tentatively pulled away one of the bricks immediately below it. The loose rubble shifted but held. She took another and another. More light appeared, giving her a surge of hope, but on the fifth brick a mass of small stones came flooding through her hard-won gap and she stumbled back.

Kamilla sighed. 'Come here, Zuzi, and get into this bed with me. If we're going to die down here, we might as well do it in comfort.'

'Babcia!'

'It's true.'

'We're not going to die.'

'Based on what evidence?'

'I'm not sure,' she admitted. 'But I'm not giving up after five little bricks.'

Babcia chuckled. 'No, Zuzi, I don't suppose you are, God bless you.'

There was more of a shake in her voice now and Zuzi felt her way back to the bed to give her a hug. Her grandmother lay there stiffly but did not pull away and that told Zuzi plenty.

'How's your wound?'

'Painful.' Zuzi patted gently down Babcia's body, trying not to notice how thin and frail she felt. When she got to her stomach area, Babcia let out a gasp of pain and she felt worrying moisture seeping through her clothes. 'I'm bleeding, aren't I?'

'A little.'

'We need your lovely doctor again.'

'He's not *my* doctor.'

'Not yet, but you like him, don't you?'

'Babcia! This is hardly the time or place.'

'On the contrary, I'd say it's exactly the time and place. What else have we got to do?'

'Dig our way out,' Zuzi shot back, standing up again.

She probed at the bricks, keeping her eyes firmly on the beams above them, and carefully removed a few. There was a glint amongst the darkness and, hope rising, she shifted more. 'There's something here, something bright and, oh!' Her hand closed around it and she tugged it from the rubble.

'Babcia, look!' It was the silver cross, one arm bent and one jewel cracked, but otherwise intact. She crossed to place it in her grandmother's hands. 'God is with us,' she told her.

'I pity Him,' Kamilla said drily, but she clasped the cross and began murmuring the Lord's prayer as Zuzi returned to her brick-picking.

It seemed a hopeless task. Every time she removed a brick, another slid into the hole and she feared that Babcia was right and they were going to die down here, either of the building collapsing on them, or, more slowly, of thirst. Both options made her shudder.

Eventually, worn out, she slid onto the bed with Kamilla. 'It's a sorry way to go, Babcia.'

'It is as He wills.'

Her grandmother was holding the cross tight, her eyes fixed on it in the sparse light. She looked ghostly pale, as if she was checking out already, and fear shuddered through Zuzi. She could just about cope in here with Babcia alongside her; if she had to do it alone, she might go mad.

'Stay strong, Babcia, and help will come.'

Kamilla shook her head. 'I fear not – not for you and I, and not for Warsaw. The whole city might as well be as buried as we are for all the attention the so-called Allies are paying us.'

'That's not true. Hana saw Emil, didn't she? Mr Churchill will send aid.'

'From Italy! It's the Russians we need.' She clasped Zuzi's hands. 'Such irony, Zuzi. All these years we've kept my father's handcuffs on the wall to remind us how the Soviets enslaved us and now we're waiting for them to ride in as saviours. We've been foolish, I fear.'

Zuzi feared she might be right but she couldn't let that in now.

'Well, we're here and we have to get ourselves out,' she said, returning to the rubble pile. 'It's not like we have anything else to do, is it?'

She pulled at the nearest brick. It was stuck and, frustrated, she pulled harder. It came away in her hands, but with it a rush of others so that she had to scramble back onto the bed to stop them crushing her feet.

'Good work, Zuzi,' Babcia said drily.

Zuzi bit her lip to resist snapping at her but then they heard a sound, a beautiful, magical sound: voices.

'Here!' Zuzi shouted, creeping cautiously back across the rubble pile. More light seemed to be getting into their alcove and she could definitely hear voices. 'We're in here! It's me, Zuzi, and Babcia Kamilla. We're here. We're alive!'

'Zuzi?' came the reply, faint but gloriously distinct. 'Zuzi! Thank the Lord. We're coming. Stay safe. We're coming.'

'Thank you! Thank you so much.'

Zuzi went back to Babcia's bed, her legs weak with relief. Someone was there. She couldn't tell who but someone was there, someone who knew her name and who would do all they could to get them both out.

'Hold on,' she said to Babcia Kamilla. 'Rescue is coming.'

'God be praised.' Kamilla held the cross up to the dim light which caught in the sapphire at the top, sending a flash of blue around their enforced den. 'Now, sit down for heaven's sake,

Zuzi, and don't bring it all toppling down on us before they get here.'

'I think you'll find it was me who released...'

She stopped herself. It didn't matter. All that mattered was that there were people digging through to them. She would not have to die down here, in the dark, her body slowly running out of moisture and her grandmother's corpse as her only companion. If she listened carefully, she could hear bricks being moved with methodical care above them. She longed to leap up and tear them away from this side and to stop herself, she found the edge of Babcia's covers and crawled underneath.

'We have to be patient, Babcia.'

Kamilla patted her hand. 'Not a strength for either of us.'

'No.'

Kamilla gave a small laugh.

'I'm sorry I said we were going to die. It was weak of me. I didn't mean it, Zuzi. I really want to survive and to see the bastard Nazis kicked out of our city.'

'Me too, Babcia.'

'These last five years of occupation have been like we are now – alive but only just, hemmed in on all sides by bricks that might fall down at any moment.'

Zuzi nodded into the darkness, it was a good analogy. She'd been seventeen when the Nazis had invaded and had been loving life – studying, meeting friends, talking to boys. Her future had seemed to be opening up and then, in a whine of Stukas, it had all collapsed on her. The Wehrmacht had marched in and seized Warsaw and suddenly all their favourite cafés and cinemas had been Nur für Deutsche. Their every movement had been monitored, their food rationed and their papers checked constantly by supercilious guards who treated them as if they were lucky to be allowed to live at all. In their own city! Truly Warsaw had closed in on them then and at least now, however hard it might be, they were fighting back.

'We were right to rise up.'

'Oh, we were. We had to. Heavens, Zuzi, when I joined you and your marvellous Minerki, I felt more alive than I've done since my dear Aleksander was taken from me.'

'I'm so sorry.'

'Thank you. He was a great loss. No one made my heart race like he did.' Zuzi shifted on the bed and Kamilla laughed. 'Come, Zuzi, you're an adult now. We can talk about these things?'

Zuzi wasn't sure she felt very adult but she was certainly curious.

'In what way race?' she asked tentatively.

'Go fast, flutter, pound, hammer! He was so handsome, it sent funny squiggles right down inside me.'

'In your tummy?'

Kamilla shook her head. 'Not in my tummy, Zuzi. Lower down.'

'Babcia!'

'Well, it did. He was gorgeous. Not conventionally handsome, not the one everyone was pointing to in the ballroom, but for me he always... shone.'

'That's lovely.'

'I was pretty cross about it at first, I can tell you. It was the first ball of the season and it upset all my plans. I had no intention of falling for anyone. I was going to have a lovely, giddy, few months. I was going to dance with every young man in Warsaw. And then in walked Aleksander Dąbrowska and that was it – I didn't want to dance with anyone but him.'

Zuzi giggled. It sounded incongruous in their dusty hole but Babcia was so indignant at finding love that she couldn't help herself.

'And he felt the same?'

'Luckily. We had one dance and then he took my card from me and he wrote his name in every single one of the slots. He even crossed out any I was already contracted to and wrote his name over the top of them. I should have been furious but I was already counting the beats until the next dance started. We married two months later and it felt like forever. I simply couldn't wait to get him into bed.'

'Babcia!' Zuzi was truly shocked.

'Oh, grow up, girl. It's allowed. We all expect men to want to bed their brides, but the truth is that if the man is the right one, the bride is every bit as eager.'

'And that's... I mean, God doesn't, well, mind that?'

Now it was Babcia's turn to laugh, so long and loud that Zuzi feared her merriment would bring the bricks right down on top of them.

'No, Zuzi, God does not mind that. He made us to fit together, you know, and we should honour that and enjoy it.'

It was a curious idea. Zuzi had seen couples pressed up close together in the darker alleyways. She'd seen them stare into each other's eyes and cling to each other's hands but it had always looked like a bit of a show, a playact for the rest of the world – a 'look I found someone' charade. And yet, there was no denying the fire Bron set going inside her; was this, then, a good thing?

'Your mother and father were much the same, you know,' Babcia went on insouciantly. 'It was clear from the start that they were enjoying their marriage. Bless them, they used to come over for dinner once a week when they were first wed and they were very polite and dutiful but it was quite clear they couldn't wait to get home and tear each other's clothes off.'

'Babcia, please!'

She laughed again.

'Have you never felt them, Zuzi – the squiggles?'

Zuzi felt heat flood into her cheeks.

'Maybe. I'm not sure I'd call them squiggles. More...' She flushed but it was dark and close and she did so want to know if this was the right way to be. 'More like fire.'

Kamilla clapped. 'I'm delighted to hear it, girl. It'll be that young doctor, of course.'

'Babcia, stop it!'

But Babcia clearly had no intention of stopping. She grabbed at Zuzi's hand, clutching it tightly. 'I won't, Zuzi, because it's important. If he makes you feel that way, that's glorious. It's God telling you that you'll make wonderful babies with him.'

'Babcia!'

'And that you'll have fantastic fun in the process. Don't shy from that, girl. Grab it. Grab *him*! Goodness, we've all spent far too many days locked beneath the Nazi jackboot and if you can escape this oppression in the bed of a handsome, kind, decent young man, then go right for it.'

'Isn't it about love?' she asked hesitantly.

'Of course! But it's about lust too, my dear girl – that's what makes the union between a man and a woman so different to any other relationship, so specially, wonderfully different.' She tugged Zuzi close. The shouts from outside were getting louder and the beams creaked ominously over their heads. 'You're a bright, lively, passionate young woman, the very spit of your old grandmother when I was younger, and I love seeing that in you. Promise me you'll give love a chance, girl! Lust too. Trust me, they're what makes all this painful living business worthwhile.'

'If you say so, Babcia.'

'Oh, I do. So, promise me.'

Zuzi laughed self-consciously.

'I promise I will give love a chance.'

'Lust too.'

Zuzi sighed and tried to suppress the surge of excitement that Babcia's words had set loose in her. All these disorientating feelings she had when Bron was around were normal, were permitted, were to be *followed*?! It was a heady thought indeed.

'Do you think...?' she started but then noticed that Babcia's grip had gone limp in her own. 'Babcia? Babcia, wake up, hang on. They're coming.' She could see the nearest bricks moving. 'Babcia, please.' Tears clogged her dry throat. 'Don't die, Babcia. Don't—'

'Can't a woman get any rest?' Babcia muttered, making her gasp out loud in relief, and just then, a handful of bricks rolled down the pile and a shaft of light shone into their cave, catching in the silver cross in Babcia's hands and lighting up the jewels so that her tired face seemed bathed in myriad colours.

'We did it, Babcia! We made it. They came for us.'

'Who came?'

Babcia grabbed Zuzi's hand to pull herself up to sitting as another brick was removed and a face peered anxiously through the gap – a young, serious, undeniably handsome face.

'Bron!' Zuzi cried and then looked to Babcia, who wiggled her eyebrows at her in such a ridiculously suggestive manner that they both burst out laughing.

'Sorry,' Zuzi gasped through her laughter. 'It's just such a relief, such a, a...'

But then she ran out of words because Bron was stepping through the gap and taking her in his arms and she swore he was going to kiss her right there, in front of her grandmother. The 'squiggles' raced around her stomach and, yes, maybe a little lower but for once she didn't try and squash them, but let them draw her eyes upwards to his. And yes, he was going to kiss her and...

The beam creaked and they leaped apart. Babcia groaned.

'Let's get you out of here,' Bron said, hastening to her side.

'No rush,' she said. 'Please, don't mind me.'

But the moment was lost and as Zuzi went to help Bron lift her dear, priceless grandmother free of their dark cave, she could only hope it would come again. For now, though, they were stepping into the semi-fresh air of Warsaw, thickly warm with sunshine and an acrid fire somewhere nearby but still a million times better than the dust of their underground hole. Orla was there, hugging her tight, with Magda and Jacob rushing in and Hana trying to throw her arms around them all and it felt wonderful.

'We're free!' she said.

It wasn't really true. With the Germans closing in on all sides and the Russians still kicking their red heels over the Vistula, it was far from true but right now, surrounded by family and friends and with air in her lungs to enjoy them all for another day, it felt free enough. Zuzi looked to her grandmother and remembered her promise to give love, in all its glorious guises, a chance. For the first time she felt that it would be a joy to do so. There was just the small matter of a war to win first...

TWENTY-FOUR
17 AUGUST

HANA

Hana grabbed a brush and swept, hard, at the floor of what had once been the gracious ground floor of Babcia Kamilla's grand townhouse and was now Piekarnia Dąbrowska in the parlour to the left, and the John of God Hospital in the dining room to the right. Their world was closing in but at least the family were all still together, they could care for Babcia in her own home, and the bakery was going again, albeit in a painfully reduced capacity. However often they swept, the marble tiles were never clean. Stare Miasto was burning and the ash of too many homes, businesses and bodies blew in constantly. The Nazis, frustrated at not being able to penetrate the medieval quarter's narrow streets with their bully-boy tanks, had brought in a range of hideous weaponry to do the job and the streets rocked to their deathly sounds day and night.

There were the mammoth shells from the monstrous Karl-Gerät and now the attacks from what they had learned was a 'Nebelwerfer rocket launcher' but all called the Kowa for its mooing bellow as it spewed up its six-fold explosion. The shells flew hard and fast and the Nazis filled them with a range of hellish substances, from sulphur powder to gooey petroleum jelly that spattered itself over everything and everyone as it exploded.

People had taken to living in the cellars of the city, crowded into nooks blocked off with screens or furniture in an attempt to create some privacy from the endless run of liaison officers, soldiers and stretcher-bearers tracing their way underground. Somehow, under great pressure, the Krybar battalion were still holding the power plant at the river side of Śródmieście and they had light to chase away the worst of the shadows, but with the endless dust, fire and cries of pain, there was nothing cosy about underground Warsaw. Some talked about surrender; others shouted them down.

'We've come this far,' they would protest, 'why stop now?'

'Because we'll all die.'

'We won't. The Allies are coming. The Allies are coming to save us.'

Hana prayed the diehards were right but if the Allies were coming, they were taking their time. Every night she clamped herself to Babcia's radio, desperately listening for 'One More Mazurka' to ring out the news that the planes would be flying in with supplies, but every night it played another tune and she had to go to bed in their own cellar-nook without a glimpse of Emil's precious violet.

Hana brushed harder, chasing the dust of Warsaw out of their sanctuary. She was exhausted after a day running messages to the AK units around Stare Miasto, but Babcia's house felt like a precious refuge and trying to keep it nice made her feel she had some control over their lives. Behind her, Magda was bringing bread through from the kitchen to serve to the patient queue of customers. Her hair was nearly all grey now, the pretty blonde leaching away with every day of the embattled uprising, but her smile was determinedly intact. She'd fashioned a makeshift counter from Babcia's fine sideboard, and she laid out bread on her prettiest crockery but, despite her best efforts, it made a poor show.

Flour was increasingly hard to come by and Magda was only managing to keep going because Zuzi's Minerki had blasted into the cellars of the Haberbusch and Schiele brewery and released a precious store of barley. After some experimenting, Magda had found a way of crushing the grain in coffee grinders and Jacob had spent most of yesterday going round those houses still standing to look for the little machines. It was laborious work and only made the roughest of flours but everyone was grateful for what they could get and the Piekarnia Dąbrowska was busy day and night. Hana worried her mother was not getting anywhere near enough rest but Magda just said they could 'sleep once we're liberated', rolled up her sleeves and kept baking – fighting in her own, loving way.

Hana flinched as the telltale whine of the Stukas rang across Warsaw once more. The Nazi planes came endlessly, the first attack at 8 a.m. and then every half hour until dusk, in a hellish clockwork. Their bombs would flash silver in the sun as they twisted downwards like overgrown fireflies, and then they would smash into someone's house, sending flames dancing towards the relentless sun and people screaming onto the street. So far Babcia Kamilla's house had stayed miraculously intact but it must only be a matter of time.

Hana glanced through to the hospital in the once elegant dining room. Orla and Bron had rescued what beds and supplies they could from the ruins of the John of God and set up Babcia in the prime bed. It was her own, grand four-poster – minus the posts because they'd had to saw them off to get it down the stairs – and it seemed apt for their elegant grandmother, save that it made her look wasted and small. Bron had done his best to sew up her stomach again, but the Warsaw air was more brick dust than oxygen these days and it was almost impossible to keep wounds clean. Babcia was relying on her father's handcuffs, hung on the wall above her, and the family's silver cross, set on a makeshift altar by the door. These, she said, represented the strength of man and the protection of God, and between them, they would triumph. Hana admired her optimism.

Sharing it was harder.

'Hana! Hana, you have to come!' Jacob came charging through from the makeshift ward. 'It's on the radio!' he said and her heart leaped.

'The planes are coming?'

Jacob frowned, then shook himself. 'No, not that, but it's good. Come and listen.'

Hana set the broom aside and went with him. Magda came too, the little queue of customers following her like sheep. Inside, Hana saw Orla in her nurse's apron and Bron in his not-so-white coat. Baby Nella was sitting in bed with Kamilla, playing with her rosary beads. The remains of her young mother had been dug out of the rubble of the John of God and buried beneath a simple cross, alongside far too many others, and the baby was officially alone in the world. Sister Maria was trying to find a family to adopt her but everyone in Warsaw was having enough trouble keeping their own loved ones alive without taking on a nine-month-old orphan so for now she was sticking with the Dąbrowskas.

Orla hitched Nella onto her hip with newly practised ease as Jacob turned up the radio and Hana saw the stretcher-bearer, Eduard, cross over to join them, so that they looked for all the world like a ready-made family. Her heart ached for Emil and she touched her fingers to her ring as everyone gathered around the radio set, sitting alongside the silver cross at the edge of the room.

'There are scenes of great joy across the city,' the Polish reporter was saying and Hana glanced eagerly out of the door, but all she could see was a young woman racing for cover as a Stuka took a run of shots at her on his way back from bombing people out of their houses.

'People are lining the streets, cheering and throwing flowers on the parades of soldiers...'

'Parades? Where?'

'... as they march up the Champs Elysées to the tune of '*La Marseillaise*'.'

'Paris?!'

'Paris,' Jacob confirmed. 'It's been liberated.'

'That's marvellous,' Hana gasped but Magda shushed her.

'Listen, sweetie.'

'President de Gaulle today arrived to thank General Eisenhower's troops for marching to help the brave resistance who rose up against the collapsing Germans to nobly secure their city for France.'

There was silence in the ward. Hana looked around the curious gathering of patients, medics, family members and bakery customers and saw every one of them fighting to take in what this meant.

'So,' Orla said slowly, 'the French resistance rose up and took their capital city.'

'That's right,' Jacob agreed.

'And the American forces marched in and helped secure it for them?'

'Yes.'

'After how long?'

'The radio is saying three days.'

'Three days?' The words went around the room like a sacred whisper. It was August twenty-fifth – exactly twenty-five days since the Polish resistance had risen up to secure Warsaw and yet still they were here. Alone.

'What have they got that we haven't?' Orla asked.

'Americans,' Eduard spat. 'I heard that Eisenhower wasn't

even intending to take Paris. It wasn't "of strategic importance" in the march on Berlin, but when the resistance rose up, they wrote to appeal to him for help and he sent several battalions immediately.'

'Immediately!' Again, the word ran around the little crowd, louder this time – and angrier.

'So,' Zuzi cried, stepping into the room, 'is it because we're not as important as Paris? We don't have a fancy metal tower, or a load of snooty art, or, or...'

'Croissants?' Eduard suggested bitterly.

'Our bakeries have the best pastries in the world,' Jacob said stoutly. 'Especially Mother's.'

Magda reached out and ruffled his head.

'Thank you, son, but I'm afraid we're simply too far east. Paris got the Americans, Rome got the British, we get the Russians...'

'It's not fair,' Zuzi exploded. 'We're the *first* ally. We joined the British way before the French did, and the Italians were fighting *against* them for two years. The Polish navy is patrolling the North Sea against the U-boats. The Polish infantry were the ones who finally took Monte Cassino...'

'And the Polish pilots helped win the Battle of Britain,' Hana put in sadly.

'Exactly! We saved them and they're happy to let us be bombed day after day after day. What sort of allies are they?'

'A rubbish sort,' the doctor, Bronislaw, agreed, looking at Zuzi with shining admiration.

Goodness, Hana thought, as her sister returned his gaze with one that was burning as fiercely as any house in Stare Miasto. Zuzi had been fired up since she and Babcia had escaped from beneath the John of God. She'd been talking about how her Minerki were going to attack the Telephone Exchange, acting as if it was the easiest task in the world to blast Nazis out of a concrete tower. Hana had suggested that, if the attack went ahead, she could look out for the maps that had been so cruelly stolen from Marek back in the mists of a time before the uprising, and Zuzi had bouncily agreed that she would. It had perplexed Hana, but now she could see where she was getting her new-found energy from.

It seemed that everyone was in love, except her. That's to say, she *was* in love but Emil felt so far away that remembering what it had been like to be with him was like trying to imagine a frosty day in the heat of the summer, or a time when you could walk around your city without Nazis controlling your every move, or even a day without bombers and rocket launchers blowing up buildings all around you – impossible.

'Three days,' she repeated bitterly. 'If the Russians had done that for us, like they said they would when Moscow Radio told us all to rise up, then we'd have been liberated for twenty-two whole days. We'd be out in this sunshine, bathing in the Vistula, picnicking in the Saxon Gardens, welcoming our government back to Poland, like the French are doing – the French, who capitulated, who *collaborated*!'

She felt arms going around her and realised only when Magda started stroking her hair and murmuring to her, as she'd done when she'd been young and suffering from one of the many perceived injustices of childhood, that she was shouting. But, so what? This wasn't getting less jam than her sisters, or having her favourite toy stolen, or not being allowed to play on the swing. This was a betrayal of her city and her country in favour of other more 'Western' ones and it hurt like hell.

She pushed her mother gently away. 'I'd better get back to work. No doubt Bór will have messages to send about this.'

Magda loosened her hold but didn't let go. 'Are you sure, Hana? You seem... tired. I don't think—'

'We're all tired,' Hana interrupted. 'Orla is tired from treating the people the Nazis are burning with their evil chemistry. Zuzi is tired from blasting passageways through cellars because it's not safe for our citizens to walk their own streets. Jacob is tired from working with his tank platoon – aged thirteen. Babcia is tired because she's taken a bullet in the stomach and been buried beneath the hospital that was trying to help her mend. And you, Mama, you're tired from trying single-handedly to feed everyone in Stare Miasto. We're all tired but we have to keep going or else we'll be annihilated. Let the Parisians throw flowers onto their tanks, we need to drive ours into the enemy lines that are advancing day by dark day while the rest of the world parties in the Champs Elysées.'

She pulled away and marched for the door, bristling with rage.

'Just stay safe, Han-Han,' Magda said and the pain in her voice cut through Hana's anger like nothing else would.

'I will, Mama,' she said, forcing herself to summon up a smile. And that was when she heard it – the broadcast was ending and there, signing off, was 'One More Mazurka'. She stared at the radio. 'That's it!' she cried. 'That's the signal for the planes!'

'You see,' Orla said, 'they haven't abandoned us after all.'

'No,' Hana agreed, 'look at them kindly letting Polish pilots fly to the aid of the Polish capital. So noble.'

But she couldn't stop a smile forming and she went round to give every one of her family a hug – even a protesting Jacob – before she skipped out the door to head back to Bór's HQ. The planes were coming and she fully intended to be there to wave them in.

Three hours later, standing in the shadow of half a church as the throb of a Halifax aeroplane came through the light cloud, Hana felt her heart pounding as loudly as a machine gun. It was ridiculous, she knew that. Even if, by some miracle, one of the planes was Emil's, it wasn't as if she could actually see him. It wasn't as if he would land amongst the rubble, jump out of his cockpit and take her in his arms. It wasn't as if he could stroke her hair or put his arm around her waist or press his lips to hers...

She closed her eyes, snaking her arms around herself as if they were his, and leaning into the imagined embrace. She'd dreamed of him so many times during the long, dull years of the occupation. It had been partly to stop tormenting herself with insubstantial longings that she'd started studying architecture and, to be fair, it had led her to something else she was truly passionate about. The dreams had subsided but these last weeks, with death always a few footsteps away, they had returned with a passion. She didn't want to die without seeing him again.

The engine noise grew and she opened her eyes, berating herself for wasting the possibility of having him at least nominally close. She scanned the dark sky and suddenly there they were, breaking through the clouds like angels.

'Go, go, go!' Czajnik called and Hana rushed to light her lamp and get into position.

They were back out on the ghetto land, the eastern side this time where, in the heady first days of the uprising, Zuzi, Jacob and Babcia had been part of the group who'd liberated the Gęsiówka concentration camp. How they'd celebrated! Hana could picture Zuzi dancing on top of the newly created barricades as everyone in Wola rushed to throw their precious furniture on top to keep the Nazis out. Just a few days later, most of those same people had been gunned down in cold blood and it was only thanks to Eduard that their own dear Orla had made it out alive.

'Hold those lights high, ladies!'

Hana held hers up but, as if they'd also heard the leader's command, the Nazi searchlights flashed on and several beams swooped malevolently above Warsaw, picking out the incoming planes with evil accuracy.

'Don't you dare,' Hana hissed at them.

The planes were close and she peered up, desperately searching for the bright hope of a purple flower. The anti-aircraft guns were firing fierce ack-acks that seemed to go straight into her overworked heart. But still the planes came and now the bomb doors of the first one were opening and packages were falling out, as if it were Christmas and St Nicolas was making an airborne delivery. The parachutes opened and the precious containers floated slowly down towards them, landing with gentle thuds and cheers from the other girls. Hana was too fixed on the planes to bother. The first one came and went with no violet, the second too, but the third...

She held her lamp to the side so its light did not confuse her straining eyes and, yes, there it was, unfurling its heart-shaped petals as it dropped its presents on Warsaw.

'Emil,' Hana whispered. Then louder, 'Emil, Emil!' as if he might somehow hear her and know that she was still alive, as she now knew that he was. 'Emil!'

'Sssh!' Czajnik chided. 'Do you want the Germans shooting at us all?'

'Sorry,' she muttered because she was endangering the group and that wasn't fair. Yet, every part of her wanted to wave her lamp, and shout and stamp, and tell Emil that she loved him and couldn't wait to marry him when this madness came to an end.

There were two more planes coming and Hana glanced over, trying to be sure that she was guiding them in correctly. So it was that she heard, rather than saw, the sharp, metallic sound of a rocket connecting with a fuselage. So it was that she turned her head to see a brave silver plane shudder in the night sky before dipping and turning and careering down to earth, the vibrant violet on its underside flashing into a streak of purest purple as it spun faster and faster and, with a splash and a vicious hiss, plunged into the Vistula.

Her hands went to her mouth and the lamp crashed into the rubble at her feet, sending shards of glass and sparks of flame around her as if she, too, were being consumed by the rocket. She sank to her knees as the other girls came running, but she couldn't see their wide eyes or their concerned hands. All she could see was a streak of violet descending into the river, taking her dreams and her hopes and her plans for the future crashing down with them.

'Emil,' she moaned. And then, louder, 'Emil!'

But Emil was gone and even if Hana ripped her voice out of her throat and threw it to the smoke-filled skies above Warsaw he would not come back. Hana had no groom and no future and no hope and it was hard to see what the point of any of this was any more.

TWENTY-FIVE

19 AUGUST

ORLA

'Please, Han-Han, eat something.'

Orla crouched next to her big sister, holding out the bowl of soup Magda had cobbled together from the scraps they'd scavenged out of the pantries and stores still standing in Stare Miasto. It was getting harder and harder to find food and people were getting thinner by the day, none more so than Hana, who'd been nothing but a ball of misery ever since she'd seen her fiancé's plane shot down two days ago.

Zuzi had been out asking about the pilot but the plane had sunk to the bottom of the Vistula, the pilot with it, and with the Germans still holding the bridges and, therefore, the river, there was no retrieving him. The only consolation seemed to be that Emil Andrysiak was lying at rest close to his fiancée, but it was not much consolation. Ever since his loss, Hana had either been carrying messages around Warsaw on autopilot or, as now, huddling in the corner of the hospital, body limp and eyes vacant. Orla hated seeing her like this, but could find no way to coax her out of her distress.

'Please, Han-Han, for me?'

Hana did raise her head at that, but simply gave Orla a weak smile and then looked past her into the middle distance where, Orla presumed, she was seeing images of her lost future. Orla sighed and, handing the soup to a grateful patient, sat on the floor next to Hana and simply held her. Hana cuddled up tight, clutching her arms around Orla as if she was holding onto life itself. Orla stroked her hair, sang softly and prayed that her love could somehow keep Hana together until her heart mended enough for her to want to move on again.

'How is she?'

She looked up and saw that Zuzi had crept into the dining-room hospital. She was dark with the ash that coated everything these days and her eyes were rimmed with tiredness but still full of compassion for their suffering sister.

'Sad,' Orla said succinctly.

Zuzi nodded. 'Poor Hana. I didn't realise how much she'd been relying on seeing Emil again. Stupid of me. I can't imagine what it must be like to feel that way about someone.'

'Can't you?' Orla asked lightly, glancing across the room to where Bronislaw was checking a patient over.

'No,' Zuzi said tightly. 'I thought, for a day or two, that maybe I could, but seeing what it's done to Hana has put me right off again. I'm just not one for this romance stuff.'

Orla shook her head at her.

'It doesn't have to be "romance", Zuzi. There don't have to be hearts and flowers and serenading. It's about connecting with someone, being fascinated by them, wanting to know everything about them – wanting to be with them.'

'Is it?'

'Of course.'

'Cos in those silly books you read, it all seems to be about being swept off your feet, which sounds pretty damn uncomfortable to me.'

Now Orla couldn't stop herself laughing. 'I agree.'

'You do?'

'I do. I don't think of love like that at all. I think of it far more as finding someone who opens up the door to knowing where your feet want to go.'

Zuzi squinted at her.

'You're very strange sometimes, little doe. Is that how this Eduard chap makes you feel then?'

Orla felt herself blush. 'We weren't talking about me, we were talking about Hana.'

'Well, now we *are* talking about you. Does he?'

Orla had forgotten how damned direct her sister could be. She shifted uncomfortably, but then Eduard came rushing into the hospital with his fellow stretcher-bearer and she couldn't stop herself smiling. And what was wrong with that? There was precious little else to smile about around here.

'He does,' she said firmly. 'That's to say, I think he could, in time, when we get to know each other more and, and... and I'd better go and help. Here, you hold Hana.'

She prised herself away from her sister and got up to go and help Eduard find a bed – or, rather, a space on the floor – for the new patient. Bron came running too and Orla glanced back to see Zuzi, sitting stiff-backed next to Hana, tentatively stroking her sister's hair and watching them intently.

Bron, she was delighted to note, kept glancing Zuzi's way and, as they examined the patient's badly broken hand, she said casually, 'Any nice young lady waiting for you back in Łódź, Bron?'

'None at all,' he said instantly, head down over the patient. 'I'm totally free, should, er, should anyone ask. Not that...' He shook himself. 'This is a grave wound. Fetch me water please, Orla.'

'I'll try.'

She ran through to the kitchen but all the buckets of water had been used up.

'Sorry,' Magda said from the table where she was kneading a huge lump of dough. 'I had the last of it for this bread – if you can call it bread.'

She grimaced at the rough substance she was trying to knead into life and Orla grimaced back. Now she'd have to make a trip to the well. The AK had set a guard on it and they prioritised medics so she shouldn't have to wait long but it always felt like there were more important things to do. She was hugely grateful, therefore, when Jacob popped up at the door.

'I'll fetch you water.'

Orla looked at him in surprise. It wasn't like her little brother to be voluntarily helpful; perhaps the AK was doing him good.

'Thank you, Jacob.'

'Anything for you, sis.' She squinted at him and he gave her a sudden wink. 'Besides, it'll give me a chance to try out my new helmet.'

From behind his back, he produced a grand, spiked, Prussian-style helmet.

'Where did you get that?'

'Babcia's bedroom. She says it belonged to Great-Grandfather Kaczper, the one Papa was named after. She asked me to fetch her a new nightgown, and I found the helmet and she said I could have it and I should wear it with pride, so...' he plonked it on his head and picked up a bucket in each hand, '... here I go!'

Then he was off. Orla looked to Magda who smiled shakily.

'He's doing very well but, Lord help me, I do worry about him running around with fancy helmets and stolen mines and tanks, as if it's all one big game.'

Orla gave her mother a hug. 'It's scary, I know, but he's

probably best like that. He could just as easily be killed hidden away in a cellar.'

It was a terrible truth. Every day scores of buildings collapsed under the weight of enemy firepower. Babcia's house, on the eastern, river side of Stare Miasto, had so far survived unscathed but as the Germans wheeled their hideous rocket launchers closer, they were increasingly at risk. Bron was talking about moving the hospital into the cellar and whenever they had a free moment they went down to try and clear enough space for their many patients, but with the relentless attacks, free time was hard to come by.

'I'd better get back and help,' Orla said to Magda. 'Send Jacob through when he gets back. We need the water urgently and Babcia will love to see him in that helmet.'

'Will do.'

Magda was forming her loaves now, her face creased with fierce determination, though Orla knew that beneath her apron, her big mother's heart was breaking for poor Hana. For Warsaw. For them all. And, yet, what could any of them do, but carry on?

The loaves were rising already, as the sticky August heat continued into the back end of the month, and Magda certainly wasn't short of places to cook them – the embers of what was left of the once beautiful Old Market place would be as hot as an oven. Orla's stomach rumbled hungrily and she shook her head at herself for her preoccupation with food. It seemed that humans could get used to all sorts of horrors far more quickly than they could cope with the most basic drives of hunger and thirst and she gratefully accepted the crust that Magda handed her, chewing on it as she returned to the hospital.

Her spirits lifted when she saw Eduard fastening the infamous handcuffs and chains – rescued from the rubble of the John of God – onto the end of Babcia's bed and she glanced around to see if there was time to join him. Bron had bandaged the AK lad's hand to seal it from the dirty air until water could be found and he was apparently applying his doctorly skills to Hana's distress. Or, more accurately, chatting to Zuzi. Or, even more accurately, scuffing words around with Zuzi as neither of them seemed able to relax in each other's company.

Smiling, Orla slid up to Eduard at Babcia Kamilla's bedside and put an arm around his waist. It was probably very forward of her but watching her sister's awkward flirtation made her grateful for her own more straightforward romance.

'It's my favourite nurse!' Eduard placed his hand over hers, warm and reassuring. 'How do you think your babcia's handcuffs look?'

'Fantastic!'

Orla wasn't actually sure the grim shackles improved the elegant bed, but Babcia looked happy with them and that was what counted. Her wound had been ripped open again when the John of God had collapsed around her, allowing the unavoidable ash and dirt of siege Warsaw into her flesh, and it was continuing to ooze pus in an alarming way. Orla bathed it whenever she could, using the finest vintages from the winemaker's cellar in the foolish hope that the posher the chateau the greater its healing properties. It was doing little good, however, and yesterday Kamilla had suggested she, 'let me drink it instead, darling – it'll do me far more good that way.' By the looks of the level in the bottle she'd been doing just that and she smiled woozily at Orla.

'They cannot cuff us for long.'

'Too right, Babcia,' Orla agreed robustly though it was hard to see how this was going to end.

The Germans were sending in more and more firepower, the Allies, since the tragic night Emil's plane had crashed into the Vistula, were nowhere to be seen, and the Russians were sitting with their feet up on the far shore, apparently watching the horror show with glee. The Warsawians had risen up to free their city but, unlike in Paris, no one had lifted more than a little finger to help. It didn't seem fair to Orla, but what did she know about it? Personally, she thought it might be time to surrender before more people died, but she knew that wasn't in the Polish spirit so wasn't saying it out loud.

Behind her, she saw Jacob returning with the water and beckoned him over. He sat on Babcia's bed, chattering eagerly about how the helmet had saved him from a sniper bullet. Orla prayed that was more his imagination than reality, but Babcia was drinking it in and it was good to see her animated.

'Thank you for your help,' she said to Eduard.

'Anything for you.' Orla stood on her tiptoes to place a quick kiss on his lips. 'My angel,' he murmured and it felt like they were all alone, no blood, no ash, no heat, no suffering – just the two of them, in their own little world.

But then she heard Bron calling, 'Nurse!' and pulled herself reluctantly away.

'I really hope this isn't an amputation,' she moaned.

'You don't like them?'

'Would you?'

'No, but I'd rather be assisting than going through it.'

Orla sighed. 'You're so right. I'm useless.'

He held her close. 'You are not. You're bold and strong and caring and...'

'And incapable of holding some suffering man's limb without fainting.'

'That's part of the caring. Tell you what, why don't I do it?'

'Sorry?'

'If all it takes is holding the poor man down, I can do it as well as you.'

'True, but you're a stretcher-bearer.'

'Not really, Orla. I'm a farmer turned reluctant soldier, turned stretcher-bearer. I've birthed more lambs than I've shot guns or carried men. We're all doing what we can to survive. So

– you go and nurse some people and I'll go and hold onto a limb. Deal?'

Orla stared up at him, this kind, straightforward, honest man that she'd had the astonishing luck to find in her life.

'Deal,' she agreed and kissed him again.

'Nurse!' Bron called, more desperately, and they hastily separated.

Orla watched Eduard stride across to Bron, saw him nod keen agreement to his aid and almost fainted with relief – which was even more pathetic than fainting at the operation. Tutting at herself, she was turning to check on Hana when a high-pitched wail from the corner stopped her.

'Nella!' The baby had started awake in the cot they'd fashioned from the bottom drawer of Babcia's Kammler dresser, and Orla darted over to sweep her up. 'There, there, sweetie. You're well, you're all well.'

Nella quieted but Orla felt guilty again. Things were far from well in Nella's young world. Her mother was dead, her home gone. Sister Maria was talking to the nuns about taking her into their orphanage but they already had many lost children and Orla hated the thought of the nine-month-old stuck with no one of her own to love her. Setting her on her hip, she took her over to her sisters, hoping that maybe her innocent face would draw Hana out of her distress.

Zuzi leaped up with relief when she reached their corner. 'Orla, thank heavens. I've got to go back to work. We're preparing to attack the Telephone Exchange and I've been away too long already.'

Orla looked at her, aghast.

'The Telephone Exchange? That huge concrete tower? The one that looks like a medieval fortress?'

Zuzi shifted.

'That's the one. Some old man who used to work there has

dug a tunnel into the basement so we can get in and blow them up from beneath.'

'Won't that be terribly hard?'

'Not our simplest job, but that building gives the Nazis far too much control over Śródmieście.'

'But the Nazis hold the whole of the Saxon Gardens between here and there,' Orla objected. 'So how will you get there?'

Zuzi shifted.

'Across a bit of a minefield,' she admitted, putting up a hand to forestall Orla's protests. 'Don't worry about it, we're Minerki – mines are what we know.'

'Your own mines, not theirs.'

'Same difference. And it has to be done, we need to get the Nazis out of Śródmieście if we're going to evacuate people to there.'

'People? Us, you mean? Leave Stare Miasto?'

'It's hardly an idyll, Orls.'

'I know! But, leave it? All of us? How? You're not going to have *us* crawling across minefields, are you?'

'No!'

'So…?'

'Ask Hana.'

Orla looked to the floor to see that her eldest sister had, at least, looked up. 'How would we get out, Hana?'

Hana sat up taller.

'The sewers,' she said and a curious gleam came into her eyes.

'The sewers?' Orla asked, horrified. 'Aren't they dark and dirty and dangerous?'

'They are,' Hana agreed, nodding with something strangely like eagerness. 'But they don't have any Nazis in them.'

'Hana's boss has been travelling through them, right, Han?'

Zuzi supplied, sending Orla a secret look that said that she, too, had clocked their sister's new animation.

'He's not my boss, but he's my old tutor and, yes, Agaton has been all the way to Żoliborz and back. A few of the liaison girls and some of the postal scouts have been using the route too.'

'But not you?'

'No. I didn't want to, before...' Tears choked her but she brushed them fiercely aside and stood up so fast that both Zuzi and Orla had to leap back to avoid her. On Orla's hip, little Nella gave a happy clap but Orla was suddenly feeling less pleased at her sister's sudden restoration.

'Hana, you're not thinking of—'

'Volunteering? Too right I am. Why not? Someone has to. Do you want to stay here while Stare Miasto burns around us?'

'I... no. But—'

'Someone has to step up and sort it out. Agaton says they've got people putting in rope handles and signs to make it safer. Drawing maps too. I can do that, girls. I'm good at that.'

'Yes, but Hana, the danger—'

'Doesn't feel like it matters quite as much any more.' She grabbed at their hands. 'Emil died flying hundreds of miles to try and bring us aid, so surely I can manage to walk through a little poo?'

'It's not the poo,' Orla objected. 'It's the rest of it. I know you're grieving, Han. I know it all feels dark and desperate and I'm so, so sorry you won't get a future with Emil, but we love you too, right, Zuzi?'

Zuzi nodded awkwardly. 'I don't, you know, say it much, but Orla's right, Hana. We don't want to lose you.'

'Someone has to do it.'

'But does it have to be you? Think about how much you're hurting from losing Emil. Would you wish that on us?'

'Of course not.'

'Because that's exactly what it'll be like for us if you... you know, don't make it out.'

Orla felt a rush of love for spiky Zuzi. She hugged her, pulling Hana in with them too. 'Zuzi's right, Han. It'd tear us apart to lose you.'

Hana hugged them back. 'I know, girls. I feel the same and it means a lot, really it does, but we have to get out of here. If Zuzi can get to Śródmieście and attack the Telephone Exchange to make it secure for us, surely I can go down a sewer to forge a way there for everyone else?'

'Hana—'

But the eldest Dąbrowska sister was fired up now. 'I've been pathetic but no more. Take care, girls – see you at sunfall, yes?'

'Hana—'

'See you at sunfall.'

'See you at sunfall, Hana,' Orla agreed resignedly and with a last hug, her big sister was gone.

Orla looked to Zuzi, who shrugged. 'I guess she's got to do what she's got to do. As have I. Take care, sweetie.'

She blew Orla a kiss and then she, too, was gone, off to blow things up in the name of freedom. Orla leaned against the wall and hugged Nella close. On the far side, she could see Bron and Eduard leaning over the operating table and hear the grind of the saw and the wails of the poor man who was losing his hand. Nearby, Jacob was on the end of Babcia's bed, regaling her with some tale of AK derring-do and Babcia's eyes were shining with pride. How come everyone else in her family was so brave? Or, more to the point, how come she wasn't?

She hung her head, letting Nella play with her plaits as she tried not to cry, but then she felt a warm arm around her shoulders and looked up to see Magda at her side.

'Hana's gone back to work already?'

Orla nodded. 'She's going to go down the sewers, Mama.

And Zuzi is going to cross a minefield and blow up the Telephone Exchange. They're so brave.'

'So reckless.'

Orla shook her head. 'No. It's definitely brave. Papa would be proud of them if he was here.'

'As he would of you, sweetie.'

Orla gave a dark laugh. 'Hiding away in a hospital where I'm not even much use as a nurse?'

'No! I told you at the start of all this – we fight in our own ways. You do it by caring for everyone and looking after them and keeping the whole family together.'

'Mama... It's nice of you to say, but it's hardly what Tata meant when he said we had to keep fighting, is it? Hana and Zuzi are cut in his mould and I...'

She trailed off.

'You are, maybe, cut in mine?'

'What?'

Magda put a finger under her chin and drew her face round to look at her. 'Am I bold and brave and daring?'

'Well, no, but you're Mama. You're here to, to...'

'Care for everyone and keep the family together?'

'Yes. And you do it wonderfully.'

'As do you, Orla my sweet, as do you. And more than the family, besides.' She pulled a crust of raisin bread from her apron pocket and handed it to Nella, who grabbed it and sucked happily on it. Orla bounced her on her hip and Magda smiled. 'Caring for people is not, you know, such a bad skill. Your father, after all, loved me for it and I know – I am totally certain – that he would love you for it too.'

'You are?'

'Not everyone can blow things up, sweetie. Some people have to put them back together.'

Magda kissed her, then was up and gone, off to get her loaves from the ovens to feed the starving people of Warsaw.

Orla watched her go with love. She'd always thought she was meant to be brave and fierce like her father, but her mother was a wonderful role model too.

Feeling happier, she went to drop Nella at the end of Babcia's bed to be amused by Jacob's wild stories and rushed to mop the brow of the poor man Bron had bandaged up.

'Thank you, Nurse,' he said faintly and her heart ached for him, as it ached every day for all of them. She understood that it was weak to surrender but was it better to die? She had a horrible feeling they were in danger of finding out.

TWENTY-SIX
20 AUGUST

ZUZI

Zuzi crouched down at the entrance to the tunnel, trying to be brave and strong and fierce and all the other things she knew her father would have expected of her, but in the fading torchlight, this hand-dug passageway looked very rickety. Crossing the minefield had been bad enough but at least she'd had training in that and the Minerki had made careful, steady progress in the dark, not setting off a single enemy device. Now here they were, before the Telephone Exchange, or rather beneath it, and it seemed their challenges had only just begun.

She glanced up to the man who'd dug the subterranean passage, a doughty sixty-six-year-old with white hair and wrinkles carving grooves down his weather-beaten face.

'Are you sure it's safe, Albert?'

Albert tipped his workman's hat at her. 'I'd swear my life on it, miss. I know it doesn't look like much but I was forty years an engineer and I know how to put a decent prop in.'

Zuzi smiled up at him. However daunting his tunnel, the man was a hero. He'd apparently reported to the AK at the start of the uprising, begging to be allowed to join, but with so few weapons for the trained soldiers, they'd turned him away. Undeterred, he'd been single-handedly digging into the Telephone Exchange – his place of employment back in the prosperous years between the wars – using a small shovel and a bucket. Two days ago, he'd broken into the basement and now Zuzi and the other twelve remaining Minerki were travelling down his tunnel to set the mines that would, hopefully, forge the way for the AK to take the crucial building.

'It's a very impressive piece of work,' she told him.

'Least I could do. And I'll be right behind you, so you young ladies get in there and blast those bloody Nazis to hell!'

Zuzi saluted him and headed down as, really, what else was there to do? She thought of Hana, plunging into the maze of sewers beneath the city, and told herself she could do this. Her big sister had seen her off with a fierce hug and a reminder to find the maps that the Gestapo had taken off her fellow student before the uprising. Zuzi had forgotten all about the incident but clearly her sister had not and, although a few maps didn't seem worth much to Zuzi, she'd gladly agreed. Anything to see Hana smile again.

Her feet found the first of three stones Albert had set into the initial slope and she was uncomfortably reminded of the ancient steps into the tomb where they'd carried Babcia Kamilla after she'd been shot. Sweet Orla had been working calmly away down there amongst actual skeletons, so Zuzi could cope with the few worms that were their only companions in this tunnel.

Bronislaw had been in that tomb too, operating on coffins, and the thought of him warmed her in welcomely distracting ways. As she crawled under the road towards the Nazis' lair, she focused on her disconcerting conversation about him with Babcia Kamilla. They'd been underground then too, though not voluntarily so. They were all becoming moles!

A patter of dislodged soil at her side made her jump.

'Just a little loose earth,' Albert's soothing voice said at the rear of their small group and Zuzi forced herself to push past it.

What had Babcia said? 'God made us to fit together and we should honour that and enjoy it.' It was a tantalising idea. Zuzi wasn't sure of the exact mechanics but she knew that when Bronislaw was in the room she wanted to be near to him – as near as it was humanly possible to be. She'd thought that made her some sort of sinner, but, if Babcia was to be believed, it might be an entirely natural response. Drawing in a deep breath as the tunnel got even narrower, she allowed herself to imagine what it might be like to kiss Bronislaw, to step up close to him and reach an arm around his neck and press her lips to—

'We're here,' the girl behind her hissed and Zuzi wasn't sure whether to be relieved or sorry.

Maybe you should get on and kiss him for real, she told herself and the bold thought gave her the courage to step into the large basement and look around. She would do this job to the best of her ability, she would get out, and she would find Bron and tell him that she liked him. Well, she might. Doing that felt scarier than throwing grenades into a bunch of heavily armed Germans, so she pushed her wanton thoughts aside and focused on the job in hand.

The other Minerki were with her now, plus Albert. Their accompanying AK platoon were catching them up and Zuzi flushed with embarrassment as their leader, Kapitan Szymon Ancel, took a place at her side. If he could see her thoughts! Still, she'd seen him dancing very close to his beautiful redhaired wife the day they'd first built the barricades, so perhaps he'd had these feelings himself. Perhaps everyone had. Perhaps...

The last of the AK stepped into the room and Zuzi sucked in her breath, for standing there, complete with Prussian helmet, was her little brother. Had Jacob been there all along, crawling behind her across the minefield in the dark? She might have been even more nervous if she'd known.

'Jacob?' she stuttered.

'Reporting for duty, ma'am.'

'It's not a game,' she snapped, more sharply than she should.

He flinched but didn't back away. 'I'm not playing.' He lifted a pistol. 'I'm deadly serious.'

'Where did you get that?'

He looked briefly abashed. 'Off a man who... doesn't need it any more.'

'He died?'

'Lots do.'

'Which is precisely why I'm worried about you.'

'And I about you,' he shot back. She stared at him and he sidled closer. 'It's painful waiting around, hoping you all come back home. It's easier being out here taking part.'

Zuzi sighed. 'I can see that. Just, please, Jacob, be careful.'

'If you will, I will.'

He held up his crooked little finger and, with a half-smile, she hooked her own into it and they mock-shook on their deal. Zuzi had no idea what Magda would say if she could see them, poised to storm an enemy stronghold, but she had to admit that it was reassuring having him here.

'Has everyone got their kit?' Tosia asked in a whisper and Zuzi told herself, once again, to concentrate. She looked in her pack for her mines and grenades, checking they all had their pins securely fastened, the memory of her stupid incident with the courgettes sharpening her mind instantly. Letting a grenade off early in here could bring half the soldiers of the Third Reich down on them. It was a sobering thought and she looked to the ceiling, as if she might be able to see the German defenders through it.

'Remember, there's not that many of them,' Tosia whispered. 'And they should be tired and hungry. We've had the building under siege for days, stopping any new supplies getting in, so hopefully they'll be weak.'

No one said that, with few supplies in Warsaw, they were all weak. Magda had sent Zuzi with some precious bread and she pulled it out and handed it around. The Minerki fell on one loaf gratefully and she handed the other to Szymon for his men.

'God bless you,' he said, patting her arm and she felt a rush of longing for her own father, too long gone from them.

'This one's for Tata,' she whispered to Jacob, who nodded.

'See you at sunfall?'

'See you at sunfall.'

They set their mines above a rough staircase up to the battened-down hatches, positioning them carefully beyond the supporting beam so they didn't bring the whole structure down on themselves. Zuzi rolled out the wire fuses, remembering the endless drills last summer. How bored they'd got back then, but how well it was paying off now.

The group moved slickly into place and Tosia looked to Szymon. 'Ready?'

He looked around his men and nodded. 'Ready.'

'Then let's do this! Zuzi – over to you.'

Zuzi lit one of her precious supply of matches and put it to the fuse. It crackled brightly and they all crouched in the far side of the basement as it flickered along the wire, turned upwards to the devices clinging to the wall and then caught. The boom echoed deafeningly around the basement and they cowered back as the hatches blew apart, flying upwards in a hundred splinters of ancient wood. The AK had ladders ready but the mines had been accurate enough to leave the stairs in place and Zuzi watched as, Jacob at the rear, they ran up them.

'Let's go, Minerki.'

Zuzi headed upwards. Her heart was pounding now, the

blood surely pumping around her body at twice its normal rate. She could hear shouts in frantic German above them and, as the AK ahead opened fire, she prayed like she'd never prayed before that Jacob would be safe. Then suddenly a grenade was landing right near her feet and she had to dive through a doorway and scrabble away before it exploded. A desk broke apart, sending fragments everywhere. A splinter glanced off Zuzi's shoulder but there was no time to complain. She could hear footsteps coming down the stairs and, on instinct, whipped a grenade from her pack and threw it through the doorway.

The explosion and the scream of pain seemed intertwined and then there was silence. On the floors above they could hear fighting, but in the corridor nothing. Slowly, Zuzi crept out and peered around the door frame. A man in a German uniform was lying, spreadeagled across the iron banister, a great hole in his chest where Zuzi's grenade must have caught him full-on. She put her hands over her mouth as vomit rose up in her throat.

She'd done that. She'd ripped a man apart and almost visibly torn his heart from his body. Yes, he was a German, yes, he was the enemy – a living exemplar of the cruel treatment they'd all received for the last five years – but he was a man, someone's son, someone's brother, maybe someone's husband. In Germany a woman would weep, as Hana had been weeping for Emil, and all for possession of a concrete tower. It seemed so futile but already she could hear the AK calling for back-up and Tosia was running past her, grabbing her arm and pulling her upwards.

'Don't think about it, Zuzi. Don't look, don't care and don't think. We've got to keep ourselves alive.'

Zuzi nodded and followed her leader, but the building was full of smoke and confusion and stank of cordite and blood.

'Stand back,' Tosia cried and sent a grenade up the stairs.

A man toppled down, shouting in rage and fear, to land,

twitching at their feet. Tosia and another girl lifted him up and flung him bodily over the banister into the central atrium below. He landed with a crack and Zuzi edged forward to see, but already they were heading upwards. Always upwards. And always to more of the enemy. This was like the Prudential all over again but tighter and more intense.

Daylight seeped into the carnage, and then, as the sun rose fully, it striped through the barred windows, making mystical patterns in the swirling smoke. Zuzi saw a Prussian helmet run past several times and thanked God but the fight was hard and it took hours to secure each floor. The AK were slowly pushing the Nazis upwards but they weren't going without a fight and several AK had to be carried down to be handed to medics or, worse, hastily buried in the rubble beyond the door.

Then a shout went up: 'They've hung out an SOS.'

Zuzi ran to the window of their secure position on the third floor and saw a distress flag flying high above on the sixth. They made their way cautiously up to join the AK on the fourth and she was delighted to see Jacob with Szymon. They were all watching tensely for what might happen outside but, apart from some desultory shooting from the Nazi positions far down the road, nothing did.

'Now what?' Zuzi asked.

'Now we go again,' Szymon said. 'Force them right up to the top and we'll have them trapped.'

'How many of them are there?'

'Hard to tell. Maybe a hundred.'

'A hundred?' Zuzi looked around their group – eleven Minerki and twenty AK soldiers, plus Jacob. 'How do we manage that?'

'Because,' came back the immediate reply, 'we have you.'

'We're going to have to use all our trickery,' Tosia said. 'I want mines on this ceiling, then we can retreat to the next floor, roll long fuses and literally take the floor out from under them.'

'Cool,' Jacob said but not with his usual verve.

He looked pale and Zuzi longed to pluck him out of the group and send him home to Magda but knew he would hate her for it. Instead, once they had laid their mines and everyone had retreated to the third floor to take cover, she took the chance to squeeze in next to him beneath a table.

'How are you doing, Jacob?'

'Good. I'm good, Zuzi. I killed a Nazi.'

'Me too,' she said. 'Not nice, is it?' He looked at her, surprised, and she slipped an arm around his shoulder and gave him a quick hug. 'I know they're the enemy but they don't feel quite that way up close, right?'

'Right,' he agreed on a long outrush of breath and Zuzi hated that he'd had to learn this most brutal of lessons at such a tender age, then hated the Nazis all over again for it – though not enough to want to see them dead at her feet. It was most confusing.

'Fuse,' Tosia ordered and there was no time for thinking, for she had to step out and set a match to the long run of wire heading up the stairs to the ceiling above.

She lit it and darted back in with Jacob. The light flared along the wire and out the door. Zuzi clutched Jacob close and he clutched back and then came an almighty boom followed by the clatter of falling beams and boards and what was almost certainly men. The ceiling above them visibly buckled but held, then Szymon was shouting the AK up the stairs, guns ready, to clear the fourth and fifth floors. Zuzi held quietly onto Jacob and he did not protest until Szymon shouted down, 'all clear,' and, with a darting kiss on Zuzi's cheek, he shot off to rejoin the men.

Zuzi crawled out and looked at her fellow Minerki. They were all, like her, covered in dirt and soot and rubbing at exhausted eyes. They'd been fighting for hours and were making progress but it wasn't over yet.

'Weapons stock-check,' Tosia instructed and they opened their packs and pulled out what supplies they had left. There were precious few – certainly not enough to take out a hundred Nazis if they chose to come storming down.

But all had gone very quiet above. Straining, Zuzi heard Symon whispering his troops into position up the stairs and glanced out, glad to see Jacob was firmly at the back. She knew, from all she'd seen around Warsaw, that her brother was far from the only youngster wielding a gun in the unequal fight, and that numbers were so short they were badly needed, so she appreciated Szymon's rough care for her brother. Even so, her heart was in her mouth as the men crept up the stairs, but moments later there were shouts of triumph and, then, confusion.

'They're gone! Where the hell are they gone?'

'Go, girls,' Tosia urged and they shot out and ran up the stairs, past the gaping maw of the fifth floor and on to the sixth and final one. The top of the building was one big, open attic space and, bar a run of complex telephone machinery, it was totally empty.

'Where are they?' Tosia demanded.

A curious noise came echoing back in response, like a mystical creature bellowing.

'There!' It was Jacob, darting over to the far corner where a huge metal tube provided a watertight conduit for various wires and, it would seem, enough space for panicked Nazis to slide down.

'Where does it go?' Szymon leaned right out, then turned back. 'The basement! The bastards have got all the way back down to the basement. Go, go, go!'

They hammered down the stairs and there, in the big entrance hall they saw several Nazis tugging on the main door, desperately trying to get out.

'Freeze!' Szymon roared in first Polish and then German. 'Guns down. Hands up!'

The enemy soldiers glanced at each other, but it was clear they were trapped and they looked frayed and past caring. Szymon motioned for them to throw their guns into the centre, the AK covering them from the balustrade that conveniently looked over the lower hall. One by one they did so and moved, hands held high, to stand against the far wall. More and more came out of the basement and Zuzi stood there and watched as they handed themselves into AK custody, babbling for mercy.

'Decorum,' Szymon instructed his men. 'These soldiers are prisoners of war under the Geneva Convention which we, as soldiers ourselves, recognise fully.'

'Banditen,' one of the Nazis muttered but he was hastily hushed by his fellows and, as the AK gathered up the guns and ammo – treasure indeed – and ushered them out under fierce guard, realisation ran through Zuzi.

'We did it!' She clasped at Tosia. 'We did it. We took the Exchange!'

'We did.' Tosia looked as dazed as Zuzi. It was the first serious AK victory in days and it took time to sink in but they could hear cheering and jeering on the street as some of Szymon's men marched the prisoners out, while the rest checked the building for rogue soldiers.

'Wait till we tell Hana and Orla,' Jacob said, leaping up and down, and that's when Zuzi remembered.

She grabbed at the first senior-looking prisoner.

'You,' she said, trying to recall her schoolgirl German. 'Where are the maps?' He stared at her. 'The Karten. The Stadtplan.'

'Stadtplan! Ja.' He nodded keenly and pointed sideways into an office.

Zuzi looked to Szymon and Tosia for permission and got a curious nod in return. She strode into the room, Jacob in tow, and looked around. The office was as highly organised as she'd expect but had little in the way of files. Then she spotted a cabinet in one corner, the drawers handily labelled, including one marked 'Karten'. She yanked it open and there, in a neat manilla folder, was a set of maps clearly marked as: 'Warsaw – Future plans.'

She snatched it up and waved it at Jacob. 'Oh Jacob, this is going to cheer Hana right up.'

The reality of their victory was sinking in and she grabbed his hands and danced him around the German-free office.

'She'll need it,' he giggled. 'If she's been down the sewers, she is going to stink!'

'Come on then,' she said, giggling with him and pushing aside her darker fears about the dangers of the underground maze. 'Let's make sure this place is secure and get ourselves home, hey?'

'Home!' Jacob agreed and Zuzi, weary to her very bones of fighting and of death, thought a single word had never sounded sweeter. She just prayed home was still there, for nothing was certain in Warsaw any more.

TWENTY-SEVEN

HANA

Hana blinked back tears, but they kept on coming. The fumes were so acrid that her eyeballs felt like they were on fire, making it even harder to see down the endless passageways, lit only by the roving beam of Agaton's torch. At least he kept it up in the higher part of the sewer, playing over the dripping bricks, and not into the sludge that was flowing around her ankles and often up to her knees. Hana did not want to see what she was shuffling her way through. The endless soft bumps and sticky wisps against her stockinged legs were enough to make her want to throw up and she was very grateful for the lavender her boss had tied around her neck to counteract some of the worst of the smells.

'Stop here.'

She did as instructed, though she had to physically will her legs to do so because they were screaming at her to get out of here, to run, run, run to the nearest manhole cover and scramble up the metal steps to fresh air and open skies above. That, though, would be madness. The sewer was oval, its curving sides steep so that your feet were on a constant angle and it was all too easy to lose them and fall into the... Hana shuddered and gripped her fingers tight into the higher bricks either side at the thought.

'Can you hold this?' Agaton asked. His voice was low but it still echoed around the tunnel, ghost-like. He handed her a looped metal nail while he fished a hammer out of his pack, splaying his legs, star-like, to keep himself steady. 'Thank you.'

He paused, listening carefully, but there was nothing to be heard bar the rush and squelch of the sewage around their feet, so he set the nail against the mortar at waist height and hammered it in with strong strikes that played around them over and over like an endless drum roll. Hana looked up and down the sewer in terror. If there were Germans nearby, they could easily open up a manhole cover and throw a grenade down. There would be nowhere to go if metal-laden fire came towards them and she would be struck down and...

The hammer blows faded away and there was just the flow of human detritus once more.

'Good,' Agaton said, taking a coil of thin rope from his pack and tying one end to the loop. 'Onwards.' He set off and she willed herself to follow, but her feet seemed to be stuck to the bricks. He stopped and shone the torch over her. 'Are you well, Fiolet?'

The name threatened to undo her. She fumbled for her ring but could not feel it beneath the gloves she was wearing. Suddenly all she could see was a streak of purple, no longer heart-shaped, but a line of death plunging into the Vistula, taking all her hopes for the future with it. Suddenly all she could see was Emil, dazed and only half-conscious, perhaps burned and bloodied, battling to get out of his cockpit beneath the fast-flowing water – battling and failing.

'Fiolet! Look at me. Here. Look into my eyes.' Agaton was

holding her by the shoulders now. 'Stay with me, girl. I'm here. We're together. We can do this.'

She looked into his eyes, blue and kind and willing her to respond.

'Can you call me Hana?' she whispered.

'Hana? Of course. No problem. You're doing so well, Hana. Really. Now, look, we need twenty steps to the next nail. Can you count to twenty?'

The mundane question almost made her laugh. 'Course I can count to twenty.'

'I should hope so too. What use would an architect be if they couldn't count, hey? And you're going to be a great architect, Hana. You've got a real talent for it.'

'You're only saying that to stop me panicking.'

Now Agaton did laugh. 'I'm not, but if it does that too then so much the better. Now – twenty, come on. One, two...'

'Three, four...' Hana joined in obligingly and the numbers did help, driving her feet forward and giving her something to focus on other than the endless darkness ahead and the eye-stinging mush below. Then, somehow, they were at twenty and stopping to hammer in the next nail.

'Where are we?' she whispered.

'Below Leszno Street. This is the northerly E-sewer. It runs from Stare Miasto to Żoliborz. The other major lines also run north to south, with A furthest west then B and finally C closest to the river, extending into D further south. The rest of the tunnels are smaller and cut east–west between them. There are maps, but the Nazis have them, of course.'

That reminded Hana. 'My sister is part of the attack on the Telephone Exchange today.'

Agaton raised an eyebrow in the low light. 'Your family are brave.'

'No more than any other in Warsaw right now. But the point is, I asked her, if they succeed...' She paused as the thought of Zuzi not succeeding threatened to crowd in on her, but the rap of Agaton's hammer on the next nail brought her back. 'To see if she could spot the maps. You know, the ones that...'

'Poor Marek took from the class?'

She nodded and he gripped one of her hands.

'That was clever thinking, Hana. And I truly hope she succeeds. The Exchange is critical to our defence of Śródmieście. And those maps – they are our hope, our future. They will allow us to rebuild the city, and to rebuild it even better than it was before those bastards took it.'

Again, Hana thought of Emil spiralling to his death. Life with him had been her future, the focus of all her night-time dreams, but she had taken up her architectural studies to distract herself from that, and to give herself something else in case. She'd always known he might die, had always, indeed, known it was likely – those were a pilot's odds – and at least she had found something that truly inspired her. She looked at Agaton. This man, bravely travelling the sewers to make them safer for others to follow, was a brilliant architect forced, by circumstance, to work like a mole in the effluent of the city. If he could do it, so could she.

'Our future,' she repeated and it echoed down the tunnel like a lover's promise.

She had wanted a more personal future – a husband, babies, a home to make nice – but if that was not to be her destiny, she would embrace a wider, more communal one. She would work and she would study and she would be part of the team who would raise Warsaw out of the Nazi ashes.

First, though, she had to get through this sewer.

'Leszno Street,' she said. 'So we'll head up the line of Elektoralna next and then below Grzybowska.'

Agaton smiled at her.

'Spot on. Keep that in your mind, girl, because when we get

out of here, I want maps. Sewer maps – consider it your homework.'

Hana nodded. Homework felt like something from another world; a happier world. Maps of the sewer system weren't quite as glamorous as those for a bold new expressway, but for now, they were what was needed. As she trod along, picturing the streets above them and ticking them off in her mind, the sewers seemed a little less dark and the stink a little less unpleasant and the tears, slowly, cleared from her eyes.

They reached their final destination – a manhole on Prosta Street in Śródmieście – a surprisingly short time later. Hana's head was full of streets and intersections and all she wanted was some paper to note it down, but as a group of AK lads helped her out, she forgot that. She stood, spinning slowly and taking in the scenes around her in disbelief.

'It's so... so normal!'

She'd known that the AK held an area of some thirteen square kilometres in the modern centre of Śródmieście, and that most of the Nazis' attacking power was being focused on the more northerly Stare Miasto, but she hadn't realised quite how gloriously free that made it down here. The streets were full of people strolling around in the sunshine. The buildings were almost all standing and even had glass in their windows. There were cafés, with tables out on the pavement, and people were chattering over coffee and cakes as if there was no uprising, or even any war. At the far end of Prosta Street, she could make out a giant barricade, but it was doing its job perfectly and here, behind it, civilian Warsaw was truly free.

'Astounding, isn't it?' Agaton said to her. 'Like a totally different city. You see, now, why we need to make it safe to evacuate people out to here?'

Hana nodded eagerly and looked north towards Stare

Miasto, marked out by the pall of black smoke hanging above it. A mere kilometre away, people were living in cellars, scrabbling for food and water and waiting to be buried alive by a Stuka or a Kowa slamming into the remains of the buildings above them. Over there, Orla was nursing people with fearsome burns, and Magda was battling to find enough flour to make even the roughest of bread, and Zuzi was...

She grabbed at one of the AK men who had helped them out of the manhole. 'What's happened with the Telephone Exchange?'

His broad grin was all she needed. 'They took it. The AK took it.'

'And the Minerki?'

'Oh yes. Those women are so fierce! If I could get one of them in my—'

He remembered who he was talking to and stopped but Hana, buoyed up by surviving the sewers and finding a Warsaw where life still looked like something worth living, laughed. The Exchange was barely two streets away and that hopefully meant Zuzi was somewhere near.

'My sister is one of those women,' she told the lad, 'and if you got anywhere near her, she'd eat you alive.'

He cringed as his fellows roared with laughter. But then one of them said, 'Looks like you might get eaten right now – here they come!'

Hana followed where he pointed and, sure enough, strolling cockily down the street, backpacks over their shoulders, hair wild, and hips swaying in clothing black from the smoke of their own explosives, were the Minerki. And there, at the front, grinning fit to burst, was her sister.

'Zuzi!' She ran into her arms, coughing at the fumes embedded in her clothes. 'You reek of smoke.'

'It's better than what you reek of, Hana. Looks like we both need a wash.'

Hana sighed. 'I'd kill for a wash.'

'Good job you made it to Śródmieście then. Look.'

Zuzi pointed to where a big well was giving bucket after bucket of fresh water to a patiently waiting queue of civilians. Hana gasped and, with a shy doff of his cap, the AK lad who'd been lusting after the Minerki rushed off. Waving his pass to get to the front of the queue, he returned with a bucket full of the clearest water Hana had seen since the start of the uprising. Another lad passed her a cup and she dipped it in and drank deep, savouring the crisp, fresh taste like the finest wine, before cupping her hands and sluicing the water over her face.

It felt so good, as if she was washing off not just the dirt of the sewer but of the last three agonising weeks, from fleeing Wola, to the dark battle of the cemeteries, to the John of God collapsing and the daily grind of trying to live in Babcia's once beautiful house, now a battling bakery and hospital. They had to get everyone out of Stare Miasto, and the sewers – those dark carriers of waste – might turn out to be the perfect lifeline. She would draw the maps immediately. Oh but...

She turned to Zuzi. 'Did you get the maps?'

Zuzi quirked an eyebrow at her. 'You mean, was the fighting hard, sis? Did it go well? Did you get hurt? How's Jacob?'

'Jacob?' Hana looked at her sister, stunned. 'He was fighting with you?'

'He was – and very well too. He's currently drinking schnapps with the rest of his platoon in the secured Telephone Exchange.'

'Schnapps, Zuzi? He's too young for schnapps.'

'As he is too young for riding tanks and firing a gun, but he seems to be doing both of those so it's hard to stop him.' Zuzi shook her head. 'What's this doing to us, Han-Han?'

She looked sideswiped and Hana nudged at her. 'Stopping us asking after our loved ones, that's what. I'm sure the fighting was very hard, Zuzi, but it clearly went well as you were victorious and you are standing before me, as beautiful as always, so I assume you're not hurt.'

Zuzi rolled her eyes. 'I'm not beautiful.'

'Shall we ask Dr Bronislaw about that?'

'Hana – hush!' Zuzi looked very discomfited and swiftly changed the subject. 'As it happens, I did find a folder...'

She reached for a backpack and drew out a manilla folder, so very like the one that Hana had last seen snatched from Marek before the Gestapo had gunned him down, that she felt her knees wobble and had to clutch at the nearest thing to stay upright – which happened to be Agaton's arm.

'Sorry,' she said, embarrassed, but her one-time tutor was as fixated on the folder as she'd been and paid her no heed.

'May I?'

Zuzi nodded and handed it over. Hana leaned in as Agaton reverently opened it up and stared. Inside were maps and sketches – but none they had seen before.

'Is it not the right thing?' Zuzi asked.

'It's not the thing we were thinking of,' Hana said, 'but it's something important for sure.'

She stared at the papers. They were marked as Warsaw at the top but looked nothing like the city she knew. They were dated from 1940, signed by someone called Pabst, and the writing, now she looked more closely, was all in German.

'What *is* this?' Agaton breathed. 'See here – this is the Vistula and this is the east bank, but on the west... There's no Stare Miasto, no Jerusalem Avenue, not even an east–west road of any sort, let alone an expressway, just this arterial route around...' he peered closer, almost choking, 'around what looks like a complex of, of alpine-style houses.' He looked up at Hana. 'These aren't our beautiful ideas for Warsaw, but what the Nazis want to do with Her. This is the Third Reich's plan for our beautiful capital – a transit stop on the route east, run by Polish slaves living on the east bank and a load of German oafs in their cuckoo-clock houses in the middle. It's a travesty. An utter travesty.'

Hana fought to take it all in.

'Would they really do that? Wipe out centuries of beautiful buildings to put up some wooden chalets? What about the Brühl Palace, what about the citadel and the Royal Castle and the glorious buildings of the Market Place?'

Agaton gave a dry laugh.

'Glorious buildings of the Market Place, Hana? I thought you were all about modern design?'

Hana shifted.

'I was. That's to say, I am, but only alongside the old, not at the expense of it. Our buildings are what define us. What mark out our history, tell our story. You cannot wipe them out.'

As if in answer, a line of Stukas whined overhead, and flung their bombs into the already burning line of Stare Miasto.

'This is why they're annihilating us,' Hana whispered. She remembered something the Gestapo had said to Marek: 'This is not your city to map out. It's ours. You shouldn't even be here, any of you. Hitler wants you gone. He wants Warsaw turned into a transit post for our empire in the east.' She stared at Agaton. 'It was their plan all along and the uprising is giving them the perfect excuse to carry it out!'

Agaton nodded grimly.

'But it won't work. The Poles have resistance running through their blood and they won't give in. We've been running an underground government, an underground state and an underground army throughout their damned occupation and now we are quite literally running the whole city underground. Warsaw's cellars and sewers will keep her people alive, Hana, and that's what truly counts. When this is over, when they are defeated, we will still be here. Buildings can be rebuilt, it's the spirit of the nation that we are fighting to keep and you girls are a vital part of that. Well done today.'

He clapped Hana and Zuzi on the back and closed the folder. 'I shall be taking this to the higher-ups immediately. Then I shall be paying a visit to the Exchange prisoners. Someone knows where *our* maps are and I intend to find them. But for now – how about a meal in that glorious café right there?'

'Yes please!' they squealed.

'And then back down the sewers to home.'

Hana groaned. The last thing she wanted was to go back into the darkness but Orla and Magda and Babcia Kamilla were still in Stare Miasto and they had to get them – and everyone else – out of there before the beautiful medieval area was nothing more than cinders and graves.

TWENTY-EIGHT
22 AUGUST

ORLA

'It's for the best,' Orla told Nella, sat tight on her hip as they made their way through the cellars towards the convent. 'They'll be able to look after you there. They're lovely, really they are. Nuns, you know, so very sweet, very, er loving. They'll take care of you like I can't because I'm always rushing around and I can't give you the attention you deserve, can I? I can't be your mama.'

She was babbling, she knew, and the people crouched in the alcoves and makeshift rooms along the way were giving her funny looks, but she had to keep talking or she might lose her nerve. The cellars were eerily dark. The power plant was somehow still in AK hands but several sections had been badly bombed and it was running low on fuel, so light was as rationed as everything else. Often people had to make do with candles or gas lamps, or the ghastly flicker of the fires up above; they were all living in the shadows these days.

Sister Maria had found Nella a place at the Convent of the Benedictine Sisters of the Perpetual Adoration of the Holy

Sacrament and given Orla time off to take her there, so it would be churlish to say no, wouldn't it? And foolish too. Her time was taken up with nursing the increasing number of wounds and burns incurred by both the AK soldiers and the innocent people of Stare Miasto, and far too often Nella was left on the end of a patient's bed, or crawling around in what were, frankly, unsanitary conditions for a little one.

Magda often had her, sitting her up in the smart family high chair, chattering to her as she tried to cobble together bread for starving Warsawians. Babcia liked to have her on her bed, but she tired easily and Orla didn't dare leave Nella unattended for fear she would crawl up onto her grandmother's still festering wound. Babcia had a fever and Orla could only pray that it was her body generating the heat to attack the infection, for they had little else to treat it with. But it made her woozy and weary and the baby could not be left with her.

No, the nuns were the best option. And, besides, as Babcia Kamilla had quietly said to her the other day, she had to think of her own life after the uprising. Eduard was a lovely young man, her grandmother had told her, and it was clear they could make a happy life together, but what man would want another's child? It was best if little Nella went to the Sisters of the Sacrament. Orla had wanted to ask Eduard but had been unable to find a way to do it without sounding presumptuous, so here she was, on her way to the convent. And it would be the best thing for the child, really it would. Though, if so, why did she feel so damned guilty?

Life in Stare Miasto was hard. Hana and Zuzi had told them about the wonders of the near-normal existence in Śródmieście and it seemed impossible to believe people were dining out a few streets away. Jacob, at least, had stayed in the modern centre with Szymon's platoon, holding the Telephone Exchange. It was a relief to them all to know he was relatively safe and he was doing a wonderful job of collecting flour and sending it through the sewers with Hana, who was taking the route regularly. She and her fellows were starting to be known as Kanalarki – canal-travellers – though Zuzi, jealous of her Minerki label, still insisted on calling them sewer rats. Orla found it funny watching her sisters sparring over their roles, but she didn't like to think too closely about the dangers both of them were enduring.

Hana had sat up on Babcia's bed with Orla last night describing the trip through the sewers and, even though she suspected her sister had spared them the worst of the details, it sounded horrific. Hana said that they were looking to evacuate all AK, medics and ancillary staff to Śródmieście if no external help came in the next few days and Orla wasn't sure which scared her more – being stuck amongst the burning remains of Stare Miasto or going into the sewers.

'At least you won't have to do that, sweetie,' she said to Nella as she reached the end of a run of cellars and had to take the stairs up to the outside. 'The nuns will be part of the surrender and no one is going to hurt nuns, not even the Nazis. You'll be safe with them.'

Above ground, the air was fiercely hot. A house across the street was burning. The front wall had been blown away and the one-time inhabitants were huddled together watching their lovingly decorated rooms being eaten up by the greedy flames and sent down on them in clouds of sticky ash.

'Go into the cellars,' Orla urged them.

The mother looked at her, her eyes wild. 'It's burning. It's all burning.'

'Go into the cellars,' Orla said again, taking her shoulders and gently turning her away as the top floor collapsed in on itself, toppling two beds and a cot into the inferno. 'Get your children down below.'

'What's the point?' the woman asked. 'We're done for.'

But she still put her arms around her children and led them

down to join the many other refugees beneath the earth. A painted PW had fallen with the wall and Orla turned her head away from the shattered pieces of the once bold AK symbol, trying not to see a message in its ruin. Dust filled the air and she pulled her collar up over her mouth and tried to do the same for Nella, though the baby tugged it crossly away and rubbed at her eyes.

'Let's go,' Orla said to her, turning her steps towards the barricade at the end of the road.

It was manned by two weary AK soldiers, little older than Jacob, but seeing her with a baby they stepped forward like true gentlemen to draw her in tight against the sandbags.

'Fritz is in that building up there,' one of them told her, pointing to an apartment past the barricade, 'but he shouldn't see you with the glare of the fire.' He grimaced. 'Every cloud...'

Orla thanked him. Holding Nella close, she ducked her head down and, at his signal, dashed along the back of the barricade to get across the street. There she could dip back down into the cellars on the far side and take the final underground run to the convent.

The Sisters of the Sacrament had been in Warsaw since 1688, an institution of the city seen only through their beautiful church of St Kazimierz when they opened it to the public for feast day services. They were a closed community and had not allowed any outsiders into the convent for centuries, but on the first day of the uprising, an AK officer had knocked on their door and respectfully asked to be allowed to station a platoon there. The convent was on the eastern edge of Stare Miasto, high above one of the most solid sections of the ancient walls, and so, he had explained to the Mother Superior, a perfect vantage point for defence.

A holy woman first, but a Pole a close second, the Holy Mother had not hesitated, but welcomed the men – the first males to ever cross the sanctified threshold – and installed them in her office. It had been a coveted post, with access to the nun's kitchen and extensive gardens, but the nuns had gone on to throw open their doors to the homeless and orphans, and now their food was as short as anyone else's. Their love, however, was boundless and Orla was sure Alicja would be happy to have them caring for her daughter.

'Here we are,' she said brightly to Nella, though the child was grizzling unhappily at the dark, dusty journey.

The Minerki had blasted this route right into the convent cellar and she could take the steps up into the cloisters. The old arches were beautiful and gave Orla an instant feeling of security, although they were far from peaceful, lined as they were with destitute families making paltry homes in the alcoves. A nun stood up from praying with one group and came to Orla.

'Can I help you, child?'

'Thank you, yes. I have an orphan...'

She indicated Nella, who took one look at the woman in her austere gown and wimple and buried her face in Orla's shoulder. The nun gave Orla a kindly smile.

'Perhaps it would be best if you brought the little mite through yourself? This way.'

Orla followed her down the cloister towards what must, in happier times, have been a gracious and peaceful chapter house but was now crammed full of cots and beds of all shapes and sizes. Babies sat in every cot, and toddlers played between them with a variety of makeshift toys. There had to be over a hundred children in here.

'So many?' she gasped.

The nun put her hands together.

'War is cruel, child, especially on those not actively engaged in it.'

Orla had seen that day in day out at the hospital but it seemed more starkly obvious here. All these children had been deprived of their parents and left to be brought up by strangers just to fulfil some maniac's desire to turn the world German.

'It's hateful,' she said.

'It is, my dear, but we cannot let the hate suck us in. We must fight it with love.'

'Is love as powerful as a Nazi tank?' Orla asked morosely, but the nun was swift to answer.

'Oh, my child, it is far, far more powerful. For love, you see, will exist long after we are gone, long after the tanks are rusted and the men who ordered them into our country are in their graves. Love is more than just one person, or even two people, love is the sum of those good humans who take the time to care for each other, whatever is going on around them, and that cannot be wiped out by any weapon, however brutal.'

Orla smiled at her. 'You're right.'

'It is as Jesus taught us – "love your neighbour as you love yourself".'

'I wish he was here to tell the Nazis that,' Orla said, and the nun chuckled.

'That would be a wonder indeed, but as He cannot, it is down to us to carry His message. Peace will come, I know it, and some of us will be here to see it. That is enough.'

She bowed her head in a brief prayer and Orla watched, in awe of her goodness. She was right, of course, but Orla couldn't help a selfish wish to be one of those who *were* here – and for her family too, not to mention Eduard.

'Anyway,' the nun said, looking up again, 'Jesus also said "suffer the little children to come to me", so shall I take this sweetie?' She put out her hands for Nella, but Nella burrowed even deeper into Orla. 'Come now,' the nun said, more crisply, 'this lady has other people to look after.'

Other people to look after. The words bounced hollowly around inside Orla's head. Nella had been in Orla's arms when her mother had died, not five metres away, and an anonymous nun was telling the little girl she was less important than 'other people'.

'What's her name?' the nun asked.

'Nella,' Orla told her. 'Daniella. She was named after her father, Daniel, who was killed last year.'

'Poor thing,' the nun crooned but she was looking round the room, and who could blame her? There were a hundred children needing her attention. And only one Nella.

'I'm not sure about this,' Orla spluttered.

'Best done quickly, child. Come.'

The nun reached out suddenly, grabbing for Nella and setting her into a cot with another baby, a sickly-looking little boy who set up a loud wail at his new companion. Nella pulled herself to standing, clinging to the bars, tears streaming down her face as she stared at Orla.

'Best you get going, child. It's harder if you draw it out and—'

'Mama!' The word came from Nella's mouth, loud and clear. Orla stopped dead and stared at her. 'Mama,' she said again, reaching out her little arms.

Orla's heart broke. She couldn't do this. It might be chaotic and unsanitary at Babcia's, but at least there were people there to love Nella, including Orla herself. And, yes, it might mean that Eduard did not want to be her husband, but if he was the sort of man to turn his back on an orphan, maybe he wasn't the husband she needed anyway.

'Nella!' She stepped over and swept the little girl back into her arms.

'This is sentimentality, child,' the nun tutted.

Orla touched her hand to her heart, feeling it almost physically swell with a rush of protective affection for the baby clinging tightly to her.

'No, Sister,' she told her, 'this is love.'

The nun smiled and nodded. 'In that case, God bless you and see you safe.'

Orla bowed her head for the blessing and then, with a silent apology to the other children she could not carry with her, she clasped Nella tight and headed back down the cloisters, back down the stairs and home to her family. She felt the child's fingers tangle in her hair, her little legs clamp around her waist, and her heart beat against her own, and clutched her close as she ducked beneath Warsaw once more. Nella was her daughter now; she was a Dąbrowska and she would stay with them for as long as they all had breath.

TWENTY-NINE

ZUZI

Zuzi pulled her chair closer to Kamilla's bed, straining to hear her grandmother's breathing, terrified it was going to stop. It was the middle of the night and she should be asleep. She was certainly tired enough but Tosia had said yesterday that she was moving the Minerki to Śródmieście to help attack the Nazis around other strongholds and she wanted this time with her grandmother before she had to go.

Orla and Hana were asleep in the one-time living room next door, little Nella peacefully tucked between them. Zuzi hadn't been surprised when her sweet-natured sister had returned with the baby yesterday. She'd seen the city's crammed orphanages in her work and could imagine that leaving the girl who'd so quickly become a part of their family's world would have been beyond Orla. Having her to care for her was complicated, perhaps, but with the house already crammed with patients and refugees, what was one more?

It was curiously peaceful. The Nazis didn't usually attack at night as, with no Allied aircraft challenging the Stukas in the skies, they could raid with impunity beneath the bright sun. That made daytimes precarious but did at least offer some respite in the softer hours of darkness. Many civilians were sleeping in the day now, huddled down in the cellars, and came out for some air at night, tracing their way silently around the rubble of their former homes like ghosts.

Zuzi looked awkwardly around. Bronislaw was working tonight but the disturbingly handsome doctor was, thankfully, over in the far corner tending to a man with burns down one side. The burn injuries were often the worst, turning huge patches of skin a raw, inflamed red that pulsed painfully if left open to the hot, dust-filled air of Warsaw. One of the hospital's greatest challenges was to find enough bandages to bind them against the worst of the exposure and many patients were wrapped in strips torn from sheets, blouses and shirts.

If Zuzi found any textiles on her trips to attack-sites, she brought them back for Orla and Bron, but they were usually filthy and, with water so terribly short, it was impossible to get them clean enough to wrap around the tender skin. Wounded Warsaw was spiralling in on itself and they had to get people out to Śródmieście, but there were thousands trapped in Stare Miasto and, even with the sewers offering a semi-safe passage, they would never get them all out. Many, besides, would not be up to making the journey; Babcia was one of them.

'Breathe, Babcia,' she urged, then wondered if that was mean.

Should she be asking her dear grandmother to fight to stay in this life, or be inviting her to surrender to God and join her husband and son in a better place? The wound in Kamilla's stomach was still oozing unpleasantly and Zuzi reached for her grandmother's hand as she remembered the battle in the cemetery when she'd been shot. She'd been so full of life that night, throwing grenades of her own making into Bartek's 'kill box', screaming 'that one's for Kaczper' as she sent a Nazi to his death. Scrolling further back in her memories, she could see her grandmother blowing a pigeon out of the tree with such gay aplomb to impress her undoubted skills on Tosia and join the Minerki. Oh, she'd been wonderful that day – so passionate and determined and alive.

Zuzi sighed. It was only three weeks ago that she'd stood on top of the barricades in Wola as Babcia triumphantly stuck their hated portrait of Hitler on top for the enemy to shoot at, but it felt like almost another lifetime. For three glorious days the uprising had been a success, a liberation. They'd been so pleased with themselves, so proud that they'd opened the door of Warsaw for the Russians. But the Russians hadn't come and the Nazis had brought an arsenal from hell down on them, and now here they were – living in smoke and shadows.

'How's she doing?'

Bronislaw had trodden so lightly that Zuzi hadn't heard him come up and she jumped as he leaned over the patient, his chest brushing her hand where it held Babcia's. Fire flared in her belly and, yes, a little lower, and she remembered Babcia telling her that these discomfiting feelings were: 'God's way of telling you that you'll make wonderful babies with him.' Bron was looking curiously at her and that thought was not helping, so she battled to push it away and look at him as a professional.

'Not good I don't think, Doctor.'

He sat down on the chair at her side.

'I've told you, Zuzi, call me Bron. Please.'

She dared to look at him and he looked back with such concern and care that this time the feelings were less like fire and more a warm blanket wrapping around her.

'Not good I don't think, Bron.'

He placed his hand over hers. 'You need to prepare yourself.'

Tears clogged her throat and she could only nod. It was

exactly what she'd been thinking but hearing someone else say it made it all too real.

'She's suffering?' she choked out.

'I don't think so, no, but her body has had enough and is quietly shutting down.'

Now the tears did fall. She turned away to try and hide them, but Bron, unfazed, put his arm around her shoulder and pulled her to him, wiping them gently with his finger.

'God will take care of her now, Zuzi.'

'He'll do a better job than we have,' she said wryly, looking around the cluttered, dirty remains of Babcia's once beautiful house.

'You've been remarkable, all of you. You have a wonderful family, Zuzi, and seeing you with your sisters is so lovely. You obviously have a tight bond.'

'One that survives us squabbling constantly?'

'Yes. It's the best kind. You can disagree with someone and still love them. They can irritate the hell out of you, but you'd still do anything for them.'

Zuzi looked at him. He had pulled her gently away from Babcia's bed, his arm still around her and his face was close to hers as they whispered in the muted light of the hospital at night. Looking into his eyes she felt the horrors of Warsaw receding into their own shadows, leaving them in a tiny, perfect world of their own.

'Is that how you feel about your family?'

'Oh yes.' A smile spread instantly across his face and Zuzi's heart lifted to see it.

'Can you tell me about them?'

He looked surprised. 'I'd love to. But do we have time? Should you not be resting?'

'Talking to you is rest enough.'

Goodness, she hadn't meant to say that out loud, but it was true all the same and he squeezed her shoulders.

'Thank you. I'm, I'm not sure where to begin...'

Zuzi leaned into him.

'Orla says your mother is a midwife.'

'She is.' His eyes shone. 'And a wonderful one. The best in Łódź, I swear. Mind you, that was a nuisance when I was a child. We could never go anywhere without a message coming. If we had a meal out, or went to the cinema, or even the park, sooner or later we'd hear: "Could Midwife Kaminski please report to the telephone." And she'd be off, kissing us apologetically goodbye and going to bring some other child into the world. I used to resent it when I was small, complain that other families got to see more of her than we did, but as I got older I learned to love her dedication to her duty. And, besides' – he shot Zuzi a sudden cheeky grin that set the fire burning inside her again – 'there were as many people bringing us treats to say thank you as calling for her services. There was never a shortage of cakes and pies in our house.'

'She sounds wonderful,' Zuzi said. 'And your father? Bartek? He seems a good man too.'

'Oh, he is, though the man you know is not the one I grew up with. He was a printer back in Łódź; a quiet, unassuming man, not the warrior you see here in Warsaw.'

'War changes people, I suppose.'

'Brings out a different side of them, certainly. My father was always fiercest in the protection of his family, and with my mother and brother in the camps...'

'He's desperate to get them free.'

Bronislaw nodded. 'As am I, though I am not, I fear, as warrior-like as Tata.'

'My mother says we all fight in our own way,' Zuzi said.

He sent her a grateful smile.

'She's right. Honestly, Zuzi, if I had to go in and do what you do, I'd be hopeless. I'd get myself blown up in the first strike and then what use would I be to anyone? You're amazing.'

Zuzi shifted but his arm stayed tight around her and there was nowhere to go.

'Thank you,' she managed. 'But I'd be useless with the whole caring for people thing. I'm far too impatient.'

'We fight in our own ways?'

'Exactly.'

'I like that.' He paused, still looking into her eyes. 'But I also think you're amazing.'

The fire flared, hot and insistent inside Zuzi. This man, this gorgeous, clever, capable man thought she was amazing. She wanted to lean in, to press her lips to his, but that would surely be far too forward.

'What are your brothers' names?' she stuttered.

He blinked. 'Zander and Jakub.'

'Jakub? Like mine?'

'Yes, but my little brother is in a labour camp somewhere. Both of them are. The last we heard they'd been sent to somewhere called Mauthausen and I can only pray they are together there and they are safe.'

Zuzi tried to conceive what it would be like not knowing where Hana and Orla were and her heart ached just with the imagining of it.

'That must be so hard. When did you see them last?'

'February 1943. The Gestapo raided our house and took all three of them away. Tata and I were tipped off and hid with kind friends for a few days but when we heard that Mama, Zander and Jakub had been shipped away, we fled for Warsaw. Tata had been introduced to Bór when he'd been forging documents for the Jews in Łódź ghetto, and they were swift to offer him a role in the AK. I volunteered too but when they found out I was a doctor, they sent me to the John of God and I've been learning there ever since.'

'February 1943.' Zuzi shook her head. 'That's a year and a half ago.'

'One year, six months and fifteen days,' he said, then blushed. 'I keep a tally.'

'I don't blame you. I would too. Family are everything.'

'Yes.' His arm was still around her shoulders, his face centimetres from hers. 'I always think,' he said, his voice husky, 'how lucky my parents were to find each other, to be so happy together, for it has made us, their children, happy too.'

Zuzi nodded. 'My parents the same, though it did mean my mother was torn apart when Tata died.'

'He was executed?'

She fought tears once more, but she had speak out for him. Had to bear witness.

'They flung him off the balcony of the Pawiak prison with a noose around his neck.'

Bron gasped. 'In front of you?'

'Yes. In front of all of us. We were made to watch at gunpoint. It was, was...'

'Unspeakable?'

'No,' she shot back. 'I mean, yes, it feels that way but we have to speak about it, don't we? We can't be silent in our suffering. People must *know*. They must know what these monsters did to us – what they're still doing to us. They must know about the ghettos and the camps – that those bastards are exterminating our Jewish population in cold blood and now they're after the rest of us. They must know about the massacre in Wola and the bombing of our hospitals. What the Nazis are doing to Poland isn't war, Bron, it's annihilation – cold-blooded, calculated annihilation.'

Her voice had risen and she bit on her lip to silence herself. Bron gave a low moan and she stilled, looking deep into his eyes. She tried to remember what Orla had said about romance – something about it not being hearts and flowers but a deep connection with someone. She wanted that, wanted it now. She leaned towards Bronislaw and he responded instantly, bringing his lips to hers, the mere touch of him sending her whole body singing. His hand went around the back of her head, pulling her in, and she returned his kiss, their little world exploding in the touch of their mouths. Zuzi forgot war, she forgot occupation, she forgot bombs and nooses and miserable sickbeds, she forgot the fire raging through Warsaw and let herself drop into the one raging between herself and this amazing man.

'Zuzi.' He moaned her name against her lips and she ran her hands down his back, pulling him even closer. 'I want you, Zuzi.'

'Bron, I—'

'I mean I want you in my life. Always. I want you as my—'

But at that moment, Babcia Kamilla cried out. Horrified at herself, Zuzi tore her gaze from Bronislaw's, yanked out of his arms, and ran back to her grandmother.

'Babcia? Babcia, are you hurting?'

Kamilla clawed for her hand.

'Not for much longer,' she rasped. 'I am going to Aleksander, Zuzi. I'm sorry to leave you all but I, I...' She gasped for breath and Zuzi clutched at her hand, willing her to hold on.

'Zuzi,' Bron said behind her but she could not talk to him, not now. She had kissed him, had thrown herself into his arms, neglecting her grandmother, and she was ashamed of herself. Whatever Babcia had said about following her feelings, she would not have meant at the expense of the comfort of your family and most definitely not at the expense of herself.

'Fetch my sisters,' she choked out.

She felt Bron leave her side and forced herself to ignore the cold shudder that his absence sent through her. This was not about her now.

'We love you, Babcia,' she said.

Babcia recovered her breath enough to tut.

'Love,' she muttered, scathingly, but then broke into a soft smile. 'What more is there?'

Then Orla and Hana were scrambling in at Zuzi's side and Magda came running from the kitchen. She swept Kamilla's silver cross off the makeshift altar and brought it over, holding it above the bed. Kamilla's milky eyes fixed on it and she smiled again.

'Take care of each other,' she said with new energy. 'Take care of the family. Take care of Warsaw.'

And then, with the softest of sighs, she closed her eyes.

'Is she gone?' Hana sobbed.

Zuzi had no idea and was grateful when Orla leaned over, feeling for a pulse with new expertise, before nodding sadly.

'She's gone.'

'Gone to God,' Magda said. 'And to her dear Alekzander and Kaczper.'

Her voice broke and Zuzi slid a hand into hers. Her mother looked surprised but held onto it tightly as she laid the silver cross on Kamilla's bosom and they bowed their heads in shared grief. Zuzi's head whirled. How could breath just stop like that? How could life just end? She had seen it all around her for three long, dark weeks, but Babcia Kamilla had always seemed to have enough life in her for five people, and to see that extinguished dug deep inside her – deep where she had been indulging wanton passions just a heartbeat ago. It had been wrong of her. There was a war on here, a hard, vital, urgent war, and she had to focus on that.

In the corner, Bronislaw hovered, but there was no time for romance right now and she never should have let herself be distracted by it. 'Take care of Warsaw,' Babcia had asked of them with her final breaths and, her heart breaking at the loss of the woman on whom she had modelled herself all her life, she vowed to do so until their beloved, broken city was free at last.

THIRTY
25 AUGUST

HANA

They buried Babcia, not with a grand mass in a beautiful basilica attended by hundreds of well-dressed mourners, but in a hasty ceremony in her own back yard between Stuka attacks.

'It's not what she would have wanted,' Magda fretted.

'It's a warrior's burial,' Zuzi said stoutly.

'We're here and that's what counts,' Orla added.

Hana supposed it was and moved closer into the huddle of her family as they waited for a break in the bombing to go out and bless their grandmother's final resting place. It had hit them all hard. Someone had gone to Śródmieście to fetch Jacob, and Szymon Ancel had brought him back personally and was standing respectfully to one side. Poor Jacob looked lost as he pressed close to Magda, a child once more, despite the Prussian helmet clutched tightly under his arm. Hana hated to see it but was glad he was with them. So many families were divided, stuck in different parts of Warsaw with only the valiant work of the postal Scouts keeping them in touch. The Dąbrowskas were lucky to still be together and they needed to stay close right now.

Orla was weeping openly, cuddling Nella and letting her tears soak into the baby's soft hair, and Hana envied her youngest sister her easy grief. Zuzi, in contrast, stood rigid, her arms wrapped around herself as she fought not to cry. Bronislaw was hovering, as he had been hovering all night, but Zuzi was resolutely refusing to look his way and Hana willed her spiky sister to let this lovely man into her life. They all needed comfort and Zuzi more than most. She'd been closest to Babcia, and had been with her both when she'd been shot and when the hospital roof had collapsed. Hana feared Zuzi took her death as her personal responsibility and hated to see her suffering.

The Stukas cleared from the skies and the priest, crossing himself, stepped hastily out onto what had once been a beautiful lawn to begin the service before the next wave came whining in on Warsaw. He took his place at the head of the mound of earth covering Babcia and the family joined him. Eduard had dug the grave at first light, before heading off on his stretcher-bearing duties, and he and Bronislaw had laid Kamilla to rest wrapped in her wedding sheets, carefully saved at the bottom of a carved wooden chest.

At least they had Babcia's body to bury and pay their last respects, Hana thought. Emil's was deep in the Vistula, unknown and unmarked, save by the writing on her heart. She would get him a proper grave one day, when this was over, but for now burying her grandmother felt mixed up with burying her fiancé and she bowed her head at the priest's hasty intonations and prayed for them both.

The grave, at least, was marked in a way fitting for a woman of Babcia Kamilla's pride and stature and Hana looked, through tears, at the grand silver cross standing brightly amongst the many wooden ones already filling the ruined garden. Babcia's once beautiful flowerbeds had been scorched by the endless fires, so the only colours marking her grave were the jewels in her cross, but they shone fiercely in the relentless sun, casting incongruously pretty patterns across the dark earth beneath which she lay. Hana was glad of this reminder of beauty on God's scorched earth.

'May the good Lord bless and keep her soul, Amen.'

The priest bowed his head and they all repeated 'Amen', the word barely out before the telltale whine of a Stuka sent them scurrying back into the building, their funeral as interrupted as everything else in beleaguered Warsaw. Hana paused in the doorway to look back and the cross seemed almost to wink at her as the light flashed down on it off the silver side of the passing bomber. She smiled at last.

'Look,' she said to the others. 'Even in death, Babcia Kamilla is shouting defiance at the enemy.'

Orla and Zuzi came close, arms around each other, and as Hana glanced from one to the other, she felt the ever-present duty of care to her younger siblings.

'She'd want us to be happy,' she said.

'*You're* not happy,' Zuzi shot back.

Hana swallowed. 'I'm sad at losing Emil, yes, but I'm happy I still have all of you.'

'For now.'

'Don't say that,' Orla protested, hitching Nella higher on her hip. 'We just have to stay alive and, somehow, things will improve.'

She kissed the baby's soft nose and Hana watched her fondly. 'Is Eduard glad Nella is back with us?' she dared to ask.

Orla shrugged. 'I haven't had much chance to talk to him, with...' She gestured to the grave. 'But it was my decision and I'm sticking by it.'

'Quite right.' Hana looked at her youngest sister, saw new

steel in her shoulders, and admired her for it. 'You did a good thing, Orls.'

'I did? Babcia would probably call me a sentimental fool and I am – sentimental, that is – but I don't think that's so foolish any more.'

'I think it's brave,' Hana told her stoutly. 'Don't you, Zuzi?'

'What?'

'Don't you think it's brave to allow sentiment to rule yourself?'

'Sentiment? No. Well, not right now, not in wartime. Babcia told us we had to care for Warsaw.'

'She also told us we had to care for each other.'

'And I will.' Zuzi looked at Hana and Orla with ferocity. 'I'd die for you both. Mama and Jacob too.'

Hana swallowed. 'Thank you, I think, but that's not quite what I meant.' She plucked up her courage. 'I think Bronislaw wants to talk to you…'

She indicated the still hovering doctor but Zuzi shook her head.

'No time. I've got to get back to work. Babcia would expect it of me – and of you too.'

'Babcia would understand—' Hana started but, with a sharp kiss for them both, Zuzi was turning away. 'Take care, Zuzi!' Hana called after her. 'See you at sunfall, yes?'

'See you at sunfall,' Zuzi called over her shoulder and then she was gone, off into the remains of Stare Miasto to fight on, and Hana could only pray the grief she was holding far too tightly to herself would not cloud her judgement in the perilous situations ahead.

'I suppose I'd better go too,' she said reluctantly to Orla.

If she was honest, she was weary of war, weary of hunger and pain and grief. She meant it about being happy to still have her family but it felt as if all they were doing now was clinging onto each other, adrift on a crumbling lifeboat, far from shore.

Warsaw had risen up, sent out a message of defiance to the world, and the world had not listened. The world, it seemed, did not care about them and she could not help glancing back to Babcia's body in its shallow grave and wondering how many of them would be laid next to her before this was over.

'Come on,' she told herself crossly, 'Babcia would not approve of this sort of snivelling self-pity.' She would, as Zuzi had said, tell her to get back to work. And really, what else – save curl up in a useless ball and weep – was there to do anyway?

An hour later, Hana stood in Bór's HQ, looking in concern at her boss. He'd been having headaches since the dark day when the tank had exploded outside his office and it was clear today was a bad one. His eyes were screwed up against the endless sunshine pouring in through the windows and his fingers were scrubbing at his temples as if trying to dig the pain out.

'Should you not be in bed, sir?' Hana asked nervously.

'No time for that,' came the abrupt response and Hana supposed that was true, but could not imagine trying to run this nightmare feeling the way he did. His wife was apparently still alive somewhere in Warsaw, with his two-year-old son and another baby due at any time, but he could not be with them and that must be terrible. Hana was sure she wouldn't have got this far without her family to cuddle up with every sunfall and her heart ached for the AK's strained commander. She looked nervously to Agaton, who stepped forward.

'We're almost ready to evacuate Stare Miasto, sir, and I think the Homeland Council should go first. The radio is on its last legs and what use is a command centre if it cannot make contact with those it's meant to be commanding?'

'Fair point,' Bór grunted and Hana thought she saw relief cross his brow. 'And Śródmieście is still solid, you say?'

'Rock solid, sir.'

'I don't need to surrender?'

'Surrender?!' Agaton cried and Bór winced again. 'Sorry, sir, but why would you surrender?'

'Some people are calling for it. They think our situation is hopeless. Is it hopeless, Agaton?'

Hana saw her boss hesitate, but he recovered and answered stoutly, 'Not if the Allies help.'

Bór sighed. 'I message London every day. The Americans have vast supplies in some warehouse, waiting to be flown to us once Stalin lets them use Russian bases, and Churchill has instructed the RAF to fly from Brindisi again.'

Hana felt her heart, already battered from this morning's sorrows, throb with new pain. Pilots would be flying but Emil Andrysiak would not be among them. There would be no violet over Warsaw but that did not lessen the value of the supplies his fellows would so bravely bring.

'That's excellent news, sir,' she forced out.

'Excellent,' Agaton agreed. 'We will send messages to all the troops immediately. Usual signal on the BBC?'

Bór nodded and closed his eyes. Hana saw him fight the pain in his head and wished Mr Churchill and Mr Roosevelt could see the pressure this man and his brave city were under. She was under no illusions that Mr Stalin would care – Russians were as inured to Polish suffering as Germans – but perhaps, if the Western Allies could witness the horrors of life here, the men who had liberated Rome and Paris might force his hand for Warsaw.

'We will let them know and will put plans for evacuation of yourself and your staff into motion, sir. Warsaw needs you safe.'

Bór smiled wearily.

'I'm not sure I'm so good for Warsaw,' he said, but then visibly shook off his doubts and gave Agaton a sharp salute. 'Onwards! Thank you, Agaton.'

He wrote out the new directive with an almost steady hand and gave it to Agaton. He and Hana left the office and she reached for the slip to start doing the rounds of the AK units, but Agaton held it back.

'I know where the maps are, Hana.'

Hana stared at him. 'Marek's maps? How? Where?!'

'How is simple. I paid a visit to our Exchange prisoners and they were... persuaded to offer up the information.'

'You didn't torture them?'

Agaton gave her a wry smile.

'I don't think I've got that in me even if I wanted to. No, I merely employed my most persuasive German and told them that the information might buy them a pass to a POW camp in the countryside. The bastards hate being trapped in the city as much as we do.'

'They get out and we're stuck here?'

'They are sent away to the forest and we remain to hold our city.'

Hana nodded grimly. 'So where are our maps?'

'In the university.'

Hana groaned. The university buildings, at the top of the Saxon Gardens, had been held by the Wehrmacht garrison throughout the uprising and were protected by the fortified corridor the SS murderers had forged through that area from Wola.

'Your prisoner told you that?'

'He was very certain. They're in the one-time history department, he said, in an office on the ground floor. Someone has stuck one on the wall, apparently, and they cross buildings out on it whenever they blow them up.'

'Bastards,' Hana burst out. 'Treating us like we're some sort of board game.'

She hated the thought of a group of thuggish Nazi soldiers gleefully marking off people's hard-earned homes as they went up in smoke. Did they have a tally of people they'd murdered, too? A book running on how many Polish limbs had been lost, perhaps? It made her blood boil, but they were helpless before the German firepower.

'The maps are all lost to us then?' she said sadly. 'Both the plans of the existing buildings and the proposals for the new ones?'

It was a small matter, she supposed, compared to people's lives, but it felt like yet another cruel injustice being heaped on the Poles.

'Maybe.' Agaton patted her arm. 'And maybe it's better this way. Maybe it means that when we finally get our city back – what remains of it – we'll have to build it anew. It will be a chance to forge a totally modern, purpose-built city.'

'Like the Bolsheviks do?'

'I suppose so. Only less austere.'

'But what about our history? What about all that the palaces and civic buildings and townhouses say of hundreds of years of civilisation?'

Agaton looked at her and smiled. 'Hark at you, my little modernist!'

Hana went to the glassless window-opening and looked out across Stare Miasto. Skeletons of once-proud buildings stood stark against the bright sky, their contents exposed to view, their dignity stripped by enemy fire. It made her sad. These buildings had stood witness to so many events in Warsaw's chequered history. Some of them had been here since it had supplanted Kraków as Poland's capital in 1596 and that was a point of pride for Warsawians. The city had never, perhaps, been as picture-book pretty as its southern counterpart but the heart of the nation had beaten within it. *Still* beat within it, even if the body that held it was being battered into non-existence.

'Modern design is good,' she said carefully. 'But it is best when it stands as a counterpoint to the old. We should add to the rich architectural history of our cities, not replace it.'

Agaton smiled sadly at her. 'War has taught you wisdom.'

She sighed. 'If that's what it takes, I'd rather stay foolish. Besides, what can we do? The enemy are annihilating our rich architectural history every single day and it would seem that they also have the maps that would allow us to restore it. We're stuck, Agaton.'

'Unless we get them back.'

'Sorry?'

'One of my platoon used to work at the university. He was a professor of Classics, but that's beside the point. He says the sewers run right below it. He was friends with a history professor who lectured on them as an example of nineteenth-century design, and used to regularly take students down a manhole in the rear quadrangle behind his department to see it for themselves.'

'I'm sure they loved that!' Hana laughed.

'It was a curiosity for them; now it's a necessity for us. And I'm thinking that—'

'If we could get to that manhole, we could sneak into the buildings and find the maps?'

'Exactly.'

'It's an excellent idea.'

Agaton grabbed her arm. 'It isn't, Hana. It's crazy. Whoever attempted it would be smuggling themselves into the heart of the Wehrmacht, and only a fool would do that.'

'A fool with a very worthy aim.'

'But a fool all the same. It's too risky.' He smiled at her. 'We can build new buildings.'

'We can,' Hana agreed, 'just like we can take new people into our family – but if they are all new, is it the same family?'

'More wisdom, Hana?'

She laughed. 'I don't know about that. War might teach us wisdom but maybe, despite that, it forces us to act like fools.'

Agaton put up a hand. 'It's too risky, Hana. Now come on – we've got messages to deliver. We don't want those planes arriving without a welcoming committee, do we?'

He was off and Hana followed him automatically, but her head was spinning like a streak of violet heading into the Vistula. People took risks to capture buildings, to hold barricades, to kill enemy leaders, so why not to find the maps that might enable them to rebuild their city? Was not national pride as big a gain as a small square of territory? The reward was less immediate, perhaps, but no less tangible in the long run of Warsaw's history. Emil had taken a huge risk flying his plane here to try and help the city and he had paid the price. Should she not, then, take her turn?

'Take care of Warsaw,' Babcia had urged them with her final breaths and perhaps this was the way that Hana could do that? At least it would be something positive. She was very aware that she'd made the family swear not to take too many risks, but that had been back at the start of the uprising, when it had looked like it might actually succeed. Now Babcia was dead and Emil was dead and the game had changed. In the middle of a war zone, what, at the end of the danger-strewn days, was really *too* risky?

THIRTY-ONE
28 AUGUST

ORLA

'I know it's disgusting, but it's all we've got.' Orla smiled apologetically at the patient to whom she was feeding the thin soup Magda had cobbled together from the brewery barley. 'Spit the husks out.'

'We're all husks,' the young man groaned. 'The world has spat us out.'

Orla privately agreed but what good did it do anyone to be negative?

'My sister tells me the British are sending planes again,' she said brightly.

That was true, though Hana had said it with a dark tone, laced with grief for the one pilot who would not be flying in. If she was honest, Orla could barely remember Emil Andrysiak. She'd only been thirteen when he'd had to flee Warsaw at the start of the war and she'd been far too wrapped up in her own affairs to pay much attention to her big sister's fiancé. She had hazy recollections of a tall man with dark hair, a dapper moustache and brown eyes that shone whenever he looked at her sister. More vivid was the picture of how Hana's had shone back. Orla and her friends had been making their first forays into romantic fiction at the time and Hana's engagement had seemed like their favourite stories come to life. Now it was over.

'Will the British bring ammunition?' the soldier asked, pushing himself up eagerly, although his left arm was too mauled to ever hold a weapon again.

'Food, hopefully,' Orla shot back. 'Now come on, more soup.'

He groaned but let her feed him another spoonful of the rough broth. The men were calling it plujka – spit-soup – because of the endless husks but there was no time to sieve them out before serving and, besides, if you chewed on them, you could get a little more sustenance. Or at least distract your empty tummy for longer.

August was nearly at an end but the uprising was not. Orla recalled the heady beginning when they'd thought they'd only need to hold their merry barricades for three or four days before the Russians came to seal their liberation. A month had passed since then and the Russians seemed happy to sit still, their much-vaunted plan to blast through to Berlin abandoned in favour of watching the Poles burn. Orla tried not to hate anyone but it was hard right now.

'We'll soon be heading to Śródmieście,' she said to the soldier, 'and I'm told it's like normal over there. They even have cafés and restaurants.'

'With better soup than this?'

'Can't be much worse.'

He chuckled but then shook his head at his broken arm. 'They won't evacuate useless lumps like me though, will they? They'll leave me here for the Nazis to take out.'

'All AK who can walk are to be evacuated, I'm told.'

'Really?' His eyes lit up. 'Right, Nurse, let me out of this bed.'

'Not until you eat your soup,' she said sternly.

He groaned but obediently opened his mouth for the next spoonful and Orla shovelled it in. A happy giggle from the kitchen made her glance over and she smiled to see Nella laughing at Magda playing peek-a-boo with her from behind a frying pan. The baby was as thin as the rest of them but cheery and Orla thanked God a hundred times a day for stopping her leaving her at the orphanage.

Hana had guided the Homeland Council through the sewers last night and returned exhausted but triumphant. Several of the forty staff, including the government delegate, were well over sixty, so expecting them to travel over a kilometre though five-foot sewers had been a big ask. They had, by the sounds of it, been as brave as you would expect of the men leading the uprising and they had all made it. That was good, she supposed, but what had they come to, that travelling bent double through the darkness, knee-deep in a thousand people's poo, was an attractive option?

She shuddered at the thought of enduring it herself, but Stare Miasto was becoming an inferno of falling down walls, so there was little choice. The Nazis were well into the western edges and Babcia's house, on the eastern side, was now within range of their damned rocket launchers. Yesterday, one of the grand houses two doors down had been hit by a huge incendiary and it had only been Bartek's platoon rushing to pull down the intervening building that had saved the one remaining hospital in the area. It would only be a matter of time before they took a hit themselves and Orla had tended too many people writhing in agony from massive burns to consider that prospect with anything other than total panic.

'Come on then,' she said as the man made it valiantly to the end of the soup, his bed a mass of spat-out husks. 'Let's have a go at walking.'

He gladly flung back his sheets and swung his legs over the

side of the bed, putting his good arm around her shoulders for support to heave himself onto his feet. He wobbled and blinked his eyes madly as he fought to overcome the dizziness of being upright for the first time in days, but then steadied and took a firm step forward.

'Good,' Orla said. 'That's really good.'

He took a few more and she went with him, talking encouragingly all the way and trying not to wonder how on earth he would manage through a sewer. Over at the door she saw Eduard arrive. Her heart lifted at the sight of him and then she felt bad because it inevitably meant some other patient to fit into the overcrowded room. Even so, knowing he was alive and well gave her hope and she offered him a little wave that she was relieved to see him return. They'd barely had a moment alone together since she'd come back from the orphanage with Nella and she had no idea how he felt about it, but it wasn't important right now. There would be no future to worry about if they didn't stay focused on surviving the present.

'That's probably enough for now,' she told her patient. Magda was bringing a new cauldron of soup into the hospital and she should go and serve others. 'Let's turn you round and... Oh no!'

The unholy mooing sound of the Kowa rockets cut through the air and everyone in the room froze, waiting the agonising seconds of silence before the six deadly impacts sounded out. Only Nella chattered on, blissfully unaware of the threat, and Orla drank in her childish babble before, with a sickening crack, a silver shell broke through the side wall, embedded itself in Babcia's favourite sideboard and exploded, sending wood flying. Orla flung herself and her patient to the ground, barely hearing his cry of agony over the other wails of pain and alarm and the telltale crackle of fire. Two more rockets hit and the walls shook. They held – for now – but the shells must have been impregnated with sulphur for the fire was spreading fast, licking across the floor and greedily latching onto the wooden furniture and cotton sheets.

'We have to get out!' Orla screamed through the rapidly thickening smoke.

Nearby, Magda had been knocked over, her precious soup spilling across the floor and, momentarily, killing some of the flames. Orla ran to drag her up and push her towards the door. It was still standing but the frame was catching and they wouldn't have long to get through. She looked frantically around for Nella but could see nothing in the chaos. Those patients who could were staggering out, arms over their heads to protect them from the ferocity of the flames as they started to consume the wooden ceiling beams. The heat was unbearable and the smoke clagged in Orla's eyes and throat. She pulled her blouse over her face and blinked madly.

'Nella?! Eduard?!'

She battled to remember where she'd last seen her beau. He'd been by the door. He'd definitely waved at her from the door, but had he gone inside? Was he lying, broken, beneath one of the beams as too many of their patients were?

'Orla, you have to get out.' A man grabbed her arm and she thought it was him but as he leaned in closer, she saw it was Bronislaw.

'Eduard,' she moaned.

'Eduard will look after himself. Come on.'

'Nella won't,' she protested and that's when she heard it – a baby crying. 'Nella!'

To her left, a section of wall had collapsed, opening up a big hole through which some of the smoke rushed. Through the clearer air, Orla saw the worst sight possible – the baby girl, stuck in her high chair in the middle of the flaming kitchen.

'I have to get her.' She tried to dive back in, but Bron was holding her tight. 'Let me go! I have to get her.'

Orla yanked free and took two steps into the room. All the

beams were on fire and the heat was scorching. Nella was maybe ten steps away and she forced herself on but then someone pushed her aside and dived in, sweeping the baby and the chair into his arms and turning back, coughing and spluttering.

'Eduard!'

'Out!'

His eyes were wild as he charged towards her and she did as he bid, rushing for the door and stumbling into the street to leave space for him to escape. For one, two, three heart-stopping seconds he did not come, but then he burst through the door frame and staggered into her arms. He was gasping for breath and Nella was wailing fit to burst but Orla thought she'd never heard sweeter sounds for it meant they were here. They were alive.

'Oh Eduard, you saved her.' She took the baby from the smoking chair, holding her close, then stared up into his dear face. 'You saved Nella.'

'Of course I did,' he said, putting his strong arms around them both. 'She's ours, isn't she?'

Orla burst into tears. 'Ours?'

'Yes. That is, if you'll have me. If you'll let me share her with you? If you'll let me share your life?'

'Share my...? Eduard, of course. That is, I— Eduard, are you hurt?'

He'd let go of her and dropped to his knees and she looked down in horror. Was he injured after all? Had the smoke got into his lungs?

'Orla Dąbrowska,' he said, and he did not sound too hoarse, did not, indeed, sound unwell at all. 'Will you do me the honour of becoming my wife?'

'I...' Her heart soared. 'Yes! Oh Eduard, yes, I—'

'Move please, folks. We need to get away from this building.'

An AK fire officer came bustling up, hauling Eduard unceremoniously to his feet and they had to stagger away together, their moment interrupted, though for all the right reasons. Moving to the open square at the end of the street, they huddled together as Babcia's beautiful house, so long a haven for the family and many more besides, collapsed in a fiery rage. Orla saw Magda being checked over by Bronislaw and a handful of patients taking shaky seats on piles of rubble and her heart broke at how few had made it out. But then she remembered…

She turned to Eduard. 'Did you just ask me to marry you?'

A smile spread across his face. 'I did. Did you just say yes?'

'I did!' She ran to Magda, tugging him after her. 'We're getting married, Mama!'

'God be praised.' Magda threw her arms round her, then kissed Eduard roundly on both cheeks. 'Welcome to the family, dear boy. You're a Dąbrowski now.'

'Well, technically Orla will be…' he started, but stopped himself and grinned. 'Being a Dąbrowski sounds wonderful, doesn't it, Nella?'

He lifted the baby out of Orla's arms, holding her to the skies, and Magda clapped for joy. Hana and Zuzi came running up the street, staring at the burning building in horror. Orla waved.

'Here!' she called, her voice croaky but strong. 'We're over here. We're safe. And we're getting married!'

Then her sisters were upon her and they were one big tangle of love, with Eduard stuck right in the middle but apparently happy to be there. Orla was on the street with no home and no food and no spare clothing but, she swore, she'd never been happier. She just hoped it would last…

PART THREE

We are thinking of world opinion if anti-Nazis in Warsaw are in effect abandoned. We believe that all three of us should do the utmost to save as many of the patriots there as possible. We hope that you will drop immediate supplies and munitions to the patriot Poles of Warsaw, or will you agree to help our planes in doing it very quickly? We hope you will approve. The time element is of extreme importance.

URGENT AND MOST SECRET MESSAGE
FROM PRESIDENT ROOSEVELT AND MR
CHURCHILL TO MARSHAL STALIN 20
AUGUST 1944

THIRTY-TWO

4 SEPTEMBER 1944

ZUZI

Zuzi tugged awkwardly at the skirts of the dress Mama had made her wear. It felt peculiar around her legs after a month in AK trousers and tunic but not, she had to admit, unpleasant. Besides, even she might draw the line at being a bridesmaid in a scruffy old uniform and the very fact that they were here and free and able to dress up and escort Orla to the altar was a cause for celebration.

The family had escaped Stare Miasto through the sewers with the rest of the AK three evenings ago. It had been a night of terror. They'd had to huddle in groups of fifty in the backstreets, waiting with their assigned guide, or Kanalarki as everyone now knew them, for their turn to be signalled forward by the mass of AK around the key manhole in Krasinski Square. It had been surrounded by huge sandbank walls to protect it from the Nazi snipers in the Saxon Gardens and fiercely guarded to stop civilians storming it. A rigid pass system had been in place, with only AK and ancillary staff allowed, but their family had all made it.

Hana, their personal Kanalarki, had secured a pass for Magda as a vital cook and no one would have had the heart to turn away Nella, bound to Eduard's broad chest with an altar cloth recovered from a bombed-out church. The baby had, perhaps, had the luckiest escape, for the night before they'd fled, the Sisters of the Sacrament had been attacked by Stukas, the bombs dropping right into the heart of the church as they led Stare Miasto's many homeless in prayer. Their beautiful church had collapsed in on itself and few had made it out alive.

'God told me to keep Nella,' Orla had said, shaking all over.

'And you were wise enough to listen,' Eduard had told her fondly. 'We are very, very blessed.'

Whether it was God's blessing or pure luck Zuzi was not sure but the Dąbrowskas had prayed uncomfortably for the thousands of wounded AK and civilians left behind. Bór, Hana had told them, had received letters from the Allies saying that combatant status had finally been secured for the AK, meaning that the Germans had to take them into honourable imprisonment as soldiers, rather than shooting them as spies. That might have meant little, save that the worst of the SS units had been sent away from the city and the Wehrmacht were holding a level of control once more. They were still Nazis, so no one trusted them a centimetre, but they were Nazis with some sense of military order and the AK could only hope that the people left behind in Stare Miasto would be treated humanely.

Zuzi had to admit that at one point, halfway down the sewer, with the stench of human waste mixing potently with the stench of human fear, she'd almost wished for surrender. She'd thought, as the wail of someone losing their mind in the rat-ways had echoed down the tunnel, a labour camp – even a Nazi one – would be better than this. But then, somehow, they'd battled on, one hand on the rope hammered into the bricks, the other on the shoulder of the person in front, and had been spat out into a miracle.

Śródmieście was still as mind-blowingly normal as it had been when Zuzi had travelled here to take the Telephone Exchange. True, they had to share a house with three other families, but they had a bedroom of their own and Magda had been offered use of the kitchen for the new Piekarnia Dąbrowska. It wasn't a patch on the original shop, or even on the version she'd operated out of Babcia's grand dining room, but they had flour here and even sugar and raisins, and Magda was in her element baking for the thousands crammed into the area. Even the church in which Orla and Eduard were saying their vows to each other was still intact.

As the organ rang out, Orla took Jacob's arm and stepped without a moment's hesitation through the doors and up the aisle so that Zuzi and Hana had to hasten to stay close behind her.

Jacob walked proudly, his back straight and his arm strong for Orla. He'd acquired a full uniform to go with his helmet and looked suddenly so like their father that Zuzi had to grab the back of the pew to stay upright.

'Kaczper,' Magda whispered as they drew close, clearly seeing it too, but then the boy stepped into a colourful patch of low light shining through the still intact stained window and she wiped a tear from her eye and smiled encouragingly at her son.

Hana moved across to put an arm around their mother and Zuzi guiltily wished she'd thought of that. She was too like her grandmother, that was the problem. Kamilla thought showing emotion was vulgar and Zuzi was right with her on that though, oh, how she wished their grandmother could have been here today. She'd have been so happy to see the family standing together at the altar.

Zuzi wished they'd at least brought the cross with them to bless this family occasion. They'd found it poking up from the rubble of Babcia Kamilla's house when the wind had finally blown the flames out and had almost taken it with them to remember her by but, in the end, they'd agreed it was best left standing guard over its buried owner and that no one, however hard they tried, would ever forget Babcia. Even so, it was as tough not having her here as it was not having their father, and it was all Zuzi could do to keep the tears inside where Babcia would have wanted them.

She glanced to the windows of the pretty domed roof above, hoping that she was looking down from heaven to see their happiness, then turned back to Orla, watching her little sister in awe as she reached Eduard and beamed openly at him. Orla looked beautiful. The simple white dress donated by a kindly citizen suited her but it was the glow of happiness that made her truly shine. Zuzi watched, amazed by how happily she was including little Nella – smiling away in Magda's arms – and awed by how easily and readily Orla could give herself into the care of another human without any apparent fears for her independence.

'What if you find out that you don't like him?' she'd asked her little sister last night.

'I'm sure some days I won't,' Orla had replied easily, 'but I'll always love him, so we'll work it out.'

It was such simple faith and Zuzi was, she had to admit, rather jealous of it.

'But how do you *know* that?' she'd demanded.

Orla had laughed and kissed her. 'Because, silly, that's exactly how it feels with you and Hana.'

'But you didn't have to choose us.'

'I'll have even more chance of making it right with someone I *have* chosen.'

She'd been so sweetly sure of herself that Zuzi hadn't had the heart to push further, to ask how you knew that you'd chosen correctly, or – perhaps more to the point – how the other person knew. She supposed that sweet-natured Orla didn't have to worry about that because who would ever tire of a life with her? Zuzi, however… She had a nasty feeling that any man, once he got to know her, would run a mile.

She glanced across to the opposite pews and saw Bronislaw standing there, looking gorgeous in a borrowed suit with, for perhaps the first time since Zuzi had known him, no one else's blood on his clothing.

As if sensing her, Bron looked over and stared right back in a way that made her long to push everyone between them out of the way and throw herself upon him. But that would be most indecorous and, besides, she was not her sister. She had more things to do than wrap herself around a man – even if, for the life of her, she couldn't remember what they were right now.

'Eduard and Orla, have you come here to enter into marriage without coercion, freely and wholeheartedly? the priest asked.

'I have,' they replied at virtually the same time.

The congregation let out a joyous laugh at their eagerness. There was precious little happiness in Warsaw right now and these two people, staring lovingly at each other, were to be treasured and encouraged. The doors had been left open to let in the last light of this late summer day and, although the service had started with just those family and friends who'd made it out of Stare Miasto, others crept into the rear pews as the ceremony proceeded, eager to be a part of the joyous occasion. The roar of approval when the priest pronounced Eduard and Orla man and wife made them both jump comically and turn from gazing into each other's eyes to see a mass of people cheering their love.

'Thank you,' Orla said, blushing sweetly. 'Thank you so much.'

Then she looked to Eduard, who took her chin tenderly in his big hands and kissed her, and the applause grew even louder.

'Three cheers for the bride and groom,' Szymon Ancel called and everyone obliged.

Szymon had got away from AK duties for the afternoon to escort Jacob to the church. He'd brought his wife and children along and the four of them stood happily in a pew. They were Jewish but love was love in any religion and they looked as delighted as anyone else to be at the happy ceremony. Watching them, the parents cuddling together while Tasha and Amelia jostled each other for the best view, was like seeing a reminder of happier times – of the normal life Warsawians had risen up to get back and that seemed to be receding further and further away from them – and Zuzi smiled to see it.

The Germans were busy securing Stare Miasto, but not one refugee from there was in any doubt that they would soon be coming for Śródmieście, and the AK were frantically regrouping. British planes had flown in yesterday night. Hana had not volunteered to go out and light their way, but she had stood with Zuzi at the window of their borrowed house and watched the myriad white parachutes opening like airy jellyfish, her eyes searching the underside of every plane. There had been no violets but she had refused to cry.

'I knew he wouldn't come,' she'd said stiffly. 'I know he's dead. I saw his plane crash into the Vistula and there's no way anyone could survive that.'

Even so, Zuzi had known her big sister had been desperately hoping the new planes would provide a miracle and had ached at its lack. Love, you see, it only created pain. Again, Zuzi looked across the church, again, Bronislaw was looking straight back. She glanced to Orla and Eduard as they came apart, beaming bashfully, and remembered what it had been like to kiss him, how every part of her had come alive in his embrace. Then she remembered Kamilla's cry of pain yanking them apart and was ashamed of herself. Whatever she felt for Bron was not the pure, genuine love between Orla and her groom. God knew that and had punished her by taking Babcia away when she'd kissed him.

She tore her eyes away and saw, just beyond Bron, his father, Bartek. He, like so many, was still in his uniform, ready to go back on duty when the reception was over. Magda had been madly baking little treats with kindly offered ingredients and they were on trays in the vestry, alongside a number of bottles of very nice-looking wine that, over here in Śródmieście, people were still drinking, rather than pouring on gaping wounds. Zuzi had walked through the streets envying her fellow Warsawians their experience of the uprising as little more than an inconvenience at the barricades, while also praying that it stayed that way to the end. Whenever that might be.

'Let us pray!'

The priest's soft voice interrupted her restless musings and, chastened, she bowed her head as he asked for God's blessing on the bridal couple, their families and all of Warsaw.

'I present to you, Mr and Mrs Dąbrowski'

The crowd gave another hearty cheer but Zuzi and Hana looked at each other in astonishment.

'Dąbrowski' Zuzi whispered to Orla, who gave them a broad wink.

'I'm not the sap you think, hey, Zuzi?'

'I didn't think... That is, I don't... But, even so – he's taking your name?'

Eduard looked across. 'It's a good name,' he said, then looked around, embarrassed, and added in a whisper, 'and better than a German one right now.'

It was a fair point. Zuzi had almost forgotten, with Eduard so intimately involved in the AK, that, however unwillingly, he had marched into Warsaw as part of the murderous Dirlewanger SS group. Even so, Zuzi couldn't imagine having a husband who took her name, dearly as she loved it. It would be wrong, surely? Far more natural for her to become, say, Kaminski...

She tutted at herself and Hana and Orla looked at her in surprise.

'I think it's lovely,' Hana said.

'Oh, me too,' Zuzi agreed hastily. 'Very lovely. Welcome to the family, Eduard.'

'And Nella,' Orla said happily. 'She's going to be a Dąbrowska too.'

Zuzi hugged her. It was so easy in Orla's world. She saw what she wanted, opened her arms and welcomed it in. Easy and, perhaps, sensible. She glanced again to Bronislaw, but he was talking to his father and this time he didn't see her. Well fine, she had bridesmaid duties anyway. Probably. If she could work out what they were.

Moving through to the vestry, she picked up a plate of pastries, handing them politely round the impromptu mass of guests and ignoring her mother's exaggerated look of surprise. But the plate was soon empty and, returning for more, she found her way blocked.

'You look beautiful, Zuzi,' Bronislaw said.

She flushed and brushed at her borrowed dress, only succeeding in covering it in pastry crumbs from the empty plate.

'You prefer girls in skirts then?'

'I prefer you to other girls, whatever you're wearing.'

'Oh. Thank you. I think.'

'How are you?'

His voice, as so often, was serious. Usually she liked it but today, envying Orla's easy happiness, she wanted things light.

'Fantastic, thank you. Delighted to see my sister so happy.'

'Of course. And you – are you happy, Zuzi?'

His concern grated on her.

'I think I can afford to be happy for Orla for one day, without needing my own petty needs serviced, thank you.'

He looked taken aback and, to be fair, it had come out more harshly than she'd intended.

'I'm sure you can,' he said. 'I just... I've been worried about you since, you know...'

'Since I kissed you?' she challenged.

'Since we kissed each other,' he corrected gently. 'I meant more since your grandmother died.'

'Ah. Yes.' Zuzi felt tears spring to her eyes and was furious with him for doing that to her. 'Thank you so much for bringing sadness to this happy day.'

Bronislaw looked stricken.

'I didn't mean to do that, Zuzi, truly. It's better, I find, to keep the dead alive in our speech than to hide our sorrow away, but I apologise if I've spoken out of turn.'

He made a good point but, still, this was her family's occasion so it was up to her to make the points. If any had to be made at all.

'No matter,' she said. 'And now, if you'd let me past, I have snacks to pass around.'

'An important job.'

'It is.'

'I meant it.'

He spread his hands wide and Zuzi felt mean. She was meant to be welcoming their guests, not making them feel bad.

'Sorry,' she said. 'I'm such a grump. Bet you don't prefer me to other girls now.'

'Oh, I do. I'm simply sorry that you don't prefer me too.' He gave a slight bow, his dark eyes still fixed on her. 'I'll leave you to enjoy your evening.'

Then he was backing away and when Zuzi put her hand out to stop him, the plate she was still holding caught on the vestry door and smashed, making everyone jump and stare at her. Someone clapped, others laughed and she had to scramble away to avoid their stares. By the time she'd recovered herself, Bronislaw had gone.

'Damnation,' she swore and then glanced to the statue of Christ with a hasty, 'Sorry.'

'What should I do?' she whispered to herself.

'Go after him,' came the answer, loud and clear and, to her relief, in Orla's soft voice.

Zuzi turned to her, embarrassed to have been caught. 'Chase him? No way!'

'Why not?'

'He might feel... Might think...'

'That you like him? Would that matter?'

Zuzi was pretty sure that it would, but Orla's beautifully simple way of looking at life was very hard to refute.

'You're not to worry about it,' she said firmly. 'It's time for you to dance with your groom.'

Hana, coming over, clapped agreement. 'Absolutely, it is. And look, these two talented men can give us a tune.'

She indicated two older men who'd come into the Dąbrowski wedding carrying fiddles. They eagerly got them out of their cases and someone pushed back the pews as they took up position at the foot of the altar. They struck up a merry folk tune and the church was transformed into a dance hall, with Orla and Eduard at its heart. Zuzi looked around the exuberant celebrations in astonishment. Four days ago, this pair had been spluttering their way out of a burning building and now they were taking the first dance of their married life amidst a rapt crowd. It was a true miracle.

She felt the tune pull at her feet and looked around for Bronislaw. She could apologise. She could tell him she *did* prefer him to other men. That much was true and it was hardly a declaration of love or commitment or any of that other deep stuff. Spotting him near the door, she screwed up her courage to walk towards him, but she had barely taken three steps before the lights went off with a loud and horribly final click, plunging the wedding and every one of its guests into darkness.

THIRTY-THREE

ORLA

'Eduard?'

Orla clutched at her groom as the lights went out and felt his arms around her, warm and assured.

'Don't worry, sweetheart. It's probably just a fuse.'

Orla laughed lightly at the reminder of a time when their only problems were dodgy wires but she was still terrified that this was some new German weapon and a bomb would come roaring into her brand-new marriage before it was even consummated. Slowly, however, her eyes adjusted and she could see, in the last threads of sun outside and the two big candles on the altar, that everyone was safe. There was no whine of Stukas, no mooing of Kowas and no rattle of machine guns, just the soft chatter of a hundred confused guests.

People ran outside to see what was going on but returned saying there appeared to be no cause for alarm. The priest produced more candles from a cupboard in the vestry and people lit them and stuck them in candlesticks, plant pots and glasses around the church until the whole place was a-sparkle.

'Even better than before,' Eduard said. 'Now, where were we?'

He signalled the fiddlers who picked up their instruments to resume their tunes but barely had they got five bars in before the doors rattled and an AK soldier burst in.

'It's the power station! The Nazis have taken the power station!'

Orla sank her head against Eduard's shoulder.

'Could they not have waited one more day?' she moaned.

'Or not got it at all. I hope too many people haven't been hurt.'

Orla felt instantly guilty. The brave men of the Krybar battalion had made a heroic effort to hold the besieged power plant and must have been exhausted when the Nazis struck. She prayed Hana was right about them now taking the AK as honourable prisoners and that they would be well treated, but it was bad news for those Warsawians left in the city. Even here, in the relative peace of Śródmieście, life would be hard without electricity and, worst of all, they had to assume that if the Nazis had hit the power plant, they were planning another major attack. Already the various AK members who'd been happily whirling partners around the church were heading for the door and their wedding party was dissolving into the darkness.

Bartek came up, offering his apologies. 'I'm so sorry. Duty calls.'

'When doesn't it these days?' Eduard said sadly.

Bartek leaned in. 'It doesn't for either of you. Not tonight. And you won't need much light either.' He shook Eduard's hand and gave Orla a kiss on her cheek. 'God bless you both.'

Then he was gone and Kapitan Szymon Ancel also came up to wish them joy before heading into the night, leaving his wife and daughters dancing in a quiet circle.

'The Nazis spoil everything,' Orla moaned to Eduard.

'Not everything,' he whispered back, his voice low and throaty. 'We still have each other. And if the party is over...'

Orla felt herself blushing but it wasn't an unpleasant feeling and, as she looked up into Eduard's eyes, she knew he was right. There would be time for dancing when the war was over. Tonight was for them.

'Let me say goodbye.'

'Of course.'

A kind older lady had lent them her nearby apartment for the night – a pretty little studio flat with a kitchenette, two chairs, a tiny table and a large bed.

'Perfect!' Magda had clapped when they'd gone to look at it yesterday and she and the lady had exchanged a wicked look that had sent Orla scurrying to the window to check the view – or at least pretend to. Then, on the way back to their shared house, Magda had explained what she'd called 'the facts of life' to Orla in simple, no-nonsense terms that had made the whole thing sound rather peculiar.

'Isn't it a bit awkward?' Orla had asked, trying to put the angles together in her head.

'A bit,' Magda had agreed, 'but that's half the fun and it will feel perfectly logical once you get started. Don't worry, Orla, you've got a good man there. He'll look after you. Just be sure to tell him what makes you feel good.'

Orla had agreed that she would but, to be honest, the whole conversation had left her feeling more bewildered about her marriage bed than before, and now she was almost in it.

She found Hana first.

'We're going to go, Han.'

'Oh yes!'

'Not like that.' She leaned into her big sister. 'When you were, you know, engaged...' It came out all wrong and she cringed. 'Sorry, forget it. I'm sorry, Han-Han, that was awful of me.'

Hana kissed her. 'No, it wasn't. What did you want to ask?'

'Only if Mama had a, you know, "chat" with you?'

'About sex?' Orla glanced around, embarrassed, and Hana grinned at her. 'We didn't get that far, no, but I wouldn't worry, Orls. You like kissing him, don't you?'

'Oh yes!'

'Then it'll be fine.' She gave her a big hug. 'See you tomorrow. Have fun!'

'See you tomorrow.'

Hana let her go as Zuzi came bounding over. 'Off to take your groom to bed, hey, little sis?'

'Zuzi!'

'It's true, isn't it? Are you worried? Don't be. Babcia told me it was wonderful.'

'She did?' Orla and Hana gasped together. 'When?'

'When we were stuck under the rubble. Said she loved doing it with Dziadek Aleksander and...' she looked around, 'that Mama couldn't wait to get home with Tata when they were first married.'

The three of them looked at each other, pulled disgusted faces, then burst out laughing.

'What's up with you?' Magda demanded, bustling up.

'Nothing, Mama,' Hana managed but then Zuzi giggled and Orla joined in and even Hana was chuckling again.

'You three!' Magda said. 'You're like a coven of witches. What's got into you?'

'Just happy,' Orla said.

'Not as happy as you will be soon,' Magda retorted, and that set them off again. Magda shook her head at them, and chucked Nella, sitting happily on her hip, under the chin. 'You don't think we'd have so many babies if it was no fun, do you? Don't you worry, you'll all be at it soon enough.'

'Not me,' Hana said. 'Not with Emil gone.'

Magda put an arm around her. 'There'll be other men when you're ready, sweetie.'

'Nope. Buildings, that's what I'm focusing on now.'

'Buildings?' Magda squinted at her but wisely chose not to pursue it further. 'Fair enough. But you, Zuzi, you'll—'

'Not be bothering with men any time soon, thank you very much,' Zuzi snapped.

Magda suppressed a smile. 'I see. Well, in that case, Orla – enjoy yourself for everyone.'

'Mama!'

This was all too much for Orla. She kissed them and turned to look for Jacob, who would surely not bother her with embarrassing conversation, and he came bundling into her, lifting her off her feet.

'Got to go, Orls, sorry. AK need me.'

'Stay safe, Jacob.'

'Course I will. See you at sunfall, yes?'

'See you at sunfall,' they chorused and then he was off and Magda was turning Orla towards Eduard and it seemed that her marriage was truly about to begin.

Eduard laid her on the bed, two candles flickering softly either side, and sat down next to her.

'My beautiful, beautiful bride,' he said, bending to kiss her. 'I can't believe how blessed I am to have found you.'

'Found me – and tied me to a ladder,' she teased gently.

He groaned. 'You saved me, Orla.'

'Nonsense.'

'No, really, you did. I was angry and lonely and confused. I didn't want to join Dirlewanger's lot but they gave us no choice and it was easier to go along with them than stand up and be shot.'

'I'm glad that you did,' Orla said, pulling him down to kiss him again. 'Or we wouldn't be here now.'

He shuddered.

'True, but I could so easily have got you killed. Other girls were killed. There are other men out there deprived of their brides because of the likes of me.'

'Because of the likes of *Dirlewanger*,' she corrected him gently. 'We've all done bad things in this war.'

'You haven't.'

'Haven't I? When the fire raged in Babcia's house, did I save the nearest people? No. I looked for Mama and you and Nella. I wanted my own people safe.'

'That's natural.'

'And so is trying to save your skin.'

She kissed him again, more deeply and he responded hungrily.

'I can't believe I've got you, Orla. I can't believe you're mine. I'm going to make you so, so happy, I swear it.'

'And I you,' she said against his lips. Then she was tangling her fingers in his hair, pulling him closer and his fingers were going to the buttons of her borrowed dress, his lips not far behind, and Magda was right, it all felt logical – so wonderfully, gloriously, deliciously logical that she thought perhaps she would do it again. Twice ideally. She and Eduard had promised each other a lifetime together but who knew, in war-torn Warsaw, how long a lifetime might last and Orla was determined to make the most of every minute granted to them.

THIRTY-FOUR
18 SEPTEMBER

HANA

'You're not going to like this,' Hana told her family. 'But it's something I've decided I've got to do.'

She fought to keep her voice as steady and determined as her words because it *was* something she had to do, but that didn't make it something she was looking forward to, or something her family would approve of.

They were gathered in the bedroom they shared, waking up for another day on the forefront of the uprising. The only ones not sleeping with them were Orla and Eduard, who'd made themselves a marital nest in a store cupboard in the makeshift hospital they, along with Bronislaw, were helping to run down the road. There was little room for anything in there but a mattress, however, so they usually came back here to eat and had just arrived with steaming cups of tea for everyone.

They'd been as bouncy as puppies in the three days since their wedding. Marriage clearly suited Hana's little sister and that was lovely to see, really it was, but, oh, it hurt. Orla was living the life she should have had, while she was having to make herself a new future.

'Yesterday, I went up the Prudential tower,' she told her family.

'How is it?' Zuzi asked. 'I don't know how it's still standing with that hole in its side.'

The tower had taken a nasty direct hit from a Stuka the other day and looked as if some mythical monster had taken a bite out of it.

'Steel superstructure,' Hana told her. 'Excellent design.'

'Fascinating,' Zuzi said drily. 'And Babcia's flag?'

'Battered, but still flying.'

'Like us all,' Magda said sagely. 'But why does this matter, Hana sweetie?'

Her mother was looking at her with such concern and Hana hated to make her worry, but this was war and risks had to be taken.

'It matters because while I was up there, I got to see out over Warsaw and our poor city looks awful.'

Hana closed her eyes, remembering the scar of a view. She'd only gone to the top because the AK sentry had refused to take her message to the platoon stationed there. She could have done without the long climb but with the power out across the city there'd been no lift, so no choice. Plus, when she'd agreed and he'd got up to thank her, he'd been leaning on a stick, his leg in plaster, and she'd forgiven him his apparent laziness. In truth, the chance to see the top of the building that had been the first capture of the uprising had excited her – until she'd made it up there.

Warsaw had ranged around her, scorched and broken. To the north, Żoliborz had still looked relatively intact and to the south, Czerniaków the same, but Wola had been a desert and Stare Miasto an ash heap. Even the luxurious Śródmieście was badly pockmarked and now the Nazis were coming for it in earnest. From up there, she'd been able to see the Kowa rocket launchers, hideous, six-barrelled weapons of destruction, as they were wheeled into the Saxon Gardens ready for the assault, and her blood had chilled at the thought of hearing that deathly mooing once more.

'We're going to have to surrender,' she told her family, forcing her eyes open and drinking in the far better sight of her loved ones.

'That's not true, Hana,' Zuzi said stoutly.

'I think it is,' Orla put in. 'Sister Maria has been asked to represent the Red Cross in negotiations for a ceasefire to release civilians.'

All eyes swung to her.

'Really?' Magda asked. 'People really want to leave?'

'Oh yes,' Orla said. 'Thousands of them.'

'The Nazis will put them into labour camps.'

'Maybe but at least they won't bomb them there. They're hungry and homeless and just want to escape.'

'I can see that,' Magda said. 'But we've come this far, so it seems a shame to stop the fight.'

'We've got no ammunition to fight with,' Jacob said. 'Our platoon in the Telephone Exchange has only got enough bullets to man one gun. If the Nazis come for us, we're done for.'

'But the Allied planes...'

'Are bringing more,' he agreed, 'which is wonderful, but so few packages actually land in our sectors. It's better if they drop in Żoliborz, but then people have to carry them to Śródmieście overnight and it's very dangerous. Plus the planes keep getting...'

He stopped himself but Hana finished the sentence in her head – 'shot down'. Didn't she know it!

'Our only hope is if the Americans come,' she said.

'And will they?' Zuzi asked eagerly.

'Bór says Churchill is pushing Stalin to let them use his bases to refuel but he keeps making excuses.'

'Like what?' Orla wailed. 'I don't understand how he's getting away with it. He's meant to be our ally.'

'He's meant to be Britain and America's ally,' Hana corrected her gently. 'He's never actually reopened diplomatic relations with Poland and apparently he's denouncing the uprising as a…' She coughed, but they had to know the true situation. 'A "reckless adventure".'

The whole family sucked in an outraged breath.

'But he encouraged it,' Magda protested. 'Moscow Radio told us to rise. They told us they were coming and we were to rise up ready to meet them.'

'Stalin's memory is, it seems, very selective. He's calling the AK "bandits" and telling the world that his Polish communist army is the only one liberating the country.'

'What Polish communist army?' Jacob demanded.

'The one he made up out of the soldiers he imprisoned when he invaded us at the start of the war. Now they have to march under the Soviet banner. Or, rather, *not* march, as they're being held on the other side of the Vistula with the rest until…'

'Until the Poles and the Germans destroy each other and he can march in unimpeded,' Eduard finished wearily. 'He's no one's ally but his own.'

They looked bleakly at each other. They'd been brought up in the understanding that Poland had enemies on either side but Stalin's grand alliance with the West had lulled them into a false sense of security.

'He'll be the end of us,' Magda said weakly and Orla leaped over and hugged her.

'Not if we surrender, Mama.'

'But then it will all have been for nothing.'

The Dąbrowskas sat there, their tea cooling in their mugs as the terrible truth of this paradox sank in. Hana cleared her throat.

'We can't think like that,' she said. 'We have to forget what's gone before and focus on what we can do in the time ahead. Which is why...' she swallowed, 'I have to get the city maps back from the Nazis who stole them.'

The others stared at her.

'The what?' Jacob asked.

'The city maps. They hold intricate details of all the streets and houses, sketches of the old buildings. If we're to rebuild Warsaw, we need them.'

Magda looked at her curiously.

'Old buildings, Hana? I thought you were keen on the new. Modern design, isn't that what you've been telling us we need? Surely here's your chance.'

Hana smiled at her mother.

'I did think that, but I never meant for us to lose all that had gone before. Well, maybe some of it – the ugly, impractical stuff – but not all. Our history is in the bricks of our city. Our identity as Warsawians has been forged by our environment and that should not be taken away from us.' She looked around, warming to her theme, for she had thought of little else since Agaton had told her where the plans were. 'Poles should be able to honour the Sigismund column, or the Tomb of the Unknown Soldier. They should be able to see the Royal Castle and the beautiful merchants' houses. They should be able to walk amongst their ancestors, even as they forge new paths.'

She stopped, suddenly feeling self-conscious, but then Zuzi clapped and the rest of her family joined in and she had to blushingly ask them to stop.

'Where are these maps?' Magda asked nervously.

'In the university.'

'The university where the Wehrmacht garrison is stationed?'

Hana nodded grimly. 'But I'm told the soldiers are in the main buildings. The ancillary ones, like the history department where the maps have been stored, are very lightly guarded.'

'But still guarded?'

'Yes.'

Magda leaped up. 'You don't have to do this, Hana. You're not a soldier.'

'There'll be soldiers with me. Bartek and his crack platoon have volunteered.'

'So why do they need you?'

'Because I'm the Kanalarki, Mama – the one who knows the sewers, the one who can get them there.'

Magda closed her eyes and Hana saw her lips moving in prayer, but then she opened them again and looked deep into Hana's own.

'If you feel you have to do this, daughter, then who am I to stop you? But, please, make sure you're also the one who gets them out again.'

'I will, Mama.'

Her mother's grip on her shoulders was tight, her words run through with emotion.

'Because, you see Hana, Warsawians' identity may have been forged by their environment but mine – mine has been forged by you. You and your sisters and your brother. Yes, I'm a baker but only because your father... your father could bake no more. Above all else, I'm a mother. You are the monuments of my life and I do not want you toppled.'

Then she was crying and they were all tumbling together in a big, rough hug and Hana sucked in their love like her very lifeblood.

'I'll come back,' she promised, pulling gently away.

Zuzi stepped up next to her. 'And so will I.'

'Sorry?'

She linked an arm through Hana's. 'You didn't think I'd let you go alone?'

'Zuzi, you don't have—'

'And, besides, you never know when you might need a Minerki to blow something up. Come on, Han-Han, let's go and get these maps.'

They entered the sewer at Krzyska Street. It was less than three hundred metres from the university but the main C-drain would only take them a short way before they'd have to turn off into the unexplored maze of side tunnels. Hana was to lead the way and felt the weight of responsibility for the lives of the five AK soldiers who were accompanying her plus, of course, her dear sister. Agaton should have been coming too but this morning he'd taken a nasty piece of shrapnel in his right leg and exposing a wound like that to the filth of the sewers would be madness. He'd tried to talk her into waiting, but they knew that the Nazis might break into Śródmieście very soon and she'd assured him she could manage the route alone. Now she had to prove it.

There were no maps for these side sewers or, at least, none in their possession. Hana's only guide would be her inner compass and the calculations she and Agaton had spent hours working on. She knew how many steps in any combination of directions it would be to reach the manhole his colleague remembered, but she also knew how disorientating it was in the endless darkness of the sewers, especially the smaller ones.

'Do you have your sticks?' she whispered to her little platoon.

They waved them at her in the faint light from her torch. Hana had not had to travel down many of the smaller sewers before but there was a regular run between Śródmieście and the Riverbank, and the Kanalarki who trod it had shown her their technique for negotiating the three-foot-high hell. It involved placing a sturdy stick in front to support your weight, then bunny-hopping forward to meet it, again and again until you made it out. It placed your nose mere centimetres from the effluent, which took some getting used to, but prevented you from slipping into it and, with the water and power off, many people were tipping their waste into holes in the rubble instead of down the drains so the level was quite low.

Hana carefully measured out the fifty steps she and Agaton knew would take her to the first of the side sewers. From there, she needed to be about thirty hops east and seventy north. Across open ground it would have been simple; down here, she was going to have to try and calculate the direction of the tunnels and take them into account. Their only hope was that the nineteenth-century British architect who'd built the system had favoured rigid grids where possible so there would be fewer diagonals to confuse her counting. Sure enough, the first side sewer was set at a promising right angle to the main one – due east then. Drawing a deep, acrid breath, Hana planted her stick and took her first hop.

Within twenty hops her back was aching and her thighs burning and she knew from the laboured wheezing behind her that the others were suffering too. She could hear Zuzi working hard to regulate her breathing, not wanting to admit she was struggling and, although Bartek had picked his shortest men, they would be finding it even harder. She couldn't afford to get this wrong and lead them further than necessary. Five hops more and there, to her left, was another right-angled tunnel, heading north. Did she take it, hoping there would be one going east, or did she go onwards to connect with another going north? She fought to think. She only needed thirty hops east in total, so it was surely a better bet to turn north.

'This way,' she whispered back, taking the turn, and was

offered some relief when, barely ten hops in, they came to a manhole and could straighten beneath it.

'Good work, sis,' Zuzi whispered.

Hana was grateful for the support and just prayed her sister was right. As the others stretched out, she marked her course on the sweaty skin of her hand, fighting to concentrate. She and Agaton had asked everyone they came across to remember any manholes from the happy days when they'd simply been something you walked across, rather than relying on for your life. Few had been able to do so, but yesterday they'd found a water engineer with expert knowledge and, although he hadn't worked in the university grounds, he'd identified covers outside them at Królewska, Traugutta and Obozna. According to the calculations in her head, she was at Królewska, and being able to picture the streets above ground steadied her. She could do this.

She pushed on, taking another turn right and another very swiftly left. They had to be close, but then she came to a crossroads, four sewers spanning temptingly out in all directions, and felt her head start to spin. There was an increase in waste here, suggesting the garrison were still happily using their lavatories. Hana was certain they were under the university but the complex was large and they couldn't afford to come up at the front, where the bulk of the enemy soldiers were stationed.

She paused. The men behind were breathing hoarsely and she had to move fast. She stared at her hand, checking off the rough hops north and east and forcing herself to remember the angles. She had to go north twenty more hops at the most, but which was north? The fumes were spiralling into her mind, making it spin, but her gut was pulling her to one tunnel and, with little else to go on, she had to trust it.

'This way.'

'Right behind you,' Zuzi whispered.

Again, she was grateful for the vote of confidence but her

heart pounded in her chest as she led the group on. Twenty hops, twenty-one, twenty-two. Had she got it wrong? Would she have to turn them back and try another way? They would surely hate her for that.

But no!

Three more hops and she felt the rush of air that indicated a manhole. Hastening forward, she looked up at the metal steps and the circular lid above and prayed it was the right one. If her gut had let her down, she could be leading all of them to their deaths.

'Is this it?' Bartek asked her.

'I hope so.'

He patted her shoulder. 'Wherever it is, we'll sort it. Ready, lads?'

The men nodded and Hana edged round to stand next to Zuzi as Bartek took the ladder upwards and put his hand to the cover. She felt Zuzi's hand sneak into hers, as it had when they were little girls facing something new, and she clutched it tightly as Bartek eased the lid upwards. No one shot at them.

'Good start,' Zuzi whispered.

Bartek lifted it further and peered out.

'Coast clear,' he whispered down. 'Bushes to the immediate right. Head up as quietly as you can and straight into those, one at a time. Yes?'

'Yes, boss.'

Bartek moved the lid away, pushed himself up and was gone. The next man followed and the next, until the last one was indicating it was the girls' turn. Suddenly the sewer, for all its dank, dark stink, felt like the ultimate in safety, but Hana had brought them here and could not hesitate now. Grabbing the first of the metal rungs, she headed upwards, glad to have Zuzi at her back.

She came out, blinking in what felt like lurid starlight, and dived for the bushes. Zuzi was right behind her, the last AK bringing up the rear and tugging the manhole cover back into place, as if they'd never stepped through it at all.

'Is this the right place?' Bartek hissed.

Hana looked frantically around. Agaton's friend had drawn them a sketch of the history department but he'd been a classics professor not an artist and it had been rough. It had, however, clearly shown two buildings at right angles to each other and in front of them was only one. Hana bit her lip, but then she saw the rubble covering the ground to the left – the second building had obviously been bombed and the bricks taken off for some barricade. The criss-cross paths meeting at a fountain in the middle were still there and either side of the big door were two concrete globes, just as the man had shown.

'It's the right place,' she said on a relieved outbreath.

'Then let's go.'

There was no obvious sign of life, so Bartek signalled them into a dash across the quadrangle to crouch either side of the stairs. Hana felt like something out of a film and had to remind herself that any drama here would come at the expense of her life.

'Go!' Bartek hissed again and the AK pounded up the steps, Zuzi hot on their tail, dragging Hana along.

The doors were unlocked and they rushed them. Two guards were sitting inside, playing cards by the light of a gas lamp. They leaped up but before they could shout a warning Bartek and his right-hand man drew knives from their belts and slit their throats. The guards slid to the ground, instantly limp. Hana stood, transfixed by their blood leaking onto the oak boards but then snapped to her senses.

'This way.'

The first office on the right, Agaton had said, and she dived for the door, finding it, like the first, unlocked. Bartek nudged her aside to enter ahead of her but the room was deserted and they filed in and shut the door gratefully behind them. Now it was Hana's turn. She ran for the big map chest at the centre, Zuzi at her side.

'Manilla folder?' her sister asked in a whisper.

'Most likely. But anything you can find.'

They eased open the drawers, trying to be both speedy and silent. Hana was very aware of the AK patrolling tensely around the edges, covering the door and the big windows looking back out onto the quadrangle and the manhole cover that would be their escape. It was all quiet.

'Here!'

She grabbed a folder in the second drawer and opened it up. There, shining bright white in the moonlight coming in through the glass, were the maps that Hana had last seen Marek handing to the Gestapo before his death. She gave a thumbs-up to Bartek and thrust them into her backpack, adding everything else in the drawer and a few folders from the next one down too. She would have loved to comb the whole room but she had what she'd come for and she mustn't risk their lives too far.

'We can go.'

Bartek nodded and motioned the AK towards the door. They gathered behind him as he peered cautiously out but all still seemed to be quiet. Hana's heart pounded. They were going to do this! She would be able to take Agaton his maps and, whatever else happened to Warsaw, someone would be alive at the end of it to take the city forward with at least an imprint of its precious past to support it.

They crept to the door, the pack pleasingly heavy on Hana's back. Bartek edged it open and peered out. He gave a short nod but then came a shout from round the side of a building and, to Hana's horror, four Nazi soldiers came into the quadrangle. One of them pointed to their footsteps, clear in the dewy grass, then, drawing their guns, they headed straight towards the door, and Hana's little group huddled behind it.

THIRTY-FIVE

ZUZI

They were coming at pace – four soldiers, the silver Nazi eagle on their tunics flashing in the moonlight and their fingers cocked on the triggers of their Lugers. There was no time for Zuzi to think, no time to do anything but draw a grenade from her belt, pull the pin and, stepping into the gap in the door, lob it straight at them.

'For Tata,' she hissed as it turned tip over tail through the night and hit the ground right between them, blasting on impact. 'And for Babcia!'

One of them fell, two staggered sideways and the other dropped into a defensive crouch. It was all the time they needed.

'Go!' Bartek urged his men and led the charge himself, shooting the crouched man, while his fellows took out the two on the ground.

One ran for the manhole cover, yanking it up and they leaped down it.

'Jump,' someone called from down in the sewer and Zuzi saw hands reaching up.

'You go,' she urged Hana.

There was another shout and two more men came round the corner. Bartek, still standing guard, shot one, but then she heard him curse as his bullets ran out. She grabbed a grenade.

'Go!' she screeched at Hana and was glad to see her jump but then a shot was ringing out and the screech was all Hana's.

Zuzi flung the grenade in fury. It hit the oncoming Nazi in the stomach and exploded in a sickening shower of blood and guts. It made her want to throw up but there was no time for such indulgences. Hana had tumbled into the sewer and, with a quick glance to see hands still waiting, Zuzi flung herself after her.

'Hana,' she gasped. 'Where's Hana?'

'I'm here.' She'd never been more relieved to hear her big sister's voice. 'I'm here, Zuzi. I'm fine.'

She did not sound fine but, then, none of them did. Bartek was coming down now, securing the lid above them, but it would surely not be long before more soldiers came running and it would take them moments to work out which way they'd gone. They could only pray that the tiny tunnels would put them off – though it would also make their own escape tricky.

'Are you hurt?' she gasped to Hana.

'Just a graze. I'll be all right. I can get us out of here. Come on.'

She grabbed one of the sticks they'd left at the bottom of the ladder and set off. Zuzi went straight behind her and was worried to see her sister's movements looking lopsided. The sticky, gunky sewage was flowing fast and once they ducked into the three-foot-tunnel it required total concentration to stay above it. Hana's head was bobbing worryingly and when they reached the first crossroads, she looked around as if she had no idea where she was.

Zuzi put a hand on her back. 'Hana, let me lead. You can lean on me.'

'My job,' Hana muttered, staggering slightly.

'*Our* job,' Zuzi told her. 'I'll lead and you can tell me where to go, yes?'

Hana put a hand to the brick wall and Zuzi could see in the dimming light of her torch that she was gritting her teeth.

'Yes,' she agreed weakly. 'Thank you, Zuzi.'

'It's what sisters are for,' she told her crisply, squeezing past. 'Put your hand on my back and let's go.'

She felt Hana touch her back, lightly at first but with increasing pressure as they inched their way along the next tunnel. Somewhere far back, they heard the sound of grating metal and a German voice echoed down the tunnel, terrifyingly loud. They moved faster. A grenade sounded out and light flared towards them but they had taken the turn and were thankfully out of the line of any shrapnel blast. The water would surge, she knew, and she paused, bracing herself against the sides, very glad she had as Hana fell against her.

'Are you still there, Han-Han?'

'Still here,' she said weakly.

'Where was your graze?'

'My leg.'

'Does it hurt?'

'A little.'

Zuzi knew an underestimation when she heard one and sent a fervent prayer up through the tunnel bricks, through the earth, through whatever street was above them and to God in His heavens, to protect her sister. She'd lost Babcia to a Nazi bullet; she was not going to lose Hana too.

'Come on, sweetie. It's not far. Just a walk in the woods really, like when we were younger, remember?'

'With Orla's deer?'

Hana's voice sounded worryingly sing-song but at least she was talking.

'Just like that. Dear little doe, always chasing after those pretty creatures.'

Zuzi pushed on as fast as she could. She'd memorised the turns on the way here and counted her way along to the next one. Another grenade blast sent the sludge surging around them once more but then the Germans must have gone to tend to their dead for the sewer fell silent of all but their laboured breathing and her silly prattle.

'And you, Han-Han – you were always looking for that hut. Remember that hut?'

'The shepherd's one?'

'The shepherd's one, yes, with the pictures carved around the door. Remember the pictures?'

'Was there one of a sheep dancing?' She was slurring now and her weight was so heavy on Zuzi's back that every hop was a huge effort, but there was no way she was going to stop.

'There was. We loved that dancing sheep. And one knitting too. Do you remember the one knitting, Hana?'

She could hear her own voice fading as she struggled for breath.

'You're doing brilliantly, Zuzi,' Bartek said from behind Hana. 'We'll make it, we'll get her home.'

Home! The word echoed crazily down the sewer. Where was home now? Twice, their family house had been taken from them.

But the family is still standing, Zuzi told herself sternly. *Including Hana.*

She did not want to think what the filthy flow around them might be doing to her sister's wound. There were a number of rocks and broken fragments of who-knew-what in the water and several times she heard Hana gasp in pain and willed her onwards with every fibre of her being.

After what felt like an eternity, they reached the manhole where they'd paused to rest on the way and Zuzi straightened, taking Hana in her arms and looking into her eyes. She didn't like what she saw. Hana was struggling to focus, her eyes set in some wild world of her own and, glancing down, Zuzi saw blood running from her leg into the sewage. She looked in panic to Bartek.

'Let's get her back,' he said calmly. 'Let's get her back to Bron.'

The name flared in Zuzi, a beacon of hope. She'd watched Bron dig a bullet out of Babcia's stomach and knew that, if it had not been for the hospital collapsing, he would have saved her life. She pictured him, standing patiently at an operating table waiting for her, and it was enough to drive her onwards again. Her feelings for the man were confused, but her trust in his skill was total.

'Come on, Han-Han,' she said. 'Not much further.'

Bartek took the pack from Hana's back, hefting it easily onto his own. He pulled a flask from his pocket and held it to her lips.

'Emergency vodka. Drink it.'

Hana obeyed and her eyes widened in shock but focused once more.

'Zuzi?' she said, confused. 'What are you doing down here?'

'Getting you home, sweet one. Getting you all the way home. Now, come on – final push.'

The last of the small tunnels was only, by Zuzi's memory, some twenty hops, but they seemed to take twice as long as before. Even with Bartek supporting her from behind, Hana was a dead weight across her back, and she was so relieved when they burst into the main sewer and could almost stand in the comparable luxury of the five-foot space.

'Give her to me.' Bartek swept Hana into his arms, limp

and still dripping blood from a wound Zuzi could not even bring herself to look at. 'Now, let's go.'

Zuzi went after him, her eyes fixed on her sister, her feet following her automatically, though every part of her body was screaming in agony. It reminded her of Bartek carrying Babcia Kamilla away from the cemetery battle and she could only pray this injury would not end the same way. They'd secured Hana's precious maps but at what cost Zuzi had no idea. She felt the sewer closing dizzily in on her and had to put a hand to each side to keep herself from tumbling into the stench below. Noises seemed to be filling her ears – German shouts, grenade blasts, shots. She looked all around but could see only bricks, bricks and more bricks, curving towards her, threatening to crush her.

She staggered.

'I can't...' she started, but stopped herself. She could and she had to. She had chosen to come and she would not let everyone else down by falling. Even so, her legs were wobbling like jelly and darkness began to close in until suddenly, above her, she saw a circle of light. Kind voices were urging her upwards and she thought that perhaps, after all that effort to get Hana back, it was she who had died and gone to heaven.

'No,' she shouted. 'I don't want to die.' But then strong arms were lifting her and a soft breeze was kissing her face and she sucked in breath after blessedly sweet breath as she fought her way back to life.

Had Hana done the same?

'Zuzi?' A handsome face swam into focus above her. 'Zuzi, speak to me.'

'Bron!' He smiled and she reached up and grabbed at the lapels of his stained white coat. 'Save her. Please, Bron, save my sister.'

'I'll do my best,' he promised but his voice was grim and, as she looked around and saw Hana lying next to her, her lower leg a mangle of flesh and bone, she feared that her sister's hard journey home was only just beginning.

THIRTY-SIX

ORLA

Orla uncurled herself reluctantly from Eduard's arms and stretched out in the tiny store cupboard they called home, relishing the last minutes of their brief rest before the nightshift began. Nella had a cardboard-box crib at the end of their mattress for night times but if they were both on duty, she stayed in the house with Magda. Bakeries, even struggling ones, were less unpredictable than hospitals and Orla wanted Nella to have as stable a time as possible. A ridiculous aim, perhaps, given the dire situation in Warsaw, but an aim all the same.

'I suppose we have to get up,' she said to her husband, who reached sleepily for her.

'Can't we just stay here forever?'

It was tempting. Her marriage bed, even in a cupboard, had proved as delightful a place as her mother had promised and there were days when she resented every minute spent out of it. But there was a war on and they did not have the luxury of a honeymoon. Sometimes, when they lay spent in each other's arms after a snatched moment of passion, Eduard would talk to her about the places he would take her and Nella once this was over and, cuddled up with him, listening to his soft talk of beaches and mountains and cottages in the hills, Orla could truly believe it possible. Then someone would shout out in agony from the hospital and she would be dragged back to the reality of war and suffering.

'Why can everyone not just be content with what they have?' she'd complained to Eduard more than once.

'Some people are greedy,' was all he'd had to offer.

Hitler, in Orla's opinion, was the greediest man in the world, possibly excepting Stalin, and it was Poland's fate to be stuck between the pair of them. It had ever been thus.

She let Eduard pull her back into his arms for another kiss but then she heard the clatter of the doors ramming open and a cry of 'Nurse!' followed by a louder, more urgent one of 'Orla. Oh, Orla, come now, please!'

'Zuzi,' she gasped and leapt to her feet, grabbing her dress from the side of Nella's crib and scrambling it on, tearing the hem in her haste.

Eduard had leapt up too, pulling on his trousers and shirt to follow her into the hospital. The sight that met Orla's eyes was the worst she had ever seen, even over the last month. Bartek was carrying Hana, Bronislaw running ahead of him and calling for space on the operating table, and Zuzi weeping at his side. Hana lay limply across Bartek's broad arms, coated – as were Bartek and Zuzi – in filth and with her stockings ripped apart to reveal a gaping wound in her left calf. The flesh was so badly torn open that Orla could see her sister's bone, sickly white amidst the filth, and the glint of a bullet bedded within it. Her head swirled but she fought it, leaning briefly back against Eduard to give herself the strength to join her sisters.

'What happened?'

'Bullet,' Zuzi said shortly. 'And then a long, long walk

through the sewers. I think her leg got battered by the debris in the water. It's torn it apart.'

Orla could see that and ran round to Hana's head.

'Is she alive?' She pressed a hand to her big sister's chest and felt the beat of her heart against it. 'She is. Thank God.'

'Tata!' Bron called from the operation table. 'Bring her over. Quickly. And someone fetch water, or wine or... or any sort of liquid at all. We have to get it as clean as possible.'

Orla nodded agreement but couldn't make her legs leave Hana and it was Zuzi who ran off to grab a bucket and sluice it unceremoniously over the battered leg. Hana came round with a start and looked up into Orla's eyes, her own filled with fear.

'Orla. What's happened? Where am I?'

'You're in hospital, my love,' Orla told her, dropping into the safety of her well-practised nursing tone. 'You've got a nasty cut on your leg but Bron is here and we're going to sort it out for you. All will be good soon, don't you worry.'

'It hurts,' Hana moaned. 'What happened?'

'You were shot.'

'At the university,' Zuzi put in. 'Remember? The Nazis came round the corner and one of the bastards shot you as you were getting into the sewer.'

Orla screwed up her face against the picture forming in her head of her two crazy-brave sisters scrambling away from enemy fire.

'The maps,' Hana gasped. 'Did the maps make it?'

'Oh yes. Bartek has them on his back.'

'That's good. That's— Ow!' Someone had brought wine and Bronislaw was pouring it onto the raw flesh. Hana scrabbled for Orla's hand and clutched at it. 'It's bad, isn't it, Orls? It's really bad. I'm not going to die, am I? You won't let me die?'

'I won't let you die,' Orla agreed hotly. She might not be

brave or bold or daring but she could – and *would* – care for her family with the ferocity of a lioness with a cub.

'Where's Mama?' Hana whimpered. 'Will someone fetch Mama?'

'I will,' Zuzi said and she was off, darting for the door leaving Orla temporarily alone with their wounded sister.

She felt herself start to panic and glanced to Bron.

'How is it?' she asked as quietly as she could.

The look he gave her chilled her bones. She looked back down at her sister's leg but she'd seen too many such injuries to be in any doubt about what Bronislaw was telling her. The lower leg was torn beyond repair and the only option was to cut it off to save the rest. But she couldn't do that. Holding a stranger's leg had made her faint away; holding her sister's would break her.

'No,' she whispered.

Bron reached across and gave her hand a quick squeeze.

'You don't have to do it, Orla. I understand.'

Eduard stepped up, saying, 'I'll help.'

But at that, Hana clung tighter to her hand. 'Don't leave me, Orla. I'm frightened.'

Orla looked down at her big sister, terrified herself. Hana was the eldest, the calm, confident, organised one. Zuzi was the wild child, and Orla – Orla was just Orla, quietly getting on with things, safe in the knowledge that her big sisters would look after her. Now, though, the tables were turned. Hana needed Orla to look after *her* and Orla could not let her down.

'I won't leave you,' she said. She set her shoulders and looked to Bronislaw. 'I can do it,' she told him. 'For Hana, I can do it.'

The saw, when Bronislaw lifted it, looked like a gaping monster from hell. Orla felt sweat break out on her temples at the thought of it biting into her sister, but Eduard was there to mop it away with his handkerchief. She focused on Hana as Bartek produced his flask and encouraged her to drink the rest of the vodka. Hana seemed hideously lucid now.

'Are you going to cut it off?' she asked Orla. Orla bit her lip. 'You can tell me. It's only a leg, isn't it?'

'Half a leg,' Orla hedged.

'The bottom half, I hope?' Hana asked, a little manically.

Orla wasn't sure if it was the pain or the vodka talking but she tried to smile all the same.

'It's going to hurt, Han-Han.'

'But you'll be here?' Fear flashed again across Hana's face. 'You'll be here with me?'

'For every minute.'

'Ready?' Bronislaw asked.

Eduard was having to mop the young doctor's brow too and Orla pitied Bron his gruesome task. She remembered that very first day of the uprising when all had seemed to be going so well and then the hospital doors had flung open and they'd faced the first amputation. It had become a horribly familiar task for poor Bron, but not one that ever got easier. And now it was her own dear sister in his care.

'Make it fast,' she begged him.

'As fast as I can. Hold her down.'

Orla drew in a deep, deep breath and placed a hand on her sister's thigh. Hana had her other hand tight in her grasp so it was Eduard who held her foot steady.

'Now,' Bron said and he dug the saw into her slender leg.

Hana screamed. Orla pressed down and leaned as far over as she could, looking deep into her sister's eyes.

'I'm here, Hana. I've got you. It'll be over soon, I promise.'

She could hear the grind of the saw, as she had on that very first day of the uprising, and feel the blood leaking onto her hand. It had shocked the hell out of her then. Little shocked her now, but having to see her dear sister go through it was hell itself.

'I love you, Han-Han,' she said.

Hana's eyes were lolling in her head and she was moaning in a high-pitched, desperate way. Orla leaned over, kissing her face, and stroking her sweat-stained hair back with the press of her lips as she held her tight to the operating table.

And then, with a crunch as the saw broke through and bit into the wood of the extemporised operating table, it was done. Hana had, thankfully, passed out and as Eduard took the limb quietly away, Bron turned to Orla.

'I'm going to try and seal it with ligatures instead of cauterising. There's a French surgeon using the technique to great success and I've been reading up about it. It will take longer but it'll be less brutal.'

'Thank you.'

Orla had to bite hard on her lip to keep herself at the operating table, but was at least spared the sizzle of raw flesh that had made her vomit that first night of the uprising. Bronislaw worked slowly but patiently until at last he was finished and the bleeding was stopping.

'We need to dress it.'

Orla nodded and peeled her hand away from Hana's, still clutching her own, vice-like, through unconsciousness. She reached down to the torn hem of her dress and ripped a long strip off the bottom. It was the cleanest dressing she could think of, though still far from clean enough for her liking. She looked at the sewage clinging to Hana's skirt and dreaded to think what might have wormed its way into her wound to lurk in her flesh, infecting it from within.

'Bastards!' she yelled at the ceiling. 'All she wanted was a few maps and you had to do this to her. Bastards. Bastards!' And then she was saying it over and over and Eduard was taking her hands and clasping her tight against him so she could roar her fury into his chest.

'She's still alive, Orla,' he said gently. 'She's still with us and we must do all we can to keep it that way.'

He was right, of course. Her shouting obscenities at an uncaring enemy was going to help no one and so, smoothing down what was left of her dress, she fetched wine and her cleanest cloth and slowly and meticulously began cleaning every last centimetre of the gaping wound. And if her tears fell endlessly onto it, so much the better. They, at least, might have the power to heal.

Magda arrived with Zuzi just as they were binding the stump, Jacob in frightened tow. Magda had Nella in her arms and Orla took her, hugging her adoptive daughter as Magda lifted a still limp Hana into her arms, crushing her close against her bosom.

'My baby, my poor baby.'

Hana's eyes fluttered open and she peered up at her.

'Mama.' She gave a half-smile then a grimace of pain. 'I'm sorry, Mama.'

'Sorry! Don't be sorry, my beautiful, just be strong, as you are always strong. We're here for you, all of us.' The Dąbrowskas gathered around her bed. 'You *will* get better, you *will* recover, and you *will* build a new Warsaw for us all, I know it.'

'If they don't kill us first,' Hana muttered grimly.

Orla felt everyone look to her and knew that she was usually the one who provided the bright-eyed hope in these situations but her eyes were still too full of tears to see anything.

'I...' she started, but could find no more words and was grateful when Jacob looked up and said, 'What's that?'

'What?' Eduard asked.

'Planes,' he said. 'Listen, I can hear planes.'

Orla strained to hear over the echoes of Hana's screams

ricocheting in her head, and realised he was right. There were engines in the sky but they didn't sound anything like the whine of the Stukas, or even the steady hum of the British Halifaxes.

'What sort of planes?' she asked, confused.

And that's when Syzmon Ancel burst into the hospital.

'The Americans!' he cried. 'The Americans are coming at last!'

They ran outside and saw a mass of huge planes in the blue skies above Warsaw, as if God had sent them a horde of silver angels. Orla stood with Eduard, staring up in astonishment as they drew closer. The long-awaited Liberators were enormous and there had to be at least fifty of them, flying almost wing to wing so that their shadows covered the city with welcome shade.

'It's a miracle,' Orla breathed.

All around, people were rushing out of their homes, pointing and cheering and dancing around the war-torn streets. In Orla's arms, Nella lifted her little hands towards the silver angels, trying to touch their shiny sides. The sun flashed off the planes and, as they got close, they could even see the pilots leaning out of their windows to wave. At the far end of the street, behind their barricade, the Germans were frozen, watching the imposing display, their little bullets clearly futile against the bulk of the American aircraft.

'Liberators!' Szymon shouted, and the big planes certainly felt like they heralded freedom.

'Is this it?' Orla asked Eduard. 'Is this the Allies coming to save us? Have we made it?'

She felt joy pump around her body, pushing away the dark fear of Hana's amputation less than an hour ago. The Americans came with food and medicines. Just as exciting, they came with tolerance. They were the most westerly of the Westerners and surely if they were here to help, Warsaw was saved. They would drive out the fascist Nazis, and stop the Russians imposing communism, and Poland would be able to live in peace and freedom.

'Look!' someone shouted, pointing an excited finger upwards.

Everyone did so, to more cheering, as the bomb doors of the first planes opened and packages began to spill out, white parachutes opening to let them drift gently to the ground. Orla watched, incredulous at this sudden turn in the Warsawians' fortunes. All this time they'd thought they were forgotten, but the Allies had been battling to get to them – and now look.

Magda had stayed inside with Hana, but Jacob and Zuzi scampered forward with many others to reach the first of the containers. They were dark green and bomb-shaped but these bombs brought salvation not destruction. Jacob flipped the catches on the sides of the nearest one and dived eagerly inside, then grimaced.

'It's just letters,' he said in disgust. 'What are we meant to do with letters?'

'See them safely to the people they're addressed to,' Orla suggested. 'These could bring huge hope from loved ones elsewhere.'

'I suppose,' Jacob grunted. 'But they're not as good as chocolate, are they?'

'Or morphine,' Zuzi added and with that, Orla had to agree.

Szymon took the sacks of letters off to the postal scouts for distribution and the Dąbrowskas scrambled for the next bomb-from-heaven. The wind was getting up and a number of the precious packages were blown west, over the German barricades. Orla could weep at the thought of the enemy getting their much-needed supplies, but still they were falling from the skies and she forced herself to focus on the ones she could reach instead of wasting energy bemoaning the ones she could not.

To her right, an unseemly scrap broke out as precious foodstuffs spilled out of a package. Jacob darted into the middle of it, but then Szymon was back with several of his men, shouting for order.

'The AK will take care of distribution,' he announced.

'Like they've taken care of the city?' someone shot back bitterly. 'We wouldn't be in this mess if it wasn't for your lot's petty power games.'

'Petty power...?' Szymon gasped. 'I escaped the ghetto last year. I've seen first-hand what the Nazis can do to a nation and they were coming for the Poles. They've had plans to destroy the city all along, and they would have done it – done it with all of us in it. Rising up was our only chance of escape.'

'Well, it hasn't worked.'

'Maybe it has now.'

He indicated the last of the gloriously shiny American planes still dropping goods across Warsaw and his opponent huffed.

'I hope so. I truly hope so. Now, chocolate – please.'

Szymon and his men started the tricky task of fair distribution. Orla admired them their discipline but couldn't help being glad when Jacob darted back to her side with two contraband bars.

'Take it to Hana,' she said. 'Take it to Hana and tell her that's the taste of freedom.'

'Are you coming, Orls?'

'In a minute. Can you take Nella too? I want to see if there are any medicines.'

She gave the wriggling baby to her grimacing brother and turned to hunt. Most of the packages seemed to hold guns and ammunition. She knew they needed those to defend themselves but it made her heart ache to see the arrival of more weapons to create hurt instead of medical supplies to soothe the too many already wracking the Warsawians. The last of the American planes were disappearing over the horizon and the Nazis were shooting at the people trying to retrieve their prizes.

'Have you no humanity?' Orla yelled in their direction.

In reply, a bullet pinged off a wall behind her and Eduard threw her to the ground.

'It's not worth it, my darling girl. It's nearly over. Leave them to their hate and keep yourself alive for my love.'

She kissed him, long and deep, until someone kicked at her foot and she looked up to see Zuzi standing over them, hands on hips.

'Sorry to interrupt but I thought you might be interested in this.'

She held something up but, with the planes gone, the sun was shining once more and Orla could not see. She scrambled up, keeping tight to the wall.

'What is it?' Then she saw – a large, white bag with a red cross on the front. 'Medicines!'

Eduard was up too and they took it from Zuzi and all went into the hospital.

'Bron!' Orla called. 'Look – Zuzi's found medicines.'

'She's amazing,' he said, rushing over to look inside, and Zuzi blushed furiously.

'Have you not got it together with this lovely man yet?' Orla whispered to her sister and Zuzi blushed even more.

'There are more important things than kissing right now,' she said primly.

Orla grinned.

'That's true, sister dear, but it's a lovely way to pass the time.'

'Orla! You're so shallow.'

'To prefer kissing to shooting?'

'No. That's fair, generally speaking, but we have a war to

win. We're close. The Russians have let the Americans use their airbases at last and someone just told me that the Red Army is on the march again. Tosia says the Minerki are being asked to go out to Czerniaków.'

'Why?'

Zuzi jumped up and down in excitement.

'Because the AK holds a landing stage down there and the Russians are sending the First Polish Army over.'

'The communist one?'

'Does it matter at this stage? With the Americans in the sky and the Russian Poles crossing the river, we have to be close to victory. Then we can set about mending our people and rebuilding our city. Come on – let's tell Hana. It'll be as good a medicine for her as anything in that bag.'

She had a point and Orla took her arm and followed Bron to Hana's bed. Jacob was already there with Nella, feeding the eldest Dąbrowska morsels of chocolate with Magda's eager encouragement. There was morphine in the first aid parcel and even, miracle of miracles, some penicillin to attack any infection in her sister's severed leg.

'We're going to get you better, Han-Han,' Orla promised as the family gathered around her bed. 'We're going to get you better and we're going to be free. Any day now, we're going to be free.'

THIRTY-SEVEN
20 SEPTEMBER

ZUZI

'Yes!'

Zuzi cheered with four other Minerki and Bartek's skeleton platoon as, with a boom and a loud creak of metallic pain, the Poniatowskiego Bridge collapsed into the dusk-pink waters of the Vistula. It was sad to see the magnificent piece of engineering ripped apart but what it meant for Warsaw was important. Bridges could be rebuilt; freedom was what counted.

'They're retreating,' Tosia cried, grabbing Zuzi's hands and dancing her around on the riverbank. 'The Nazis are leaving Warsaw. We've won!'

'Not quite yet,' Bartek said cautiously but he was smiling as he stared across the water to the broken metal. 'But it must only be a matter of time.'

The Nazis had blown both bridges up on the city side, which could only mean that they'd given up hope of stopping the renewed Russian advance any other way. And it wouldn't work, as they could clearly see the Red Army on the far bank, bringing flat-bottomed pontoon boats up from the south to cross. For the last two days, Soviet tanks had pounded the eastern bank and now they'd taken it and were poised to attack the city proper. They'd heard reports that the First Polish Army – made up mainly of those men taken when Russia had invaded Poland at the start of the war and then released to fight alongside them in 1941 – was going to cross, and now they could actually see them preparing. Somehow, Stalin had been talked into helping the insurgents and liberation must be mere days away.

Zuzi thought back to before the uprising when she, Hana and Orla had watched the Volksdeutsche fleeing for the station in a mad panic, and the Wehrmacht troops straggling through the city in retreat from the Red Army. Warsaw had risen up to pave the Russians' way into the city and the Russians had delayed and delayed, putting them through a hell that had robbed the Dąbrowskas of two homes, many friends, Babcia Kamilla's life and Hana's leg. It had been a high price but at last, it seemed, they were coming.

The glorious American planes had, sadly, not returned as the weather had turned suddenly towards autumn, bringing thick cloud that would prevent the clumsily large aircraft from flying. It seemed darkly ironic that while Stare Miasto had burned unaided, the sun had shone fiercely down, but now aid was available, the clouds had closed in. The sceptical were muttering that perhaps God did not want Warsaw free, but that was just hunger talking. God moved in mysterious ways and if He wished to send help by boat instead of plane, that was fine by Zuzi.

Besides, word had come that the Russians were going to deliver supplies too, probably this very night, and the Minerki were on standby to collect them. Zuzi had no idea what had gone on in the corridors of power but she was very glad of the Allied pressure and could only pray that if Stalin was working with Churchill and Roosevelt to rescue Warsaw, they would have some protection against his imperialist greed. The invasion of Poland had started this damned war and surely the world would hail Her liberation together.

'Planes!' Tosia called.

Zuzi looked into the blood-red skies over the river and saw the dark shapes coming towards them. They were far smaller than the American planes and flying far, far lower, so low in fact that Zuzi had to resist the urge to duck as they sped down the line of the Vistula, sweeping over the sinking bridge arches and turning into Warsaw. Bartek's men had pulled out torches and were signalling their position and Zuzi saw the doors open and packages begin to fall. Everyone, it seemed, was sending Warsaw gifts and she ran up the slope from the river onto the open plain where they were dropping.

Then ran back again, fast.

The Russians were delivering goods in wooden crates without any parachutes and they were falling at speed and hitting the ground with loud cracks. Zuzi ducked into the Warsaw sailing club they were using as their base and watched as more and more fell, many cracking open on landing and spilling their goodies across the earth.

'Why are they doing that?' Zuzi gasped.

'They're too low to use parachutes,' Tosia said from the next doorway. 'They wouldn't have time to open.'

'So, fly higher,' Zuzi gasped, as a crate landed metres from her and split open, sending shards of wood flying like shrapnel so that she had to press herself to the inside wall to avoid being skewered.

'Then it drifts into the German zones,' Tosia called and Zuzi was glad to hear she was still alive.

The planes were almost done now, the pilots heading off over Warsaw to take potshots at the Nazis before turning for home. Once the coast was truly clear, the AK crept out to find crates everywhere, like a birthday party gone mad. Zuzi saw two of Bartek's lads scaling a tree to rescue one from the uppermost branches and two more staring in puzzlement at the domed roof of a nearby church where one had lodged itself against the drain.

'Let's take those on the ground,' Tosia called and, nodding, Zuzi ducked out to the nearest one.

Guns were spilling promisingly from it, but when she picked up the first, she saw that the barrel had been twisted on landing. A second one had lost its trigger and a third was split open.

'At least there's ammo,' Tosia said, lifting up boxes full of bullets, but when they looked more closely, they saw that they were – obviously, she supposed – of Russian manufacture and therefore useless in the Polish weapons, designed to work with British and German-captured ammunition.

'Perhaps the weapons experts can do something with it?' Zuzi suggested but the weapons experts were back in Śródmieście so little use to them in the southern reaches of the city. She looked across the river. It was almost dark and the Vistula was an inky stretch before her but on the far side, busily moving lights marked the Russians positions.

'If the Red Army come, they'll surely bring guns?' she said.

'They will,' Tosia agreed. 'And maybe other packages have done better than ours.'

Some certainly had. The one cushioned by the tree was intact and the men gleefully loaded their new Russian guns, pointing them towards the German positions, still thankfully out of range on the western edges of Czerniaków. Bartek had managed to break a hole in the domed roof of the church and rescue the crate to find more weapons. Those on the ground, however, had yielded little. Several holding precious grain had split wide open, scattering it across the dirty ground, though two Minerki still diligently scooped up as much as they could in the hope that a good boil would kill the worst of the germs.

One box had clearly held grenades, several of which had, predictably, lost their pins on landing and blown up the entire lot. When the little group laid out their gains, they were poor indeed.

'Better than nothing,' Bartek said determinedly. 'At least it means they're with us now. And the boats may come in the morning.'

He was right, Zuzi supposed, and she lay down to sleep with the rest of her gang praying that the dawn would bring new hope.

It did. She was shaken awake by Tosia at the first threads of light.

'Listen, Zuzi.'

She strained to do so and heard, above the quiet snores of the AK soldiers, the distinct plash of oars. She grabbed at her boss.

'They're coming?'

'Sounds like it. Come on.'

Zuzi shook the others awake and they stumbled down to the shore to see, through the autumnal mists, a mass of pontoon boats heading to their landing stage. The AK ran to take up defensive positions with their new guns and Zuzi, Tosia and the two other girls rushed onto the stage with Bartek to help them moor.

To their huge surprise, the first officer to jump out was a woman. Tall, blonde and striking, she came striding towards them with her hand held out.

'Janina Blaszczak,' she introduced herself in fluent Polish. 'Leader of the Third Pomeranian Infantry division of the First Polish Army.'

Tosia rushed to shake her hand, the others following, as Janina's troops leapt out of the boats and began assembling on the slope. A shot rang out from upriver, at the edge of the destroyed bridge, signalling that the Nazis had not yet abandoned their positions, and Bartek hurried to get them into the sailing club.

'Thank you so much for coming,' Tosia said to Janina as they brought up the rear.

'I've been champing at the bit to get over to you for weeks,' she replied.

'So, what's been the hold-up?'

She shrugged. 'Awaiting instruction from Moscow, which can take forever.'

'Awaiting instruction?' Zuzi gasped. 'While we all burned?'

She shrugged again. 'Welcome to Stalin's world. You'll get used to it.'

'We will not,' Zuzi said hotly.

Janina looked at her in surprise and Tosia put a warning hand on Zuzi's arm.

'Let's get these troops settled, shall we?' she suggested. 'And fed. Have you brought food?'

Janina shook her head. 'We were told supplies had been dropped by plane?'

Zuzi and Tosia exchanged dark looks.

'Not many of them made it,' Tosia said carefully. 'You do have weapons?'

'Of course.'

'Excellent.'

Janina shifted. 'Though I wouldn't say many of our troops are crack shots.'

Zuzi stared at her, confused. 'Why not? Are you not an army?'

'Sort of. That's to say, yes, of course, but we've brought in a lot of new recruits along the way and they're not fully trained.'

'Not *fully*?'

'Not at all, really. We've done drills while we were waiting to cross, but most of our weapons were only issued last night, so it's not been easy.'

Zuzi looked to Tosia again. What on earth was going on here? Why would you send green men into battle?

'You can't be *all* new recruits?' she said.

Janina ran a finger under her collar and looked around.

'Not all,' she agreed, though her tone was not convincing. 'It was felt by Moscow that it would be a good idea to send the, er, fresh men first to be sure we could make it.'

'First?' Zuzi seized on this. 'So, there are more coming?'

'Oh yes,' Janina agreed, but again her words were not matched by her tone. She glanced to her troops which, now Zuzi looked properly, she could see were a load of bemused-looking young men in a mish-mash of uniform items worn over rough farming smocks. 'We were assured you had a strong force in the city and that we were merely here as back-up.'

Zuzi ground her teeth.

'If we had a strong force, Janina, do you not think we'd have control of Warsaw by now? We rose up because Moscow Radio incited us to do so with assurances that the Red Army would be there within days to finalise our liberation. That was a month and a half ago, and here we are, hanging on by a thread. You lot are our lifeline.'

'Lifeline?' Janina visibly swallowed. 'Well, we'll do our best.'

It was not encouraging and Zuzi felt her hopes for this invasion twisting as badly as the barrels on the Russian guns.

Four days later and Zuzi's worst fears were realised. The next night had brought more of the First Polish Army but none with experience or weaponry, merely providing the skeleton AK group with additional mouths to feed for little military advantage. Zuzi had talked to some of them and found them to be parochial mountain farmers, press-ganged into the Red Army's

Polish force with little idea of how to fight and even less about the political situation. Many only vaguely knew there was a war on; two of them had never even heard of Hitler.

'You must know Adolf Hitler,' Zuzi had raged. 'The Nazi "Führer", the man who's systematically invaded almost every country in Europe over the last five years in his egomaniacal quest for world domination.'

'What's Europe?' one lad had asked in reply.

Zuzi had despaired.

It had been clear that leading these country farmworkers against the might of the German army would be madness, especially as, after a few desultory shots to cover the second landing, the Red Army proper had paid them no attention at all. Yesterday, when the sun had come out from behind the clouds, Zuzi had seen their soldiers sunbathing on the riverbank, playing volleyball and picnicking. Meanwhile, from the west, Himmler had set Dirlewanger's SS thugs on Czerniaków and they were attacking with their usual brutal aplomb. The sailing club had taken a direct hit from a rocket launcher and the AK and their innocent helpers had had to retreat to abandoned houses further inland where they could do little more than huddle miserably together, clutching empty stomachs.

'I want to help,' many of the young Poles had told Zuzi. 'I want to free the Motherland.' But wanting to and being able to were very different things.

It was clear the Russians had sent these young men to be as much a sacrifice as the abandoned AK and that Stalin had never intended to come to Warsaw's rescue. He'd simply dangled the suggestion of help to prevent Bór from negotiating a surrender. Thousands more would die and that was exactly how Stalin wanted it.

Zuzi thought about the sketches she'd rescued from the Telephone Exchange showing some Nazi called Pabst's crazy ideas to destroy their centuries-old capital in favour of a mock-alpine transit town. No doubt Stalin had something similar planned, only with more concrete and less wood. Both Germany and Russia saw Warsaw simply as an area in which to set up their own people; the Poles were a necessary and little-regretted sacrifice on the way to that goal.

Their only hope was the Western Allies, but no more shiny Liberators had been seen in the sky and yesterday Janina had brought them word that Stalin had blocked use of his airfields again. She had also reported that, with the Germans closing in on Czerniaków, they were sending boats to take the First Polish Army back across the river. Sure enough, the useless soldiers had slipped back the way they'd come and the AK were on their own again.

'What do we do?' Zuzi asked Bartek.

'We have to get back to Śródmieście. The Germans will overrun Czerniaków within a day or two and we can't be here then or...'

He stopped himself but Zuzi did not need his discretion. She knew full well that if the Nazis caught them 'consorting' with Russians, they would execute them on the spot. And that was if they were lucky. The women, especially, might be saved for the SS's more bestial habits and even starting to think about that made Zuzi cold to her bones.

Oh, she missed her family. She'd come out here to pave the way for the army that would liberate them and instead found herself trapped in a different part of the city from those she loved. She thought of broken Hana and prayed she was still alive and healing with the American medicine. She thought of Orla, newly married and caring for their sister, of Jacob, battling to remain a bright-eyed fighter in the face of the endless grind of death. She thought of Magda, still trying to bake for all Warsaw while she fretted about the fate of her children. 'Above all else, I'm a mother,' she'd said to them. 'You are the monuments of my life and I do not want you toppled.'

Zuzi peered out at the German tanks creeping closer and knew that she did not want to be toppled either. All reports, however, indicated that the enemy had closed off their escape routes north.

'How do we get back?' she asked nervously.

Bartek grimaced. 'They've got the sewers and the river covered so that leaves us only one way.'

'Overland?'

He nodded grimly. 'I've been on the radio to Agaton in HQ and we've identified an access point at Jerusalem Avenue. There's an AK barricade there that isn't well covered by the Germans. They have a few snipers in buildings nearby but if we gather our remaining weapons and mount a full charge, we might make it. Or, at least, some of us might.'

'*Some* of us?'

'It's better than none.'

Put like that, she supposed he was right, but they were not odds she fancied. Bartek put warm hands on her shoulders.

'I'm sorry, Zuzi.'

'It's not your fault.'

'I asked you and the other Minerki to accompany us. I led you into this situation and now, I promise, I'm going to get you out.'

'We chose to come, Bartek. We can take care of ourselves.'

He smiled. 'You certainly can. My Bron's picked well.'

'Picked?'

'I know he cares for you, Zuzi.'

'He told you that?'

'Not directly, but there's not been much time for father-son chats around the campfire. He talks about you all the time though, and I've seen the way he looks at you. I used to look at my wife like that, I know I did.'

'And will again when you get back to her.'

'If merciful God permits, I most certainly will. I'll sweep

her into my arms and cover her with kisses and make sure she knows that she's the most wonderful woman in the world.'

'I really hope you do.'

'Me too, but I won't make it to her sitting here like a fairground duck, so we have to try.'

'We have to try,' Zuzi agreed, her heart pounding already.

'We go tonight so let's hit the food stores – we'll run better on full stomachs.'

Zuzi agreed and eagerly ate her share of the final rations, but several hours later, when, after crawling through acres of allotment on her belly, she found herself crouched at the end of Jerusalem Avenue, eyeing up the exposed run to the AK barricade, the food churned sickeningly inside her. She looked at the apartment blocks on either side. If there was even one German sniper in any of the windows, he'd be able to take most of them out undisturbed.

'Grenades,' Tosia said, shoving a bag of filipinkas at her. 'Our job is to stay tight to the walls, two of us on each side, and if we see anyone firing, to fling one at them. Don't try and be heroic, ladies. Let the men do as they wish, our aim is to get over the barricade alive. Understood?'

'Understood,' Zuzi and the others agreed sombrely.

'Great. Last one to the other side makes the tea, yes?'

Zuzi tried to say yes, but it stuck in her throat. Suddenly she wished she'd written a loving note to her family that might be found on her body. She hadn't told them what they meant to her enough. She'd been too like Babcia, preferring to keep her feelings to herself than to lavish them on those that so deserved them. She—

'Ready?' Bartek asked grimly.

No, Zuzi wanted to scream but what was the point? She would never be ready and this had to be done.

'Ready.'

'Go!'

Then they were out, charging towards the AK barricade some hundred metres away. Zuzi followed Tosia, keeping tight to the wall as the AK shot down the centre, guns raised to both sides. At first, all seemed good. At first, it looked as if any Germans who'd been stationed here had been redeployed, maybe even to attack the sailing club they'd not long abandoned. That would be a beautiful irony, she thought, as she made it maybe halfway up. But no!

The first shot rang out and an AK soldier went down screaming and tripping a second who was fired on before he could get up. Zuzi pressed herself against the wall, scrabbling for a grenade. The shots had come from the opposite side and she flung her first filipinka towards the window she thought the sniper was hiding behind. It fell way short, almost taking out two of their own men.

'No,' she whimpered, grabbing a second and trying to remove the pin, though she was shaking too much to grip it.

'Be more Babcia,' she told herself sternly.

Steadied, she threw a second. It flew through the window and exploded inside, but more shots were ringing out and it was clear that the Nazis had called up their reserves.

'Run!' Bartek shouted, turning back to look for her.

She forced her legs to carry her, scraping along the wall as she gained ten metres, twenty.

'Come on, Tata!' she heard someone call and, through the fog of exertion and fear, she saw Bron at the barricade, urging his father on. He spotted her, and his hands went to his mouth before he leaned urgently forward and cried, 'Come on, Zuzi!' Instinctively she veered towards him as a shot ricocheted off the wall she'd just abandoned.

Someone let out a sob and she thought perhaps it was her but it was hard to tell in the chaos. More of the AK were falling but they were shooting at their attackers with deadly accuracy. One Nazi fell from a window, another slumped across a windowsill. Zuzi pressed herself into a doorway, mere metres from the barricade. Eager AK soldiers were opening a gap and urging them on. Hands were reaching out and she remembered them reaching up for her in the sewer. The AK had caught her then and they would catch her now. She had to go for it, but the gap was on the far side of the street and she'd have to leave the wall to get there.

Ten more steps. Bartek was ahead of her, leading his men bravely forward, and that's when the machine gun fire rang out, a vicious rat-a-tat of menace. Zuzi braced herself for a strike but felt nothing until she saw Bartek hit the ground, clutching at his chest. Then her heart spiked as if she'd taken a direct hit.

'No!'

'Zuzi, get down!' Tosia called.

She obeyed instinctively, grabbing for a grenade. The Nazi leaned out, a satisfied smile on his face as he saw Bartek writhing on the ground and, filled with raw, burning hatred, Zuzi stood up, planted her feet, and threw. The grenade arced up and over him and she saw his eyes follow it in almost comic shock before it exploded behind him and he fell from the window, hitting the street head first.

'Serve you right,' Zuzi hissed.

There were no more shots. That man had either been the last of the Nazis or his remaining fellows had fled. Zuzi looked to Bartek, just metres away, and saw blood spilling thickly from between his fingers where they clutched at his brave heart. This was the man who had carried Babcia Kamilla to safety, Hana too; now Zuzi had to repay his aid. She moved towards him, but someone beat her, leaping the barricade and negotiating too many dead bodies to clutch him in his arms.

'Tata. Oh Tata, I'm here. I've got you. Don't die, Tata.'

Zuzi sank to the ground, amongst the corpses of her fellows, and watched, eyes stinging with pain as Bronislaw cradled his father. Around her, everything else seemed to fall to silence and she could only hear the two men.

'God is calling, Bronislaw,' Bartek said to his son, his voice hoarse but clear. 'He is calling and I must go to Him. I'm sorry. I love you, son. I love you so much. Your brothers too. You will tell them that?'

'Of course, Tata. But don't give up. *Please*. I can make you better.'

'It's too late, Bron.'

'It can't be.' Bronislaw's voice broke and Zuzi's heart with it. 'What's the point in me becoming a doctor if I can't save *you*.'

Bartek clutched at his hand. 'You will save many, son, and you will think of me when you do and know how proud I am of you. Of all of you.'

Bartek fought for breath and Zuzi listened to Bronislaw weeping.

'Find your mother, Bron,' Bartek gasped out. 'Find her for me and take care of her. God knows, dearly as I love you three, I love her above all things on this earth. She is the kindest, bravest, most beautiful woman I've ever known.' He clawed at Bron's hand for the strength to get out the words. 'Truly, being married to her completed my life. I wish it could be longer.' His voice choked. 'I wish it could be much, much longer but just one day with my Ana would have been enough and I thank God for the many wonderful years He granted us. You will tell her that?'

'I'll tell her, Tata, I swear it. And I'll look after her for you.'

'I know you will,' he said but his voice was fading, the effort of his final words draining the life from him before Zuzi's eyes. 'You're a good lad. You deserve a love like I had. You deserve...'

The words failed in Bartek's throat and with a small cry, he went still. Zuzi felt sadness spike through her but, as Bronislaw leaned in close over his father, his body shaking with grief, she knew that her own sorrow was nothing in comparison to his. She longed to go to him, to hold him, but was not sure she'd be welcome. And then he looked up to heaven, his eyes translucent with sorrow, and she knew that she *had* to help. She *had* to go to him. This man was suffering and she loved him. She loved him! It could not and should not be denied any longer.

She crawled to the other side of Bartek and put a hand over Bron's where it clutched his father's body tight. He slowly pulled his eyes from the skies and looked into hers and she held his gaze, strong and sure.

'I'm here, Bron,' she said softly. 'I'm here for you. Always.'

THIRTY-EIGHT

HANA

Hana lay in the darkness, her eyes turned to the moon glinting through the sliver of a window in their basement hideout. It was fat and round and bright – unlike everyone below. A plane flew across the front of it in a graceful silhouette and a tear ran down Hana's face. She did not bother to wipe it away.

It was hopeless. The Russians were sitting on the far riverbank laughing at Warsaw while the Nazis pounded modern Śródmieście with the ferocity they'd brought to medieval Stare Miasto. Meanwhile, the rest of the world had turned its back, ashamed to even look at what they were allowing to happen to the capital city of the first ally. Poland was being carved up between Germany and Russia as surely as she'd always been. Hana thought of her grandfather's handcuffs, once so proudly displayed on Babcia's wall and now deep in the rubble with her, and felt that they were not so much a symbol of pride as a tragic truth of her country's endless destiny.

Not that politics really mattered now. What mattered was that she was huddled in a basement with her family with no power, little water and less food. So many AK were dead, so many more wounded and mutilated, like herself. Most of her fellow liaison girls were gone and even Czajnik had fallen. She was lucky, really, that her immediate family were still alive and, yet, they weren't so much living as clinging on. And for what?

Another tear ran down Hana's cheek and she shifted in bed, feeling the gap where her leg should be like a vast chasm. The wound was healing, or so Orla kept telling her with irritating brightness, as if she were a child who could be jollied into feeling better. And it was true that she didn't feel ill now; but she didn't feel well either.

What was the point of it all? She had her family and she loved them to bits but they were changing. When this was somehow over, Orla would live with Eduard, and Zuzi, it seemed, with Bron. They'd come back from the terrible loss of Bartek so firmly together that Hana suspected they were every bit as married as Orla and Eduard – and good for them. A priest would be found if they ever got out of here and Hana reckoned, after all they'd been through, that God would bless their union. If God was even still watching.

She shook herself. There was no point in descending into the darkness with Warsaw, even if it did feel as if her personal power plant had been switched off. Agaton had been to visit her the other day, bringing the retrieved maps and trying to engage her in discussion about the Warsaw of the future, but when he'd sat on the edge of her bed, she'd instinctively gone to move her leg away, before realising it was no longer there to move, and all she'd been able to think about was what those maps had cost her.

'We'll get you a prosthetic,' Bronislaw kept telling her. 'There've been astounding advances in that field recently – I did a dissertation on it before the war – and there will be even more once it's over because...'

'Because there will be so many cripples around?' Hana had finished bitterly.

She knew she wasn't being the calm, measured older sister they expected her to be, but, frankly, why should she? At the start of this war, she'd been the one with the fiancé and the dreamy future and now Orla and Zuzi had that and all she had to look forward to was a fake leg.

'You are not a "cripple",' Bron had told her sternly.

'No,' Zuzi had agreed, tight at his side, 'you're you, Hana Dąbrowska, with a little bit missing.'

She'd wanted to scream then, because it wasn't a "little bit". Maybe, as a proportion of her overall body, it was a small amount, but it made her incomplete and marked her out as someone to be pitied and she hated that.

'I'll look after you,' Magda told her, over and over, and Hana loved her mother for that, truly she did. But she was the eldest daughter, the sensible child, the one who did the looking after, and she didn't like it the other way round.

The moon was curving out of her sight and she could see the pink gleam of yet another day, looking as determinedly perky as her damned sisters despite the clear evidence that it would bring only horror and hurt. Sometimes Hana tried to remember what it had felt like to dance on the barricades back at the start of August when the sun had been as hot as their hopes, but it was impossible. Besides, she'd never dance again, even if they got free to do so.

'Pathetic, Hana Dąbrowska,' she told herself. There were thousands dead, thousands more with wounds that were festering and dragging them into a slower, more painful ending. All she'd lost was a "little bit" of her leg and she should be grateful but it was hard.

'Hana?' She looked round to see Magda standing over her holding a rough bread roll. 'It's not much but you should have it.'

'Why?' Hana asked dully. 'Because I'm a cripple?'

'No, stupid, because you're awake first. Early bird catches the worm!'

Hana forced a smile and tried to shake off her melancholy but it had its hooks firmly into her. She sat up on her pillows and nibbled at the bread. It was more grit than flour but her stomach was as empty as her heart and, despite herself, she savoured it.

'I'm sorry I'm being such a grump, Mama,' she said.

Magda sat on the bed and put an arm round her. 'In case you hadn't noticed, my sweet, we're all being grumps.'

'Orla and Zuzi aren't,' she said, indicating her sister, asleep on a mattress nearby. 'They're in love.'

'That's true, but they're still hungry and weary and fed up. They want to get on with married life instead of, of... Oh I'm sorry, Han-Han, that was insensitive of me.'

Hana twisted wearily on her redundant engagement ring.

'Not at all, Mama. You spoke the truth. And I know how they feel. I wanted to get on with married life with Emil, but the Germans came and forced him away and now he's at the bottom of the Vistula.' She turned to Magda on a sudden thought. 'What happened to my leg, Mama?'

'You were shot, Hana, escaping from—'

'No, no. I know that. I mean what happened to the actual leg?'

'I'm not sure. Why?'

'Because maybe I should throw it into the river, to be with him. A fitting tribute, do you not think?'

'I do not,' Magda said sternly. 'Don't get hysterical, Hana my love, it doesn't suit you.' She was right of course but it was hard to care any more. Magda hugged her close. 'I know how you feel, truly I do. I still miss your father constantly. I miss him when I wake up alone. I miss him when one of you does something funny or sweet or stupid and I want to turn to him and share it. I miss him every time I bake – and I bake all day long. I understand.'

Hana squeezed her hand. 'I'm so sorry, Mama. It's horrible, isn't it?'

'Horrible.'

They sat there quietly together as Hana nibbled her way to the end of her roll and the rest of Warsaw woke to another day of shelling. Around them, the others began to stir, but then there was a knock at the basement door and it lifted to show a bright young face peering in on them.

'Is there a Hana Dąbrowska in here?'

Hana looked to Magda puzzled.

'She's over here,' Magda called.

'Excellent.' A young lad scrambled down the ladder into their hidey-hole and came scampering across. 'Letter for you.'

'Letter?'

Hana stared in astonishment at the airmail envelope, feeling its thin folds beneath her fingers.

'Came in the sack from the Americans,' the lad said cheerily. 'Hope it's good news.'

Then, with a tip of his cap, he was gone and Hana was left staring down at the writing on the front. It was directed to Piekarnia Dąbrowska in Wola, and that address felt so very familiar and yet so very alien, although it was only two months since the SS had driven them away from their precious home. The handwriting, too, was heartbreakingly familiar and yet impossibly distant.

'It's from Emil,' she whispered.

How long ago must he have written this? How much time must it have spent winging its way around Europe while its writer flew to his death? She looked at Magda. 'I'm not sure I can bear to read it.'

Magda took it gently from her and turned it over and over. More light was creeping through the little window and Hana could see Emil's neat handwriting through the flimsy paper. She grabbed for it. She couldn't *not* read it. These must be his final words to her before his last flight and, bittersweet though they would be, at least they would let her revel for a few wonderful moments in what might have been.

Magda handed her a knife and she slit along the opening, careful not to cut any of his precious words. And that's when she saw the date, written clearly at the top of the page – 01.09.1944. She stared at it, then looked to her mother.

'Emil died in August,' she said. 'August seventeenth. I saw it. I saw him go down. I saw the violet go into a spin, I saw the plane crack open and sink into the water.'

Magda put a hand on hers and Hana could feel it shaking.

'Read it, Han-Han,' she urged and, drawing in a deep breath, Hana did so.

My dearest, darling Hana,

I thought that the longer we were apart the easier it might get, that time might dull the pain of missing you, but if anything, it has only made it worse. Every night before I go to sleep, I picture your beautiful face and imagine the impossible deliciousness of kissing your lips and when I wake up it is almost as if you have actually been there. For a moment, life feels unutterably sweet and then reality slams into me like a grenade and my heart aches afresh.

I just want this evil war to be over, my sweet. I just want to get out of this damned plane and take you up the aisle and build a house in which to make our future life together. I don't want adventure, or medals or the camaraderie of my fellow pilots – though all those are good – I just want to step over a small threshold to eat dinner with my wife. Is it so much to ask of the world?

I pray daily – hourly – that you are alive and well, Hana.

Now more than ever. I hate the thought of you trapped in Warsaw and only the knowledge that you are with your lovely family makes it anywhere near bearable. I hope you are keeping each other safe and that you will come out of the other side and into my arms.

God, I am sure, is watching over us – at least as best as He can do while man runs rampant across his creation. Certainly, He is watching over for me, for last month he sent me a fever. I cursed at first because it meant I could not fly my second sortie to Warsaw. I railed at my weakness, failing you when it was most critical but, oh Hana, the young man who took my place was shot down somewhere on the trip and never returned.

My plane, painted with a violet for you, my sweet girl, was lost, while I lay in my bed sweating my way to wellness. Can you believe it? God wants us to be together, I know He does. Hold on, my beautiful Hana, my sweetheart, my soon-to-be-wife. Hold on and one day this will be past and we will be together.

All my love,

Emil

'He's alive!'

Hana leapt instinctively out of bed, wobbled on her right leg, but then steadied herself against the bedhead and waved the letter triumphantly.

'He's alive!'

Instantly her sisters were awake and flinging themselves into her arms so that she toppled backward onto the bed.

'He's alive!' she cried again, twisting her ring with a surge of joy, seeing in its pretty purple heart the renewal of all her hopes.

Zuzi and Orla took up the refrain like a song. It was still dark and they were still hungry and helpless and scared, but joy had found its way between the cracks of their suffering and they let it lift them and nourish them and keep them safe. Their happiness lilted through the cracks of the Warsaw dawn. It woke Jacob and brought Bronislaw and Eduard running, others with them, unsure exactly what scrap of happiness had fallen to one of them but glad to snatch at it all the same.

And then, into the little crowd, came a liaison officer with news: surrender.

The news spread rapidly and Warsaw buzzed with it, shame battering up against relief, horror mingling with delight. There would be an end. Jacob flung open the door to their hideout and they all headed out, Hana in Eduard's arms, Nella in Orla's. It was quiet, beautifully quiet. No planes flew across the broken city and more and more people crept out of their houses to look around, peering into the faces of their fellow survivors, trying to gauge if it was true. Then the official notification blared out from the remaining street-speakers and radios:

> *The Homeland Council wish to inform you, the brave people of Warsaw, that Commander Bór has negotiated a surrender with the German command. It felt vital to us that, since we have not received the assistance expected, we should save what is most dear to us, namely the biological substance of the nation. May God bless you all and may Warsaw's bloody ordeal move the conscience of the world and inspire the triumph of law and justice.*

As the buzz finally settled into a steady reality, the Dąbrowskas came together, stunned.

'Surrender?!' Zuzi said, shaking her head. 'Now? After all this?'

Magda waved to their tiny underground hideout. '*Because of all this*, Zuzi. We simply cannot go on much longer.'

'Babcia Kamilla would not like it,' Zuzi said mulishly.

Hana nudged Eduard to set her down on a lump of rubble, adjusting her balance carefully.

'Babcia Kamilla is dead,' she said to the others, 'and she will not want any of the rest of us in heaven with her for many years yet.'

'But we've got this far,' Jacob objected, going to stand next to Zuzi.

'And been heroes to do so,' Orla told him.

'Heroes don't surrender,' he insisted, though his voice wobbled at the end.

Hana felt for her brave young brother, who should have spent his teenage summer playing with a football, not with guns. She reached out a hand to him.

'Do you expect *me* to fight on, Jacob?'

He grabbed at her hand. 'Of course not. You're... injured.'

'You were going to say crippled, and you'd be right, but I think, perhaps, we are all crippled now – by hunger and loss and sheer lack of anything with which to defend ourselves. We have fought honourably and we have suffered much and maybe now – tragic as it is – we just have to be grateful we are still alive.'

'It's not very noble,' he mumbled.

'It's not,' Zuzi agreed, putting an arm around him, 'but Hana's right.' He looked up at her, surprised, and she put her hands up. 'I know, I know. I was the one keenest to fight, I was the one who wanted to blow up the Nazis and we did. We did everything that was asked of us and more, so much more. But we were only ever meant to be an advance force – a welcome party for the Red Army. They didn't come, Jacob. They betrayed us. Remember that day when the guns went silent?'

They all looked at each other, picturing the moment in

their cosy bedroom on the top floor of Piekarnia Dąbrowska when they had heard the Russian guns go silent – shortly before the blood-curdling cries of the attacking SS.

'I nearly died that day,' Orla said quietly.

'I nearly died in the ruins of the hospital with Babcia,' Zuzi said.

'And I nearly died in the sewers,' Hana agreed quietly. 'It's enough.'

Magda smiled at them all.

'It's definitely enough. Your father would be so, so proud of you all – and so, so keen for you to live on.' Hana felt them all gather close around her, their love like a warm glow even in this coldest of moments. 'Even Babcia would agree,' Magda went on. 'She asked us to take care of each other and to take care of Warsaw, and we can do that best, now, with peace.'

'Peace!' Hana agreed, and the word rang around their weary family like a bell. 'Peace has to be the aim now. And surrender will be temporary. The Allies *are* coming, however slowly, and the Nazis *will* be defeated. The Homeland Council is right – we must save our "biological substance"; we must save our family. And when the time comes, together, we must rebuild.'

'She's back!' Zuzi said. 'Our big sister is back, sensible and calm and strong again.'

'Shut up, you,' Hana berated, swiping at her, but Zuzi kissed her and then they were all hugging, drawing in the sorrow of surrender and its sweet, sweet relief.

When they finally disentangled, Hana felt for Emil's precious letter in her pocket. She pictured Agaton's maps, gained at such cost, but there now to form a blueprint for Warsaw's future. It had not been for nothing and she would be a part of it. She would get out of here, she would find Emil, and she would rebuild their city stronger and prouder and freer than ever before.

THIRTY-NINE
4 OCTOBER 1944

HANA

'Are we ready?'

It was a ridiculous question. How, after sixty-four days of proud uprising, could they possibly be ready to hand themselves over to the arrogant Nazis who had pounded them with brutal disregard for any of the basic rules of war? How could they put themselves into the hands of men who had sent sixfold rockets into their hospitals and churches? How could they trust their bodies to those who had massacred their families and friends? And yet how could they not?

In war, losers had few choices.

'We are not losers,' Zuzi had insisted when Jacob had miserably put this to the family last night. 'We won our pride, we won our right to stand up for our own, we won the chance to be heard.'

'It's just that no one was listening,' Bron had said sadly, his arm tight around her shoulders.

It still made Hana fiercely jealous but, bound to hope, she

could use that to fire her dreams of the future. And besides, where they were going none of them would have their men close, and for her sisters' sakes she hated that.

They had spent two agonising days deciding how to surrender. The AK members and ancillaries had a stark choice – they could either walk out of Warsaw in their armbands and be taken as prisoners of war, or remove them and go as citizens to labour camps. Either way they would be segregated and either way they would be at the mercy of the Nazis; it was simply a question of which route might offer them a greater chance of survival. The Germans had put the Wehrmacht, rather than the SS, in charge of the surrender and had signed a treaty agreeing to treat the AK as an official armed force, protected by the Geneva Convention. The civilians, however, were drifting in a no-man's land, theoretically also protected but in a way that was far harder to monitor.

It had been an agonising decision but, to everyone's surprise, it had been Orla who had made it in the end.

'We went into this as AK, so we should go out of it as AK. Did we not join for Tata, to honour his request to carry on the fight?'

They'd paused, remembering the dark morning when they'd been forced to watch their beloved father and husband thrown to a casual death over the balcony of the Pawiak prison. Then Magda had nodded firmly.

'We did, Orla. And we will continue to do so.'

The fight might not look as it should right now. It might not look like blazing guns and triumphant barricades and captured tanks, but it was there all the same, in the hearts of the people standing in long lines waiting for the outward surrender. It was there in the hearts of the Dąbrowskas.

Hana shifted as a trumpet called for silence. She was in a wheelchair, rescued from a broken house by Zuzi and Jacob and mended by Eduard, and much as she disliked it, at least she could sit up tall before the Nazis who had put her in it. And, of course, it had a secret of its own, one that made her smile even through the pain of this bitter morning.

She watched, heart aching for her one-time boss, as Commander Bór stepped out from the ranks of generals to hand himself over. He looked tired and old but held himself proudly. Hana had heard tell that his wife was alive and well and that she had, just two days ago, given birth to his second son – a child with, it seemed, the wisdom to wait for the bombs to stop. She prayed Bór would get to see them soon but for now, like the rest of them, he was heading into captivity.

The commander was wearing a simple, dark brown overcoat with his AK armband on the sleeve – his way of insisting to the Nazis that this, rather than the official uniform designated in the Geneva Convention, was sufficient to be honourably treated as a combatant. This had been agreed as part of the surrender and they could only hope the Nazis would stay true to it, as it was what they were all wearing, their armbands tattered and faded but still proudly in place.

'Attention!'

Agaton called their group to order as the barricade opened up before them and they were sent down the wide reach of Lwowska Street towards Plac Zbawiciela where they would surrender the tools of their various trades. Zuzi went first with Tosia and the last of the Minerki, holding rolls of fuse wire over their shoulders. Jacob pushed Hana behind them, his Prussian helmet on his head, his gun over the handle of her wheelchair and her liaison satchel clutched in her lap. Magda was at their side, holding a loaf of bread, and Bronislaw, Eduard and Orla – Nella on her hip – brought up the rear of their little group with their medical bags held tight in their hands.

All around them, others did the same. A chaplain stood in bright, if dusty, robes, to bless them as they passed through and they marched with shoulders back and heads held high, refusing to look at the German soldiers lining the route, or the photographers and film crews gleefully recording their humiliation for the Führer.

'It won't last,' Jacob muttered to Hana. 'They'll be the ones marching to imprisonment soon enough and theirs will last forever.'

'And still not be long enough,' Hana replied, shifting on the padded cushion which Agaton had been kind – and cunning – enough to bring for her last night. She half smiled but the ordeal was not over yet. They might have reconciled themselves to surrender but the humiliation was still painful, and the fear of wherever they were going intense.

Wehrmacht soldiers stood in the square, holding large wicker baskets into which any guns or other weapons had to be thrown. The AK tossed them in with deliberate lack of care, forcing the soldiers to bend to pick up one that had missed the target. The Wehrmacht were young and looked embarrassed, but Hana could find no pity for them. This was all their fault. Someone began singing the national anthem, 'Jeszcze Polska nie Zginęła' – Poland Is Not Yet Lost – and it was taken up with alacrity, the rousing tune showing the enemy that the Poles refused to lie down, that this was but a momentary blip in a centuries-long crusade for freedom.

From the square they were divided into several paths out through the city and the Dąbrowskas were marched north, eventually turning into Miodowa Street where the prisoner parade halted. Up at the front people were being loaded onto trains out to POW camps and those waiting their turn shuffled uncertainly, wary now that the official surrender had been achieved with dignity. But then Nella strained in Orla's arms, tugging to get down and pointing into the charred remains before them.

'What is it?' Orla asked, letting her stand.

The little girl clutched tight to her hand and pointed again.

'Look,' Zuzi cried. 'It's Babcia's cross!'

Sure enough, there, perched almost cockily on top of a mound of rubble, sat the beautiful silver cross, its jewels picking up the sun as they always had and casting a rainbow of light across the blackness of Stare Miasto.

'She's with us!' Magda cried, clasping her hands together.

'Well done, Nella,' Orla said, bending to her adopted daughter. Nella beamed and then, letting go of Orla's hand, took four determined steps towards the cross before falling onto her nappy-covered bottom. The family laughed out loud and everyone stared, attracted by the happy sound.

'You walked, Nella!' Eduard cried, picking her up and swooping her into the air. 'You walked for Tata! And just in time too.'

He pointed to where, up ahead, people were being sifted into male and female lines, then pulled Orla close in against him, Nella between them. Zuzi ran to Bronislaw and Hana's heart ached for them both.

'Why can't we stay together?' Orla moaned.

'It won't be for long,' Eduard assured her. 'The Allies are marching so fast through France that they're almost at the German border.'

'And once we are gone,' Zuzi put in, 'the Russians will doubtless march on defenceless Warsaw.'

'And through to Berlin,' Bron added gently, stroking her hair. 'Then it will be Germany surrendering and we will be free. We must choose somewhere to meet.'

'Somewhere in Warsaw?' Magda asked, looking round at the ruins.

'Sadly not. Not yet. Not until we can rebuild and...'

He glanced to Hana but there were still soldiers on guard and he stopped himself.

'Łódź,' Bronislaw suggested. 'That's my hometown and it has not been destroyed as Warsaw has. There's a beautiful cathedral there – St Stanislaus – where we can find each other. Let's say 5 p.m. every day, without fail, until we are all together once more.'

'Will that be necessary?' Orla asked nervously.

'It will. They will scatter us to the winds but the winds will bring us back. And then – then we will return to Warsaw.'

'Return,' Hana agreed. 'And rebuild.'

She reached down, sliding a hand beneath her bottom, ostensibly to adjust her cushion but, in reality, to feel for the plans hidden tight within the feathers, ready, as the Dąbrowskas were ready, to rise again.

The sound of an engine cut through the air and everyone looked up to see three planes swooping in on Warsaw. Many dived for the ground, screaming.

'The bastards have betrayed us already,' Zuzi cursed.

'I don't think they're Stukas, sweetheart,' Bron soothed and Hana would have smiled to hear it, save that she was worried Zuzi was right. Were the Nazis playing them false? Had they organised this charade of a surrender only to get them into the open as targets for the Luftwaffe to remove from the earth? She reached for Jacob's hand on one side and Magda's on the other, as her sisters huddled with their menfolk behind, but then Jacob laughed.

'Bron's right – they're Halifaxes! They're British planes, here to show us their support.'

The German soldiers looked furiously up as their prisoners pointed and cheered at the three planes dipping down to fly low across Warsaw. Their bomb doors opened and they released a beautiful shower of red and white ticker tape, like a glorious Polish flag in the sky, broken up but all there ready to be put back together again.

And that was when Hana saw it – bright and clear as the lights from Babcia's cross, a violet shone from the underside of the first plane. She squinted into the sky and she swore that she saw Emil, leaning from the window and saluting them in honour of all they had been through and promise of better times ahead. And then he was gone.

'I'll see you at sunfall,' Hana cried after him through happy tears. 'I'll see you at sunfall for tea.'

EPILOGUE

5 NOVEMBER 1945

This is the stark truth. We were treated worse than Hitler's satellites, worse than Italy, Romania, Finland. May God, who is just, pass judgement on the terrible injustice visited on the Polish nation, and may He punish accordingly all those who are guilty. Your heroes are the soldiers whose only weapons against tanks were revolvers and bottles of petrol. Your heroes are the women who tended the wounded, cooked in bombed-out cellars and comforted the dying. Your heroes are the children who went on playing in the ruins. Immortal is the nation that can muster such universal heroism. For those who have conquered, and those who live will fight, will conquer and will bear witness again that Poland has not perished yet, so long as we still live.

The battle is finished but from the blood that has been shed, from the common toil and misery, from the pains of our bodies and souls, a new Poland will arise – free, strong, and great.

HOMELAND COUNCIL OF MINISTERS' FINAL ADDRESS TO THE POLISH NATION

MAGDA

'Ladies and gentlemen of Warsaw, it is my huge pleasure to call to order the very first meeting of the Association of Architects. Our mission: to rebuild, repair and renew this, our soon-to-be-beautiful-again capital of Poland.'

The president stretches his arms wide to encompass the charred remains of Warsaw and the crowd gathered before his makeshift stage cheer wildly. They have a huge task before them, but they come to it with passion, energy and goodwill and that, Magda believes, is half the battle. She has always said that people must fight their own way and that goes for the city as well as its inhabitants.

Besides, right at this moment, it is enough to be here, back in Warsaw, back together. It has not been an easy journey. Magda was sent to Oflag IX-C near Erfurt with Hana, Zuzi, Orla and little Nella and they fought for survival until the Americans brought blessed liberation in early April 1945. It took them over a month to get transport to Łódź and three more weeks of turning up to church every evening before Bronislaw, who'd been sent, to his disgust, to work in a German hospital, found them and took them to live with his mother Ana.

Ana Kaminski had somehow made it back from Auschwitz alive, as had her nurse friend, Ester. Their tales of the place were enough to turn the brightest of hearts black with horror and that, Magda sensed, was not even the half of it. Both women would bear the scars of the camp forever but they were awe-inspiring in their desire to fight for a better future. Magda liked Ana instantly and they went daily together to pray for their lost husbands' souls in St Mary's Church – and for the return of the rest of the family.

It was an agonising month-long wait for Eduard and Jacob who finally staggered in one gloriously sunny day in July. They had been sent to the gruesome Stalag X-B near Bremen, not liberated until the end of April, then Jacob had been ill and Eduard had stayed to nurse him to health before travelling. Their arrival triggered great rejoicing – and Zuzi and Bron's wedding barely days later. The pair, bless them, all but sprinted to the altar. Magda stood side by side with Ana to watch the simple, happy ceremony, smiling to see her spiky middle daughter, once so reluctant to give herself to love, falling so thoroughly into its glories.

'I'm delighted the war brought my son such happiness,' Ana told Magda as they clutched each other's arms in a brave attempt to fill the hole forced on both of them by the untimely death of their dear husbands.

'They'll probably argue quite badly,' Magda said ruefully, looking her fiery daughter up and down with a knowing eye.

'And make up quite wonderfully,' Anna replied calmly. 'Some couples are just made that way.'

Magda glances at them now, arm in arm at this vital meeting of Warsaw's returning citizens. The Dąbrowskas moved back here a month ago, bringing sturdy self-build huts with them from Łódź for makeshift homes. The city is ruined. Even after the very last Poles were marched out, Hitler did not stop his wanton destruction. He sent Himmler in with vast teams of Brandkommandos – fire troops – to systematically burn and pull down street after street after street. Almost 80 per cent of the buildings standing when he marched over Poland's borders on 1 September 1939 are gone – bombed, burned and demolished – and few that remain are safe to inhabit.

Not that that has stopped the Warsawians, who have been returning in droves since VE Day last May. Over two hundred thousand of them now live, like the Dąbrowskas, in tents, sheds and makeshift rooms amongst the rubble. Magda knows because daily she feeds as many of them as she can. Piekarnia

Dąbrowska operates out of a rough wooden kiosk, in a row of similar shops, but people flock to it all the same. There is flour, at least, brought in by the Allies in truckloads, as if that might somehow make up for abandoning them to the mercy of their enemies. It does not make up, but the flour is good and the bread nourishing and, really, what point is there in recriminations? It is time to look forward, which is why thousands of Warsawians are here today to hear the architects speak about their future.

There are many decisions ahead of them but the key ones have been made: Warsaw will stay as Poland's capital; money will be poured into her regeneration; and they will combine modern buildings with the recreation of old ones, most notably those in the market square at the heart of Stare Miasto. Babcia Kamilla would be glad of that, Magda knows, and hopes she is looking down on them all, Aleksander and her own dear Kaczper with her.

Already the committee has put out an appeal for pictures of Warsaw as it once was, for postcards and artwork, for maps and plans. Paintings by a famous artist called Canaletto are being loaned to them from private collections all over Europe to aid the restoration and although it is hard to see how the committee will get even halfway to their goal, their energy is wonderful.

On the stage behind the president stands his main operational team led, amongst others, by Agaton, back to his true identity as Stanisław Jankowski. He stands proudly in front of enlarged copies of many maps, recovered by his own team and by others with similar foresight. At his side, to Magda's enormous pride, stands his assistant, Hana Andrysiak, both feet firmly planted, although one is entirely made of wood. She has no stick, but leans discreetly on the arm of her husband for support and it swells Magda's maternal heart to see them together after far, far too long.

Hana and Emil have been married just six weeks. It took Emil a long time to be released from the RAF and longer, having been repatriated to England, to make it back to Poland to claim his bride. Hana was terrified to face him when he first arrived in Łódź, afraid that her missing leg would cut a hole in his love for her, but Magda was delighted to see that he did not even notice it, so intent was he on drinking in her face. When she shyly pointed it out, he dropped to his knees and kissed the stump, thanking God for keeping the infection from claiming any more of the woman he loved.

'A bit over-dramatic,' Zuzi said from the sidelines.

Magda tutted her but Hana simply laughed and said that, frankly, after the dark tragedy of losing her leg, Emil could be as dramatic as he liked. Besides, the delay had given her time to learn to walk on her wood-and-leather limb, and it was easily hidden beneath the skirts of the first proper wedding dress for any of the Dąbrowska sisters. Magda's eldest daughter may have had to wait longest for her wedding, but she had the finest ceremony, with plenty of food and wine and even lights that stayed on to the end. It was a magnificent party, after which all three of her girls headed for Warsaw, via honeymoons of their own.

Magda clutches her arms around herself, imagining them to be Kaczper's holding her close as she considers their three daughters and their husbands. Hana and Emil will not argue but will certainly tussle intellectually, especially now that Hana is training full-time as an architect and Emil returning to his love of history as a junior lecturer here in Warsaw. The university buildings, as a continued Wehrmacht base during the destruction, are some of the few still standing, and the irony has not escaped the family that Hana's new husband will be teaching in the very building in which she risked her life for the maps now on display to the whole city.

Magda sighs at the thought of the terrible night when they brought Hana in bleeding from her injured leg. She hadn't wanted her precious girl to go on the crazy mission, hadn't wanted her to risk herself for a few maps. And had she not been proved right? For all the good it had done her. But that, too, was motherhood and here were the maps, the starting point for regeneration for them all, so perhaps Hana was right too.

Magda smiles and turns her eyes to Orla and Eduard. They will not argue either, she is sure, because neither of them are made for combat. He is a good man, training to be a plumber, and every bit as soft as his wife. Little Nella is already being brought up in a household that believes more in the power of hugs than slaps and if Magda's eyes do not deceive her (and they rarely do), her youngest daughter is carrying another child – a new Dąbrowska to carry on the miraculously surviving line.

'Oh Kaczper,' she whispers. 'I wish you could see them now.'

He would be so proud of his children. Even Jacob, who chafed against the restraints of school when he first returned to the makeshift arrangements set up in the Saxon Palace (another survivor of the destruction because Hitler fancied it for himself), is settling down, finding a passion for science that is thankfully more constructive than his previous passion for tanks and guns. Too many young Warsawians have grown up in conflict and they must learn to live in peace. It is not always easy, especially with Stalin taking control.

Magda shivers at the thought. The city did not want communist rule any more than they wanted fascist occupation but the city does not get much say – save in its own shape. That, for now, will have to do. The fight for true liberation goes on but if it can be channelled into houses and palaces, civic buildings and expressways, then at least no one will be hurt.

There has been enough hurt.

It is time to make Warsaw great once more – the perfect place to bring up the new generation of their family, united and secure.

Magda closes her eyes and sees Kaczper, her dear husband, standing on the Pawiak balcony exactly six years ago, his chest bare to the November air and his head high. Oh, she loved him then, as she'd loved him from the instant she'd set eyes on him as a trainee baker. So many times she'd run her hands over that broad chest, had cuddled up to it, feeling safe from everything in his arms. The Nazis threw him over the balcony as if he was nothing when, in truth, to her at least, he was everything.

'It would gladden your big heart to see your daughters happy,' Magda tells him under her breath.

'I do not want you to weep,' he said on that dread day, 'but to live and to love – and to fight.'

'Well, Kaczper,' she tells him, opening her eyes again and smiling through her tears, 'we fought with all we had. We clung to life with all we had. And now, my own dear heart, we will love with all we have, all the way to the final, gloriously free, sunfall.'

A LETTER FROM ANNA

Dear reader,

I want to say a huge thank you for choosing to read *The Secret Message*. This novel developed from *The Midwife of Auschwitz* as I knew that Stanisława Leszczyńska's (the real-life inspiration for my heroine Ana Kaminski) husband, Bartek, and son, Bronislaw, had fled to Warsaw and been part of the Warsaw Uprising. I only had time for some brief research into this fascinating period of WW2 history but it was enough to want more. When I decided to follow Tasha Ancel's story for *The War Orphan*, it was a chance to explore further as she, too, came from Warsaw. I was therefore fascinated to be able to delve deep into the uprising for this new story which follows the three fictional Dąbrowska sisters but features, as side roles, Bartek, Bronislaw and Tasha and her family.

If you want to keep up to date with all my latest releases, and receive a free short story, *The Woman Who Hoped*, just sign up at the following link. Your email address will never be shared and you can unsubscribe at any time.

www.bookouture.com/anna-stuart

The story of the Warsaw Uprising is a hard one. The people of the city rose up, as instructed, fulfilled their brave resistance to the Nazis brilliantly, taking large swathes of the city ready for full liberation, and were then left to face renewed Nazi attacks largely alone. Their fate, both as individuals and as a people, was tragic, but their courage and endurance was – and is – an inspiration to me and I hope it has been so for you too.

If you enjoyed this novel, I'd be very grateful if you could write a review. I'd love to hear what you think, and it makes such a difference helping new readers to discover one of my books for the first time. I also love hearing from my readers – you can get in touch via social media or my website.

Thanks for reading,

Anna

www.annastuartbooks.com

facebook.com/annastuartauthor
x.com/annastuartbooks
instagram.com/annastuartauthor

HISTORICAL NOTES

The Secret Message is a novel about an entirely fictional family. The three Dąbrowska sisters are figments of my imagination but they are, I hope, representative of the very real Warsawians who rose up so bravely to help the Red Army win back their beloved city, and who were betrayed in the worst possible way. Here are a few notes for those who would like to know a little more about the history of the Warsaw Uprising.

Poland – Land of Occupation

The Nazis were not the first to occupy Poland – far from it. This vast, fertile, well-organised country sits, to its detriment, between Russia and Germany, and has been the target of one or other throughout history. The country was forced to become a Russian Protectorate in 1716 and then partitioned between Austria, Prussia and Russia in 1797, with a treaty removing the word 'Poland' from all official documents.

In effect, the country ceased to exist for the next 123 years but the Polish spirit was kept alive in the hearts of the people. The 'January Uprising' of 1830 and the 'November Uprising' of 1863 were bold attempts to reassert independence. Both were ultimately doomed but gave the Poles a blueprint for insurgence, as well as their national anthem – 'Poland Is Not Yet Lost' – and the stirring Chopin Études that would blare from the barricades in August 1944.

Polish independence was finally granted as part of the First World War armistice in 1918 and there followed a period of huge prosperity with great advances in music, the arts, science, housing, education and government intelligence. Small wonder that, in 1939, the Poles were so bitterly opposed to the renewed invasion by both Germany and Russia – the age-old enemies between whom they would find themselves tragically caught in the Warsaw Uprising.

The Polish Resistance

When I first started researching the Polish underground, I was expecting something like the French maquis – rough groups of local insurgents, working bravely but without much coordination (at least until de Gaulle got the Free French movement going). What I found, instead, was an entire state operating underground.

From the moment Warsaw was forced to surrender, the key mechanisms of government, judicial and social systems reset in a clandestine manner. The cabinet fled to London and operated from there as a fully recognised government (as did those of a number of other occupied countries), issuing advice and instruction to brave leaders within Poland. There was an underground nationwide civil service, and a judicial system, complete with courts and sentences for Polish criminals, so that it could be seen that the country was still operating fully, albeit in secret.

There was also a massive education system, ensuring – at great risk – that Polish youth were still taught when the German occupiers had, cruelly, denied them any right to attend school or education. Classes like Agaton's, shown in the novel, were a matter of daily life with huge numbers of brave teachers standing up to continue the schooling system beneath the Nazis' noses. There was also, of course, an army, run by many of Poland's top generals, with Bór (the code name for General Tadeusz Komorowski) heading it up, and a whole ranking system of commanders.

The many years of cruel occupation in Poland's history had solidified her spirit of resistance – and her ability to organise it. This was not a coalition of guerrilla groups but an entire country functioning beneath the Nazi radar, recruiting and training and waiting for their chance to strike back. The Warsaw Uprising was that chance and but, I believe, for the lack of support from Poland's supposed allies, should have been a glorious one.

The Minerki

These were a very real troop of all-female sappers, led by Antonina Mijal, code name Tosia, who performed astonishing feats both before and during the Warsaw Uprising. As shown in the novel, they were key to the taking of both the Prudential tower on the opening day and the Telephone Exchange (known locally as the PAST-a building) on 20 August. They also helped blast through hundreds of cellar walls to create the underground city that kept so many of the Warsawians alive throughout the horrific bombing of August and September.

The Kanalarki

This was also a real designation, though a less defined group than the Minerki, as it was a term that came to be given to all the brave people – mainly youngsters – who travelled through the sewers to carry messages and escort evacuees. The idea of travelling through tunnels beneath the city sounds, at first, rather like a *Boys' Own* adventure, with an almost comic touch always ascribed to human sewage, but there was nothing funny about it at all.

If you go to the Warsaw Uprising Museum (an astounding place and well worth a visit), you can step into replicas of both the larger oval sewer and the smaller side ones. Clearly they are empty, clean, and lit, but even without the hideous addition of darkness, swirling effluent and the danger of Nazi attack, they are claustrophobic, back-breaking tunnels. There are many heartbreaking stories of people losing their minds down there, or having horrible accidents that left corpses floating with everything else in the cramped spaces. The fumes were almost overwhelming and the long, long time it took people to travel the relatively short distances stand testimony to how tricky it was. I was keen to take Hana down the sewers to stand testimony to the bravery of the hundreds of Kanalarki in the uprising and, although it broke my heart, felt it important to show her taking an injury as so many of them did.

The Scouts

I mention the Scouts a few times in the context of training the younger AK members and, although I didn't have the space to go into it in any detail in the novel, this was a big feature of the Armia Krajowa (Home Army). The scouting movement started under Baden-Powell in Britain in 1908 but soon spread across Europe and was eagerly embraced in Poland. Given the constant threat from enemies either side, the movement there had an inevitably military bent and Scouts were involved in all major conflicts from 1919 onwards in ancillary roles.

Much training, for both sexes, was combat-orientated, and when the first Polish city of Poznan was taken on 10 September 1939, a large body of Scouts left with the retreating army, marching 270 km to Warsaw to join resistance forces. On 27 September, the moment the underground movement was officially formed (a day before surrender to the Germans), the Scouting movement put themselves officially at the disposal of the underground army. They wore a grey uniform so, during the war, became known as Szare Szeregi (Grey Ranks), enabling them to sign propaganda leaflets and messages as SS, in an ironic play on their occupiers' secret police. Many brave Scouts as young as twelve lost life and limb to the Nazis, and they were a significant force in the uprising.

PW

The PW symbol, painted on the walls by lads like Jacob, was an important mark of defiance during occupation. It first came into being during the Wawer massacre – one of the first large-scale massacres of Polish civilians by German troops 26–27 December 1940. The initial meaning of the initials PW was Pomścimy Wawer – We shall avenge Wawer – and at first, Polish scouts painted the whole phrase on walls, but it was soon abbreviated to PW. In early 1942, the AK organised a contest to design an emblem and it was won by Anna Smoleńska, a Scout, who combined the letters P and W into the 'Kotwica' – Polish for anchor – and this was the design most commonly used going forward. Over time, the PW of the Kotwica came to also stand for Polska Walcząca – Fighting Poland – and then Powstanie Warszawskie – Warsaw Uprising. I hope stories like this one can remind the world where hatred and over-zealous nationalism can take us as a society and encourage us all to embrace each other in a more loving peaceful way.

W-hour

For the sake of narrative simplicity, I have not shown the timings in the lead up to W-hour in all their complex detail. Bór did issue the order to rise at around 5 p.m. on 31 July, but it had to first go to Monter, the code name for Colonel Antoni Chruściel, the commander of Warsaw who I sadly didn't have space to include in the novel. The order didn't actually go out, therefore, until about 7 p.m., just one hour before curfew, making it very hard for messengers to get it distributed until the next morning. As a result, many AK commanders did not know about the order until hours before they had to assemble their troops – no easy matter in an occupied city, with the Nazis getting wind of something in the air. It has been estimated that possibly as many as 40 per cent of the AK were not in position for W-hour and this was part of the reason that several key strongholds – such as the Brühl Palace and the railway stations – were not taken. Another reason was that, even had they all been there, there simply weren't enough AK – and certainly not enough firepower – to take those very well-defended sites, and the leadership should perhaps have realised that in advance.

There was much argument between the leaders of the AK about whether to rise up and when to do it. Now is not the time to cover that in detail but certainly several well-informed people were telling Bór that the Germans had sent reinforcements against the Russians, and also – knowing their likely treachery – warning him not to rise until the Red Army actually crossed the Vistula.

It is likely that Bór was under huge pressure at this point, with tension reaching boiling point in the city. The government in London were behind the uprising, suggesting that the British also were, and there was a very real fear that if they failed to rise before the Russians came, they would be handing them their city on a plate. At the end of the day, I think Bór gave the command because, as I say in the novel, he felt that the young soldiers of the AK, utterly fed up of the oppression and brutality of their occupiers, were going to rise anyway and it was better that there was some central command. He was an honourable man, in an impossible position, and had the Russians simply done as they'd promised, it would all have worked out well.

AK Weapon Shortages

Weapon shortages during the uprising were a huge problem and the AK leadership does have to take some responsibility for that. As shown in the novel, the original plan for the uprising was for it to be out in the country to block the Nazi retreat, and it was changed within only weeks of W-hour to be in Warsaw itself. That meant that weapons hidden all over Poland had to be brought back into the capital and given this was an occupied city, closely patrolled by Nazi troops, that was not an easy job. The protocol of only two people knowing about any one cache was also problematic. It was undoubtedly needed as AK were regularly captured and tortured, but as so many died in the first days of the uprising, it meant that some went undiscovered. Large caches were found intact in Warsaw years after the uprising that would have been so very useful during it.

However, the uprising was only ever meant to last a maximum of five days before the Red Army came in and the AK had enough to last out that period and, indeed, longer. They were never going to last the two months that the uprising turned into without outside help. Churchill was racked with worry about Warsaw and did all he could to persuade Stalin to let the British and American pilots help, but Stalin was playing his own vicious game and Roosevelt, in thrall to 'Uncle Joe' and more concerned than Britain about securing his ongoing help for the war in the Pacific, was not prepared to push him.

The AK were, therefore, left to draw on their own considerable resources. The mass manufacture of 'filipinkas' kept them going far longer than should have been possible, as well as very strict – and doubtless hugely frustrating and scary – protocols on when to fire, and the manufacture of all sorts of home-made guns and rocket launchers. Many, many civilians were drawn into production of these fireside weapons and it is testimony to the Warsawians' ingenuity and productivity that they lasted as long as they did before surrender.

Stalin's Tactics

There has been much debate amongst historians about how calculated the Russian abandonment of Warsaw was. It is certainly true that the Germans sent out unexpectedly strong reinforcements to keep the Red Army on the other side of the Vistula at the end of July, but also true that it only held them up for a few days. The more I have read of the Warsaw Uprising, the more convinced I am that Stalin cold-bloodedly left the citizens to rot.

Moscow Radio, as shown, incited the people of Warsaw to rise up to allow their army swift entry but when the people did so, Stalin not only refused to enter, but also publicly denied having anything to do with it. Meanwhile, Hitler sent in the SS against the Poles and Stalin made no effort to even send up Russian planes against the Luftwaffe. He actively obstructed other Allied efforts, refusing to let either the British or the Americans use Russian airbases – far, far closer to Warsaw than their own – and it seems to me all this can only be seen as a very calculated way of having the Polish capital ruined to make it easier for him to take it for his own.

Even worse, as shown – albeit briefly – in the novel, as September ground on and the AK were seriously considering surrender, Stalin sent in just enough hope to keep them fighting to the bitter end. There is some argument that Russians always did their supply drops without parachutes to allow the planes to fly lower for greater accuracy, but the crates carrying the food and arms were just not strong enough to take the fall and almost everything they dropped was useless. It was a very clever show of help that actually offered no help at all.

This was also true of the so-called Polish Army when Moscow finally allowed them to cross the river in boats. This army, note, was made up of the prisoners the Russians had taken when they invaded Poland as aggressors in 1939. Many of them had been sent to Siberia or kept in terrible conditions and their assimilation into Stalin's army was as much lip service to Polish aid as the supply drops. They were under-equipped and under-trained and many, as shown, were peasants dragged into the march. The story of some of the Polish recruits not having heard of Hitler is a true one and shows the remote lives these young men had been leading before Stalin pulled them into the Red Army and sent them to Warsaw as pretend aid for the insurgents.

Stalin was playing the long game. He wanted to win the war, yes, and was happy to join the Allies to achieve that, but his main goal was to create the Soviet Union – his own, eastern empire – and he would stop at nothing to achieve that. The Westerners thought they were negotiating with him on gentlemanly terms, but Stalin had little intention of using them as anything other than a means of getting exactly what he wanted – the whole of Eastern Europe, tight behind his Iron Curtain.

The people of Warsaw were some of the first victims of that brutal, calculated policy. Sadly, they would be far from the last with communism crushing many countries in the post-war years, leading up to the dramatic building of the Berlin Wall, as explored in my novel *The Midwife of Berlin*.

The SS and the Wola Massacre

The story of Orla being tied to a tank is based entirely on a true episode, one of many equally horrific ones in the Wola massacre that signified the start of the Nazi fight-back. Sadly for Warsaw, Hitler handed command of breaking the AK to Himmler, his vicious right-hand man and commander of the SS. Himmler wasted no time in sending in his most brutal, undisciplined gangster groups.

Oscar Dirlewanger was a sadistic criminal who had rampaged through Belarus for the year leading up to the Warsaw Uprising, wreaking terror on the local population. His men were soldiers in name only and had far more in common with a terrorist gang – out for their own gain. They were gleeful in their killing, rampant in their looting and brutal in their sexual attacks on women. Hitler was happy to let them ravage the city he hated and the poor people of Wola stood no chance.

Eduard is also based on true stories of young men pulled into the Dirlewanger Group as they marched. Many were sickened by the so-called soldiers' vicious tactics and sought to escape by any means, including taking their own lives. I was glad to give Eduard a second chance in the arms of gentle Orla.

The Rebuilding of Warsaw

The astonishing story of the rebuilding of Warsaw is not one that I had room to fully explore in this novel, though I hope I have shown the roots of it in the determination of the people to make it great again, even while it was being destroyed. Hana's bid to fetch the plans is fictional but based on various true sorties to find and save every map that could be kept to preserve the blueprint of the historic Warsaw the Germans destroyed.

Warsaw was devastated in a way that is hard to truly get your head around. The population of Poland's capital went from 1,300,000 in 1939 to 900,000 at the start of August 1944 to 153,000 in January 1945. Over 200,000 people died during the uprising and, after surrender, approximately 600,000 survivors were deported into the crumbling Reich. In the end, many civilians were simply released into the countryside to fend for themselves, but the fear on surrender was that they would all be sent to camps so many chose to leave as AK in the hope they would be treated honourably as POWs.

With its people gone, the entire city of Warsaw was wiped out. As mentioned in the novel, Hitler brought in troops to raze those parts not already bombed into non-existence, pouring huge resource into this in the back end of 1944 – a time when that manpower was sorely needed elsewhere for the retreating Nazis. He truly hated Warsaw. The Pabst Plan of 1940 is a real document, showing the Nazi intention of turning the grand city into a mere staging-post on the route east (genuinely complete with alpine chalets for the intended German citizens) and, even in defeat, Hitler was desperate to wipe it from the map. He failed.

The Poles made a bold decision to keep Warsaw as their capital after the war and put huge resources behind its restoration. There was modernisation too, along the vast east–west expressway mentioned in the novel, but huge swathes of the city – mainly in the historic Stare Miasto– were recreated from plans, photos, paintings and human memory. Stanisław Jankowski was a real architect (and a real, and very successful AK leader as Agaton) and a key part of the restoration and I was delighted to be able to make Hana his fictional assistant.

If you visit Warsaw now – and I strongly recommend you do – you would be hard-pressed to know that you are not looking at Renaissance townhouses but at twentieth-century recreations. The market square is, to all intents and purposes, a stage set, but a perfect and lovingly created one that stands testimony both to Warsaw's ancient heritage and her far more recent resilience and determination.

The Ghetto Uprising

There were two uprisings in Warsaw of which the 'Warsaw Uprising' was the second. The first, mentioned several times in the novel, was in 1943 and was, I'm afraid, equally tragic. This was the Ghetto Uprising, when the last of the Jews in the barbaric ghetto at the centre of Warsaw rose up against their Nazi guards to avoid being sent to certain death in Treblinka.

The Nazis were as quick to persecute Jews in Warsaw as elsewhere, making them wear Star of David armbands within weeks of the occupation – although they were blue and white in Warsaw, not the yellow we usually see elsewhere. The ghetto was set up in November 1939 and would become the largest of some eight hundred across Europe, having close to 400,000 inhabitants at its peak. Then, from January 1942, the Nazis began shipping Jews out of the ghetto to Treblinka, an extermination camp, built solely for killing them.

As mentioned in the novel, it didn't take AK spies long to work out that many people were going in and none were coming out and to join the dots. Warnings went back to Warsaw but there was little anyone could do to stop the inhumane transports. By April 1943, the ghetto was down to its last few thousand inhabitants and, having correctly anticipated its liquidation, two groups of clandestine fighters rose up on 19 April, using weapons largely smuggled in by the Warsaw AK. The brutal fighting went on until 8 May, with those outside the ghetto able to hear constant gunfire and explosions and see Jews jumping from top storeys to avoid flames. Almost all the Jews inside the ghetto were killed, but a few escaped to hide in the darkest corners of Warsaw. Amongst those were my fictional

Ancel family, whose story is explored more fully in *The War Orphan*.

The Ghetto Uprising was a tragedy, ending in inevitable destruction, but those watching were very impressed by the heroism of the Jewish fighters and amazed that so small and poorly armed a group could keep the Germans at bay for so long – it was to be, in part, the inspiration for the wider Warsaw Uprising just over a year later.

The Handcuffs on the Wall

The handcuffs and chains on Babcia Kamilla's wall are inspired by a true story – that of Countess Maria Tarnowska. This bold, strong woman led a distinguished life in various parts of the world as the wife of a key Polish diplomat, before becoming a leading figure in the Polish Red Cross, heading up the medical efforts during the Warsaw Uprising. She features briefly in the novel as Orla's Sister Maria but there was not enough space to do her full story justice.

One notable detail, told in her memoir, however, I could not resist including. It was Countess Maria's father who was imprisoned by the Russians during the 1883 and sentenced to eight years' hard labour in the Siberian mines. He escaped and was reprieved by the Tsar, returning to Warsaw where he kept the handcuffs from his time in Siberia on his wall to symbolise the Polish determination never to be enslaved. I chose to give these, along with something of their owner's dignified ferocity, to Babcia Kamilla, but those who wish to know more about Countess Maria should seek out her fascinating memoir – *The Future Will Tell*.

Extracts from Real Documents

The Oath of Allegiance of the AK, Stalin's letter to the Polish prime minister, the letter from Churchill and Roosevelt to Stalin, and the heartbreaking Homeland Council of Ministers' final address to the Polish nation are all extracts or translated paraphrases of real documents. I chose to include them to back up the story with a glimpse into some of the high-level political wrangling going on behind the scenes. The 'litany for the Polish people' is also cited in direct translation and shows, I think, the fighting spirit at the core of even the nation's prayers.

Bór's orders have not survived to give verbatim, but I hope that my version of them is close to the truth and the statement that the Homeland Council must save the 'biological substance of the nation' is true and a phrase that has passed into Polish history. I can see why, as the people – the brave, bold, resilient people – of Warsaw were the heart of the uprising and their spirit survived, bringing them flocking back to the utterly ruined city in 1945 to start its astonishing rebirth.

POW Routes

Most POWs were sent out of Warsaw via the Western railway station in the south of the city, but there was a second route via the 'Gdansk Station' in the north, between Żoliborz and Stare Miasto. Some may well have been loaded there, to ease crowding, and I chose to send the Dąbrowskas that way so I could take them past Stare Miasto, scene of much of their suffering and Kamilla's burial place, as it felt fitting for my characters to see it one last time before they were forced away.

The Warsaw Uprising is a tale of unbelievable endurance and community spirit. It was not, of course, perfect harmony and I have tried to show a little of the reservations of some of the

HISTORICAL NOTES 385

population, thrust into a brutal siege that lasted far longer than it ever should have done. Given the tough conditions, however, and the heartbreaking lack of support from outside, this too-little-known Second World War story seems to me one of huge courage by everyday people and I hope readers have enjoyed it.

References for Historical Documents:

- Oath of allegiance for the Armia Krajowa: as cited in the Warsaw Uprising Museum
- Message from Churchill and Roosevelt to Stalin: Marxists.org archive (https://www.marxists.org/reference/archive/stalin/works/correspondence/02/44.htm)
- Message from Stalin to Stanisław Mikołajczyk: LSE Digital assets (FPARF, f. 06, inv. 6, fold. 23, file 242, p. 31)
- Homeland Council of Ministers' final address to the Polish nation: broadcast on Błyskawica radio station, Warsaw, 3 October 1944.

ACKNOWLEDGEMENTS

This novel is dedicated to five wonderful women – writer friends that I have met while trying to make my way in this crazy business, and who have made it a little less crazy, and a lot more fun. I met the lovely Julie Houston on my first Romantic Novelists Association conference way back in 2008 and, both new writers in a field of pros, we hit it off straight away. The following year, up in Cumbria, we met Tracy Bloom. Tracy and I found, to our great surprise, that she had grown up in my Derbyshire village and now lived barely ten minutes away. Our regular stamps around Kedleston Park putting the writing world to rights have been invaluable to me.

Four years ago, with our kids growing up, the three of us decided we'd like to sort ourselves out a retreat – nothing fancy, just a cottage with a bedroom each to write in, some home-cooked food, and maybe a bottle or two of wine for the evenings! Julie brought along her new-found writer friend, Debbie Rayner, and Debbie swiftly became our new-found writer friend too. The retreat was a huge success, both in terms of productivity and bonding, and from that point on it has been a regular spring and autumn feature. And two of my favourite weeks of the year.

Various other people have joined us, all lovely, but two years ago someone had to pull out for illness and at the RNA Industry Awards in London Julie and I 'jumped' a poor new writer who was at her first RNA event and unlucky enough to land on our table. This was Helen Conway and, fair play to her, when we suggested she might like to shut herself away in the wilds of Yorkshire with us for a week, she didn't hesitate. A little wine may have been taken, but even when she'd sobered up, Helen was keen and has been a wonderful addition to our gang. And then Sharon Sant – last into the wordy nest but definitely not least (no one is least!). I actually met Sharon (who writes as Tilly Tennant) years ago at one of Tracy's book launches and when we bumped into each other again at a Burton Library event, we got on very well and I asked her if she fancied our next retreat. Like Helen, bless her, she barely hesitated – and on nothing stronger than a cup of tea! A day into the retreat, writing at the kitchen table in her PJs, fringe in a curler, she announced that she felt very at home, and I think that's how it's been for all of us.

I am so lucky to have found this group. These five women are incredibly hard-working and dedicated to their writing, but also rich, warm, wonderful human beings that it has been my utter pleasure and pride to spend time with. I look forward to many, many more 'WordyAways' with them in the years to come.

As usual, it is my pleasure to thank the lovely team around me – my agent, Kate Shaw, my editor Natasha Harding and all the dedicated, engaged, brilliant people at Bookouture. What a publisher! I'd also like to take this chance to thank the fabulous people at the Intercontinental Literary Agency for all their hard work in securing me so many foreign deals. It's a joy to get social media messages in so many different languages (and thank heavens for Google Translate!) and my goal to see every one of my foreign editions on the shelves. What an excuse to travel!

While researching this novel, I had a wonderful trip to Warsaw and would like to pay tribute to several excellent museums there. The Warsaw Uprising Museum is a wonderful facility and was a huge help to me, both in terms of factual information and the feel of the uprising. The Jewish Cemetery was an emotional place to visit and gave me a good sense of the scenes of the battle in the cemeteries. The permanent exhibition, Destruction and Reconstruction of Stare Miasto, at the Heritage Interpretation Center was the perfect way to explore what happened to the fabric of the city, and the small but very well-stocked bookshop on the ground floor of the Telephone Exchange was a real find. We also did an excellent guided tour of the beautiful old town in which our guide, Jesús, pointed out such helpful things as the location of barricades and bullet marks in some of the walls that survived Hitler's destruction.

I would like to thank my heroic research assistant, Stuart – also my much-loved husband. He was tireless in the treading of museums and invaluable in helping me work out the geography of Warsaw, both in the present (I have zero sense of direction!) and in the past. It was down to his persistence that we found the 1940 map that was such a huge help in understanding wartime Warsaw – and he was also pretty good at sniffing out a decent bar for 'making notes'! Thank you so much, Stuart.

A final shout-out has to go to my lovely readers, many of whom regularly get in touch to let me know if they have enjoyed a book, or if they have personal stories to share. The more I study of this fascinating era of the Second World War, all across the globe, the more I find intertwining stories. It was very satisfying to me to include characters who also feature in *The Midwife of Auschwitz*, *The Midwife of Berlin* and *The War Orphan*, the interconnecting novels reflecting how people's real-life stories also overlapped in this tumultuous period of history.

The Warsaw Uprising was a tragedy – a brave people let down by political considerations that valued power over life – and it has been my honour to insert my three fictional sisters into it. I hope I have done it justice.

PUBLISHING TEAM

Turning a manuscript into a book requires the efforts of many people. The publishing team at Bookouture would like to acknowledge everyone who contributed to this publication.

Audio
Alba Proko
Sinead O'Connor
Melissa Tran

Commercial
Lauren Morrissette
Hannah Richmond
Imogen Allport

Contracts
Peta Nightingale

Cover design
Lisa Horton

Data and analysis
Mark Alder
Mohamed Bussuri

Editorial
Natasha Harding
Lizzie Brien

Copyeditor
Anne O'Brien

Proofreader
Liz Hatherell

Marketing
Alex Crow
Melanie Price
Occy Carr
Cíara Rosney
Martyna Młynarska

Operations and distribution
Marina Valles
Stephanie Straub

Production
Hannah Snetsinger
Mandy Kullar
Jen Shannon
Ria Clare

Publicity
Kim Nash
Noelle Holten
Jess Readett
Sarah Hardy

Printed in Great Britain
by Amazon